Sea Captains' Tales

The novels of Douglas Reeman

A PRAYER FOR THE SHIP
HIGH WATER
SEND A GUNBOAT
DIVE IN THE SUN
THE HOSTILE SHORE
THE LAST RAIDER
WITH BLOOD AND IRON
HMS SARACEN
PATH OF THE STORM
THE DEEP SILENCE
THE PRIDE AND THE ANGUISH
TO RISKS UNKNOWN
THE GREATEST ENEMY
RENDEZVOUS — SOUTH ATLANTIC
GO IN AND SINK!
THE DESTROYERS
WINGED ESCORT
SURFACE WITH DARING
STRIKE FROM THE SEA
A SHIP MUST DIE
TORPEDO RUN
BADGE OF GLORY
THE FIRST TO LAND
THE VOLUNTEERS

Fact

AGAINST THE SEA

Douglas Reeman introduces

Sea Captains' Tales

compiled by Alexander Enfield

C

CENTURY PUBLISHING
LONDON

Introduction copyright © Douglas Reeman 1986
Compilation copyright © Alexander Enfield 1986

This compilation first published in 1986 by
Century Hutchinson Ltd
Brookmount House, 62–65 Chandos Place
Covent Garden, London WC2N 4NW

ISBN 0 7126 0157 0

Photoset in Linotron Sabon by
Rowland Phototypesetting Ltd
Bury St Edmunds, Suffolk

Printed and bound in Great Britain by
Anchor Brendon Ltd, Tiptree, Essex

Contents

Acknowledgements

The Editor and publishers are grateful to the following authors, publishers and agents for permission to include copyright material in this collection. While every care has been taken to establish the copyright holders of all the items included, in the case of any accidental infringement, interested parties are asked to write to the Editor in care of the publishers.

The Society of Authors for 'Outsailed' by W. W. Jacobs from *Many Cargoes* and 'The Liner and the Iceberg' by C. J. Cutcliffe Hyne from *The Adventures of Captain Kettle*; the representative of the Estate of Morley Roberts for 'The Ingenuity of Captain Spink' by Morley Roberts; Rupert Hart-Davis Ltd for 'Don Alfonso's Treasure Hunt' by John Masefield from *A Mainsail Haul*; A. P. Watt Ltd for 'The Blank Shot' by Rafael Sabatini and 'The Last Laugh' by Norman Reilly Raine; Longman Group Ltd for 'The Luck of the *Tavy*' by Commander H. T. Dorling; Century Hutchinson Ltd for 'Duty' by Albert Richard Wetjen; Campbell, Thomson & McLaughlin Ltd for 'Night Shoot' by Nicholas Monsarrat; A. D. Peters & Co. Ltd for 'Dawn Attack' by C. S. Forester; Harrap Ltd for 'The Windjammer Film' by Alan J. Villiers.

Foreword

During a lifetime spent afloat, hardly a day has passed when I
have not whiled away an hour or so in my cabin with a book
about the sea. It never really bothered me if I had just spent the
previous hours completely absorbed in nautical affairs. Even
now my greatest sense of relaxation comes from delving into
the vast library of maritime literature that has been written
over the past hundred years. It would be true to say, too, that I
have found equal pleasure whether the story I was reading was
set in the exotic China Seas or the frozen Arctic waters, if the
ship concerned was a splendid old four-master or a modern
liner – for the challenge that the world's oceans present to all
those who go upon them is the very basic element of drama and
excitement. I can also be just as absorbed by stories of the great
navigators as well as those about humble seamen. I should just
add, of course, that all of them must be entertaining and
authentic!

Over the years, there have been quite a number of collections of sea stories assembled – and I have several of them on
my shelves. But what I cannot discover is one that brings
together stories specifically about sea captains. Tales in which
a captain either tells the story or features as the central
character. Tales about men commanding windjammers or
tramp steamers, pirate galleons or destroyers, tiny yachts or
submarines. And so that's what I have put together in the book
now in your hands.

I am not going to claim that all the very best stories about sea
captains are to be found here, or even that every one is the most

exciting. But what I do have is a very representative selection, ranging from the work of those great 'fathers' of the genre, Herman Melville and Captain Frederick Marryat, to the modern masters such as C. S. Forester, Nicholas Monsarrat and Hammond Innes. I have also been fortunate in that my friend, Douglas Reeman, who is perhaps today's most popular writer of sea stories, has contributed a tale of his own as well as a most perceptive and interesting introduction about man's relationship with the sea.

I expect that the rest of my sailing will now be done in an armchair, but I shall certainly be happy to spend those hours in the company of such men as are to be found in the pages of this book. I trust that you will, too.

ALEXANDER ENFIELD
Walton-on-the-Naze, Essex

Introduction

Douglas Reeman

Of all this nation's maritime heritage, and it covers over a thousand years, perhaps the most lasting is the sea story itself.

People often ask me about this fascination for sailors and ships, where it began and what sustains it today. As an island race, we often say that we have the salt in our blood, not surprising when you consider it is impossible to be born more than ninety miles from the sea anywhere in these islands.

For centuries, sailors of all kinds left our shores for reasons as varied as their craft. Curiosity led to the desire to explore beyond the horizon, and beyond the one after that. In seafaring, curiosity and courage usually go hand in hand. To seek new lands and to find trade, to wage war or to maintain the peace throughout the oceans. To sail with Nelson to the Nile or, as in two world wars, to bring back those battered convoys without which this country would have fallen.

This fascination for the sea and its many tales survives perhaps because we often find it difficult to identify with today's complicated and highly technical advances. With a constant danger of war, one is too often reminded that today's weapons have almost outstripped the minds of those who control them. The expansion of space travel, too, seems to lack a sense of excitement, mainly, I suppose, because we know we can never take part. But if you watch faces at the Boat Show, or that of a proud owner, it is all there: *I could go round the world in my own boat one day*. Of course most of us never will, but the thought that it is even a remote possibility hinges on our old affinity with the sea.

In the era of the great square-riggers – the most beautiful if the most demanding of man's creations – the sailor was always a romantic figure to those ashore. The caricature of Jack Tar with the blue jacket and a parrot on his shoulder was not so very far from the truth. The sailor was, after all, the only person who went anywhere on such a vast scale.

Even until the years between the last two great wars, travel was largely the privilege of the rich, the diplomatic corps and, of course, the military, who weekly left Southampton and Liverpool in jam-packed troopers to deal with troubles throughout the Empire. I doubt if many soldiers at the time would have thought of sea-travel as romantic.

So the sailor, with his yarns and stories of foreign places that most people could only imagine, spread the lore of the sea and left it firmly placed in our daily language. We toss expressions like 'taken aback', 'third mate', 'gone by the board' into our conversation and rarely pause to note that these and hundreds of others still in use, too often wrongly, are the language of the wooden ships and the intrepid sailorman. As a writer of sea stories myself, both under my own name and also as the pseudonymous Alexander Kent, I have cause to be grateful for this extended heritage.

When I was a boy, I read the old works of Marryat, Conrad and Melville and later naval writers such as 'Taffrail'. Although I was born into an army family, when the time came it seemed the natural thing to join the Royal Navy where I soon experienced the brutal reality of sea warfare at first hand. On convoy duty or taking part in attacks on enemy coasts and shipping, it never once occurred to me that I would one day sit down and write about it.

In the Fifties, when I wrote my first novel, it was based on my sort of war and I thought that would be that. But with a contract in my pocket I soon realised that, once again, the sea, and writing about it, was to change everything in my life. Ten years after that first book was published, I decided to launch out into a different style of writing. It was to be a series about one man, Richard Bolitho of Falmouth in Cornwall, his life and times at the turbulent height of the sailing navy in the eighteenth and nineteenth centuries. I had always held that period dearest in my heart. It gave me my first real interest in the sea, probably from when I was about nine or ten years of age, when I set foot aboard Nelson's old flagship *Victory* in Portsmouth dockyard. I thought I knew the period, historically and technically, very well so, with the pseudonym of Alexander Kent, I set to work on what has since become a worldwide series. To my immediate astonishment, I discovered I had to begin learning all over again, both about the main character and about the ships and the manoeuvres expected of them.

I found that, when I was researching the series, I thought with the viewpoint of the time: newspapers, letters and diaries soon made me feel a part of the scene I was describing. Whereas, when writing about more modern vessels, the characters are often separated or even confined in 'metal boxes', on the deck of an eighteenth-century first rate or lively frigate, most of the officers and crew are visible at any one time. The writer must learn where everyone stands, what he does and who he can hear calling to him from another part of the ship. The miles of standing and running rigging, the sizes and uses of pulling boats, weapons and how the sailors lived each working day, all had to be researched and learned with no less dedication than some first-year midshipman.

That period in our maritime history is fascinating. It was the last time of true independence, of the self-dependent sailorman. It was a world of great distances, when every vessel had to survive on her own resources. Death at sea was commonplace, and the cures for illness and injury were sometimes horrific. There are countless stories of courage, endurance and defeat. The sea in all its moods was an enemy just as it can be today for the foolhardy and the plain unlucky.

But in a ship you are constantly reminded of how much you depend on your fellow sailors. For if the sea is the enemy, the ship is also your home and you must protect it as best you can. In no other trade or calling can you discover such men who have been tempered and formed by their daily environment, the sea.

In this book there is a span of stories as broad and as varied as the oceans it touches. Many of the writers are, alas, no longer living, but on these pages their ships and their harbours, their seamen, their captains are with us like the tang of salt spray. It is difficult, almost impossible, to pick out favourites as there is a story to suit most tastes.

For me, the late Alan Villiers, included here with his 'The Windjammer Film', was *the* man of the sea. A heroic sailor himself, he knew the sea and described his love of it with written words or in his many broadcasts better than anyone I ever knew. His word pictures of ships under pyramids of sails, of the hardships and of the humour of their crews are unrivalled. 'Night Shoot' by Nicholas Monsarrat struck a ready chord. I knew him both as a sailor and an author, and I admired both roles. He wrote of 'my war' and had fought the same battles, seen the same sights on the Atlantic, the 'killing ground' as it was called. And 'Outsailed' by W. W. Jacobs, who was, I suppose, one of the first writers who drew me to reading about the sea. How many stories did he write, I wonder? There must have been hundreds. His vivid descriptions of life at sea and the salty characters he introduces us to along the way make his work everlasting.

For all those who love ships and sailors there is something between these covers.

It makes me proud to share this book with such an illustrious collection of shipmates.

DOUGLAS REEMAN

Herman Melville

BENITO CERENO

Captain Ahab, the central figure in Herman Melville's classic novel Moby Dick (1851), is arguably the most famous sea captain in maritime literature. His obsessive pursuit of the huge white whale is told with such vigour and colourful detail that it has swept generations of readers along with all the irresistible power of the sea. Herman Melville (1819–91) drew much of his inspiration for this book from the years he spent at sea after giving up his job as a bank clerk in New York. During his travels, he not only experienced the harsh life of a seaman on a whaling ship and a man-of-war but was also involved in a mutiny in the South Seas. These later episodes provided the raw material for another of his great sea novels, White Jacket, published in 1850. A third work, Billy Budd, which appeared posthumously in 1924, assured Melville's reputation as perhaps the greatest of all sea story writers, and it was, of course, turned into a remarkable opera by Benjamin Britten in 1951.

The novels by Melville that I have mentioned are widely familiar and easily obtainable. Much less so is the story that I have selected to begin this collection. 'Benito Cereno' was written in 1855 and has been rightly described as one of the most precise and carefully executed short works in American literature. Certainly it is a marvellously imaginative piece of writing and Jay Leyda, the Melville expert, believes that the character of Cereno is very much the author himself. Interestingly, the story is based on an old book that Melville found called A Narrative of Voyages and Travels in the Northern and

Southern Hemispheres by a certain Captain Amasa Delano written in 1817, and this he used to create the story of a sea captain in some ways almost as colourful and fascinating as the great Captain Ahab himself . . .

In the year 1799, Captain Amasa Delano, of Duxbury, in Massachusetts, commanding a large sealer and general trader, lay at anchor with a valuable cargo, in the harbour of St Maria — a small, desert, uninhabited island toward the southern extremity of the long coast of Chili. There he had touched for water.

On the second day, not long after dawn, while lying in his berth, his mate came below, informing him that a strange sail was coming into the bay. Ships were then not so plenty in those waters as now. He rose, dressed, and went on deck.

The morning was one peculiar to that coast. Everything was mute and calm; everything grey. The sea, though undulated into long roods of swells, seemed fixed, and was sleeked at the surface like waved lead that has cooled and set in the smelter's mould. The sky seemed a grey surtout. Flights of troubled grey fowl, kith and kin with flights of troubled grey vapours among which they were mixed, skimmed low and fitfully over the waters, as swallows over meadows before storms. Shadows present, foreshadowing deeper shadows to come.

To Captain Delano's surprise, the stranger, viewed through the glass, showed no colours; though to do so upon entering a haven, however uninhabited in its shores, where but a single other ship might be lying, was the custom among peaceful seamen of all nations. Considering the lawlessness and loneliness of the spot, and the sort of stories, at that day, associated with those seas, Captain Delano's surprise might have deepened into some uneasiness had he not been a person of a singularly undistrustful good-nature, not liable, except on extraordinary and repeated incentives, and hardly then, to indulge in personal alarms, any way involving the imputation of malign evil in man. Whether, in view of what humanity is capable, such a trait implies, along with a benevolent heart, more than ordinary quickness and accuracy of intellectual perception, may be left to the wise to determine.

But whatever misgivings might have obtruded on first seeing the stranger, would almost, in any seaman's mind, have been dissipated by observing that the ship, in navigating into the harbour, was drawing too near the land; a sunken reef making out off her bow. This seemed to prove her a stranger, indeed, not only to the sealer, but the island; consequently, she could be no wonted freebooter on that ocean. With no small interest, Captain Delano continued to watch her – a proceeding not much facilitated by the vapours partly mantling the hull, through which the far matin light from her cabin streamed equivocally enough; much like the sun – by this time hemisphered on the rim of the horizon, and, apparently, in company with the strange ship entering the harbour – which, wimpled by the same low, creeping clouds, showed not unlike a Lima intriguante's one sinister eye peering across the Plaza from the Indian loop-hole of her dusk *saya-y-manta*.

It might have been but a deception of the vapours, but the longer the stranger was watched the more singular appeared her manoeuvres. Ere long it seemed hard to decide whether she meant to come in or no – what she wanted, or what she was about. The wind, which had breezed up a little during the night was now extremely light and baffling, which the more increased the apparent uncertainty of her movements.

Surmising, at last, that it might be a ship in distress, Captain Delano ordered his whale-boat to be dropped, and, much to the wary opposition of his mate, prepared to board her, and, at the least, pilot her in. On the night previous, a fishing-party of the seamen had gone a long distance to some detached rocks out of sight from the sealer, and, an hour or two before daybreak, had returned, having met with no small success. Presuming that the stranger might have been long off soundings, the good captain put several baskets of the fish, for presents, into his boat, and so pulled away. From her continuing too near the sunken reef, deeming her in danger, calling to his men, he made all haste to apprise those on board of their situation. But, some time ere the boat came up, the wind, light though it was, having shifted, had headed the vessel off, as well as partly broken the vapours from about her.

3

Upon gaining a less remote view, the ship, when made signally visible on the verge of the leaden-hued swells, with the shreds of fog here and there raggedly furring her, appeared like a whitewashed monastery after a thunder-storm, seen perched upon some dun cliff among the Pyrenees. But it was no purely fanciful resemblance which now, for a moment, almost led Captain Delano to think that nothing less than a ship-load of monks was before him. Peering over the bulwarks were what really seemed, in the hazy distance, throngs of dark cowls; while, fitfully revealed through the open port-holes, other dark moving figures were dimly descried, as of Black Friars pacing the cloisters.

Upon a still nigher approach, this appearance was modified, and the true character of the vessel was plain — a Spanish merchantman of the first class, carrying negro slaves, amongst other valuable freight, from one colonial port to another. A very large, and, in its time, a very fine vessel, such as in those days were at intervals encountered along that main; sometimes superseded Acapulco treasure-ships, or retired frigates of the Spanish king's navy, which, like superannuated Italian palaces, still, under a decline of masters, preserved signs of former state.

As the whale-boat drew more and more nigh, the cause of the peculiar pipe-clayed aspect of the stranger was seen in the slovenly neglect pervading her. The spars, ropes, and great part of the bulwarks, looked woolly, from long unacquaintance with the scraper, tar, and the brush. Her keel seemed laid, her ribs put together, and she launched, from Ezekiel's Valley of Dry Bones.

In the present business in which she was engaged, the ship's general model and rig appeared to have undergone no material change from their original warlike and Froissart pattern. However, no guns were seen.

The tops were large, and were railed about with what had once been octagonal net-work, all now in sad disrepair. These tops hung overhead like three ruinous aviaries, in one of which was seen perched, on a rattlin, a white noddy, a strange fowl, so called from its lethargic, somnambulistic character, being frequently caught by hand at sea. Battered and mouldy, the castellated forecastle seemed some ancient turret, long ago

4

taken by assault, and then left to decay. Toward the stern, two high-raised quarter-galleries – the balustrades here and there covered with dry, tindery sea-moss – opening out from the unoccupied state-cabin, whose dead-lights, for all the mild weather, were hermetically closed and caulked – these tenant-less balconies hung over the sea as if it were the grand Venetian canal. But the principal relic of faded grandeur was the ample oval of the shield-like stern-piece, intricately carved with the arms of Castile and Leon, medallioned about by groups of mythological or symbolical devices; uppermost and central of which was a dark satyr in a mask, holding his foot on the prostrate neck of a writhing figure, likewise masked.

Whether the ship had a figure-head, or only a plain beak, was not quite certain, owing to canvas wrapped about that part, either to protect it while undergoing a refurbishing, or else decently to hide its decay. Rudely painted or chalked, as in a sailor freak, along the forward side of a sort of pedestal below the canvas, was the sentence, 'Seguid vuestro jefe' (follow your leader); while upon the tarnished head-boards, near by, appeared, in stately capitals, once gilt, the ship's name, 'SAN DOMINICK', each letter streakingly corroded with tricklings of copper-spike rust; while, like mourning weeds, dark festoons of sea-grass slimily swept to and fro over the name, with every hearse-like roll of the hull.

As, at last, the boat was hooked from the bow along toward the gangway amidship, its keel, while yet some inches separated from the hull, harshly grated as on a sunken coral reef. It proved a huge bunch of conglobated barnacles adhering below the water to the side like a wen – a token of baffling airs and long calms passed somewhere in those seas.

Climbing the side, the visitor was at once surrounded by a clamorous throng of whites and blacks, but the latter out-numbering the former more than could have been expected, negro transportation-ship as the stranger in port was. But, in one language, and as with one voice, all poured out a common tale of suffering; in which the negresses, of whom there were not a few, exceeded the others in their dolorous vehemence. The scurvy, together with the fever, had swept off a great part of their number, more especially the Spaniards. Off Cape Horn they had narrowly escaped shipwreck; then, for days together,

5

they had lain tranced without wind; their provisions were low; their water next to none; their lips that moment were baked.

While Captain Delano was thus made the mark of all eager tongues, his one eager glance took in all faces, with every other object about him.

Always upon first boarding a large and populous ship at sea, especially a foreign one, with a nondescript crew such as Lascars or Manila men, the impression varies in a peculiar way from that produced by first entering a strange house with strange inmates in a strange land. Both house and ship — the one by its walls and blinds, the other by its high bulwarks like ramparts — hoard from view their interiors till the last moment; but in the case of the ship there is this addition: that the living spectacle it contains, upon its sudden and complete disclosure, has, in contrast with the blank ocean which zones it, something of the effect of enchantment. The ship seems unreal; these strange costumes, gestures, and faces, but a shadowy tableau just emerged from the deep, which directly must receive back what it gave.

Perhaps it was some such influence, as above is attempted to be described, which, in Captain Delano's mind, heightened whatever, upon a staid scrutiny, might have seemed unusual; especially the conspicuous figures of four elderly grizzled negroes, their heads like black, doddered willow-tops, who, in venerable contrast to the tumult below them, were couched, sphinx-like, one on the starboard cat-head, another on the larboard, and the remaining pair face to face on the opposite bulwarks above the main-chains. They each had bits of unstranded old junk in their hands, and, with a sort of stoical self-content, were picking the junk into oakum, a small heap of which lay by their sides. They accompanied the task with a continuous, low, monotonous chant; droning and druling away like so many grey-headed bagpipers playing a funeral march.

The quarter-deck rose into an ample elevated poop, upon the forward verge of which, lifted, like the oakum-pickers, some eight feet above the general throng, sat along in a row, separated by regular spaces, the cross-legged figures of six other blacks; each with a rusty hatchet in his hand, which, with a bit of brick and a rag, he was engaged like a scullion in scouring, while between each two was a small stack of hatchets, their rusted edges turned forward awaiting a like operation. Though occasionally the four oakum-pickers would briefly address some person or persons in the crowd below, yet the six hatchet-polishers neither spoke to others, nor breathed a whisper among themselves, but sat intent upon their task, except at intervals, when, with the peculiar love in negroes of uniting industry with pastime, two and two they sideways clashed their hatchets together, like cymbals, with a barbarous din. All six, unlike the generality, had the raw aspect of unsophisticated Africans.

But that first comprehensive glance which took in those ten figures, with scores less conspicuous, rested but an instant upon them, as, impatient of the hubbub of voices, the visitor turned in quest of whomsoever it might be that commanded the ship.

But as if not unwilling to let nature make known her own case among his suffering charge, or else in despair of restraining it for the time, the Spanish captain, a gentlemanly, reserved-looking, and rather young man to a stranger's eye, dressed with singular richness, but bearing plain traces of recent sleepless cares and disquietudes, stood passively by, leaning against the main-mast, at one moment casting a dreary, spiritless look upon his excited people, at the next an unhappy glance toward his visitor. By his side stood a black of small stature, in whose rude face, as occasionally, like a shepherd's dog, he mutely turned it up into the Spaniard's, sorrow and affection were equally blended.

Struggling through the throng, the American advanced to the Spaniard, assuring him of his sympathies, and offering to render whatever assistance might be in his power. To which the Spaniard returned for the present but grave and ceremonious acknowledgements, his national formality dusked by the saturnine mood of ill-health.

But losing no time in mere compliments, Captain Delano, returning to the gangway, had his basket of fish brought up; and as the wind still continued light, so that some hours at least must elapse ere the ship could be brought to the anchorage, he bade his men return to the sealer, and fetch back as much water as the whale-boat could carry, with whatever soft bread the steward might have, all the remaining pumpkins on board, with a box of sugar, and a dozen of his private bottles of cider.

Not many minutes after the boat's pushing off, to the vexation of all, the wind entirely died away, and the tide turning, began drifting back the ship helplessly seaward. But trusting this would not last long, Captain Delano sought, with good hopes, to cheer up the strangers, feeling no small satisfaction that, with persons in their condition, he could – thanks to his frequent voyages along the Spanish main – converse with some freedom in their native tongue.

While left alone with them, he was not long in observing some things tending to heighten his first impressions; but surprise was lost in pity, both for the Spaniards and blacks, alike evidently reduced from scarcity of water and provisions; while long-continued suffering seemed to have brought out the less good-natured qualities of the negroes, besides, at the same time, impairing the Spaniard's authority over them. But, under the circumstances, precisely this condition of things was to have been anticipated. In armies, navies, cities, or families, in nature herself, nothing more relaxes good order than misery. Still, Captain Delano was not without the idea, that had Benito Cereno been a man of greater energy, misrule would hardly have come to the present pass. But the debility, constitutional or induced by hardships, bodily and mental, of the Spanish captain, was too obvious to be overlooked. A prey to settled dejection, as if long mocked with hope he would not now indulge it, even when it had ceased to be a mock, the prospect of that day, or evening at furthest, lying at anchor, with plenty of water for his people, and a brother captain to counsel and befriend, seemed in no perceptible degree to encourage him. His mind appeared unstrung, if not still more seriously affected. Shut up in these oaken walls, chained to one dull round of command, whose unconditionality cloyed him, like some hypochondriac abbot he moved slowly about, at times suddenly pausing, starting, or staring, biting his lip, biting his finger-nail, flushing, paling, twitching his beard, with other symptoms of an absent or moody mind. This distempered spirit was lodged, as before hinted, in as distempered a frame. He was rather tall, but seemed never to have been robust, and now with nervous suffering was almost worn to a skeleton. A tendency to some pulmonary complaint appeared to have been lately confirmed. His voice was like that of one with lungs half gone — hoarsely suppressed, a husky whisper. No wonder that, as in this state he tottered about, his private servant apprehensively followed him. Sometimes the negro gave his master his arm, or took his handkerchief out of his pocket for him, performing these and similar offices with that affectionate zeal which transmutes into something filial or fraternal acts in themselves but menial; and which has gained for the negro the repute of making the most pleasing body-servant in the world; one, too, whom a master need be on no stiffly superior terms with, but may treat with familiar trust; less a servant than a devoted companion.

Marking the noisy indocility of the blacks in general, as well as what seemed the sullen inefficiency of the whites, it was not without humane satisfaction that Captain Delano witnessed the steady good conduct of Babo.

But the good conduct of Babo, hardly more than the ill-behaviour of others, seemed to withdraw the half-lunatic Don Benito from his cloudy languor. Not that such precisely was the impression made by the Spaniard on the mind of his visitor. The Spaniard's individual unrest was, for the present, but noted as a conspicuous feature in the ship's general affliction. Still, Captain Delano was not a little concerned at what he could not help taking for the time to be Don Benito's unfriendly indifference toward himself. The Spaniard's manner, too, conveyed a sort of sour and gloomy disdain, which he seemed at no pains to disguise. But this the American in charity ascribed to the harassing effects of sickness, since, in former instances, he had noted that there are peculiar natures on whom prolonged physical suffering seems to cancel every social instinct of kindness; as if, forced to black bread themselves, they deemed it but equity that each person coming nigh them should, indirectly, by some slight or affront, be made to partake of their fare.

But ere long Captain Delano bethought him that, indulgent as he was at the first, in judging the Spaniard, he might not, after all, have exercised charity enough. At bottom it was Don Benito's reserve which displeased him; but the same reserve was shown toward all but his faithful personal attendant. Even the formal reports which, according to sea-usage, were, at stated times, made to him by some petty underling, either a white, mulatto, or black, he hardly had patience enough to listen to, without betraying contemptuous aversion. His manner upon such occasions was, in its degree, not unlike that which might be supposed to have been his imperial countryman's, Charles V, just previous to the anchoritish retirement of that monarch from the throne.

This splenetic disrelish of his place was evinced in almost every function pertaining to it. Proud as he was moody, he condescended to no personal mandate. Whatever special orders were necessary, their delivery was delegated to his body-servant, who in turn transferred them to their ultimate destination, through runners, alert Spanish boys or slave-boys, like pages or pilot-fish within easy call continually hovering round Don Benito. So that to have beheld this undemonstrative invalid gliding about, apathetic and mute, no landsman could have dreamed that in him was lodged a dictatorship beyond which, while at sea, there was no earthly appeal.

Thus, the Spaniard, regarded in his reserve, seemed the involuntary victim of mental disorder. But, in fact, his reserve might, in some degree, have proceeded from design. If so, then here was evinced the unhealthy climax of that icy though conscientious policy, more or less adopted by all commanders of large ships, which, except in signal emergencies, obliterates alike the manifestation of sway with every trace of sociality; transforming the man into a block, or rather into a loaded cannon, which, until there is call for thunder, has nothing to say.

Viewing him in this light, it seemed but a natural token of the perverse habit induced by a long course of such hard self-restraint, that, notwithstanding the present condition of his ship, the Spaniard should still persist in a demeanour, which, however harmless, or, it may be, appropriate, in a well-appointed vessel, such as the *San Dominick* might have been at the outset of the voyage, was anything but judicious now. But the Spaniard, perhaps, thought that it was with captains as with gods: reserve, under all events, must still be their cue. But probably this appearance of slumbering dominion might have been but an attempted disguise to conscious imbecility – not deep policy, but shallow device. But be all this as it might, whether Don Benito's manner was designed or not, the more Captain Delano noted its pervading reserve, the less he felt uneasiness at any particular manifestation of that reserve toward himself.

Neither were his thoughts taken up by the captain alone. Wonted to the quiet orderliness of the sealer's comfortable family of a crew, the noisy confusion of the *San Dominick*'s suffering host repeatedly challenged his eye. Some prominent breaches, not only of discipline but of decency, were observed. These Captain Delano could not but ascribe, in the main, to the absence of those subordinate deck-officers to whom, along with higher duties, is entrusted what may be styled the police department of a populous ship. True, the old oakum-pickers appeared at times to act the part of monitorial constables to their countrymen, the blacks; but though occasionally succeeding in allaying trifling outbreaks now and then between man and man, they could do little or nothing toward establishing general quiet. The *San Dominick* was in the condition of a transatlantic emigrant ship, among whose multitude of living freight are some individuals, doubtless, as little troublesome as crates and bales; but the friendly remonstrances of such with their ruder companions are of not so much avail as the unfriendly arm of the mate. What the *San Dominick* wanted was, what the emigrant ship has, stern superior officers. But on these decks not so much as a fourth mate was to be seen.

The visitor's curiosity was roused to learn the particulars of those mishaps which had brought about such absenteeism, with its consequences; because, though deriving some inkling of the voyage from the wails which at the first moment had greeted him, yet of the details no clear understanding had been had. The best account would, doubtless, be given by the captain. Yet at first the visitor was loth to ask it, unwilling to provoke some distant rebuff. But plucking up courage, he at last accosted Don Benito, renewing the expression of his benevolent interest, adding, that did he (Captain Delano) but know the particulars of the ship's misfortunes, he would, perhaps, be better able in the end to relieve them. Would Don Benito favour him with the whole story.

Don Benito faltered; then, like some somnambulist suddenly interfered with, vacantly stared at his visitor, and ended by
looking down on the deck. He maintained this posture so long,
that Captain Delano, almost equally disconcerted, and involuntarily almost as rude, turned suddenly from him, walking
forward to accost one of the Spanish seamen for the desired
information. But he had hardly gone five paces, when, with a
sort of eagerness, Don Benito invited him back, regretting his
momentary absence of mind, and professing readiness to
gratify him.

While most part of the story was being given, the two
captains stood on the after part of the main-deck, a privileged
spot, no one being near but the servant.

'It is now a hundred and ninety days,' began the Spaniard, in
his husky whisper, 'that this ship, well officered and well
manned, with several cabin passengers – some fifty Spaniards
in all – sailed from Buenos Ayres bound to Lima, with a
general cargo, hardware, Paraguay tea and the like – and,'
pointing forward, 'that parcel of negroes, now not more than a
hundred and fifty, as you see, but then numbering over three
hundred souls. Off Cape Horn we had heavy gales. In one
moment, by night, three of my best officers, with fifteen sailors,
were lost, with the main-yard; the spar snapping under them in
the slings, as they sought, with heavers, to beat down the icy
sail. To lighten the hull, the heavier sacks of mata were thrown
into the sea, with most of the water-pipes lashed on deck at the
time. And this last necessity it was, combined with the prolonged detentions afterward experienced, which eventually
brought about our chief causes of suffering. When –'

Here there was a sudden fainting attack of his cough,
brought on, no doubt, by his mental distress. His servant
sustained him, and drawing a cordial from his pocket placed
it to his lips. He a little revived. But unwilling to leave
him unsupported while yet imperfectly restored, the black
with one arm still encircled his master, at the same time keeping his eye fixed on his face, as if to watch for the first
sign of complete restoration, or relapse, as the event might
prove.

The Spaniard proceeded, but brokenly and obscurely, as one
in a dream.

–'Oh, my God! rather than pass through what I have, with joy I would have hailed the most terrible gales; but –'

His cough returned and with increased violence; this subsiding, with reddened lips and closed eyes he fell heavily against his supporter.

'His mind wanders. He was thinking of the plague that followed the gales,' plaintively sighed the servant; 'my poor, poor master!' wringing one hand, and with the other wiping the mouth. 'But be patient, señor,' again turning to Captain Delano, 'these fits do not last long; master will soon be himself.'

Don Benito reviving, went on; but as this portion of the story was very brokenly delivered, the substance only will here be set down.

It appeared that after the ship had been many days tossed in storms off the Cape, the scurvy broke out, carrying off numbers of the whites and blacks. When at last they had worked round into the Pacific, their spars and sails were so damaged, and so inadequately handled by the surviving mariners, most of whom were become invalids, that, unable to lay her northerly course by the wind, which was powerful, the unmanageable ship, for successive days and nights, was blown northwestward, where the breeze suddenly deserted her, in unknown waters, to sultry calms. The absence of the water-pipes now proved as fatal to life as before their presence had menaced it. Induced, or at least aggravated, by the more than scanty allowance of water, a malignant fever followed the scurvy; with the excessive heat of the lengthened calm, making such short work of it as to sweep away, as by billows, whole families of the Africans, and a yet larger number, proportionably, of the Spaniards, including, by a luckless fatality, every remaining officer on board. Consequently, in the smart west winds eventually following the calm, the already rent sails, having to be simply dropped, not furled, at need, had been gradually reduced to the beggars' rags they were now. To procure substitutes for his lost sailors, as well as supplies of water and sails, the captain, at the earliest opportunity, had made for Baldivia, the southernmost civilised port of Chili and South America; but upon nearing the coast the thick weather had prevented him from so much as sighting that harbour.

13

Since which period, almost without a crew, and almost without canvas, and almost without water, and, at intervals, giving its added dead to the sea, the *San Dominick* had been battledored about by contrary winds, inveigled by currents, or grown weedy in calms. Like a man lost in woods, more than once she had doubled upon her own track.

'But throughout these calamities,' huskily continued Don Benito, painfully turning in the half-embrace of his servant, 'I have to thank those negroes you see, who, though to your inexperienced eyes appearing unruly, have, indeed, conducted themselves with less of restlessness than even their owner could have thought possible under such circumstances.'

Here he again fell faintly back. Again his mind wandered; but he rallied, and less obscurely proceeded.

'Yes, their owner was quite right in assuring me that no fetters would be needed with his blacks; so that while, as is wont in this transportation, these negroes have always remained upon deck – not thrust below, as in the Guinea-men – they have, also, from the beginning, been freely permitted to range within given bounds at their pleasure.'

Once more the faintness returned – his mind roved – but, recovering, he resumed.

'But it is Babo here to whom, under God, I owe not only my own preservation, but likewise to him, chiefly, the merit is due, of pacifying his more ignorant brethren, when at intervals tempted to murmurings.'

'Ah, master,' sighed the black, bowing his face, 'don't speak of me; Babo is nothing; what Babo has done was but duty.'

'Faithful fellow!' cried Captain Delano. 'Don Benito, I envy you such a friend; slave I cannot call him.'

As master and man stood before him, the black upholding the white, Captain Delano could not but bethink him of the beauty of that relationship which could present such a spectacle of fidelity on the one hand and confidence on the other. The scene was heightened by the contrast in dress, denoting their relative positions. The Spaniard wore a loose Chili jacket of dark velvet; white small-clothes and stockings, with silver buckles at the knee and instep; a high-crowned sombrero, of fine grass; a slender sword, silver mounted, hung from a knot in his sash – the last being an almost invariable adjunct, more for utility than ornament, of a South American gentleman's dress to this hour. Excepting when his occasional nervous contortions brought about disarray, there was a certain precision in his attire curiously at variance with the unsightly disorder around; especially in the belittered ghetto, forward of the main-mast, wholly occupied by the blacks.

The servant wore nothing but wide trowsers, apparently, from their coarseness and patches, made out of some old topsail; they were clean, and confined at the waist by a bit of unstranded rope, which, with his composed, deprecatory air at times, made him look something like a begging friar of St Francis.

However unsuitable for the time and place, at least in the blunt-thinking American's eyes, and however strangely surviving in the midst of all his afflictions, the toilet of Don Benito might not, in fashion at least, have gone beyond the style of the day among South Americans of his class. Though on the present voyage sailing from Buenos Ayres, he had avowed himself a native and resident of Chili, whose inhabitants had not so generally adopted the plain coat and once plebeian pantaloons; but, with a becoming modification, adhered to their provincial costume, picturesque as any in the world. Still, relatively to the pale history of the voyage, and his own pale face, there seemed something so incongruous in the Spaniard's apparel, as almost to suggest the image of an invalid courtier tottering about London streets in the time of the plague.

The portion of the narrative which, perhaps, most excited interest, as well as some surprise, considering the latitudes in question, was the long calms spoken of, and more particularly the ship's so long drifting about. Without communicating the opinion, of course, the American could not but impute at least part of the detentions both to clumsy seamanship and faulty navigation. Eyeing Don Benito's small, yellow hands, he easily inferred that the young captain had not got into command at the hawse-hole, but the cabin window; and if so, why wonder at incompetence, in youth, sickness, and gentility united?

But drowning criticism in compassion, after a fresh repetition of his sympathies, Captain Delano, having heard out his story, not only engaged, as in the first place, to see Don Benito and his people supplied in their immediate bodily needs, but, also, now further promised to assist him in procuring a large permanent supply of water, as well as some sails and rigging; and, though it would involve no small embarrassment to himself, yet he would spare three of his best seamen for temporary deck officers; so that without delay the ship might proceed to Conception, there fully to refit for Lima, her destined port.

Such generosity was not without its effect, even upon the invalid. His face lighted up; eager and hectic, he met the honest glance of his visitor. With gratitude he seemed overcome.

'This excitement is bad for master,' whispered the servant, taking his arm, and with soothing words gently drawing him aside.

When Don Benito returned, the American was pained to observe that his hopefulness, like the sudden kindling in his cheek, was but febrile and transient.

Ere long, with a joyless mien, looking up toward the poop, the host invited his guest to accompany him there, for the benefit of what little breath of wind might be stirring.

As, during the telling of the story, Captain Delano had once or twice started at the occasional cymballing of the hatchet-polishers, wondering why such an interruption should be allowed, especially in that part of the ship, and in the ears of an invalid; and moreover, as the hatchets had anything but an attractive look, and the handlers of them still less so, it was, therefore, to tell the truth, not without some lurking reluctance, or even shrinking, it may be, that Captain Delano, with apparent complaisance, acquiesced in his host's invitation. The more so, since, with an untimely caprice of punctilio, rendered distressing by his cadaverous aspect, Don Benito, with Castilian bows, solemnly insisted upon his guest's preceding him up the ladder leading to the elevation; where, one on each side of the last step, sat for armorial supporters and sentries two of the ominous file. Gingerly enough stepped good Captain Delano between them, and in the instant of leaving them behind, like one running the gauntlet, he felt an apprehensive twitch in the calves of his legs.

But when, facing about, he saw the whole file, like so many organ-grinders, still stupidly intent on their work, unmindful of everything besides, he could not but smile at his late fidgety panic.

Presently, while standing with his host, looking forward upon the decks below, he was struck by one of those instances of insubordination previousy alluded to. Three black boys, with two Spanish boys, were sitting together on the hatches, scraping a rude wooden platter, in which some scanty mess had recently been cooked. Suddenly, one of the black boys, enraged at a word dropped by one of his white companions, seized a knife, and, though called to forbear by one of the oakum-pickers, struck the lad over the head, inflicting a gash from which blood flowed.

In amazement, Captain Delano inquired what this meant. To which the pale Don Benito dully muttered, that it was merely the sport of the lad.

'Pretty serious sport, truly,' rejoined Captain Delano. 'Had such a thing happened on board the *Bachelor's Delight*, instant punishment would have followed.'

At these words the Spaniard turned upon the American one of his sudden, staring, half-lunatic looks; then, relapsing into his torpor, answered, 'Doubtless, doubtless, señor.'

Is it, thought Captain Delano, that this hapless man is one of those paper captains I've known, who by policy wink at what by power they cannot put down? I know no sadder sight than a commander who has little of command but the name.

'I should think, Don Benito,' he now said, glancing toward the oakum-picker who had sought to interfere with the boys, 'that you would find it advantageous to keep all your blacks employed, especially the younger ones, no matter at what useless task, and no matter what happens to the ship. Why, even with my little band, I find such a course indispensable. I once kept a crew on my quarter-deck thrumming mats for my cabin, when, for three days, I had given up my ship — mats, men, and all — for a speedy loss, owing to the violence of a gale, in which we could do nothing but helplessly drive before it.'

'Doubtless, doubtless,' muttered Don Benito.

'But,' continued Captain Delano, again glancing upon the oakum-pickers and then at the hatchet-polishers, near by, 'I see you keep some, at least, of your host employed.'

'Yes,' was again the vacant response.

'Those old men there, shaking their pows from their pulpits,' continued Captain Delano, pointing to the oakum-pickers, 'seem to act the part of old dominies to the rest, little heeded as their admonitions are at times. Is this voluntary on their part, Don Benito, or have you appointed them shepherds to your flock of black sheep?'

'What posts they fill, I appointed them,' rejoined the Spaniard, in an acrid tone, as if resenting some supposed satiric reflection.

'And these others, these Ashantee conjurers here,' continued Captain Delano, rather uneasily eyeing the brandished steel of the hatchet-polishers, where, in spots, it had been brought to a shine, 'this seems a curious business they are at, Don Benito?'

'In the gales we met,' answered the Spaniard, 'what of our general cargo was not thrown overboard was much damaged by the brine. Since coming into calm weather, I have had several cases of knives and hatchets daily brought up for overhauling and cleaning.'

'A prudent idea, Don Benito. You are part owner of ship and cargo, I presume; but none of the slaves, perhaps?'

'I am owner of all you see,' impatiently returned Don Benito, 'except the main company of blacks, who belonged to my late friend, Alexandro Aranda.'

As he mentioned this name, his air was heart-broken; his knees shook; his servant supported him.

Thinking he divined the cause of such unusual emotion, to confirm his surmise, Captain Delano, after a pause, said: 'And may I ask, Don Benito, whether — since a while ago you spoke of some cabin passengers — the friend, whose loss so afflicts you, at the outset of the voyage accompanied his blacks?'

'Yes.'

'But died of the fever?'

'Died of the fever. Oh, could I but —'

Again quivering, the Spaniard paused.

'Pardon me,' said Captain Delano lowly, 'but I think that, by a sympathetic experience, I conjecture, Don Benito, what it is that gives the keener edge to your grief. It was once my hard fortune to lose, at sea, a dear friend, my own brother, then supercargo. Assured of the welfare of his spirit, its departure I could have borne like a man; but that honest eye, that honest hand – both of which had so often met mine – and that warm heart; all, all – like scraps to the dogs – to throw all to the sharks! It was then I vowed never to have for fellow-voyager a man I loved, unless, unbeknown to him, I had provided every requisite, in case of a fatality, for embalming his mortal part for interment on shore. Were your friend's remains now on board this ship, Don Benito, not thus strangely would the mention of his name affect you.'

'On board this ship?' echoed the Spaniard. Then, with horrified gestures, as directed against some spectre, he unconsciously fell into the ready arms of his attendant, who, with a silent appeal toward Captain Delano, seemed beseeching him not again to broach a theme so unspeakably distressing to his master.

This poor fellow now, thought the pained American, is the victim of that sad superstition which associates goblins with the deserted body of man, as ghosts with an abandoned house. How unlike are we made! What to me, in like case, would have been a solemn satisfaction, the bare suggestion, even, terrifies the Spaniard into this trance. Poor Alexandro Aranda! what would you say could you here see your friend – who, on former voyages, when you, for months, were left behind, has, I dare say, often longed, and longed, for one peep at you – now transported with terror at the least thought of having you any way nigh him.

At this moment, with a dreary graveyard toll, betokening a flaw, the ship's forecastle bell, smote by one of the grizzled oakum-pickers, proclaimed ten o'clock through the leaden calm; when Captain Delano's attention was caught by the moving figure of a gigantic black, emerging from the general crowd below, and slowly advancing toward the elevated poop. An iron collar was about his neck, from which depended a chain, thrice wound round his body; the terminating links padlocked together at a broad band of iron, his girdle.

'How like a mute Atufal moves,' murmured the servant.

The black mounted the steps of the poop, and, like a brave prisoner, brought up to receive sentence, stood in unquailing muteness before Don Benito, now recovered from his attack.

At the first glimpse of his approach, Don Benito had started, a resentful shadow swept over his face; and, as with the sudden memory of bootless rage, his white lips glued together.

This is some mulish mutineer, thought Captain Delano, surveying, not without a mixture of admiration, the colossal form of the negro.

'See, he waits your question, master,' said the servant.

Thus reminded, Don Benito, nervously averting his glance, as if shunning, by anticipation, some rebellious response, in a disconcerted voice, thus spoke:

'Atufal, will you ask my pardon now?'

The black was silent.

'Again, master,' murmured the servant, with bitter upbraiding eyeing his countryman, 'again, master; he will bend to master yet.'

'Answer,' said Don Benito, still averting his glance, 'say but the one word, *pardon*, and your chains shall be off.'

Upon this, the black, slowly raising both arms, let them lifelessly fall, his links clanking, his head bowed; as much as to say, 'No, I am content.'

'Go,' said Don Benito, with inkept and unknown emotion.

Deliberately as he had come, the black obeyed.

'Excuse me, Don Benito,' said Captain Delano, 'but this scene surprises me; what means it, pray?'

'It means that that negro alone, of all the band, has given me peculiar cause of offence. I have put him in chains; I —'

Here he paused; his hand to his head, as if there were a swimming there, or a sudden bewilderment of memory had come over him; but meeting his servant's kindly glance seemed reassured, and proceeded:

'I could not scourge such a form. But I told him he must ask my pardon. As yet he has not. At my command, every two hours he stands before me.'

'And how long has this been?'

'Some sixty days.'

'And obedient in all else? And respectful?'

'Yes.'

'Upon my conscience, then,' exclaimed Captain Delano impulsively, 'he has a royal spirit in him, this fellow.'

'He may have some right to it,' bitterly returned Don Benito, 'he says he was king in his own land.'

'Yes,' said the servant, entering a word, 'those slits in Atufal's ears once held wedges of gold; but poor Babo here, in his own land, was only a poor slave; a black man's slave was Babo, who now is the white's.'

Somewhat annoyed by these conversational familiarities, Captain Delano turned curiously upon the attendant, then glanced inquiringly at his master; but, as if long wonted to these little informalities, neither master nor man seemed to understand him.

'What, pray, was Atufal's offence, Don Benito?' asked Captain Delano; 'if it was not something very serious, take a fool's advice, and, in view of his general docility, as well as in some natural respect for his spirit, remit him his penalty.'

'No, no, master never will do that,' here murmured the servant to himself, 'proud Atufal must first ask master's pardon. The slave there carries the padlock, but master here carries the key.'

His attention thus directed, Captain Delano now noticed for the first, that, suspended by a slender silken cord from Don Benito's neck, hung a key. At once, from the servant's muttered syllables, divining the key's purpose, he smiled and said: 'So, Don Benito – padlock and key – significant symbols, truly.'

Biting his lip, Don Benito faltered.

Though the remark of Captain Delano, a man of such native simplicity as to be incapable of satire or irony, had been dropped in playful allusion to the Spaniard's singularly evidenced lordship over the black; yet the hypochondriac seemed some way to have taken it as a malicious reflection upon his confessed inability thus far to break down, at least, on a verbal summons, the entrenched will of the slave. Deploring this supposed misconception, yet despairing of correcting it, Captain Delano shifted the subject; but finding his companion more than ever withdrawn, as if still sourly digesting the lees of the presumed affront above mentioned, by and by Captain Delano likewise became less talkative, oppressed, against his own will, by what seemed the secret vindictiveness of the morbidly sensitive Spaniard. But the good sailor, himself of a quite contrary disposition, refrained, on his part, alike from the appearance as from the feeling of resentment, and if silent, was only so from contagion.

Presently the Spaniard, assisted by his servant, somewhat discourteously crossed over from his guest; a procedure which, sensibly enough, might have been allowed to pass for idle caprice of ill-humour, had not master and man, lingering round the corner of the elevated skylight, begun whispering together in low voices. This was unpleasing. And more; the moody air of the Spaniard, which at times had not been without a sort of valetudinarian stateliness, now seemed anything but dignified; while the menial familiarity of the servant lost its original charm of simple-hearted attachment.

In his embarrassment, the visitor turned his face to the other side of the ship. By so doing, his glance accidentally fell on a young Spanish sailor, a coil of rope in his hand, just stepped from the deck to the first round of the mizen-rigging. Perhaps the man would not have been particularly noticed, were it not that, during his ascent to one of the yards, he, with a sort of covert intentness, kept his eye fixed on Captain Delano, from whom, presently, it passed, as if by a natural sequence, to the two whisperers.

His own attention thus redirected to that quarter, Captain Delano gave a slight start. From something in Don Benito's manner just then, it seemed as if the visitor had, at least partly, been the subject of the withdrawn consultation going on – a conjecture as little agreeable to the guest as it was little flattering to the host.

The singular alternations of courtesy and ill-breeding in the Spanish captain were unaccountable, except on one of two suppositions – innocent lunacy, or wicked imposture.

But the first idea, though it might naturally have occurred to an indifferent observer, and, in some respect, had not hitherto been wholly a stranger to Captain Delano's mind, yet, now that, in an incipient way, he began to regard the stranger's conduct something in the light of an intentional affront, of course the idea of lunacy was virtually vacated. But if not a lunatic, what then? Under the circumstances, would a gentleman, nay, any honest boor, act the part now acted by his host? The man was an impostor. Some low-born adventurer, masquerading as an oceanic grandee; yet so ignorant of the first requisites of mere gentlemanhood as to be betrayed into the present remarkable indecorum. That strange ceremoniousness, too, at other times evinced, seemed not uncharacteristic of one playing a part above his real level. Benito Cereno — Don Benito Cereno — a sounding name. One, too, at that period, not unknown, in the surname, to supercargoes and sea captains trading along the Spanish Main, as belonging to one of the most enterprising and extensive mercantile families in all those provinces; several members of it having titles; a sort of Castilian Rothschild, with a noble brother, or cousin, in every great trading town of South America. The alleged Don Benito was in early manhood, about twenty-nine or thirty. To assume a sort of roving cadetship in the maritime affairs of such a house, what more likely scheme for a young knave of talent and spirit? But the Spaniard was a pale invalid. Never mind. For even to the degree of simulating mortal disease, the craft of some tricksters had been known to attain. To think that, under the aspect of infantile weakness, the most savage energies might be couched — those velvets of the Spaniard but the silky paw to his fangs.

From no train of thought did these fancies come; not from within, but from without; suddenly, too, and in one throng, like hoar frost; yet as soon to vanish as the mild sun of Captain Delano's good-nature regained its meridian.

Glancing over once more toward his host — whose side-face, revealed above the skylight, was now turned toward him — he was struck by the profile, whose clearness of cut was refined by the thinness, incident to ill-health, as well as ennobled about the chin by the beard. Away with suspicion. He was a true off-shoot of a true hidalgo Cereno.

Relieved by these and other better thoughts, the visitor, lightly humming a tune, now began indifferently pacing the poop, so as not to betray to Don Benito that he had at all mistrusted incivility, much less duplicity; for such mistrust would yet be proved illusory, and by the event; though, for the present, the circumstance which had provoked that distrust remained unexplained. But when that little mystery should have been cleared up, Captain Delano thought he might extremely regret it, did he allow Don Benito to become aware that he had indulged in ungenerous surmises. In short, to the

Spaniard's black-letter text, it was best, for a while, to leave open margin.

Presently, his pale face twitching and overcast, the Spaniard, still supported by his attendant, moved over toward his guest, when, with even more than his usual embarrassment, and a strange sort of intriguing intonation in his husky whisper, the following conversation began:

'Señor, may I ask how long you have lain at this isle?'

'Oh, but a day or two, Don Benito.'

'And from what port are you last?'

'Canton.'

'And there, señor, you exchanged your seal-skins for teas and silks, I think you said?'

'Yes. Silks, mostly.'

'And the balance you took in specie, perhaps?'

Captain Delano, fidgeting a little, answered:

'Yes; some silver; not a very great deal, though.'

'Ah — well. May I ask how many men have you, señor?'

Captain Delano slightly started, but answered:

'About five-and-twenty, all told.'

'And at present, señor, all on board, I suppose?'

'All on board, Don Benito,' replied the captain, now with satisfaction.

'And will be to-night, señor?'

At this last question, following so many pertinacious ones, for the soul of him Captain Delano could not but look very earnestly at the questioner, who, instead of meeting the glance, with every token of craven discomposure dropped his eyes to the deck; presenting an unworthy contrast to his servant, who, just then, was kneeling at his feet, adjusting a loose shoe-buckle; his disengaged face meantime, with humble curiosity, turned openly up into his master's downcast one.

The Spaniard, still with a guilty shuffle, repeated his question:

'And — and will be to-night, señor?'

'Yes, for aught I know,' returned Captain Delano — 'but nay,' rallying himself into fearless truth, 'some of them talked of going off on another fishing party about midnight.'

'Your ships generally go — go more or less armed, I believe, señor?'

24

'Oh, a six-pounder or two, in case of emergency,' was the intrepidly indifferent reply, 'with a small stock of muskets, sealing-spears, and cutlasses, you know.'

As he thus responded, Captain Delano again glanced at Don Benito, but the latter's eyes were averted; while abruptly and awkwardly shifting the subject, he made some peevish allusion to the calm, and then, without apology, once more, with his attendant, withdrew to the opposite bulwarks, where the whispering was resumed.

At this moment, and ere Captain Delano could cast a cool thought upon what had just passed, the young Spanish sailor, before mentioned, was seen descending from the rigging. In act of stooping over to spring inboard to the deck, his voluminous, unconfined frock, or shirt, of coarse woollen, much spotted with tar, opened out far down the chest, revealing a soiled under-garment of what seemed the finest linen, edged, about the neck, with a narrow blue ribbon, sadly faded and worn. At this moment the young sailor's eye was again fixed on the whisperers, and Captain Delano thought he observed a lurking significance in it, as if silent signs, of some Freemason sort, had that instant been interchanged.

This once more impelled his own glance in the direction of Don Benito, and, as before, he could not but infer that himself formed the subject of the conference. He paused. The sound of the hatchet-polishing fell on his ears. He cast another swift side-look at the two. They had the air of conspirators. In connection with the late questionings, and the incident of the young sailor, these things now begat such return of involuntary suspicion, that the singular guilelessness of the American could not endure it. Plucking up a gay and humorous expression, he crossed over to the two rapidly, saying: 'Ha, Don Benito, your black here seems high in your trust; a sort of privy-counsellor, in fact.'

Upon this, the servant looked up with a good-natured grin, but the master started as from a venomous bite. It was a moment or two before the Spaniard sufficiently recovered himself to reply; which he did, at last, with cold constraint: 'Yes, señor, I have trust in Babo.'

Here Babo, changing his previous grin of mere animal

25

humour into an intelligent smile, not ungratefully eyed his master.

Finding that the Spaniard now stood silent and reserved, as if involuntarily, or purposely giving hint that his guest's proximity was inconvenient just then, Captain Delano, unwilling to appear uncivil even to incivility itself, made some trivial remark and moved off; again and again turning over in his mind the mysterious demeanour of Don Benito Cereno.

He had descended from the poop, and, wrapped in thought, was passing near a dark hatchway, leading down into the steerage, when, perceiving motion there, he looked to see what moved. The same instant there was a sparkle in the shadowy hatchway, and he saw one of the Spanish sailors, prowling there, hurriedly placing his hand in the bosom of his frock, as if hiding something. Before the man could have been certain who it was that was passing, he slunk below out of sight. But enough was seen of him to make sure that he was the same young sailor before noticed in the rigging.

What was that which so sparkled? thought Captain Delano. It was no lamp – no match – no live coal. Could it have been a jewel? But how come sailors with jewels? – or with silk-trimmed under-shirts either? Has he been robbing the trunks of the dead cabin passengers? But if so, he would hardly wear one of the stolen articles on board ship here. Ah, ah – if, now, that was, indeed, a secret sign I saw passing between this suspicious fellow and his captain a while since; if I could only be certain that, in my uneasiness, my senses did not deceive me, then –

Here, passing from one suspicious thing to another, his mind revolved the strange questions put to him concerning his ship.

By a curious coincidence, as each point was recalled, the black wizards of Ashantee would strike up with their hatchets, as in ominous comment on the white stranger's thoughts. Pressed by such enigmas and portents, it would have been almost against nature, had not, even into the least distrustful heart, some ugly misgivings obtruded.

Observing the ship, now helplessly fallen into a current, with enchanted sails, drifting with increased rapidity seaward; and noting that, from a lately intercepted projection of the land, the sealer was hidden, the stout mariner began to quake at thoughts which he barely durst confess to himself. Above all, he began to feel a ghostly dread of Don Benito. And yet, when he roused himself, dilated his chest, felt himself strong on his legs and coolly considered it – what did all these phantoms amount to?

Had the Spaniard any sinister scheme, it must have reference not so much to him (Captain Delano) as to his ship (the *Bachelor's Delight*). Hence the present drifting away of the one ship from the other, instead of favouring any such possible scheme, was, for the time, at least, opposed to it. Clearly any suspicion, combining such contradictions, must needs be delusive. Besides, was it not absurd to think of a vessel in distress – a vessel by sickness almost dismanned of her crew – a vessel whose inmates were parched for water – was it not a thousand times absurd that such a craft should, at present, be of a piratical character; or her commander, either for himself or those under him, cherish any desire but for speedy relief and refreshment? But then, might not general distress, and thirst in particular, be affected? And might not that same undiminished Spanish crew, alleged to have perished off to a remnant, be at that very moment lurking in the hold? On heart-broken pretence of entreating a cup of cold water, fiends in human form had got into lonely dwellings, nor retired until a dark deed had been done. And among the Malay pirates, it was no unusual thing to lure ships after them into their treacherous harbours, or entice boarders from a declared enemy at sea, by the spectacle of thinly manned or vacant decks, beneath which prowled a hundred spears with yellow arms ready to upthrust them through the mats. Not that Captain Delano had entirely credited such things. He had heard of them – and now, as stories, they recurred. The present destination of the ship was the anchorage. There she would be near his own vessel. Upon gaining that vicinity, might not the *San Dominick*, like a slumbering volcano, suddenly let loose energies now hid?

He recalled the Spaniard's manner while telling his story. There was a gloomy hesitancy and subterfuge about it. It was just the manner of one making up his tale for evil purposes as he goes. But if that story was not true, what was the truth? That the ship had unlawfully come into the Spaniard's possession? But in many of its details, especially in reference to the more calamitous parts, such as the fatalities among the seamen, the consequent prolonged beating about, the past sufferings from obstinate calms, and still continued suffering from thirst; in all these points, as well as others, Don Benito's story had corroborated not only the wailing ejaculations of the indiscriminate multitude, white and black, but likewise – what seemed impossible to be counterfeit – by the very expression and play of every human feature, which Captain Delano saw. If Don Benito's story was, throughout, an invention, then every soul on board, down to the youngest negress, was his carefully drilled recruit in the plot: an incredible inference. And yet, if there was ground for mistrusting his veracity, that inference was a legitimate one.

But those questions of the Spaniard. There, indeed, one might pause. Did they not seem put with much the same object with which the burglar or assassin, by day-time, reconnoitres the walls of a house? But, with ill purposes, to solicit such information openly of the chief person endangered, and so, in effect, setting him on his guard; how unlikely a procedure was that. Absurd, then, to suppose that those questions had been prompted by evil designs. Thus, the same conduct, which, in this instance, had raised the alarm, served to dispel it. In short, scarce any suspicion or uneasiness, however apparently reasonable at the time, which was not now, with equal apparent reason, dismissed.

At last he began to laugh at his former forebodings; and laugh at the strange ship for, in its aspect, some way siding with them, as it were; and laugh, too, at the odd-looking blacks, particularly those old scissors-grinders, the Ashantees; and those bedridden old knitting women, the oakum-pickers; and almost at the dark Spaniard himself, the central hobgoblin of all.

For the rest, whatever in a serious way seemed enigmatical, was now good-naturedly explained away by the thought that, for the most part, the poor invalid scarcely knew what he was about; either sulking in black vapours, or putting idle questions without sense or object. Evidently, for the present, the man was not fit to be entrusted with the ship. On some benevolent plea withdrawing the command from him, Captain

Delano would yet have to send her to Conception, in charge of his second mate, a worthy person and good navigator – a plan not more convenient for the *San Dominick* than for Don Benito; for, relieved from all anxiety, keeping wholly to his cabin, the sick man, under the good nursing of his servant, would, probably, by the end of the passage, be in a measure restored to health, and with that he should also be restored to authority.

Such were the American's thoughts. They were tranquillising. There was a difference between the idea of Don Benito's darkly preordaining Captain Delano's fate, and Captain Delano's lightly arranging Don Benito's. Nevertheless, it was not without something of relief that the good seaman presently perceived his whale-boat in the distance. Its absence had been prolonged by unexpected detention at the sealer's side, as well as its returning trip lengthened by the continual recession of the goal.

The advancing speck was observed by the blacks. Their shouts attracted the attention of Don Benito, who, with a return of courtesy, approaching Captain Delano, expressed satisfaction at the coming of some supplies, slight and temporary as they must necessarily prove.

Captain Delano responded; but while doing so, his attention was drawn to something passing on the deck below: among the crowd climbing the landward bulwarks, anxiously watching the coming boat, two blacks, to all appearances accidentally incommoded by one of the sailors, violently pushed him aside, which the sailor some way resenting, they dashed him to the deck, despite the earnest cries of the oakum-pickers.

'Don Benito,' said Captain Delano quickly, 'do you see what is going on there? Look!'

But, seized by his cough, the Spaniard staggered, with both hands to his face, on the point of falling. Captain Delano would have supported him, but the servant was more alert, who, with one hand sustaining his master, with the other applied the cordial. Don Benito restored, the black withdrew his support, slipping aside a little, but dutifully remaining within call of a whisper. Such discretion was here evinced as quite wiped away, in the visitor's eyes, any blemish of impropriety which might have attached to the attendant from the indecorous conferences before mentioned; showing, too, that if the servant were to blame, it might be more the master's fault than his own, since, when left to himself, he could conduct thus well.

His glance called away from the spectacle of disorder to the more pleasing one before him, Captain Delano could not avoid again congratulating his host upon possessing such a servant, who, though perhaps a little too forward now and then, must upon the whole be invaluable to one in the invalid's situation.

'Tell me, Don Benito,' he added, with a smile – 'I should like to have your man here, myself – what will you take for him? Would fifty doubloons be any object?'

'Master wouldn't part with Babo for a thousand doubloons,' murmured the black, overhearing the offer, and taking it in earnest, and, with the strange vanity of a faithful slave, appreciated by his master, scorning to hear so paltry a valuation put upon him by a stranger. But Don Benito, apparently hardly yet completely restored, and again interrupted by his cough, made but some broken reply.

Soon his physical distress became so great, affecting his mind, too, apparently, that, as if to screen the sad spectacle, the servant gently conducted his master below.

Left to himself, the American, to while away the time till his boat should arrive, would have pleasantly accosted some one of the few Spanish seamen he saw; but recalling something that Don Benito had said touching their ill conduct, he refrained; as a shipmaster indisposed to countenance cowardice or unfaithfulness in seamen.

While, with these thoughts, standing with eye directed forward toward that handful of sailors, suddenly he thought that one or two of them returned the glance and with a sort of meaning. He rubbed his eyes, and looked again; but again seemed to see the same thing. Under a new form, but more obscure than any previous one, the old suspicions recurred, but, in the absence of Don Benito, with less of panic than before. Despite the bad account given of the sailors, Captain Delano resolved forthwith to accost one of them. Descending the poop, he made his way through the blacks, his movement drawing a queer cry from the oakum-pickers, prompted by whom, the negroes, twitching each other aside, divided before him; but, as if curious to see what was the object of this deliberate visit to their ghetto, closing in behind, in tolerable order, followed the white stranger up. His progress thus proclaimed as by mounted kings-at-arms, and escorted as by a Caffre guard of honour, Captain Delano, assuming a good-humoured, off-handed air, continued to advance; now and then saying a blithe word to the negroes, and his eye curiously surveying the white faces, here and there sparsely mixed in with the blacks, like stray white pawns venturously involved in the ranks of the chessmen opposed.

While thinking which of them to select for his purpose, he chanced to observe a sailor seated on the deck engaged in tarring the strap of a large block, a circle of blacks squatted round him inquisitively eyeing the process.

The mean employment of the man was in contrast with something superior in his figure. His hand, black with continually thrusting it into the tar-pot held for him by a negro, seemed not naturally allied to his face, a face which would have been a very fine one but for its haggardness. Whether this haggardness had aught to do with criminality, could not be determined; since, as intense heat and cold, though unlike, produce like sensations, so innocence and guilt, when, through casual association with mental pain, stamping any visible impress, use one seal – a hacked one.

Not again that this reflection occurred to Captain Delano at the time, charitable man as he was. Rather another idea. Because observing so singular a haggardness combined with a dark eye, averted as in trouble and shame, and then again recalling Don Benito's confessed ill opinion of his crew, insensibly he was operated upon by certain general notions which, while disconnecting pain and abashment from virtue, invariably link them with vice.

If, indeed, there be any wickedness on board this ship, thought Captain Delano, be sure that man there has fouled his hand in it, even as now he fouls it in the pitch. I don't like to accost him. I will speak to this other, this old Jack here on the windlass.

He advanced to an old Barcelona tar, in ragged red breeches and dirty night-cap, cheeks trenched and bronzed, whiskers dense as thorn hedges. Seated between two sleepy-looking Africans, this mariner, like his younger shipmate, was employed upon some rigging – splicing a cable – the sleepy-looking blacks performing the inferior function of holding the outer parts of the ropes for him.

Upon Captain Delano's approach, the man at once hung his head below its previous level; the one necessary for business. It appeared as if he desired to be thought absorbed, with more than common fidelity, in his task. Being addressed, he glanced up, but with what seemed a furtive, diffident air, which sat strangely enough on his weather-beaten visage, much as if a grizzly bear, instead of growling and biting, should simper and cast sheep's eyes. He was asked several questions concerning the voyage – questions purposely referring to several particulars in Don Benito's narrative, not previously corroborated by those impulsive cries greeting the visitor on first coming on board. The questions were briefly answered, confirming all that remained to be confirmed of the story. The negroes about the windlass joined in with the old sailor; but, as they became talkative, he by degrees became mute, and at length quite glum, seemed morosely unwilling to answer more questions, and yet, all the while, this ursine air was somehow mixed with his sheepish one.

Despairing of getting into unembarrassed talk with such a centaur, Captain Delano, after glancing round for a more promising countenance, but seeing none, spoke pleasantly to the blacks to make way for him; and so, amid various grins and grimaces, returned to the poop, feeling a little strange at first, he could hardly tell why, but upon the whole with regained confidence in Benito Cereno.

How plainly, thought he, did that old whiskerando yonder betray a consciousness of ill desert. No doubt, when he saw me coming, he dreaded lest I, apprised by his captain of the crew's general misbehaviour, came with sharp words for him, and so down with his head. And yet – and yet, now that I think of it, that very old fellow, if I err not, was one of those who seemed so earnestly eyeing me here a while since. Ah, these currents spin one's head round almost as much as they do the ship. Ha, there now's a pleasant sort of sunny sight; quite sociable, too.

His attention had been drawn to a slumbering negress,

partly disclosed through the lacework of some rigging, lying, with youthful limbs carelessly disposed, under the lee of the bulwarks, like a doe in the shade of a woodland rock. Sprawling at her lapped breasts was her wide-awake fawn, stark naked, its black little body half lifted from the deck, crosswise with its dam's; its hands, like two paws, clambering upon her; its mouth and nose ineffectually rooting to get at the mark; and meantime giving a vexatious half-grunt, blending with the composed snore of the negress.

The uncommon vigour of the child at length roused the mother. She started up, at a distance facing Captain Delano. But as if not at all concerned at the attitude in which she had been caught, delightedly she caught the child up, with maternal transports, covering it with kisses.

There's naked nature, now; pure tenderness and love, thought Captain Delano, well pleased.

This incident prompted him to remark the other negresses more particularly than before. He was gratified with their manners: like most uncivilised women, they seemed at once tender of heart and tough of constitution; equally ready to die for their infants or fight for them. Unsophisticated as leopardesses; loving as doves. Ah! thought Captain Delano, these, perhaps, are some of the very women whom Ledyard saw in Africa, and gave such a noble account of.

These natural sights somehow insensibly deepened his confidence and ease. At last he looked to see how his boat was getting on; but it was still pretty remote. He turned to see if Don Benito had returned; but he had not.

To change the scene, as well as to please himself with a leisurely observation of the coming boat, stepping over into the mizen-chains, he clambered his way into the starboard quarter-gallery — one of those abandoned Venetian-looking water-balconies previously mentioned — retreats cut off from the deck. As his foot pressed the half-damp, half-dry sea-mosses matting the place, and a chance phantom cat's paw — an islet of breeze, unheralded, unfollowed — as this ghostly cat's-paw came fanning his cheek; as his glance fell upon the row of small, round dead-lights — all closed like coppered eyes of the coffined — and the state-cabin door, once connecting with the gallery, even as the dead-lights had once looked out upon it,

33

but now caulked fast like a sarcophagus lid; and to a purple-black, tarred-over panel, threshold, and post; and he bethought him of the time, when that state-cabin and this state-balcony had heard the voices of the Spanish king's officers, and the forms of the Lima viceroy's daughters had perhaps leaned where he stood — as these and other images flitted through his mind, as the cat's-paw through the calm, gradually he felt rising a dreamy inquietude, like that of one who alone on the prairie feels unrest from the repose of the noon.

He leaned against the carved balustrade, again looking off toward his boat; but found his eye falling upon the ribbon grass, trailing along the ship's water-line, straight as a border of green box; and parterres of seaweed, broad ovals and crescents, floating nigh and far, with what seemed long formal alleys between, crossing the terraces of swells, and sweeping round as if leading to the grottoes below. And overhanging all was the balustrade by his arm, which, partly stained with pitch and partly embossed with moss, seemed the charred ruin of some summer-house in a grand garden long running to waste.

Trying to break one charm, he was but becharmed anew. Though upon the wide sea, he seemed in some far inland country; prisoner in some deserted château, left to stare at empty grounds, and peer out at vague roads, where never wagon or wayfarer passed.

But these enchantments were a little disenchanted as his eye fell on the corroded main-chains. Of an ancient style, massy and rusty in link, shackle, and bolt, they seemed even more fit for the ship's present business than the one for which she had been built.

Presently he thought something moved nigh the chains. He rubbed his eyes, and looked hard. Groves of rigging were about the chains; and there, peering from behind a great stay, like an Indian from behind a hemlock, a Spanish sailor, a marling-spike in his hand, was seen, who made what seemed an imperfect gesture toward the balcony, but immediately, as if alarmed by some advancing step along the deck within, vanished into the recesses of the hempen forest, like a poacher.

What meant this? Something the man had sought to communicate, unbeknown, to anyone, even to his captain? Did the secret involve aught unfavourable to his captain? Were those previous misgivings of Captain Delano's about to be verified? Or, in his haunted mood at the moment, had some random, unintentional motion of the man, while busy with the stay, as if repairing it, been mistaken for a significant beckoning?

Not unbewildered, again he gazed off for his boat. But it was temporarily hidden by a rocky spur of the isle. As with some eagerness he bent forward, watching for the first shooting view of its beak, the balustrade gave way before him like charcoal. Had he not clutched an outreaching rope he would have fallen into the sea. The crash, though feeble, and the fall, though hollow, of the rotten fragments, must have been overheard. He glanced up. With sober curiosity peering down upon him was one of the old oakum-pickers, slipped from his perch to an outside boom; while below the old negro, and, invisible to him, reconnoitring from a port-hole like a fox from the mouth of its den, crouched the Spanish sailor again. From something suddenly suggested by the man's air, the mad idea now darted into Captain Delano's mind, that Don Benito's plea of indisposition, in withdrawing below, was but a pretence: that he was engaged there maturing his plot, of which the sailor, by some means gaining an inkling, had a mind to warn the stranger against; incited, it may be, by gratitude for a kind word on first boarding the ship. Was it from foreseeing some possible interference like this, that Don Benito had, beforehand, given such a bad character of his sailors, while praising the negroes; though, indeed, the former seemed as docile as the latter the contrary? The whites, too, by nature, were the shrewder race. A man with some evil design, would he not be likely to speak well of that stupidity which was blind to his depravity, and malign that intelligence from which it might not be hidden? Not unlikely, perhaps. But if the whites had dark secrets concerning Don Benito, could then Don Benito be any way in complicity with the blacks? But they were too stupid. Besides, who ever heard of a white so far a renegade as to apostatise from his very species almost, by leaguing in against it with negroes? These difficulties recalled former ones. Lost in their mazes, Captain Delano, who had now regained the deck, was uneasily advancing along it, when he observed a new face; an aged sailor seated cross-legged near the main hatchway. His skin was shrunk up with wrinkles like a pelican's empty pouch; his hair frosted; his countenance grave and composed. His hands were full of ropes, which he was working into a large knot. Some blacks were about him obligingly dipping the strands for him, here and there, as the exigencies of the operation demanded.

Captain Delano crossed over to him, and stood in silence surveying the knot; his mind, by a not uncongenial transition, passing from its own entanglements to those of the hemp. For intricacy, such a knot he had never seen in an American ship, nor indeed any other. The old man looked like an Egyptian priest, making Gordian knots for the temple of Ammon. The knot seemed a combination of double-bowline-knot, treble-crown-knot, back-handed-well-knot, knot-in-and-out-knot, and jamming-knot.

At last, puzzled to comprehend the meaning of such a knot, Captain Delano addressed the knotter:

'What are you knotting there, my man?'

'The knot,' was the brief reply, without looking up.

'So it seems; but what is it for?'

'For someone else to undo,' muttered back the old man, plying his fingers harder than ever, the knot being now nearly completed.

While Captain Delano stood watching him, suddenly the old man threw the knot toward him, saying in broken English – the first heard in the ship – something to this effect: 'Undo it, cut it, quick.' It was said lowly, but with such condensation of rapidity that the long, slow words in Spanish, which had preceded and followed, almost operated as covers to the brief English between.

For a moment, knot in hand, and knot in head, Captain Delano stood mute; while, without further heeding him, the old man was now intent upon other ropes. Presently there was a slight stir behind Captain Delano. Turning, he saw the chained negro, Atufal, standing quietly there. The next moment the old sailor rose, muttering, and, followed by his subordinate negroes, removed to the forward part of the ship, where in the crowd he disappeared.

An elderly negro, in a clout like an infant's, and with a pepper-and-salt head, and a kind of attorney air, now approached Captain Delano. In tolerable Spanish, and with a good-natured, knowing wink, he informed him that the old knotter was simple-witted, but harmless; often playing his odd tricks. The negro concluded by begging the knot, for of course the stranger would not care to be troubled with it. Unconsciously, it was handed to him. With a sort of *congé*, the negro received it, and, turning his back, ferreted into it like a detective custom-house officer after smuggled laces. Soon, with some African word, equivalent to pshaw, he tossed the knot overboard.

All this is very queer now, thought Captain Delano, with a qualmish sort of emotion; but, as one feeling incipient sea-sickness, he strove, by ignoring the symptoms, to get rid of the malady. Once more he looked off for his boat. To his delight, it was now again in view, leaving the rocky spur astern.

The sensation here experienced, after at first relieving his uneasiness, with unforeseen efficacy soon began to remove it. The less distant sight of that well-known boat – showing it, not as before, half blended with the haze, but with outline defined, so that its individuality, like a man's, was manifest; that boat, *Rover* by name, which, though now in strange seas, had often pressed the beach of Captain Delano's home, and, brought to its threshold for repairs, had familiarly lain there, as a Newfoundland dog; the sight of that household boat evoked a thousand trustful associations, which, contrasted with previous suspicions, filled him not only with lightsome confidence, but somehow with half-humorous self-reproaches at his former lack of it.

'What, I, Amasa Delano – Jack of the Beach, as they called me when a lad – I, Amasa; the same that, duck-satchel in hand, used to paddle along the water-side to the school-house made from the old hulk – I, little Jack of the Beach, that used to go berrying with cousin Nat and the rest; I to be murdered here at the ends of the earth, on board a haunted pirate-ship by a horrible Spaniard? Too nonsensical to think of! Who would murder Amasa Delano? His conscience is clean. There is someone above. Fie, fie, Jack of the Beach! you are a child indeed; a child of the second childhood, old boy; you are beginning to dote and drule, I'm afraid.'

Light of heart and foot, he stepped aft, and there was met by

Don Benito's servant, who, with a pleasing expression, responsive to his own present feelings, informed him that his master had recovered from the effects of his coughing fit, and had just ordered him to go present his compliments to his good guest, Don Amasa, and say that he (Don Benito) would soon have the happiness to rejoin him.

There now, do you mark that? again thought Captain Delano, walking the poop. What a donkey I was. This kind gentleman who here sends me his kind compliments, he, but ten minutes ago, dark-lantern in hand, was dodging round some old grindstone in the hold, sharpening a hatchet for me, I thought. Well, well; these long calms have a morbid effect on the mind, I've often heard, though I never believed it before. Ha! glancing toward the boat; there's *Rover*; good dog; a white bone in her mouth. A pretty big bone though, seems to me. – What? Yes, she has fallen afoul of the bubbling tide-rip there. It sets her the other way, too, for the time. Patience.

It was now about noon, though, from the greyness of everything, it seemed to be getting toward dusk.

The calm was confirmed. In the far distance, away from the influence of land, the leaden ocean seemed laid out and leaded up, its course finished, soul gone, defunct. But the current from landward, where the ship was, increased; silently sweeping her further and further toward the tranced waters beyond.

Still, from his knowledge of those latitudes, cherishing hopes of a breeze, and a fair and fresh one, at any moment, Captain Delano, despite present prospects, buoyantly counted upon bringing the *San Dominick* safely to anchor ere night. The distance swept over was nothing; since, with a good wind, ten minutes' sailing would retrace more than sixty minutes' drifting. Meantime, one moment turning to mark *Rover* fighting the tide-rip, and the next to see Don Benito approaching, he continued walking the poop.

Gradually he felt a vexation arising from the delay of his boat; this soon merged into uneasiness; and at last – his eye falling continually, as from a stage-box into the pit, upon the strange crowd before and below him, and, by and by, recognising there the face – now composed to indifference – of the Spanish sailor who had seemed to beckon from the main-chains – something of his old trepidations returned.

Ah, thought he – gravely enough – this is like the ague: because it went off, it follows not that it won't come back.

Though ashamed of the relapse, he could not altogether subdue it; and so, exerting his good-nature to the utmost, insensibly he came to a compromise.

Yes, this is a strange craft; a strange history, too, and strange folks on board. But – nothing more.

By way of keeping his mind out of mischief till the boat should arrive, he tried to occupy it with turning over and over, in a purely speculative sort of way, some lesser peculiarities of the captain and crew. Among others, four curious points recurred:

First, the affair of the Spanish lad assailed with a knife by the slave-boy; an act winked at by Don Benito. Second, the tyranny in Don Benito's treatment of Atufal, the black; as if a child should lead a bull of the Nile by the ring in his nose. Third, the trampling of the sailor by the two negroes; a piece of insolence passed over without so much as a reprimand. Fourth, the cringing submission to their master of all the ship's underlings, mostly blacks; as if by the least inadvertence they feared to draw down his despotic displeasure.

Coupling these points, they seemed somewhat contradictory. But what then, thought Captain Delano, glancing toward his now nearing boat – what then? Why, Don Benito is a very capricious commander. But he is not the first of the sort I have seen; though it's true he rather exceeds any other. But as a nation – continued he in his reveries – these Spaniards are all an odd set; the very word Spaniard has a curious, conspirator, Guy-Fawkish twang to it. And yet, I dare say, Spaniards in the main are as good folks as any in Duxbury, Massachusetts. Ah, good! At last *Rover* has come.

As, with its welcome freight, the boat touched the side, the oakum-pickers, with venerable gestures, sought to restrain the blacks, who, at the sight of three gurried water-casks in its bottom, and a pile of wilted pumpkins in its bow, hung over the bulwarks in disorderly raptures.

Don Benito, with his servant, now appeared; his coming, perhaps, hastened by hearing the noise. Of him Captain Delano sought permission to serve out the water, so that all might share alike, and none injure themselves by unfair excess.

But sensible, and, on Don Benito's account, kind as this offer was, it was received with what seemed impatience; as if aware that he lacked energy as a commander, Don Benito, with the true jealousy of weakness, resented as an affront any interference. So, at least, Captain Delano inferred.

In another moment the casks were being hoisted in, when some of the eager negroes accidentally jostled Captain Delano, where he stood by the gangway; so that, unmindful of Don Benito, yielding to the impulse of the moment, with good-natured authority he bade the blacks stand back; to enforce his words making use of a half-mirthful, half-menacing gesture. Instantly the blacks paused, just where they were, each negro and negress suspended in his or her posture, exactly as the word had found them — for a few seconds continuing so — while, as between the responsive posts of a telegraph, an unknown syllable ran from man to man among the perched oakum-pickers. While the visitor's attention was fixed by this scene, suddenly the hatchet-polishers half rose, and a rapid cry came from Don Benito.

Thinking that at the signal of the Spaniard he was about to be massacred, Captain Delano would have sprung for his boat, but paused, as the oakum-pickers, dropping down into the crowd with earnest exclamations, forced every white and every negro back, at the same moment, with gestures friendly and familiar, almost jocose, bidding him, in substance, not be a fool. Simultaneously the hatchet-polishers resumed their seats, quietly as so many tailors, and at once, as if nothing had happened, the work of hoisting in the casks was resumed, whites and blacks singing at the tackle.

Captain Delano glanced toward Don Benito. As he saw his meagre form in the act of recovering itself from reclining in the servant's arms, into which the agitated invalid had fallen, he could not but marvel at the panic by which himself had been surprised, on the darting supposition that such a commander, who, upon a legitimate occasion, so trivial, too, as it now appeared, could lose all self-command, was, with energetic iniquity, going to bring about his murder.

The casks being on deck, Captain Delano was handed a number of jars and cups by one of the steward's aids, who, in the name of his captain, entreated him to do as he had proposed – dole out the water. He complied, with republican impartiality as to this republican element, which always seeks one level, serving the oldest white no better than the youngest black; excepting, indeed, poor Don Benito, whose condition, if not rank, demanded an extra allowance. To him, in the first place, Captain Delano presented a fair pitcher of the fluid; but, thirsting as he was for it, the Spaniard quaffed not a drop until after several grave bows and salutes. A reciprocation of courtesies which the sight-loving Africans hailed with clapping of hands.

Two of the less wilted pumpkins being reserved for the cabin table, the residue were minced up on the spot for the general regalement. But the soft bread, sugar, and bottled cider, Captain Delano would have given the whites alone, and in chief Don Benito; but the latter objected; which disinterestedness not a little pleased the American; and so mouthfuls all around were given alike to whites and blacks; excepting one bottle of cider, which Babo insisted upon setting aside for his master.

Here it may be observed that as on the first visit of the boat, the American had not permitted his men to board the ship, neither did he now; being unwilling to add to the confusion of the decks.

Not uninfluenced by the peculiar good-humour at present prevailing, and for the time oblivious of any but benevolent thoughts, Captain Delano, who, from recent indications, counted upon a breeze within an hour or two at furthest, dispatched the boat back to the sealer, with orders for all the hands that could be spared immediately to set about rafting casks to the watering-place and filling them. Likewise he bade word be carried to his chief officer, that if, against present expectation, the ship was not brought to anchor by sunset, he need be under no concern; for as there was to be a full moon that night, he (Captain Delano) would remain on board ready to play the pilot, come the wind soon or late.

As the two captains stood together, observing the departing boat – the servant, as it happened, having just spied a spot on his master's velvet sleeve, and silently engaged rubbing it out – the American expressed his regrets that the *San Dominick* had no boats; none, at least, but the unseaworthy old hulk of the long-boat, which, warped as a camel's skeleton in the desert, and almost as bleached, lay pot-wise inverted amidships, one side a little tipped, furnishing a subterraneous sort of den for family groups of the blacks, mostly women and small children; who, squatting on old mats below, or perched above in the dark dome, on the elevated seats, were descried, some distance within, like a social circle of bats, sheltering in some friendly cave; at intervals, ebon flights of naked boys and girls, three or four years old, darting in and out of the den's mouth.

'Had you three or four boats now, Don Benito,' said Captain Delano, 'I think that, by tugging at the oars, your negroes here might help along matters some. Did you sail from port without boats, Don Benito?'

'They were stove in the gales, señor.'

'That was bad. Many men, too, you lost then. Boats and men. Those must have been hard gales, Don Benito.'

'Past all speech,' cringed the Spaniard.

'Tell me, Don Benito,' continued his companion with increased interest, 'tell me, were these gales immediately off the pitch of Cape Horn?'

'Cape Horn? – who spoke of Cape Horn?'

'Yourself did, when giving me an account of your voyage,' answered Captain Delano, with almost equal astonishment at this eating of his own words, even as he ever seemed eating his own heart, on the part of the Spaniard. 'You yourself, Don Benito, spoke of Cape Horn,' he emphatically repeated.

The Spaniard turned, in a sort of stooping posture, pausing an instant, as one about to make a plunging exchange of elements, as from air to water.

At this moment a messenger-boy, a white, hurried by, in the regular performance of his function carrying the last expired half-hour forward to the forecastle, from the cabin time-piece, to have it struck at the ship's large bell.

'Master,' said the servant, discontinuing his work on the coat sleeve, and addressing the rapt Spaniard with a sort of timid apprehensivness, as one charged with a duty, the discharge of which, it was foreseen, would prove irksome to the very person who had imposed it, and for whose benefit it was intended, 'master told me never mind where he was, or how engaged, always to remind him, to a minute, when shaving-time comes. Miguel has gone to strike the half-hour afternoon. It is *now*, master. Will master go into the cuddy?'

'Ah – yes,' answered the Spaniard, starting, as from dreams into realities; then turning upon Captain Delano, he said that ere long he would resume the conversation.

'Then if master means to talk more to Don Amasa,' said the servant, 'why not let Don Amasa sit by master in the cuddy, and master can talk, and Don Amasa can listen, while Babo here lathers and strops.'

'Yes,' said Captain Delano, not unpleased with this sociable plan, 'yes, Don Benito, unless you had rather not, I will go with you.'

'Be it so, señor.'

As the three passed aft, the American could not but think it another strange instance of his host's capriciousness, this being shaved with such uncommon punctuality in the middle of the day. But he deemed it more than likely that the servant's anxious fidelity had something to do with the matter; inasmuch as the timely interruption served to rally his master from the mood which had evidently been coming upon him.

The place called the cuddy was a light deck-cabin formed by the poop, a sort of attic to the large cabin below. Part of it had formerly been the quarters of the officers; but since their death all the partitionings had been thrown down, and the whole interior converted into one spacious and airy marine hall; for absence of fine furniture and picturesque disarray of odd appurtenances, somewhat answering to the wide, cluttered hall of some eccentric bachelor-squire in the country, who hangs his shooting-jacket and tobacco-pouch on deer antlers, and keeps his fishing-rod, tongs, and walking-stick in the same corner.

The similitude was heightened, if not originally suggested, by glimpses of the surrounding sea; since, in one aspect, the country and the ocean seem cousins-german.

The floor of the cuddy was matted. Overhead, four or five old muskets were stuck into horizontal holes along the beams. On one side was a claw-footed old table lashed to the deck; a thumbed missal on it, and over it a small, meagre crucifix attached to the bulk-head. Under the table lay a dented cutlass or two, with a hacked harpoon, among some melancholy old rigging, like a heap of poor friars' girdles. There were also two long, sharp-ribbed settees of Malacca cane, black with age, and uncomfortable to look at as inquisitors' racks, with a large, misshapen arm-chair, which, furnished with a rude barber's crotch at the back, working with a screw, seemed some grotesque engine of torment. A flag locker was in one corner, open, exposing various coloured bunting, some rolled up, others half unrolled, still others tumbled. Opposite was a cumbrous washstand, of black mahogany, all of one block, with a pedestal, like a font, and over it a railed shelf, containing combs, brushes, and other implements of the toilet. A torn hammock of stained grass swung near; the sheets tossed, and the pillow wrinkled up like a brow, as if whoever slept here slept but illy, with alternate visitations of sad thoughts and bad dreams.

The further extremity of the cuddy, overhanging the ship's stern, was pierced with three openings, windows or port-holes, according as men or cannon might peer, socially or unsocially, out of them. At present neither men nor cannon were seen, though huge ring-bolts and other rusty iron fixtures of the woodwork hinted of twenty-four-pounders.

Glancing toward the hammock as he entered, Captain Delano said, 'You sleep here, Don Benito?'

'Yes, señor, since we got into mild weather.'

'This seems a sort of dormitory, a sitting-room, sail-loft, chapel, armoury, and private closet all together, Don Benito,' added Captain Delano, looking round.

'Yes, señor; events have not been favourable to much order in my arrangements.'

Here the servant, napkin on arm, made a motion as if waiting his master's good pleasure. Don Benito signified his readiness, when, seating him in the Malacca arm-chair, and for the guest's convenience drawing opposite one of the settees, the servant commenced operations by throwing back his master's collar and loosening his cravat.

There is something in the negro which, in a peculiar way, fits him for avocations about one's person. Most negroes are natural valets and hair-dressers; taking to the comb and brush congenially as to the castanets, and flourishing them apparently with almost equal satisfaction. There is, too, a smooth

44

tact about them in this employment, with a marvellous, noiseless, gliding briskness, not ungraceful in its way, singularly pleasing to behold, and still more so to be the manipulated subject of. And above all is the great gift of good-humour. Not the mere grin or laugh is here meant. Those were unsuitable. But a certain easy cheefulness, harmonious in every glance and gesture; as though God had set the whole negro to some pleasant tune.

When to this is added the docility arising from the unaspiring contentment of a limited mind, and that susceptibility of blind attachment sometimes inhering in indisputable inferiors, one readily perceives why those hypochondriacs, Johnson and Byron – it may be, something like the hypochondriac Benito Cereno – took to their hearts, almost to the exclusion of the entire white race, their serving-men, the negroes, Barber and Fletcher. But if there be that in the negro which exempts him from the inflicted sourness of the morbid or cynical mind, how, in his most prepossessing aspects, must he appear to a benevolent one? When at ease with respect to exterior things, Captain Delano's nature was not only benign, but familiarly and humorously so. At home, he had often taken rare satisfaction in sitting in his door, watching some free man of colour at his work or play. If on a voyage he chanced to have a black sailor, invariably he was on chatty and half-gamesome terms with him. In fact, like most men of a good, blithe heart, Captain Delano took to negroes, not philanthropically, but genially, just as other men to Newfoundland dogs.

Hitherto, the circumstances in which he found the *San Dominick* had repressed the tendency. But in the cuddy, relieved from his former uneasiness, and, for various reasons, more sociably inclined than at any previous period of the day, and seeing the coloured servant, napkin on arm, so debonnaire about his master, in a business so familiar as that of shaving, too, all his old weakness for negroes returned.

Among other things, he was amused with an odd instance of the African love of bright colours and fine shows, in the black's informally taking from the flag-locker a great piece of bunting of all hues, and lavishly tucking it under his master's chin for an apron.

The mode of shaving among the Spaniards is a little different from what it is with other nations. They have a basin, specifically called a barber's basin, which on one side is scooped out, so as accurately to receive the chin, against which it is closely held in lathering; which is done, not with a brush, but with soap dipped in the water of the basin and rubbed on the face.

In the present instance salt-water was used for lack of better; and the parts lathered were only the upper lip and low down under the throat, all the rest being cultivated beard.

The preliminaries being somewhat novel to Captain Delano, he sat curiously eyeing them, so that no conversation took place, nor, for the present, did Don Benito appear disposed to renew any.

Setting down his basin, the negro searched among the razors, as for the sharpest, and having found it, gave it an additional edge by expertly stropping it on the firm, smooth, oily skin of his open palm; he then made a gesture as if to begin, but midway stood suspended for an instant, one hand elevating the razor, the other professionally dabbling among the bubbling suds on the Spaniard's lank neck. Not unaffected by the close sight of the gleaming steel, Don Benito nervously shuddered; his usual ghastliness was heightened by the lather, which lather, again, was intensified in its hue by the contrasting sootiness of the negro's body. Altogether the scene was somewhat peculiar, at least to Captain Delano, nor, as he saw the two thus postured, could he resist the vagary, that in the black he saw a headsman, and in the white a man at the block. But this was one of those antic conceits, appearing and vanishing in a breath, from which, perhaps, the best regulated mind is not always free.

Meantime the agitation of the Spaniard had a little loosened the bunting from around him, so that one broad fold swept curtain-like over the chair-arm to the floor, revealing, amid a profusion of armorial bars and ground-colours – black, blue and yellow – a closed castle in a blood-red field diagonal with a lion rampant in a white.

'The castle and the lion,' exclaimed Captain Delano – 'why, Don Benito, this is the flag of Spain you use here. It's well it's only I, and not the king, that sees this,' he added, with a smile, 'but' – turning toward the black – 'it's all one, I suppose, so the

46

colours be gay'; which playful remark did not fail somewhat to tickle the negro.

'Now, master,' he said, readjusting the flag, and pressing the head gently further back into the crotch of the chair; 'now, master,' and the steel glanced nigh the throat.

Again Don Benito faintly shuddered.

'You must not shake so, master. See, Don Amasa, master always shakes when I shave him. And yet master knows I never yet have drawn blood, though it's true, if master will shake so, I may some of these times. Now, master,' he continued. 'And now, Don Amasa, please go on with your talk about the gale, and all that; master can hear, and, between times, master can answer.'

'Ah yes, these gales,' said Captain Delano; 'but the more I think of your voyage, Don Benito, the more I wonder, not at the gales, terrible as they must have been, but at the disastrous interval following them. For here, by your account, have you been these two months and more getting from Cape Horn to St Maria, a distance which I myself, with a good wind, have sailed in a few days. True, you had calms, and long ones, but to be becalmed for two months, that is, at least, unusual. Why, Don Benito, had almost any other gentleman told me such a story, I should have been half disposed to a little incredulity.'

Here an involuntary expression came over the Spaniard, similar to that just before on the deck, and whether it was the start he gave, or a sudden gawky roll of the hull in the calm, or a momentary unsteadiness of the servant's hand, however it was, just then the razor drew blood, spots of which stained the creamy lather under the throat: immediately the black barber drew back his steel, and, remaining in his professional attitude, back to Captain Delano, and face to Don Benito, held up the trickling razor, saying, with a sort of half-humorous sorrow, 'See master – you shook so – here's Babo's first blood.

No sword drawn before James the First of England, no assassination in that timid king's presence, could have produced a more terrified aspect than was now presented by Don Benito.

Poor fellow, thought Captain Delano, so nervous he can't even bear the sight of barber's blood; and this unstrung, sick man, is it credible that I should have imagined he meant to spill all my blood, who can't endure the sight of one little drop of his own? Surely, Amasa Delano, you have been beside yourself this day. Tell it not when you get home, sappy Amasa. Well, well, he looks like a murderer, doesn't he? More like as if himself were to be done for. Well, well, this day's experience shall be a good lesson.

Meantime, while these things were running through the honest seaman's mind, the servant had taken the napkin from his arm, and to Don Benito had said: 'But answer Don Amasa, please, master, while I wipe this ugly stuff off the razor, and strop it again.'

As he said the words, his face was turned half round, so as to be alike visible to the Spaniard and the American, and seemed, by its expression, to hint, that he was desirous, by getting his master to go on with the conversation, considerably to withdraw his attention from the recent annoying accident. As if glad to snatch the offered relief, Don Benito resumed, rehearsing to Captain Delano, that not only were the calms of unusual duration, but the ship had fallen in with obstinate currents; and other things he added, some of which were but repetitions of former statements, to explain how it came to pass that the passage from Cape Horn to St Maria had been so exceedingly long; now and then mingling with his words incidental praises, less qualified than before, to the blacks, for their general good conduct. These particulars were not given consecutively, the servant, at convenient times, using his razor, and so, between the intervals of shaving, the story and panegyric went on with more than usual huskiness.

To Captain Delano's imagination, now again not wholly at rest, there was something so hollow in the Spaniard's manner, with apparently some reciprocal hollowness in the servant's dusky comment of silence, that the idea flashed across him, that possibly master and man, for some unknown purpose, were acting out, both in word and deed, nay, to the very tremor of Don Benito's limbs, some juggling play before him. Neither did the suspicion of collusion lack apparent support, from the fact of those whispered conferences before mentioned. But then, what could be the object of enacting this play of the barber before him? At last, regarding the notion as a whimsy, insensibly suggested, perhaps, by the theatrical aspect of Don

Benito in his harlequin ensign, Captain Delano speedily banished it.

The shaving over, the servant bestirred himself with a small bottle of scented waters, pouring a few drops on the head, and then diligently rubbing; the vehemence of the exercise causing the muscles of his face to twitch rather strangely.

His next operation was with comb, scissors, and brush; going round and round, smoothing a curl here, clipping an unruly whisker-hair there, giving a graceful sweep to the temple-lock, with other impromptu touches evincing the hand of a master; while, like any resigned gentleman in barber's hands, Don Benito bore all, much less uneasily, at least, than he had done the razoring; indeed, he sat so pale and rigid now, that the negro seemed a Nubian sculptor finishing off a white statue-head.

All being over at last, the standard of Spain removed, tumbled up, and tossed back into the flag-locker, the negro's warm breath blowing away any stray hair which might have lodged down his master's neck; collar and cravat readjusted; a speck of lint whisked off the velvet lapel; all this being done; backing off a little space, and pausing with an expression of subdued self-complacency, the servant for a moment surveyed his master, as, in toilet at least, the creature of his own tasteful hands.

Captain Delano playfully complimented him upon his achievement; at the same time congratulating Don Benito.

But neither sweet waters, nor shampooing, nor fidelity, nor sociality, delighted the Spaniard. Seeing him relapsing into forbidding gloom, and still remaining seated, Captain Delano, thinking that his presence was undesired just then, withdrew, on pretence of seeing whether, as he had prophesied, any signs of a breeze were visible.

Walking forward to the mainmast, he stood a while thinking over the scene, and not without some undefined misgivings, when he heard a noise near the cuddy, and turning, saw the negro, his hand to his cheek. Advancing, Captain Delano perceived that the cheek was bleeding. He was about to ask the cause, when the negro's wailing soliloquy enlightened him.

'Ah, when will master get better from his sickness; only the sour heart that sour sickness breeds made him serve Babo so;

cutting Babo with the razor, because, only by accident, Babo had given master one little scratch; and for the first time in so many a day, too. Ah, ah, ah,' holding his hand to his face.

Is it possible, thought Captain Delano; was it to wreak in private his Spanish spite against this poor friend of his, that Don Benito, by his sullen manner, impelled me to withdraw? Ah, this slavery breeds ugly passions in man. Poor fellow!

He was about to speak in sympathy to the negro, but with a timid reluctance he now re-entered the cuddy.

Presently master and man came forth; Don Benito leaning on his servant as if nothing had happened.

But a sort of love-quarrel, after all, thought Captain Delano.

He accosted Don Benito, and they slowly walked together. They had gone but a few paces, when the steward – a tall, rajah-looking mulatto, orientally set off with a pagoda turban formed by three or four Madras handkerchiefs wound about his head, tier on tier – approaching with a salaam, announced lunch in the cabin.

On their way thither, the two captains were preceded by the mulatto, who, turning round as he advanced, with continual smiles and bows, ushered them on, a display of elegance which quite completed the insignificance of the small bare-headed Babo, who, as if not unconscious of inferiority, eyed askance the graceful steward. But in part, Captain Delano imputed his jealous watchfulness to that peculiar feeling which the full-blooded African entertains for the adulterated one. As for the steward, his manner, if not bespeaking much dignity of self-respect, yet evidenced his extreme desire to please; which is doubly meritorious, as at once Christian and Chesterfieldian.

Captain Delano observed with interest that while the complexion of the mulatto was hybrid, his physiognomy was European – classically so.

'Don Benito,' whispered he, 'I am glad to see this usher-of-the-golden-rod of yours; the sight refutes an ugly remark once made to me by a Barbados planter; that when a mulatto has a regular European face, look out for him; he is a devil. But see, your steward here has features more regular than King George's of England; and yet there he nods, and bows, and smiles; a king, indeed – the king of kind hearts and polite fellows. What a pleasant voice he has, too!'

'He has, señor.'

'But tell me, has he not, so far as you have known him, always proved a good, worthy fellow?' said Captain Delano, pausing, while with a final genuflection the steward disappeared into the cabin; 'come, for the reason just mentioned, I am curious to know.'

'Francesco is a good man,' a sort of sluggishly responded Don Benito, like a phlegmatic appreciator, who would neither find fault nor flatter.

'Ah, I thought so. For it were strange, indeed, and not very creditable to us white-skins, if a little of our blood mixed with the African's should, far from improving the latter's quality, have the sad effect of pouring vitriolic acid into black broth; improving the hue, perhaps, but not the wholesomeness.'

'Doubtless, doubtless, señor, but' – glancing at Babo – 'not to speak of negroes, your planter's remark I have heard applied to the Spanish and Indian intermixtures in our provinces. But I know nothing about the matter,' he listlessly added.

And here they entered the cabin.

The lunch was a frugal one. Some of Captain Delano's fresh fish and pumpkins, biscuit and salt beef, the reserved bottle of cider, and the *San Dominick*'s last bottle of Canary.

As they entered, Francesco, with two or three coloured aids, was hovering over the table giving the last adjustments. Upon perceiving their master they withdrew, Francesco making a smiling *congé*, and the Spaniard, without condescending to notice it, fastidiously remarking to his companion that he relished not superfluous attendance.

Without companions, host and guest sat down, like a childless married couple, at opposite ends of the table, Don Benito waving Captain Delano to his place, and, weak as he was, insisting upon that gentleman being seated before himself.

The negro placed a rug under Don Benito's feet, and a cushion behind his back, and then stood behind, not his master's chair, but Captain Delano's. At first, this a little surprised the latter. But it was soon evident that, in taking his position, the black was still true to his master; since by facing him he could the more readily anticipate his slightest want.

'This is an uncommonly intelligent fellow of yours, Don Benito,' whispered Captain Delano across the table.

'You say true, señor.'

During the repast, the guest again reverted to parts of Don Benito's story, begging further particulars here and there. He inquired how it was that the scurvy and fever should have committed such wholesale havoc upon the whites, while destroying less than half of the blacks. As if this question reproduced the whole scene of plague before the Spaniard's eyes, miserably reminding him of his solitude in a cabin where before he had had so many friends and officers round him, his hand shook, his face became hueless, broken words escaped; but directly the sane memory of the past seemed replaced by insane terrors of the present. With starting eyes he stared before him at vacancy. For nothing was to be seen but the hand of his servant pushing the Canary over toward him. At length a few sips served partially to restore him. He made random reference to the different constitution of races, enabling one to offer more resistance to certain maladies than another. The thought was new to his companion.

Presently Captain Delano, intending to say something to his host concerning the pecuniary part of the business he had undertaken for him, especially – since he was strictly accountable to his owners – with reference to the new suit of sails, and other things of that sort; and naturally preferring to conduct such affairs in private, was desirous that the servants should withdraw; imagining that Don Benito for a few minutes could dispense with his attendance. He, however, waited a while; thinking that, as the conversation proceeded, Don Benito, without being prompted, would perceive the propriety of the step.

But it was otherwise. At last catching his host's eye, Captain Delano, with a slight backward gesture of his thumb, whispered, 'Don Benito, pardon me, but there is an interference with the full expression of what I have to say to you.'

Upon this the Spaniard changed countenance; which was imputed to his resenting the hint, as in some way a reflection upon his servant. After a moment's pause, he assured his guest that the black's remaining with them could be of no disservice; because since losing his officers he had made Babo (whose original office, it now appeared, had been captain of the slaves) not only his constant attendant and companion, but in all things his confidant.

After this, nothing more could be said; though, indeed, Captain Delano could hardly avoid some little tinge of irritation upon being left ungratified in so inconsiderable a wish, by one, too, for whom he intended such solid services. But it is only his querulousness, thought he; and so filling his glass he proceeded to business.

The price of the sails and other matters was fixed upon. But while this was being done, the American observed that, though his original offer of assistance had been hailed with hectic animation, yet now when it was reduced to a business transaction, indifference and apathy were betrayed. Don Benito, in fact, appeared to submit to hearing the details more out of regard to common propriety than from any impression that weighty benefit to himself and his voyage was involved.

Soon, his manner became still more reserved. The effort was vain to seek to draw him into social talk. Gnawed by his splenetic mood, he sat twitching his beard, while to little purpose the hand of his servant, mute as that on the wall, slowly pushed over the Canary.

Lunch being over, they sat down on the cushioned transom; the servant placing a pillow behind his master. The long continuance of the calm had now affected the atmosphere. Don Benito sighed heavily, as if for breath.

'Why not adjourn to the cuddy,' said Captain Delano; 'there is more air there.' But the host sat silent and motionless.

Meantime his servant knelt before him, with a large fan of feathers. And Francesco, coming in on tiptoes, handed the negro a little cup of aromatic waters, with which at intervals he chafed his master's brow; smoothing the hair along the temples as a nurse does a child's. He spoke no word. He only rested his eye on his master's, as if, amid all Don Benito's distress, a little to refresh his spirit by the silent sight of fidelity.

Presently the ship's bell sounded two o'clock; and through the cabin windows a slight rippling of the sea was discerned; and from the desired direction.

'There,' exclaimed Captain Delano, 'I told you so, Don Benito, look!'

He had risen to his feet, speaking in a very animated tone,

with a view the more to rouse his companion. But though the crimson curtain of the stern window near him that moment fluttered against his pale cheek, Don Benito seemed to have even less welcome for the breeze than the calm.

Poor fellow, thought Captain Delano, bitter experience has taught him that one ripple does not make a wind, any more than one swallow a summer. But he is mistaken for once. I will get his ship in for him, and prove it.

Briefly alluding to his weak condition, he urged his host to remain quietly where he was, since he (Captain Delano) would with pleasure take upon himself the responsibility of making the best use of the wind.

Upon gaining the deck, Captain Delano started at the unexpected figure of Atufal, monumentally fixed at the threshold, like one of those sculptured porters of black marble guarding the porches of Egyptian tombs.

But this time the start was, perhaps, purely physical. Atufal's presence, singularly attesting docility even in sullenness, was contrasted with that of the hatchet-polishers, who in patience evinced their industry; while both spectacles showed, that lax as Don Benito's general authority might be, still, whenever he chose to exert it, no man so savage or colossal but must, more or less, bow.

Snatching a trumpet which hung from the bulwarks, with a free step Captain Delano advanced to the forward edge of the poop, issuing his orders in his best Spanish. The few sailors and many negroes, all equally pleased, obediently set about heading the ship toward the harbour.

While giving some directions about setting a lower stun'-sail, suddenly Captain Delano heard a voice faithfully repeating his orders. Turning, he saw Babo, now for the time acting, under the pilot, his original part of captain of the slaves. This assistance proved valuable. Tattered sails and warped yards were soon brought into some trim. And no brace or halyard was pulled but to the blithe songs of the inspirited negroes.

Good fellows, thought Captain Delano, a little training would make fine sailors of them. Why, see, the very women pull and sing too. These must be some of those Ashantee negresses that make such capital soldiers, I've heard. But who's at the helm? I must have a good hand there.

He went to see.

The *San Dominick* steered with a cumbrous tiller, with large horizontal pulleys attached. At each pulley-end stood a subordinate black, and between them, at the tiller-head, the responsible post, a Spanish seaman, whose countenance evinced his due share in the general hopefulness and confidence at the coming of the breeze.

He proved the same man who had behaved with so shamefaced an air on the windlass.

'Ah – it is you, my man,' exclaimed Captain Delano – 'well, no more sheep's-eyes now; – look straight forward and keep the ship so. Good hand, I trust? And want to get into the harbour, don't you?'

The man assented with an inward chuckle, grasping the tiller-head firmly. Upon this, unperceived by the American, the two blacks eyed the sailor intently.

Finding all right at the helm, the pilot went forward to the forecastle, to see how matters stood there.

The ship now had way enough to breast the current. With the approach of evening, the breeze would be sure to freshen.

Having done all that was needed for the present, Captain Delano, giving his last orders to the sailors, turned aft to report affairs to Don Benito in the cabin; perhaps additionally incited to rejoin him by the hope of snatching a moment's private chat while the servant was engaged upon deck.

From opposite sides, there were, beneath the poop, two approaches to the cabin; one further forward than the other, and consequently communicating with a longer passage. Marking the servant still above, Captain Delano, taking the nighest entrance – the one last named, and at whose porch Atufal still stood – hurried on his way, till, arrived at the cabin threshold, he paused an instant, a little to recover from his eagerness. Then, with the words of his intended business upon his lips, he entered. As he advanced toward the seated Spaniard, he heard another footstep, keeping time with his. From the opposite door, a salver in hand, the servant was likewise advancing.

'Confound the faithful fellow,' thought Captain Delano; 'what a vexatious coincidence.'

Possibly the vexation might have been something different,

were it not for the brisk confidence inspired by the breeze. But even as it was, he felt a slight twinge, from a sudden indefinite association in his mind of Babo with Atufal.

'Don Benito,' said he, 'I give you joy; the breeze will hold, and will increase. By the way, your tall man and time-piece, Atufal, stands without. By your order, of course?'

Don Benito recoiled, as if at some bland satirical touch, delivered with such adroit garnish of apparent good breeding as to present no handle for retort.

He is like one flayed alive, thought Captain Delano; where may one touch him without causing a shrink?

The servant moved before his master, adjusting a cushion; recalled to civility, the Spaniard stiffly replied: 'You are right. The slave appears where you saw him, according to my command; which is, that if at the given hour I am below, he must take his stand and abide my coming.'

'Ah now, pardon me, but that is treating the poor fellow like an ex-king indeed. Ah, Don Benito,' smiling, 'for all the licence you permit in some things, I fear lest, at bottom, you are a bitter hard master.'

Again Don Benito shrank; and this time, as the good sailor thought, from a genuine twinge of his conscience.

Again conversation became constrained. In vain Captain Delano called attention to the now perceptible motion of the keel gently cleaving the sea; with lack-lustre eye, Don Benito returned words few and reserved.

By and by, the wind having steadily risen, and still blowing right into the harbour, bore the *San Dominick* swiftly on. Rounding a point of land, the sealer at distance came into open view.

Meantime Captain Delano had again repaired to the deck, remaining there some time. Having at last altered the ship's course, so as to give the reef a wide berth, he returned for a few moments below.

I will cheer up my poor friend this time, thought he.

'Better and better, Don Benito,' he cried as he blithely re-entered: 'there will soon be an end to your cares, at least for a while. For when, after a long, sad voyage, you know, the anchor drops into the haven, all its vast weight seems lifted from the captain's heart. We are getting on famously, Don

Benito. My ship is in sight. Look through this side-light here; there she is; all a-taunt-o! The *Bachelor's Delight*, my good friend. Ah, how this wind braces one up. Come, you must take a cup of coffee with me this evening. My old steward will give you as fine a cup as ever any sultan tasted. What say you, Don Benito, will you?'

At first, the Spaniard glanced feverishly up, casting a longing look toward the sealer, while with mute concern his servant gazed into his face. Suddenly the old ague of coldness returned, and dropping back to his cushions he was silent.

'You do not answer. Come, all day you have been my host; would you have hospitality all on one side?'

'I cannot go,' was the response.

'What? it will not fatigue you. The ships will lie together as near as they can, without swinging foul. It will be little more than stepping from deck to deck; which is but as from room to room. Come, come, you must not refuse me.'

'I cannot go,' decisively and repulsively repeated Don Benito.

Renouncing all but the last appearance of courtesy, with a sort of cadaverous sullenness, and biting his thin nails to the quick, he glanced, almost glared, at his guest, as if impatient that a stranger's presence should interfere with the full indulgence of his morbid hour. Meantime the sound of the parted waters came more and more gurglingly and merrily in at the windows; as reproaching him for his dark spleen; as telling him that, sulk as he might, and go mad with it, nature cared not a jot; since, whose fault was it, pray?

But the foul mood was now at its depth, as the fair wind at its height.

There was something in the man so far beyond any mere unsociality or sourness previously evinced, that even the forbearing good-nature of his guest could no longer endure it. Wholly at a loss to account for such demeanour, and deeming sickness with eccentricity, however extreme, no adequate excuse, well satisfied, too, that nothing in his own conduct could justify it, Captain Delano's pride began to be roused. Himself became reserved. But all seemed one to the Spaniard. Quitting him, therefore, Captain Delano once more went to the deck.

The ship was now within less than two miles of the sealer. The whale-boat was seen darting over the interval.

To be brief, the two vessels, thanks to the pilot's skill, ere long in neighbourly style lay anchored together.

Before returning to his own vessel, Captain Delano had intended communicating to Don Benito the smaller details of the proposed services to be rendered. But, as it was, unwilling anew to subject himself to rebuffs, he resolved, now that he had seen the *San Dominick* safely moored, immediately to quit her, without further allusion to hospitality or business. Indefinitely postponing his ulterior plans, he would regulate his future actions according to future circumstances. His boat was ready to receive him; but his host still tarried below. Well, thought Captain Delano, if he has little breeding, the more need to show mine. He descended to the cabin to bid a ceremonious, and, it may be, tacitly rebukeful adieu. But to his great satisfaction, Don Benito, as if he began to feel the weight of that treatment with which his slighted guest had, not indecorously, retaliated upon him, now supported by his servant, rose to his feet, and grasping Captain Delano's hand, stood tremulous; too much agitated to speak. But the good augury hence drawn was suddenly dashed, by his resuming all his previous reserve, with augmented gloom, as, with half-averted eyes, he silently reseated himself on his cushions. With a corresponding return of his own chilled feelings, Captain Delano bowed and withdrew.

He was hardly midway in the narrow corridor, dim as a tunnel, leading from the cabin to the stairs, when a sound, as of the tolling for execution in some jail-yard, fell on his ears. It was the echo of the ship's flawed bell, striking the hour, drearily reverberated in this subterranean vault. Instantly, by a fatality not to be withstood, his mind, responsive to the portent, swarmed with superstitious suspicions. He paused. In images far swifter than these sentences, the minutest details of all his former distrusts swept through him.

Hitherto, credulous good-nature had been too ready to furnish excuses for reasonable fears. Why was the Spaniard, so superfluously punctilious at times, now heedless of common propriety in not accompanying to the side his departing guest? Did indisposition forbid? Indisposition had not forbidden more irksome exertion that day. His last equivocal demeanour recurred. He had risen to his feet, grasped his guest's hand, motioned toward his hat; then, in an instant, all was eclipsed in sinister muteness and gloom. Did this imply one brief, repentant relenting at the final moment, from some iniquitous plot, followed by remorseless return to it? His last glance seemed to express a calamitous, yet acquiescent farewell to Captain Delano for ever. Why decline the invitation to visit the sealer that evening? Or was the Spaniard less hardened than the Jew, who refrained not from supping at the board of him whom the same night he meant to betray? What imported all those day-long enigmas and contradictions, except they were intended to mystify, preliminary to some stealthy blow? Atufal, the pretended rebel, but punctual shadow, that moment lurked by the threshold without. He seemed a sentry, and more. Who, by his own confession, had stationed him there? Was the negro now lying in wait?

The Spaniard behind – his creature before: to rush from darkness to light was the involuntary choice.

The next moment, with clenched jaw and hand, he passed Atufal, and stood unharmed in the light. As he saw his trim ship lying peacefully at anchor, and almost within ordinary call; as he saw his household boat, with familiar faces in it, patiently rising and falling on the short waves by the *San Dominick*'s side; and then, glancing about the decks where he stood, saw the oakum-pickers still gravely plying their fingers; and heard the low, buzzing whistle and industrious hum of the hatchet-polishers, still bestirring themselves over their endless occupation; and more than all, as he saw the benign aspect of nature, taking her innocent repose in the evening; the screened sun in the quiet camp of the west shining out like the mild light from Abraham's tent; as charmed eye and ear took in all these, with the chained figure of the black, clenched jaw and hand relaxed. Once again he smiled at the phantoms which had mocked him, and felt something like a tinge of remorse, that, by harbouring them even for a moment, he should, by implication, have betrayed an atheist doubt of the ever-watchful Providence above.

There was a few minutes' delay, while, in obedience to his orders, the boat was being hooked along to the gangway.

During this interval, a sort of saddened satisfaction stole over Captain Delano, at thinking of the kindly offices he had that day discharged for a stranger. Ah, thought he, after good actions one's conscience is never ungrateful, however much so the benefited party may be.

Presently, his foot, in the first act of descent into the boat, pressed the first round of the side-ladder, his face presented inward upon the deck. In the same moment, he heard his name courteously sounded; and, to his pleased surprise, saw Don Benito advancing – an unwonted energy in his air, as if, at the last moment, intent upon making amends for his recent discourtesy. With instinctive good feeling, Captain Delano, withdrawing his foot, turned and reciprocally advanced. As he did so, the Spaniard's nervous eagerness increased, but his vital energy failed; so that, the better to support him, the servant, placing his master's hand on his naked shoulder, and gently holding it there, formed himself into a sort of crutch.

When the two captains met, the Spaniard again fervently took the hand of the American, at the same time casting an earnest glance into his eyes, but, as before, too much overcome to speak.

I have done him wrong, self-reproachfully thought Captain Delano; his apparent coldness has deceived me; in no instance has he meant to offend.

Meantime, as if fearful that the continuance of the scene might too much unstring his master, the servant seemed anxious to terminate it. And so, still presenting himself as a crutch, and walking between the two captains, he advanced with them toward the gangway; while still, as if full of kindly contrition, Don Benito would not let go the hand of Captain Delano, but retained it in his, across the black's body.

Soon they were standing by the side, looking over into the boat, whose crew turned up their curious eyes. Waiting a moment for the Spaniard to relinquish his hold, the now embarrassed Captain Delano lifted his foot, to overstep the threshold of the open gangway; but still Don Benito would not let go his hand. And yet, with an agitated tone, he said, 'I can go no further; here I must bid you adieu. Adieu, my dear, dear Don Amasa. Go – go!' suddenly tearing his hand loose, 'go, and God guard you better than me, my best friend.'

Not unaffected, Captain Delano would now have lingered; but catching the meekly admonitory eye of the servant, with a hasty farewell he descended into his boat, followed by the continual adieus of Don Benito, standing rooted in the gangway.

Seating himself in the stern, Captain Delano, making a last salute, ordered the boat shoved off. The crew had their oars on end. The bowsmen pushed the boat a sufficient distance for the oars to be lengthwise dropped. The instant that was done, Don Benito sprang over the bulwarks, falling at the feet of Captain Delano; at the same time calling toward his ship, but in tones so frenzied, that none in the boat could understand him. But, as if not equally obtuse, three sailors, from three different and distant parts of the ship, splashed into the sea, swimming after their captain, as if intent upon his rescue.

The dismayed officer of the boat eagerly asked what this meant. To which, Captain Delano, turning a disdainful smile upon the unaccountable Spaniard, answered that, for his part, he neither knew nor cared; but it seemed as if Don Benito had taken it into his head to produce the impression among his people that the boat wanted to kidnap him. 'Or else – give way for your lives,' he wildly added, starting at a clattering hubbub in the ship, above which rang the tocsin of the hatchet-polishers; and seizing Don Benito by the throat he added, 'this plotting pirate means murder!' Here, in apparent verification of the words, the servant, a dagger in his hand, was seen on the rail overhead, poised, in the act of leaping, as if with desperate fidelity to befriend his master to the last; while, seemingly to aid the black, the three white sailors were trying to clamber into the hampered bow. Meantime, the whole host of negroes, as if inflamed at the sight of their jeopardised captain, impended in one sooty avalanche over the bulwarks.

All this, with what preceded, and what followed, occurred with such involutions of rapidity, that past, present, and future seemed one.

Seeing the negro coming, Captain Delano had flung the Spaniard aside, almost in the very act of clutching him, and, by the unconscious recoil, shifting his place, with arms thrown up, so promptly grappled the servant in his descent, that with dagger presented at Captain Delano's heart, the black seemed of purpose to have leaped there as to his mark. But the weapon was wrenched away, and the assailant dashed down into the bottom of the boat, which now, with disentangled oars, began to speed through the sea.

At this juncture, the left hand of Captain Delano, on one side, again clutched the half-reclined Don Benito, heedless that he was in a speechless faint, while his right foot, on the other side, ground the prostrate negro; and his right arm pressed for added speed on the after-oar, his eye bent forward, encouraging his men to their utmost.

But here, the officer of the boat, who had at last succeeded in beating off the towing sailors, and was now, with face turned aft, assisting the bowsman at his oar, suddenly called to Captain Delano, to see what the black was about; while a Portuguese oarsman shouted to him to give heed to what the Spaniard was saying.

Glancing down at his feet, Captain Delano saw the freed hand of the servant aiming with a second dagger – a small one, before concealed in his wool – with this he was snakishly writhing up from the boat's bottom, at the heart of his master, his countenance lividly vindictive, expressing the centred purpose of his soul; while the Spaniard, half choked, was vainly shrinking away, with husky words, incoherent to all but the Portuguese.

That moment, across the long-benighted mind of Captain Delano, a flash of revelation swept, illuminating, in unanticipated clearness, his host's whole mysterious demeanour, with every enigmatic event of the day, as well as the entire past voyage of the *San Dominick*. He smote Babo's hand down, but his own heart smote him harder. With infinite pity he withdrew his hold from Don Benito. Not Captain Delano, but Don Benito, the black, in leaping into the boat, had intended to stab.

Both the black's hands were held, as, glancing up toward the *San Dominick*, Captain Delano, now with scales dropped from his eyes, saw the negroes, not in misrule, not in tumult, not as if frantically concerned for Don Benito, but with mask torn away, flourishing hatchets and knives, in ferocious piratical revolt. Like delirious black dervishes, the six Ashantees danced on the poop. Prevented by their foes from springing into the water, the Spanish boys were hurrying up to the topmost spars, while such of the few Spanish sailors, not already in the sea, less alert, were descried, helplessly mixed in, on deck, with the blacks.

Meantime Captain Delano hailed his own vessel, ordering the ports up, and the guns run out. But by this time the cable of the *San Dominick* had been cut; and the fag-end, in lashing out, whipped away the canvas shroud about the beak, suddenly revealing, as the bleached hull swung round toward the open ocean, death for the figure-head, in a human skeleton; chalky comment on the chalked words below, '*Follow your leader.*'

At the sight, Don Benito, covering his face, wailed out: ' 'Tis he, Aranda! my murdered, unburied friend!'

Upon reaching the sealer, calling for ropes, Captain Delano bound the negro, who made no resistance, and had him hoisted to the deck. He would then have assisted the now almost helpless Don Benito up the side; but Don Benito, wan as he was, refused to move, or be moved, until the negro should have been first put below out of view. When, presently assured that it was done, he no more shrank from the ascent.

The boat was immediately dispatched back to pick up the three swimming sailors. Meantime, the guns were in readiness, though, owing to the *San Dominick* having glided somewhat astern of the sealer, only the aftermost one could be brought to bear. With this, they fired six times; thinking to cripple the fugitive ship by bringing down her spars. But only a few inconsiderable ropes were shot away. Soon the ship was beyond the gun's range, steering broad out of the bay; the blacks thickly clustering round the bowsprit, one moment with taunting cries toward the whites, the next with upthrown gestures hailing the now dusky moors of ocean — cawing crows escaped from the hand of the fowler.

The first impulse was to slip the cables and give chase. But, upon second thoughts, to pursue with whale-boat and yawl seemed more promising.

Upon inquiring of Don Benito what firearms they had on board the *San Dominick*, Captain Delano was answered that they had none that could be used; because, in the earlier stages of the mutiny, a cabin passenger, since dead, had secretly put out of order the locks of what few muskets there were. But with all his remaining strength, Don Benito entreated the American not to give chase, either with ship or boat; for the negroes had already proved themselves such desperadoes, that, in case of a present assault, nothing but a total massacre of the whites could be looked for. But, regarding this warning as coming from one whose spirit had been crushed by misery, the American did not give up his design.

The boats were got ready and armed. Captain Delano ordered his men into them. He was going himself when Don Benito grasped his arm.

'What! have you saved my life, señor, and are you now going to throw away your own?'

The officers also, for reasons connected with their interests and those of the voyage, and a duty owing to the owners, strongly objected against their commander's going. Weighing their remonstrances a moment, Captain Delano felt bound to remain; appointing his chief mate – an athletic and resolute man, who had been a privateer's-man – to head the party. The more to encourage the sailors, they were told, that the Spanish captain considered his ship good as lost; that she and her cargo, including some gold and silver, were worth more than a thousand doubloons. Take her, and no small part should be theirs. The sailors replied with a shout.

The fugitives had now almost gained an offing. It was nearly night; but the moon was rising. After hard, prolonged pulling, the boats came up on the ship's quarters, at a suitable distance laying upon their oars to discharge their muskets. Having no bullets to return, the negroes sent their yells. But, upon the second volley, Indian-like, they hurtled their hatchets. One took off a sailor's fingers. Another struck the whale-boat's bow, cutting off the rope there, and remaining stuck in the gunwale like a woodman's axe. Snatching it, quivering from its lodgment, the mate hurled it back. The returned gauntlet now stuck in the ship's broken quarter-gallery, and so remained.

The negroes giving too hot a reception, the whites kept a more respectful distance. Hovering now just out of reach of the hurtling hatchets, they, with a view to the close encounter which must soon come, sought to decoy the blacks into entirely disarming themselves of their most murderous weapons in a hand-to-hand fight, by foolishly flinging them, as missiles, short of the mark, into the sea. But, ere long, perceiving the stratagem, the negroes desisted, though not before many of them had to replace their lost hatchets with hand spikes; an exchange which, as counted upon, proved, in the end, favourable to the assailants.

Meantime, with a strong wind, the ship still clove the water; the boats alternately falling behind, and pulling up, to discharge fresh volleys.

The fire was mostly directed toward the stern, since there, chiefly, the negroes, at present, were clustering. But to kill or maim the negroes was not the object. To take them, with the ship, was the object. To do it, the ship must be boarded; which could not be done by boats while she was sailing so fast.

A thought now struck the mate. Observing the Spanish boys still aloft, high as they could get, he called to them to descend to the yards, and cut adrift the sails. It was done. About this time, owing to causes hereafter to be shown, two Spaniards, in the dress of sailors, and conspicuously showing themselves, were killed; not by volleys, but by deliberate marksman's shots; while, as it afterward appeared, by one of the general discharges, Atufal, the black, and the Spaniard at the helm likewise were killed. What now with the loss of the sails, and loss of leaders, the ship became unmanageable to the negroes.

With creaking masts, she came heavily round to the wind; the prow slowly swinging into view of the boats, its skeleton gleaming in the horizontal moonlight, and casting a gigantic ribbed shadow upon the water. One extended arm of the ghost seemed beckoning the whites to avenge it.

'Follow your leader!' cried the mate; and, one on each bow, the boats boarded. Sealing-spears and cutlasses crossed hatchets and handspikes. Huddled upon the long-boat amidships, the negresses raised a wailing chant, whose chorus was the clash of the steel.

For a time, the attack wavered; the negroes wedging themselves to beat it back; the half-repelled sailors, as yet unable to gain a footing, fighters as troopers in the saddle, one leg sideways flung over the bulwarks, and one without, plying their cutlasses like carters' whips. But in vain. They were almost overborne, when, rallying themselves into a squad as one man, with a huzza, they sprang inboard, where, entangled, they involuntarily separated again. For a few breaths' space, there was a vague, muffled, inner sound, as of submerged sword-fish rushing hither and thither through shoals of black-fish. Soon, in a reunited band, and joined by the Spanish seamen, the whites came to the surface, irresistibly driving the negroes toward the stern. But a barricade of casks and sacks, from side to side, had been thrown up by the mainmast. Here the negroes faced about, and though scorning peace or truce, yet fain would have had respite. But, without pause, overleaping the barrier, the unflagging sailors again closed. Exhausted, the blacks now fought in despair. Their red tongues lolled, wolf-like, from their black mouths. But the pale sailors' teeth were set; not a word was spoken; and, in five minutes more, the ship was won.

Nearly a score of the negroes were killed. Exclusive of those by the balls, many were mangled; their wounds — mostly inflicted by the long-edged sealing-spears — resembling those shaven ones of the English at Prestonpans, made by the poled scythes of the Highlanders. On the other side, none were killed, though several were wounded; some severely, including the mate. The surviving negroes were temporarily secured, and the ship, towed back into the harbour at midnight, once more lay anchored.

Omitting the incidents and arrangements ensuing, suffice it that, after two days spent in refitting, the ships sailed in company for Conception, in Chili, and thence for Lima, in Peru; where, before the vice-regal courts, the whole affair, from the beginning, underwent investigation.

Though, midway on the passage, the ill-fated Spaniard, relaxed from constraint, showed some signs of regaining health with free-will; yet, agreeably to his own foreboding, shortly before arriving at Lima, he relapsed, finally becoming so reduced as to be carried ashore in arms. Hearing of his story and plight, one of the many religious institutions of the City of Kings opened an hospitable refuge to him, where both physician and priest were his nurses, and a member of the order volunteered to be his one special guardian and consoler, by night and by day.

The following extracts, translated from one of the official

Spanish documents, will, it is hoped, shed light on the preceding narrative, as well as, in the first place, reveal the true port of departure and true history of the *San Dominick*'s voyage, down to the time of her touching at the island of St Maria.

But, ere the extracts come, it may be well to preface them with a remark.

The document selected, from among many others, for partial translation, contains the deposition of Benito Cereno; the first taken in the case. Some disclosures therein were, at the time, held dubious for both learned and natural reasons. The tribunal inclined to the opinion that the deponent, not undisturbed in his mind by recent events, raved of some things which could never have happened. But subsequent depositions of the surviving sailors, bearing out the revelations of their captain in several of the strangest particulars, gave credence to the rest. So that the tribunal, in its final decision, rested its capital sentences upon statements which, had they lacked confirmation, it would have deemed it but duty to reject.

I, DON JOSÉ DE ABOS AND PADILLA, His Majesty's Notary for the Royal Revenue, and Register of this Province, and Notary Public of the Holy Crusade of this Bishopric, etc.

Do certify and declare, as much as is requisite in law, that, in the criminal cause commenced the twenty-fourth of the month of September, in the year seventeen hundred and ninety-nine, against the negroes of the ship *San Dominick*, the following declaration before me was made:

Declaration of the first witness, DON BENITO CERENO.

The same day, and month, and year, His Honour, Doctor Juan Martinez de Rozas, Councillor of the Royal Audience of this Kingdom, and learned in the law of this Intendency, ordered the captain of the ship *San Dominick*, Don Benito Cereno, to appear; which he did in his litter, attended by the monk Infelez; of whom he received the oath, which he took by God, our Lord, and a sign of the Cross; under which he promised to tell the truth of whatever he should know and should be asked, and being interrogated agreeably to the tenor of the act commencing the process, he said, that on the twentieth of May last, he set sail with his ship from the port of Valparaiso, bound to that of Callao; loaded with the produce of the country besides thirty cases of hardware and one hundred and sixty blacks, of both sexes, mostly belonging to Don Alexandro Aranda, gentleman, of the city of Mendoza; that the crew of the ship consisted of thirty-six men, besides the persons who went as passengers; that the negroes were in part as follows:

[*Here, in the original, follows a list of some fifty names, descriptions, and ages, compiled from certain recovered documents of Aranda's, and also from recollections of the deponent, from which portions only are extracted.*]

— One, from about eighteen to nineteen years, named José, and this was the man that waited upon his master, Don Alexandro, and who speaks well the Spanish, having served him four or five years; . . . a mulatto, named Francesco, the cabin steward, of a good person and voice, having sung in the Valparaiso churches, native of the province of Buenos Ayres, aged about thirty-five years. . . . A smart negro, named Dago, who had been for many years a gravedigger among the Spaniards, aged forty-six years. . . . Four old negroes, born in Africa, from sixty to seventy, but sound, caulkers by trade, whose names are as follows: the first was named Muri, and he was killed (as was also his son named Diamelo); the second, Nacta; the third, Yola, likewise killed; the fourth, Ghofan; and six full-grown negroes, aged from thirty to forty-five, all raw, and born among the Ashantees — Matiluqui, Yan, Lecbe, Mapenda, Yambaio, Akim; four of whom were killed; . . . a powerful negro named Atufal, who being supposed to have been a chief in Africa, his owner set great store by him. . . . And a small negro of Senegal, but some years among the Spaniards, aged about thirty, which negro's name was Babo; . . . that he does not remember the names of the others, but that still expecting the residue of Don Alexandro's papers will be found, will then take due account of them all, and remit to the court; . . . and thirty-nine women and children of all ages.

— That all the negroes slept upon deck, as is customary in this navigation, and none wore fetters, because the owner, his friend Aranda, told him that they were all tractable; . . . that on the seventh day after leaving port, at three o'clock in the morning, all the Spaniards being asleep except the two officers on the watch, who were the boatswain, Juan Robles, and the carpenter, Juan Bautista Gayete, and the helmsman and his boy, the negroes revolted suddenly, wounded dangerously the boatswain and the carpenter, and successively killed eighteen men of those who were sleeping upon deck, some with hand-spikes and hatchets, and others by throwing them alive over-board, after tying them; that of the Spaniards upon deck, they left about seven, as he thinks, alive and tied, to manoeuvre the ship, and three or four more, who hid themselves, remained also alive. Although in the act of revolt the negroes made themselves masters of the hatchway, six or seven wounded went through it to the cockpit, without any hindrance on their part; that during the act of revolt, the mate and another person, whose name he does not recollect, attempted to come up through the hatchway, but being quickly wounded, were obliged to return to the cabin; that the deponent resolved at break of day to come up the companion-way, where the negro Babo was, being the ringleader, and Atufal, who assisted him, and having spoken to them, exhorted them to cease commit-ting such atrocities, asking them, at the same time, what they wanted and intended to do, offering, himself, to obey their commands; that notwithstanding this, they threw, in his pres-ence, three men, alive and tied, overboard; that they told the deponent to come up, and that they would not kill him; which having done, the negro Babo asked him whether there were in these seas any negro countries where they might be carried, and he answered them, No; that the negro Babo afterward told him to carry them to Senegal, or to the neighbouring islands of St Nicholas; and he answered, that this was impossible, on account of the great distance, the necessity involved of round-ing Cape Horn, the bad condition of the vessel, the want of provisions, sails and water; but that the negro Babo replied to him he must carry them in any way; that they would do and conform themselves to everything the deponent should require as to eating and drinking; that after a long conference, being absolutely compelled to please them, for they threatened to kill all the whites if they were not, at all events, carried to Senegal, he told them that what was most wanting for the voyage was water; that they would go near the coast to take it, and thence they would proceed on their course; that the negro Babo agreed to it; and the deponent steered toward the intermediate ports, hoping to meet some Spanish or foreign vessel that would save them; that within ten or eleven days they saw the land, and continued their course by it in the vicinity of Nasca; that the deponent observed that the negroes were now restless and mutinous, because he did not effect the taking in of water, the negro Babo having required, with threats, that it should be done, without fail, the following day; he told him he saw plainly that the coast was steep, and the rivers designated in the maps were not to be found, with other reasons suitable to the circumstances; that the best way would be to go to the island of Santa Maria, where they might water easily, it being a solitary island, as the foreigners did; that the deponent did not go to Pisco, that was near, nor make any other port of the coast, because the negro Babo had intimated to him several times, that he would kill all the whites the very moment he should perceive any city, town, or settlement of any kind on the shores to which they should be carried: that having determined to go to the island of Santa Maria, as the deponent had planned, for the purpose of trying whether, on the passage or near the island itself, they could find any vessel that should favour them, or whether he could escape from it in a boat to the neighbouring coast of Arruco, to adopt the necessary means he immediately changed his course, steering for the island; that the negroes Babo and Atufal held daily conferences, in which they discussed what was necessary for their design of returning to Senegal, whether they were to kill all the Spaniards, and particularly the deponent; that eight days after parting with the coast of Nasca, the deponent being on the watch a little after daybreak, and soon after the negroes had their meeting, the negro Babo came to the place where the deponent was, and told him that he had determined to kill his master, Don Alexandro Aranda, both because he and his companions could

not otherwise be sure of their liberty, and that to keep the
seamen in subjection, he wanted to prepare a warning of what
road they should be made to take did they or any of them
oppose him; and that, by means of the death of Don Alexandro, that warning would best be given; but, that what this last
meant, the deponent did not at the time comprehend, nor
could not, further than that the death of Don Alexandro was
intended; and moreover the negro Babo proposed to the
deponent to call the mate Raneds, who was sleeping in the
cabin, before the thing was done, for fear, as the deponent
understood it, that the mate, who was a good navigator,
should be killed with Don Alexandro and the rest; that the
deponent, who was the friend, from youth, of Don Alexandro,
prayed and conjured, but all was useless; for the negro Babo
answered him that the thing could not be prevented, and that
all the Spaniards risked their death if they should attempt to
frustrate his will in this matter, or any other; that, in this
conflict, the deponent called the mate, Raneds, who was forced
to go apart, and immediately the negro Babo commanded the
Ashantee Matiluqui and the Ashantee Lecbe to go and commit
the murder; that those two went down with hatchets to the
berth of Don Alexandro; that, yet half alive and mangled, they
dragged him on deck; that they were going to throw him
overboard in that state, but the negro Babo stopped them,
bidding the murder be completed on the deck before him,
which was done, when, by his orders, the body was carried
below, forward; that nothing more was seen of it by the
deponent for three days; . . . that Don Alonzo Sidonia, an old
man, long resident at Valparaiso, and lately appointed to a
civil office in Peru, whither he had taken passage, was at the
time sleeping in the berth opposite Don Alexandro's; that
awakening at his cries, surprised by them, and at the sight of the
negroes with their bloody hatchets in their hands, he threw
himself into the sea through a window which was near him,
and was drowned, without it being in the power of the
deponent to assist or take him up; . . . that a short time after
killing Aranda, they brought upon deck his german-cousin, of
middle-age, Don Francisco Masa, of Mendoza, and the young
Don Joaquin, Marques de Aramboalaza, then lately from
Spain, with his Spanish servant Ponce, and the three young

71

clerks of Aranda, José Mozairi, Lorenzo Bargas, and Hermenegildo Gandix, all of Cadiz; that Don Joaquin and Hermenegildo Gandix, the negro Babo, for purposes hereafter to appear, preserved alive; but Don Francisco Masa, José Mozairi, and Lorenzo Bargas, with Ponce the servant, besides the boatswain, Juan Robles, the boatswain's mates, Manuel Viscaya and Roderigo Hurta, and four of the sailors, the negro Babo ordered to be thrown alive into the sea, although they made no resistance, nor begged for anything else but mercy; that the boatswain, Juan Robles, who knew how to swim, kept the longest above water, making acts of contrition, and, in the last words he uttered, charged this deponent to cause mass to be said for his soul to our Lady of Succour: . . . that, during the three days which followed, the deponent, uncertain what fate had befallen the remains of Don Alexandro, frequently asked the negro Babo where they were, and, if still on board, whether they were to be preserved for interment ashore, entreating him so to order it; that the negro Babo answered nothing till the fourth day, when at sunrise, the deponent coming on deck, the negro Babo showed him a skeleton, which had been substituted for the ship's proper figure-head – the image of Christopher Colon, the discoverer of the New World; that the negro Babo asked him whose skeleton that was, and whether, from its whiteness, he should not think it a white's; that, upon discovering his face, the negro Babo, coming close, said words to this effect: 'Keep faith with the blacks from here to Senegal, or you shall in spirit, as now in body, follow your leader,' pointing to the prow; . . . that the same morning the negro Babo took by succession each Spaniard forward, and asked him whose skeleton that was, and whether, from its whiteness, he should not think it a white's; that each Spaniard covered his face; that then to each the negro Babo repeated the words in the first place said to the deponent; . . . that they (the Spaniards), being then assembled aft, the negro Babo harangued them, saying that he had now done all; that the deponent (as navigator for the negroes) might pursue his course, warning him and all of them that they should, soul and body, go the way of Don Alexandro, if he saw them (the Spaniards) speak or plot anything against them (the negroes) – a threat which was repeated every day; that, before the events last mentioned,

72

they had tied the cook to throw him overboard, for it is not known what thing they heard him speak, but finally the negro Babo spared his life, at the request of the deponent; that a few days after, the deponent, endeavouring not to omit any means to preserve the lives of the remaining whites, spoke to the negroes peace and tranquillity, and agreed to draw up a paper, signed by the deponent and the sailors who could write, as also by the negro Babo, for himself and all the blacks, in which the deponent obliged himself to carry them to Senegal, and they not to kill any more, and he formally to make over to them the ship, with the cargo, with which they were for that time satisfied and quieted. . . . But the next day, the more surely to guard against the sailors' escape, the negro Babo commanded all the boats to be destroyed but the long-boat, which was unseaworthy, and another, a cutter in good condition, which knowing it would yet be wanted for towing the water-casks, he had it lowered down into the hold.

[*Various particulars of the prolonged and perplexed navigation ensuing here follow, with incidents of a calamitous calm, from which portion one passage is extracted, to wit:*]

— That on the fifth day of the calm, all on board suffering much from the heat, and want of water, and five having died in fits, and mad, the negroes became irritable, and for a chance gesture, which they deemed suspicious — though it was harmless — made by the mate, Raneds, to the deponent in the act of handing a quadrant, they killed him; but that for this they afterward were sorry, the mate being the only remaining navigator on board, except the deponent. . . .

— That omitting other events, which daily happened, and which can only serve uselessly to recall past misfortunes and conflicts, after seventy-three days' navigation, reckoned from the time they sailed from Nasca, during which they navigated under a scanty allowance of water, and were afflicted with the calms before-mentioned, they at last arrived at the island of Santa Maria, on the seventeenth of the month of August, at about six o'clock in the afternoon, at which hour they cast anchor very near the American ship, *Bachelor's Delight*, which lay in the same bay, commanded by the generous Captain Amasa Delano; but at six o'clock in the morning, they had already descried the port, and the negroes became uneasy, as soon as at distance they saw the ship, not having expected to see one there; that the negro Babo pacified them, assuring them that no fear need be had; that straightway he ordered the figure on the bow to be covered with canvas, as for repairs, and had the decks a little set in order; that for a time the negro Babo and the negro Atufal conferred; that the negro Atufal was for sailing away, but the negro Babo would not, and, by himself, cast about what to do; that at last he came to the deponent, proposing to him to say and do all that the deponent declares to have said and done to the American captain; . . . that the negro Babo warned him that if he varied in the least, or uttered any word, or gave any look that should give the least intimation of the past events or present state, he would instantly kill him, with all his companions, showing a dagger, which he carried hid, saying something which, as he understood it, meant that that dagger would be alert as his eye; that the negro Babo then announced the plan to all his companions, which pleased them; that he then, the better to disguise the truth, devised many expedients, in some of them uniting deceit and defence; that of this sort was the device of the six Ashantees before-named, who were his bravos; that them he stationed on the break of the poop, as if to clean certain hatchets (in cases, which were part of the cargo), but in reality to use them, and distribute them at need, and at a given word he told them; that, among other devices, was the device of presenting Atufal, his right-hand man, as chained, though in a moment the chains could be dropped; that in every particular he informed the deponent what part he was expected to enact in every device, and what story he was to tell on every occasion, always threatening him with instant death if he varied in the least; that, conscious that many of the negroes would be turbulent, the negro Babo appointed the four aged negroes, who were caulkers, to keep what domestic order they could on the decks; that again and again he harangued the Spaniards and his companions, informing them of his intent, and of his devices, and of the invented story that this deponent was to tell; charging them lest any of them varied from that story; that these arrangements were made and matured during the interval of two or three hours, between their first sighting the ship and the arrival on board of Captain Amasa Delano; that this happened about half-past seven o'clock in the morning, Captain Amasa Delano coming in his boat, and all gladly receiving him; that the deponent, as well as he could force himself, acting then the part of principal owner, and a free captain of the ship, told Captain Amasa Delano, when called upon, that he came from Buenos Ayres, bound to Lima, with three hundred negroes; that off Cape Horn, and in a subsequent fever, many negroes had died; that also, by similar casualties, all the sea-officers and the greatest part of the crew had died.

[*And so the deposition goes on, circumstantially recounting the fictitious story dictated to the deponent by Babo, and through the deponent imposed upon Captain Delano; and also recounting the friendly offers of Captain Delano, with other things, but all of which is here omitted. After the fictitious story, etc., the deposition proceeds:*]

— That the generous Captain Amasa Delano remained on board all the day, till he left the ship anchored at six o'clock in the evening, deponent speaking to him always of his pretended misfortunes, under the fore-mentioned principles, without having had it in his power to tell a single word, or give him the least hint, that he might know the truth and state of things; because the negro Babo, performing the office of an officious servant with all the appearance of submission of the humble slave, did not leave the deponent one moment; that this was in order to observe the deponent's actions and words, for the negro Babo understands well the Spanish; and besides, there were thereabout some others who were constantly on the watch, and likewise understood the Spanish, . . . that upon one occasion, while deponent was standing on the deck conversing with Amasa Delano, by a secret sign the negro Babo drew him (the deponent) aside, the act appearing as if originating with the deponent; that then, he being drawn aside, the negro Babo proposed to him to gain from Amasa Delano full particulars about his ship, and crew, and arms; that the deponent asked 'For what?' that the negro Babo answered he might conceive; that, grieved at the prospect of what might overtake the generous Captain Amasa Delano, the deponent at first refused to ask the desired questions, and used every argument to induce the negro Babo to give up this new design; that the negro Babo showed the point of his dagger; that, after the information had been obtained, the negro Babo again drew him aside, telling him that that very night he (the deponent) would be captain of two ships, instead of one, for that, great part of the American's ship's crew being to be absent fishing, the six Ashantees, without anyone else, would easily take it; that at this time he said other things to the same purpose; that no entreaties availed; that, before Amasa Delano's coming on board, no hint had been given touching the capture of the American ship: that to prevent this project the deponent was powerless; . . . that in some things his memory is confused, he cannot distinctly recall every event; . . . that as soon as they had cast anchor at six of the clock in the evening, as has before been stated, the American captain took leave, to return to his vessel; that upon a sudden impulse, which the deponent believes to have come from God and his angels, he, after the farewell had been said, followed the generous Captain Amasa Delano as far as the gunwale, where he stayed, under pretence of taking leave, until Amasa Delano should have been seated in his boat; that on shoving off, the deponent sprang from the gunwale into the boat, and fell into it, he knows not how, God guarding him; that —

[*Here, in the original, follows the account of what further happened at the escape, and how the* San Dominick *was retaken, and of the passage to the coast; including in the recital many expressions of 'eternal gratitude' to the 'generous Captain Amasa Delano'. The deposition then proceeds with recapitulatory remarks, and a partial renumeration of the negroes, making record of their individual part in the past events, with a view to furnishing, according to command of the court, the data whereon to found the criminal sentences to be pronounced. From this portion is the following:*]

— That he believes that all the negroes, though not in the first place knowing to the design of revolt, when it was accomplished, approved it. . . . That the negro, José, eighteen years old, and in the personal service of Don Alexandro, was the one who communicated the information to the negro Babo, about the state of things in the cabin, before the revolt; that this is known, because, in the preceding midnight, he used to come from his berth, which was under his master's, in the cabin, to the deck where the ringleader and his associates were, and had secret conversations with the negro Babo, in which he was several times seen by the mate; that, one night, the mate drove him away twice; . . . that this same negro José was the one who, without being commanded to do so by the negro Babo, as Lecbe and Matiluqui were, stabbed his master, Don Alexandro, after he had been dragged half-lifeless to the deck; . . . that the mulatto steward, Francesco, was of the first band of revolters, that he was, in all things, the creature and tool of the negro Babo; that, to make his court, he, just before a repast in the cabin, proposed, to the negro Babo, poisoning a dish for the generous Captain Amasa Delano; this is known and believed, because the negroes have said it; but that the negro Babo, having another design, forbade Francesco; . . . that the Ashantee Lecbe was one of the worst of them; for that, on the day the ship was retaken, he assisted in the defence of her, with a hatchet in each hand, with one of which he wounded in the breast, the chief mate of Amasa Delano, in the first act of boarding; this all knew; that, in sight of the deponent, Lecbe struck, with a hatchet, Don Francisco Masa, when, by the negro Babo's orders, he was carrying him to throw him overboard, alive, besides participating in the murder, before-mentioned, of Don Alexandro Aranda, and others of the cabin passengers; that, owing to the fury with which the Ashantees fought in the engagement with the boats, but this Lecbe and Yan survived; that Yan was bad as Lecbe; that Yan was the man who, by Babo's command, willingly prepared the skeleton of Don Alexandro, in a way the negroes afterward told the deponent, but which he, so long as reason is left him, can never divulge; that Yan and Lecbe were the two who, in a calm by night, riveted the skeleton to the bow; this also the negroes told him; that the negro Babo was he who traced the inscription below it; that the negro Babo was the plotter from first to last; he ordered every murder, and was the helm and keel of the revolt; that Atufal was his lieutenant in all; but Atufal, with his own hand, committed no murder; not did the negro Babo; . . . that Atufal was shot, being killed in the fight with the boats, ere boarding; . . . that the negresses, of age, were knowing to the revolt, and testified themselves satisfied at the death of their master, Don Alexandro; that, had the negroes not restrained them, they would have tortured to death, instead of simply killing, the Spaniards slain by command of the negro Babo; that the negresses used their utmost influence to have the deponent made away with; that, in the various acts of murder, they sang songs and danced—not gaily, but solemnly; and before the engagement with the boats, as well as during the action, they sang melancholy songs to the negroes, and that this melancholy tone was more inflaming than a different one would have been, and was so intended; that all this is believed, because the negroes have said it.

— That of the thirty-six men of the crew, exclusive of the passengers (all of whom are now dead), which the deponent had knowledge of, six only remained alive, with four cabin-boys and ship-boys, not included with the crew; . . . that the negroes broke an arm of one of the cabin-boys and gave him strokes with hatchets.

[*Then follow various random disclosures referring to various periods of time. The following are extracted:*]

— That during the presence of Captain Amasa Delano on board, some attempts were made by the sailors, and one by Hermenegildo Gandix, to convey hints to him of the true state of affairs; but that these attempts were ineffectual, owing to fear of incurring death, and, furthermore, owing to the devices which offered contradictions to the true state of affairs, as well as owing to the generosity and piety of Amasa Delano incapable of sounding such wickedness; . . . that Luys Galgo, a sailor about sixty years of age, and formerly of the king's navy, was one of those who sought to convey tokens to Captain Amasa Delano; but his intent, though undiscovered, being suspected, he was, on a pretence, made to retire out of sight, and at last into the hold, and there was made away with. This the negroes have since said; . . . that one of the ship-boys feeling, from Captain Amasa Delano's presence, some hopes of release, and not having enough prudence, dropped some chance word respecting his expectations, which being overheard and understood by a slave-boy with whom he was eating at the time, the latter struck him on the head with a knife, inflicting a bad wound, but of which the boy is now healing; that likewise, not long before the ship was brought to anchor, one of the seamen, steering at the time, endangered himself by letting the blacks remark some expression in his countenance, arising from a cause similar to the above; but this sailor, by his heedful after conduct, escaped; . . . that these statements are made to show the court that from the beginning to the end of the revolt, it was impossible for the deponent and his men to act otherwise than they did; . . . that the third clerk, Hermenegildo Gandix, who before had been forced to live among the seamen, wearing a seaman's habit, and in all respects appearing to be one for the time, he, Gandix, was killed by a musket-ball fired through mistake from the boats before boarding; having in his fright run up the mizen-rigging, calling to the boats — 'don't board,' lest upon their boarding the negroes should kill him; that this inducing the Americans to believe he some way favoured the cause of the negroes, they fired two balls at him, so that he fell wounded from the rigging, and was drowned in the sea; . . . that the young Don Joaquin, Marques de Aramboalaza, like Hermenegildo Gandix, the third clerk, was degraded to the office and appearance of a common seaman; that upon one occasion when Don Joaquin shrank, the negro Babo commanded the Ashantee Lecbe to take tar and heat it, and pour it upon Don Joaquin's hands; . . . that Don Joaquin was killed owing to another mistake of the Americans, but one impossible to be avoided, as upon the approach of the boats, Don Joaquin, with a hatchet tied edge out and upright to his hand, was made by the negroes to appear on the bulwarks; whereupon, seen with arms in his hands and in a questionable attitude, he was shot for a renegade seaman; . . . that on the person of Don Joaquin was found secreted a jewel, which, by papers that were discovered, proved to have been meant for the shrine of our Lady of Mercy in Lima; a votive offering, beforehand prepared and guarded, to attest his gratitude, when he should have landed in Peru, his last destination, for the safe conclusion of his entire voyage from Spain; . . . that the jewel, with the other effects of the late Don Joaquin, is in the custody of the brethren of the Hospital de Sacerdotes, awaiting the disposition of the honourable court; . . . that, owing to the condition of the deponent, as well as the haste in which the boats departed for the attack, the Americans were not forewarned that there were, among the apparent crew, a passenger and one of the clerks disguised by the negro Babo; . . . that, besides the negroes killed in the action, some were killed after the capture and re-anchoring at night, when shackled to the ring-bolts on deck; that these deaths were committed by the sailors, ere they could be prevented. That so soon as informed of it, Captain Amasa Delano used all his authority, and, in particular with his own hand, struck down Martinez Gola, who, having found a razor in the pocket of an old jacket of his, which one of the shackled negroes had on, was aiming it at the negro's throat; that the noble Captain Amasa Delano also wrenched from the hand of Bartholomew Barlo a dagger, secreted at the time of the massacre of the whites, with which he was in the act of stabbing a shackled negro, who, the same day, with another negro, had thrown him down and jumped upon him; . . . that, for all the events, befalling through so long a time, during which the ship was in the hands of the negro Babo, he cannot here give account; but that, what he has said is the most substantial of what occurs to him at present, and is the truth under the oath which he has taken; which declaration he affirmed and ratified, after hearing it read to him.

He said that he is twenty-nine years of age, and broken in body and mind; that when finally dismissed by the court, he shall not return home to Chili, but betake himself to the monastery on Mount Agonia without; and signed with his honour, and crossed himself, and, for the time, departed as he came, in his litter, with the monk Infelez, to the Hospital de Sacerdotes.

BENITO CERENO

DOCTOR ROZAS

If the Depositions have served as the key to fit into the lock of the complications which precede it, then, as a vault whose door has been flung back, the *San Dominick*'s hull lies open to-day.

Hitherto the nature of this narrative, besides rendering the intricacies in the beginning unavoidable, has more or less required that many things, instead of being set down in the order of occurrence, should be retrospectively, or irregularly given; this last is the case with the following passages, which will conclude the account:

During the long, mild voyage to Lima, there was, as before hinted, a period during which the sufferer a little recovered his health, or, at least in some degree, his tranquillity. Ere the decided relapse which came, the two captains had many cordial conversations – their fraternal unreserve in singular contrast with former withdrawments.

Again and again it was repeated, how hard it had been to enact the part forced on the Spaniard by Babo.

'Ah, my dear friend,' Don Benito once said, 'at those very times when you thought me so morose and ungrateful, nay, when, as you now admit, you half thought me plotting your murder, at those very times my heart was frozen; I could not look at you, thinking of what, both on board this ship and your own, hung, from other hands, over my kind benefactor. And as God lives, Don Amasa, I know not whether desire for my own safety alone could have nerved me to that leap into your boat, had it not been for the thought that, did you, unenlightened, return to your ship, you, my best friend, with all who might be with you, stolen upon, that night, in your hammocks, would never in this world have wakened again. Do but think how you walked this deck, how you sat in this cabin, every inch of ground mined into honeycombs under you. Had I dropped the least hint, made the least advance toward an understanding between us, death, explosive death – yours as mine – would have ended the scene.'

'True, true,' cried Captain Delano, starting, 'you have saved my life, Don Benito, more than I yours; saved it, too, against my knowledge and will.'

'Nay, my friend,' rejoined the Spaniard, courteous even to the point of religion, 'God charmed your life, but you saved mine. To think of some things you did – those smilings and chattings, rash pointings and gesturings. For less than these, they slew my mate, Raneds; but you had the Prince of Heaven's safe-conduct through all ambuscades.'

'Yes, all is owing to Providence, I know: but the temper of

my mind that morning was more than commonly pleasant, while the sight of so much suffering, more apparent than real, added to my good-nature, compassion, and charity, happily interweaving the three. Had it been otherwise, doubtless, as you hint, some of my interferences might have ended unhappily enough. Besides, those feelings I spoke of enabled me to get the better of momentary distrust, at times when acuteness might have cost me my life, without saving another's. Only at the end did my suspicions get the better of me, and you know how wide of the mark they then proved.'

'Wide, indeed,' said Don Benito sadly; 'you were with me all day; stood with me, sat with me, talked with me, looked at me, ate with me, drank with me; and yet, your last act was to clutch for a monster, not only an innocent man, but the most pitiable of all men. To such degree may malign machinations and deceptions impose. So far may even the best man err, in judging the conduct of one with the recesses of whose condition he is not acquainted. But you were forced to it; and you were in time undeceived. Would that, in both respects, it was so ever, and with all men.'

'You generalise, Don Benito; and mournfully enough. But the past is past; why moralise upon it? Forget it. See, yon bright sun has forgotten it all, and the blue sea, and the blue sky; these have turned over new leaves.'

'Because they have no memory,' he dejectedly replied; 'because they are not human.'

'But these mild Trades that now fan your cheek, do they not come with a human-like healing to you? Warm friends, steadfast friends are the Trades.'

'With their steadfastness they but waft me to my tomb, señor,' was the foreboding response.

'You are saved,' cried Captain Delano, more and more astonished and pained; 'you are saved: what has cast such a shadow upon you?'

'The negro.'

There was silence, while the moody man sat, slowly and unconsciously gathering his mantle about him, as if it were a pall.

There was no more conversation that day.

But if the Spaniard's melancholy sometimes ended in muteness upon topics like the above, there were others upon which he never spoke at all; on which, indeed, all his old reserves were piled. Pass over the worst, and, only to elucidate, let an item or two of these be cited. The dress, so precise and costly, worn by him on the day whose events have been narrated, had not willingly been put on. And that silver mounted sword, apparent symbol of despotic command, was not, indeed, a sword, but the ghost of one. The scabbard, artificially stiffened, was empty.

As for the black — whose brain, not body, had schemed and led the revolt, with the plot — his slight frame, inadequate to that which it held, had at once yielded to the superior muscular strength of his captor, in the boat. Seeing all was over, he uttered no sound, and could not be forced to. His aspect seemed to say, since I cannot do deeds, I will not speak words. Put in irons in the hold, with the rest, he was carried to Lima. During the passage, Don Benito did not visit him. Nor then, nor at any time after, would he look at him. Before the tribunal he refused. When pressed by the judges he fainted. On the testimony of the sailors alone rested the legal identity of Babo.

Some months after, dragged to the gibbet at the tail of a mule, the black met his voiceless end. The body was burned to ashes; but for many days the head, that hive of subtlety, fixed on a pole in the Plaza, met, unabashed, the gaze of the whites; and across the Plaza looked toward St Bartholomew's church, in whose vaults slept then, as now, the recovered bones of Aranda: and across the Rimac bridge looked toward the monastery, on Mount Agonia without; where, three months after being dismissed by the court, Benito Cereno, borne on the bier, did, indeed, follow his leader.

Captain Frederick Marryat

THE LEGEND OF THE BELL ROCK

The Englishman, Captain Marryat, who, like Herman Melville, also spent his early life at sea and then utilised his experiences as the basis of a whole series of maritime novels, has gone down in history as the 'Father of the Sea Story'. Marryat (1792–1848) went to sea in 1806 as a midshipman, and by 1820 had so proved himself that he was given the command of a sloop patrolling off the island of St Helena to prevent any escape bid by the exiled Napoleon. He later had some exciting adventures fighting lawbreakers in Burmese waters and outwitting smugglers trying to cross the English Channel with contraband goods. His reward for these successes was to be given command of HMS Ariadne, but in 1830 he decided to resign his commission and pursue an urge he had long felt to become a writer. His rich store of first-hand experiences became immensely popular books such as Peter Simple (1834), Mr Midshipman Easy (1836) and the classic novel based on the legend of the Flying Dutchman, The Phantom Ship (1839).

Captain Marryat is unrivalled when it comes to describing action at sea, and his characters are real seamen through and through. Because of his passion for characterisation and the most painstaking detail, he wrote very few short stories and only one to my knowledge that specifically features a sea captain. Andrew M'Clise who appears in 'The Legend of the Bell Rock' is an intriguing, passion-driven man, and readers *familiar with* The Phantom Ship *will find strong parallels between his fate and that which befell the doomed Dutch seaman, Captain Vanderdecken.*

There was a grand procession through the streets of the two towns of Perth and Dundee. The holy abbots, in their robes, walked under gilded canopies, the monks chanted, the censers were thrown, flags and banners were carried by seamen, lighted tapers by penitents; St Antonio, the patron of those who trust to the stormy ocean, was carried in all pomp through the streets; and, as the procession passed, coins of various value were thrown down by those who watched it from the windows, and, as fast as thrown, were collected by little boys dressed as angels, and holding silver vessels to receive the largesses. During the whole day did the procession continue, and large was the treasure collected in the two towns. Every-one gave freely, for there were few, indeed none, who, if not in their own circle, at least among their acquaintances, had not to deplore the loss of some one dear to them, or to those they visited, from the dangerous rock which lay in the very track of all the vessels entering the Firth of Tay.

These processions had been arranged, that a sufficient sum of money might be collected to enable them to put in execution a plan proposed by an adventurous and bold young seaman, in a council held for the purpose, of fixing a bell on the rock, which could be so arranged that the slightest breath of wind would cause the hammer of it to sound, and thus, by its tolling, warn the mariner of his danger; and the sums given were more than sufficient. A meeting was then held, and it was unani-mously agreed that Andrew M'Clise should be charged with the commission to go over to Amsterdam, and purchase the bell of a merchant residing there, whom Andrew stated to have one in his possession, which, from its fine tone and size, was exactly calculated for the purpose to which it was to be appropriated.

Andrew M'Clise embarked with the money, and made a

prosperous voyage. He had often been at Amsterdam, and had lived with the merchant, whose name was Vandermaclin; and the attention to his affairs, the dexterity and the rapidity of the movements of Andrew M'Clise, had often elicited the warmest encomiums of Master Vandermaclin; and many evenings had Andrew M'Clise passed with him, drinking in moderation their favourite scheedam, and indulging in the meditative meerschaum. Vandermaclin had often wished that he had a son like Andrew M'Clise, to whom he could leave his property, with the full assurance that the heap would not be scattered, but greatly added to.

Vandermaclin was a widower. He had but one daughter, who was now just arrived at an age to return from the pension to her father's house, and take upon herself the domestic duties. M'Clise had never yet seen the beautiful Katerina.

'And so, Mynheer M'Clise,' said Vandermaclin, who was sitting in the warehouse on the ground-floor of his tenement, 'you come to purchase the famous bell of Utrecht; with the intention of fixing it upon that rock, the danger of which we have so often talked over after the work of the day has been done? I, too, have suffered from that same rock, as you well know; but still I have been fortunate. The price will be heavy; and so it ought to be, for the bell itself is of no small weight.'

'We are prepared to pay it, Mynheer Vandermaclin.'

'Nevertheless, in so good a cause, and for so good a purpose, you shall not be overcharged. I will say nothing of the beauty of the workmanship, or even of the mere manufacture. You shall pay but its value in metal; the same price which the Jew Isaacs offered me for it but four months ago. I will not ask what a Jew would ask, but what a Jew would give, which makes no small difference. Have you ten thousand guilders?'

'I have, and more.'

'That is my price, Mynheer M'Clise, and I wish for no more; for I, too, will contribute my share to the good work. Are you content, and is it a bargain?'

'It is; and the holy abbots will thank you on vellum, Mynheer Vandermaclin, for your generosity.'

'I prefer the thanks of the bold seamen to those of the idle churchmen; but, never mind, it is a bargain. Now, we will go in; it is time to close the doors. We will take our pipes, and you shall make the acquaintance of my fair daughter, Katerina.'

At the time we are speaking of, M'Clise was about six and twenty years of age; he was above the middle size, elegant in person, and with a frankness and almost nobility in his countenance, which won all who saw him.

His manners were like those of most seamen, bold, but not offensively so. His eyes was piercing as an eagle's; and it seemed as if his very soul spoke from it. At the very first meeting between him and the daughter of Vandermaclin, it appeared to both as if their destinies were to unite them.

They loved not as others love, but with an intensity which it would be impossible to portray; yet they hardly exchanged a word. Again and again they met; their eyes spoke, but nothing more. The bell was put on board the vessel, the money had been paid down, and M'Clise could no longer delay. He felt as if his heartstrings were severed as he tore himself away from the land where all remained that he coveted upon earth. And Katerina, she too felt as if her existence was a blank; and as the vessel sailed from the port, she breathed short; and when not even her white and lofty top-gallant sail could be discovered as a speck, she threw herself on her couch and wept. And M'Clise, as he sailed away, remained for hours leaning his cheek on his hand, thinking of, over and over again, every lineament and feature of the peerless Katerina.

Two months passed away, during which M'Clise was busied every ebb of the tide in superintending the work on the rock. At last, all was ready; and once more was to be beheld a gay procession; but this time it was on the water. It was on a calm and lovely summer's morn that the abbots and the monks, attended by a large company of the authorities and others who were so much interested in the work in hand, started from the shore of Aberbrothwick in a long line of boats, decorated with sacred and with other various banners and devices. The music floated along the water, and the solemn chants of the monks were for once heard where never yet they had been heard before, or ever will again. M'Clise was at the rock, in a small vessel purposely constructed to carry the bell, and with sheers to hang it on the supports imbedded in the solid rock. The bell was in its place, and the abbot blessed the bell; and holy water was sprinkled on the metal, which was for the future to be lashed by the waves of the salt sea. And the music and the chants were renewed; and as they continued, the wind gradually rose, and with the rising of the wind the bell tolled loud and deep. The tolling of the bell was the signal for return, for it was a warning that the weather was about to change, and the procession pulled back to Aberbrothwick, and landed in good time; for in one hour more, and the rocky coast was again lashed by the waves, and the bell tolled loud and quick, although there were none there but the sea-gull, who screamed with fright as he wheeled in the air at this unusual noise upon the rock, which, at the ebb, he had so often made his resting-place.

M'Clise had done his work; the bell was fixed; and once more he hastened with his vessel to Amsterdam. Once more was he an inmate of Vandermaclin's house; once more in the presence of the idol of his soul. This time they spoke: this time their vows were exchanged for life and death. But Vandermaclin saw not the state of their hearts. He looked upon the young seaman as too low, too poor, to be a match for his daughter; and as such an idea never entered his head, so did he never imagine that he would have dared to love. But he was soon undeceived; for M'Clise frankly stated his attachment, and demanded the hand of Katerina; and, at the demand, Vandermaclin's face was flushed with anger.

'Mynheer M'Clise,' said he, after a pause, as if to control his feelings, 'when a man marries, he is bound to show that he has wherewithal to support his wife; to support her in that rank, and to afford her those luxuries to which she has been accustomed in her father's house. Show me that you can do so, and I will not refuse you the hand of Katerina.'

'As yet, I have not,' replied M'Clise; 'but I am young and can work; I have money, and will gain more. Tell me, what sum do you think that I should possess to warrant my demanding the hand of your daughter?'

'Produce twelve thousand guilders, and she is yours,' replied the merchant.

'I have but three thousand,' replied M'Clise.

'Then think no more of Katerina. It is a foolish passion, and you must forget it. And, Mynheer M'Clise, I must not have my daughter's affections tampered with. She must forget you; and that can only be effected by your not meeting again. I wish you well, Mynheer M'Clise, but I must request your absence.'

M'Clise departed from the presence of the merchant, bowed down with grief and disappointment. He contrived that a letter, containing the result of his application, should be put in the hands of Katerina. But Vandermaclin was informed of this breach of observance, and Katerina was sent to a convent, there to remain until the departure of her lover; and Vandermaclin wrote to his correspondent at Dundee, requesting that the goods forwarded to him might not be sent by the vessel commanded by M'Clise.

Of this our young captain received information. All hope was nearly gone; still he lingered, and delayed his departure. He was no longer the active, energetic seaman; he neglected all, even his attire.

M'Clise knew in which convent his fair Katerina had been immured; and often would he walk round its precincts, with the hope of seeing her, if it were but for a moment, but in vain. His vessel was now laden, and he could delay no longer. He was to sail the next morning; and once more did the unhappy young man take his usual walk to look at those walls which contained all that was dear to him on earth. His reverie was broken by a stone falling down at his feet; he took it up; there was a small piece of paper attached to it with a silken thread. He opened it; it was the handwriting of Katerina, and contained but two words – '*The Bell*'.

The Bell! M'Clise started; for he immediately comprehended what was meant. The whole plan came like electricity through his brain. Yes; then there was a promise of happiness. The bell was worth ten thousand guilders; that sum had been offered, and would now be given by Isaacs the Jew. He would be happy with his Katerina; and he blessed her ingenuity for devising the means. For a minute or two he was transported; but the re-action soon took place. What was he about to attempt? Sacrilege – cruelty. The bell had been blessed by the holy church; it had been purchased by holy and devout alms. It had been placed on the rock to save the lives of his brother seamen; and were he to remove it, would he not be responsible for all the lives lost? Would not the wail of the widow, and the

89

tears of the orphan, be crying out to Heaven against him? No, no! never! The crime was too horrible; and M'Clise stamped upon the paper, thinking he was tempted by Satan in the shape of woman; but when woman tempts, man is lost. He recalled the charms of Katerina; all his repugnance was overcome; and he resolved that the deed should be accomplished, and that Katerina should be gained, even if he lost his soul.

Andrew M'Clise sailed away from Amsterdam, and Katerina recovered her liberty. Vandermaclin was anxious that she should marry: and many were the suitors for her hand, but in vain. She reminded her father that he had pledged himself, if M'Clise counted down twelve thousand guilders, that she should be his wife; and to that pledge she insisted that he was bound fast. And Vandermaclin, after reasoning with her, and pointing out to her that twelve thousand guilders was a sum so large that M'Clise might not procure until his old age, even if he were fortunate, acknowledged that such was his promise, and that he would, like an honest man, abide by it, provided that M'Clise should fulfil his part of the agreement in the space of two years; after which he should delay her settlement no longer. And Katerina raised her eyes to heaven, and whispered, as she clasped her hands, 'The Bell.' Alas! that we should invoke Heaven when we would wish to do wrong: but mortals are blind, and none so blind as those who are impelled by passion.

It was in the summer of that year that M'Clise had made his arrangements: having procured the assistance of some lawless hands, he had taken the advantage of a smooth and glassy sea and a high tide to remove the bell on board his own vessel; a work of little difficulty to him, as he had placed it there, and knew well the fastenings. He sailed away for Amsterdam, and was permitted by Heaven to arrive safe with his sacrilegious freight. He did not, as before, enter the canal opposite to the house of Vandermaclin, but one that ran behind the habitation of the Jew Isaacs. At night, he went into the house, and reported to the Jew what he had for sale; and the keen grey eyes of the bent-double little Israelite sparkled with delight, for he knew that his profit would be great. At midnight the bell was made fast to the crane, and safely deposited in the warehouse of the Jew, who counted out the ten thousand guilders to the enraptured M'Clise, whose thoughts were wholly upon the possession of his Katerina, and not upon the crime he had committed.

But alas! to conceal one crime we are too often obliged to be guilty of even deeper; and thus it was with Andrew M'Clise. The people who had assisted, upon the promise of a thousand guilders being divided among them, now murmured at their share, and insisted upon an equal division of the spoils, or threatened with an immediate confession of the black deed.

M'Clise raved, and cursed, and tore his hair; promised to give them the money as soon as he had wedded Katerina; but they would not consent. Again the devil came to his assistance, and whispered how he was to act: he consented. The next night the division was to be made. They met in his cabin; he gave them wine, and they drank plentifully; but the wine was poisoned, and they all died before the morning. M'Clise tied weights to their bodies, and sank them in the deep canal; broke open his hatches, to make it appear that his vessel had been plundered; and then went to the authorities denouncing his crew as having plundered him and escaped. Immediate search was made, but they were not to be found; and it was supposed that they had escaped in a boat.

Once more M'Clise, whose conscience was seared, went to the house of Vandermaclin, counted down his twelve thousand guilders, and claimed his bride; and Vandermaclin, who felt that his daughter's happiness was at stake, now gave his consent. As M'Clise stated that he was anxious to return to England, and arrange with the merchants whose goods had been plundered, in a few days the marriage took place; and Katerina clasped the murderer in her arms. All was apparent joy and revelry; but there was anguish in the heart of M'Clise, who, now that he had gained his object, felt that it had cost him much too dear, for his peace of mind was gone for ever. But Katerina cared not; every spark of feeling was absorbed in her passion, and the very guilt of M'Clise but rendered him more dear; for was it not for her that he had done all this? M'Clise received her portion, and hasted to sail away; for the bodies were still in the canal, and he trembled every hour lest his crime should be discovered. And Vandermaclin bade farewell to his daughter: and, he knew not why, but there was a feeling he could not suppress, that they never should meet again.

'Down – down below, Katerina! this is no place for you,' cried M'Clise, as he stood at the helm of the vessel. 'Down, dearest, down, or you will be washed overboard. Every sea threatens to pour into our decks; already have we lost two men. Down; Katerina! down, I tell you.'

'I fear not; let me remain with you.'

'I tell you, down!' cried M'Clise, in wrath! and Katerina cast upon him a reproachful look, and obeyed.

The storm was at its height; the sun had set, black and monstrous billows chased each other, and the dismasted vessel was hurried on towards the land. The wind howled, and whistled sharply at each chink in the bulwarks of the vessel. For three days had they fought the gale, but in vain. Now, if it continued, all chance was over; for the shore was on their lee, distant not many miles. Nothing could save them but gaining the mouth of the Firth of Tay, and then they could bear up for Dundee. And there was a boiling surge, and a dark night, and roaring seas, and their masts were floating far away; and M'Clise stood at the helm, keeping her broadside to the sea; his heart was full of bitterness, and his guilty conscience bore him down, and he looked for death, and he dreaded it; for was he not a sacrilegious murderer, and was there not an avenging God above?

Once more Katerina appeared on deck, clinging for support to Andrew.

'I cannot stay below. Tell me, will it soon be over?'

'Yes,' replied M'Clise, gloomily; 'it will soon be over with all of us.'

'How mean you? you told me there was no danger.'

'I told you falsely; there is death soon, and damnation afterwards; for you I have lost my soul!'

'Oh! say not so.'

'I say it. Leave me, leave me, woman, or I curse thee.'

'Curse me, Andrew? Oh no! Kiss me, Andrew; and if we are to perish, let us expire in each other's arms.'

' 'Tis as well; you have dragged me to perdition. Leave me, I say, for you have my bitter curse.'

Thus was his guilty love turned to hate, now that death was staring him in the face.

Katerina made no reply. She threw herself on the deck, and abandoned herself to her feeling of bitter anguish. And as she lay there, and M'Clise stood at the helm, the wind abated; the vessel was no longer borne down as before, although the waves were still mountains high. The seamen on board rallied; some fragments of sail were set on the remnants of the masts, and there was a chance of safety. M'Clise spoke not, but watched the helm. The wind shifted in their favour; and hope rose in every heart. The Firth of Tay was now open, and they were saved! Light was the heart of M'Clise when he kept away the vessel, and gave the helm up to the mate. He hastened to Katerina, who still remained on the deck, raised her up, whispered comfort and returning love: but she heard not – she could not forget – and she wept bitterly.

'We are saved, dear Katerina!'

'Better that we had been lost!' replied she, mournfully.

'No, no! say not so, with your own Andrew pressing you to his bosom.'

'Your bitter curse!'

' 'Twas madness – nothing – I knew not what I said.'

But the iron had entered into her soul. Her heart was broken.

'You had better give orders for them to look out for the Bell Rock,' observed the man at the helm to M'Clise.

The Bell Rock! M'Clise shuddered, and made no reply. Onward went the vessel, impelled by the sea and wind: one moment raised aloft, and towering over the surge; at another, deep in the hollow trough, and walled in by the convulsed element. M'Clise still held his Katerina in his arms, who responded not to his endearments, when a sudden shock threw them on the deck. The crashing of the timbers, the pouring of the waves over the stern, the heeling and settling of the vessel, were but the work of a few seconds. On more furious shock – she separates, falls on her beam ends, and the raging seas swept over her.

M'Clise threw from him her whom he had so madly loved, and plunged into the wave. Katerina shrieked, as she dashed after him, and all was over.

When the storm rises, and the screaming sea-gull seeks the land, and the fisherman hastens his bark towards the beach, there is to be seen, descending from the dark clouds with the rapidity of lightning, the form of Andrew M'Clise, the heavy bell to which he is attached by the neck, bearing him down to his doom.

And when all is smooth and calm, when at the ebbing tide the wave but gently kisses the rock, then by the light of the silver moon the occupants of the vessels which sail from the Firth of Tay have often beheld the form of the beautiful Katerina, waving her white scarf as a signal that they should approach, and take her off from the rock on which she is seated. At times, she offers a letter for her father, Vandermaclin; and she mourns and weeps as the wary mariners, with their eyes fixed on her, and with folded arms, pursue their course in silence and in dread.

James Runciman

THE LOST SKIPPER

For a number of years, James Runciman ran his fellow Englishman W. Clark Russell hard in the sea-story popularity stakes. Like Russell (who is included in this collection as the author of 'Can These Dry Bones Live?'), his books positively reeked of the salt of the ocean and were similarly based on hard-won experience. Runciman (1850–1918) was born in that great old port of Liverpool, and was away on sailing ships when still in his early teens. Unlike Clark Russell, though, he actually began writing while he was still at sea, and his name was firmly established before he settled on dry land in the early 1880s. An early admirer of Runciman's work was Frank T. Bullen, himself to become a famous maritime writer, who commented in 1901: 'Runciman's yarns most truly hold the mirror up to nature in a manner unexcelled by any other marine author living or dead.' The reader may now judge for him or herself the validity of this claim for a man whose work has, I think, become unjustifiably neglected. It gives me more than a little pleasure to be returning 'The Lost Skipper' to print after almost one hundred years – and I hope you will agree!

The *Mariana* was swung outside the bar, in order that her compass might be adjusted.

While she was travelling slowly round in circles Thomas

Hardy, the skipper, stood on the bridge with his wife, and received the directions of the man who was making out his new compass cards.

After an hour's delay the pilot boat came alongside, and Tom said: 'Now, Jenny, my dear, we shall have to let you over the side. Good-bye; I will send you a letter from Port Said.'

Jenny Hardy put her arms round her husband's neck, and said: 'You will find us just the same when you come back; and mind, Tom, not a drop! I think I shall break my heart if you take it again.'

Hardy replied, with a tremor in his voice: 'I cannot promise anything, my dear, but I will struggle my very hardest. If I can get over the first week of the hot weather without touching the drink, I will come back without breaking the pledge. It is the confounded heat that always tempts me.'

There was a good deal of reason for Mrs Hardy's caution.

Tom was one of the finest seamen on the coast; he had been brought up in the old school, and when he was only eleven years of age he knocked up and down in a clumsy old collier brig. Before he was twelve he was shipwrecked on the *Galloper*, and landed home on a bitter winter day in his shirt-sleeves. While he was second mate he was once blown north to the verge of the Arctic Circle, where two of the crew lost their feet through frostbite. There was no kind of adventure usual to merchant seamen that he had not gone through, and there was nothing connected with his trade that he did not know better than most other men. He was an active fellow, of the blonde Scandinavian type – red-bearded, yellow-haired, deep of chest, and muscular to an extraordinary degree: he could go up a backstay hand over hand with hardly a wriggle of the legs; he could jump over a rope-yarn held four feet ten inches above the deck, and when he performed this feat he came down with a light, buoyant thud which testified to the springiness of his limbs. No danger ever scared him; and when he was in a sailing-vessel he let neither wind nor weather delay him when once the hatches were on. He was the terror of timid mates, on account of his way of carrying sail. He made a little fortune for the owners of one fine barque, but it was at the expense of almost tearing her to pieces. He once carried away two suits of sails in the course of a single voyage; and he kept the barque going at eleven knots from the Rock of Lisbon to the Downs. He might have been a wealthy man before he was forty years old, for his luck was wonderful, and his skill was only equalled by his good fortune. But he had one failing.

It happened that when he was an apprentice he fell off the main-yard and hurt his head. There was a big ugly indentation just over his right temple, and there was no doubt that his brain was affected to some degree. He had no particular craving for alcohol, but if he once so much as tasted spirits, he became silly, and was no more responsible for his own actions until it was out of him. That was his little failing. Times out of number he had been pardoned, for the fellow had the knack of inspiring affection and confidence, even among those who had seen him during his maddest fits of drunkenness, yet no one knew when or where he would break out again.

He was once running a smart little brig on a roundabout voyage to Malta, Venice, Naples, and Cardiff; he was rattling up the Adriatic at about eight knots, when one of the men happened to displease him. Hardy had taken a glass or two of spirits, and his mad temper got the better of him; he picked the man up and threw him overboard. Then, with incredible heartlessness (which he repented in his sober moments), he cracked on and left the poor drowning wretch. It happened that a pilot-boat was running under the stern of the brig, and the man was picked up. The felucca carried the waif into Venice, and a prosecution was ordered. Mr Tom had to pay a fine of £25, which considerably lessened the profits of his voyage. At Cardiff he threw a man down the hold, and very narrowly escaped a prosecution for manslaughter.

By the time he got round to London his crew were up in arms against him, and one dark night he heard one man say to another: 'Can you see the swine?'

'I don't know whether you can see, but I am going to let you feel me,' said Tom, and he thereupon inflicted such a terrible beating upon the poor squealing Dutchman that he made a case for the hospital.

Hardy was very heavily fined for this, and not a penny was left to him when he came to reckon up accounts.

Such was the skipper of the *Mariana* – a wild, undisciplined man, a compound of tenderness and ferocity, stupidity and shrewdness, cruelty and kindness, gallantry and superstition – in short, a kind of man who might have been a pirate or a Scripture reader, according to the circumstances in which he was thrown, for his ferocity was strongly tempered by intense religious feeling. He would have been the most brutal pirate in the whole of the Spanish Main, and he would have been a kindly and helpful visitor had his fate compelled him to labour among the poor.

The *Mariana* had a very good run to Port Said, and then Tom wrote home to his wife thus:

DEAR JENNY, – I write these few lines, hoping they will find you in good health, as they leave me at present. We have had a good run, and she is a nice smart boat. We can get twelve knots out of her when the wind is dead astern and we can put the square sails on her, and she goes nine very easy. I was very near having a drink as we were passing Gibraltar, but you will be glad to hear that I have managed so far without taking any stuff, and I believe I shall get through the voyage all straight. Tell Nance that I can't wear the comforter, because the weather here is so hot that you could sleep on deck at night if it were not for the moon making you blind. I go on deck in pyjamas, but not, of course, here, but after we left Malta and our decks was all frizzling like anything with the heat. Dear love, I hope we shall have a good haul this voyage, because I want to see you dressed as well as the rest of them, and if we stop at Marseilles on the way home I will get you a lump of silk, so you can cut all the lot of them out. We have got to take of lot of Arab firemen, and I doubt if the beggars vex me I shall be breaking some of their backs. The queer thing about Arabs is that if you hit them they tumble down directly, and you have to be pretty rough on them to do any good. With best love, I am your faithful husband,

THOMAS HARDY

Not long afterwards a telegram from the owners reached Jenny. The message simply said: '*Mariana* arrived at Bombay. She is to run for two years between Shanghai and Hong Kong. Charter arranged this day.'

Jenny was very glad, although she hardly liked to think of poor Tom frizzling out on that scorching coast; but two years at £20 a month meant a lot of money, and the woman's heart was rejoiced.

Things went on very smoothly, and Mrs Hardy drew her half-pay quite regularly. Once the owner said: 'I am glad Captain Hardy is doing so well; we are quite satisfied with him, and we have a strong notion of renewing the charter.'

Tom was very lucky in certain private speculations of his own, and in four months he earned eighty pounds over and above his wages. Every letter that reached England carried the same cheering tale of temperance and success, and the wife was as happy as the day was long, for she thought to herself, 'If he can only go on for five years like this he will be able to retire, and not have to go to sea any more in the stormy weather.'

On one glorious summer morning she went up the river in a passenger-boat to the great town where the owner's office stood. Everything seemed hopeful, and even the grimy banks were almost joyous under the pouring discharge of sunshine.

One of the clerks in the outer office looked ominously at Mrs Hardy as she took her seat, and presently a messenger said: 'Mr Brown would like to see you privately in the inner office.'

The colour faded from the woman's face, and a black foreboding seemed at once to blot out the brightness of the sunshine.

Mr Brown motioned his visitor to a chair. With a sudden effort he came right to the heart of the business. 'Mrs Hardy, I am sorry to say there is no half-pay for you this month; I thought everything was going on well. The fact is, we have been obliged to unship your husband, for conduct which you will probably understand.'

Jenny fell back on the chair, and the good-natured owner stuttered, 'Nay, nay! take a glass of water. You see, we have to be strict in these matters, and we could not keep a man who might lose our vessel any day. I'll strain a point and give you five pounds; but of course you must see we have our own interest to consider. Good-morning, madam; I am very sorry it has happened.'

Jenny felt as though a bar of iron had been bent across her head, and she walked home in a dazed condition. All night long she sat in a dream in the little parlour, surrounded by the quaint ornaments that Tom had collected from all parts of the world. She saw nothing, thought nothing; and even the babble of her little girl fell upon her ears as if she had been deaf.

The owner was quite right – Tom Hardy had broken out with a vengeance. During a sudden fit of temper he had been induced to take a glass of champagne with a genial stevedore, who wanted to 'pull him round'. One bottle led to another, and before midnight Tom Hardy was mad drunk. Next day he carried on the most extraordinary capers: he hired a carriage with four ponies, and occupied himself with driving full gallop until his beasts were foundered, and he had to hand over a pretty fair sum by way of compensation for broken knees. He went on board the vessel and invited a jolly party of seven skippers, who kept up a carouse until eight o'clock next morning. By that time Hardy was frantic. He kept his legs, it is true, but his brain was absolutely distraught, and his actions were those of a lunatic. He began with his old practice of knocking men about; and one poor wretch whom he shot overboard with a terrific left-hander would never have risen again if the drags had not been promptly employed by the English water-police.

After three days, during which time he never ate any solid food, he was on the verge of an attack of delirium tremens, and the vessel had to go to sea, with Hardy drunk on the bridge. In running out through a very difficult water-way he slapped the pilot's face, bade that functionary hold his jaw, and proceeded to put the engines full speed ahead.

A smart Yankee brigantine was towing out in front of the *Mariana*; the sailing vessel yawed slightly, and Hardy, who was attempting to accomplish a close shave, struck her on the quarter with the bulge of the steamer's starboard bow, and surged forward, bumping heavily, and making frightful havoc amongst the standing rigging.

After tearing his way clear he gave a wild halloo of defiance, and plunged ahead at twelve knots.

Of course the *Mariana* was detained at her port, and, as Hardy was scarcely sober even then, his explanation of the affair to the agent was so very lame that a telegram was sent to England. The reply came promptly: 'Discharge him instantly.'

The *Mariana* was lying at her moorings when the prim agent

stepped aboard about eight o'clock in the morning. Tom had a fearful headache; his eyes were bleared; his hand was shaking, and he was casting anxious glances over his left shoulder as if he expected some one was coming behind him.

The agent said, 'I must ask you to go ashore, Mr Hardy. I have orders to put another captain aboard at once.' And on that very afternoon the drunken skipper took his baggage ashore.

Two years went by, and Jenny Hardy's savings were completely exhausted. She had written to her husband saying:

DEAR TOM, — I don't care what you do; you are always the same to us. I will live as well as I can until you get back, and nobody shall ever know that anything is wrong with you. We shall have to go short, I expect, of things to eat; but I shall always be nicely dressed when I go out. It's a bad job, but there is no use moaning about it; and I will try and keep your fault from being made public as well as ever I can. Do come home, dear, as soon as you can, and you will find us just the same if you have not a penny, or a coat to your back. We send you kisses, and I am your own faithful wife for good luck or bad.

Little by little the store of savings had dribbled away, and at last poor Jenny came to the end of her hoard. One morning Nance said, 'I am so hungry, mother. As I came along the street I saw a lump of bread close beside the gutter, and if no one had been looking, I should have picked it up. I seem as if I could eat my bootlaces.'

The woman put her arms round the girl, and said, 'My bonnie bairn, I have not a bite to give you, and I dare not go and sell my shawl, or all the folks in the town would know it. We will starve just one day more, and perhaps God will be good to us if we say our prayers to-night.'

With hunger biting at her very vitals, the brave little body went out day after day, and kept a cheery face in the presence of all the townsfolk. Some few of our people knew the real state of affairs, for gossip travels fast in so small a community, but no one could get a word out of Mrs Hardy.

She was fainting with hunger after two days' starvation, when her big, burly brother came home from sea.

She met him smiling, and he sat down in the kitchen.

His first inquiry was rather startling: 'No fire, Jenny! what's up?'

'I didn't think it was cold enough for a fire, Ralph dear.'

'By George! you must have a harder skin than I have got, then. Let us have a cup of tea, old girl.'

Then Jenny fell on the strong man's breast and buried her face against him. She said, 'Oh, Ralph dear, we are starving; we have not a penny, nor a bit of bread, nor a morsel of coal.'

'The blazes you haven't!' said the sailor, jumping up.

'Oh, my dear, it is all through drink, the drink, the weary drink. He has lost his ship, and he has never written for more than two years, and I didn't like to tell you, or else I would have written out to you to America. Just keep it quiet, Ralph honey, for I pray to God every day, and I go to the church every Sunday and pick out pieces in the Prayer-book like what I wish to say; and I know my lad will come back to me, for all his being so cruel as to leave us so long without a word.'

When she finished the sailor man was sobbing heavily.

He said, 'Damn! God forgive me. I have got my two years' voyage-money here. Now, look here, you must let me lodge with you, and take care of my coin; and mind it's your own. I have a good mind to skelp you, you little duffer – starving your bairn for fond pride, and leaving all the lot of us in the dark. Why, my chums would have thought me a pretty scoot if they had known I let my sister go a-hungering.'

Within an hour a load of coals drew up at the door, and little Nance and her mother had the first mouthful of meat they had tasted for many a long day.

When Tom Hardy woke to a sense of the situation after his discharge, he felt as though suicide was his only resource. He fixed his bleared eyes on the slimy water as he tramped up and down the quay, and again and again he had an impulse to throw himself forward, and end everything in those black depths. His reputation was gone; he was friendless in a foreign land; and his wild debauch had left him with very little money.

He stayed in a low tavern amidst a riotous set of English sailors, but the shock had sobered him, and he clenched his teeth.

'Never another drop, not if I have to lie and grovel. And I will not go back to my wife and children until I have regained my character.' So he growled in his extremity.

It happened that the Chinese Government was occupied just then in routing out a nest of pirates, who frequented the winding waters of the marsh lands, and preyed ferociously on the trading boats.

Tom was wandering aimlessly among the shipping, when he met a smart, aristocratic-looking man, dressed in a naval uniform.

The aristocrat politely raised a finger and touched his hat; he then said, 'Pardon me, sir; you are of the merchant service, are you not?'

Tom answered, 'Yes, sir; late captain of the *Mariana*.'

'Ah! are you the fellow who got us into the mess with the Yankee Government?'

'Well, sir, I am afraid I am, and I have suffered for it. I have lost my ship, lost everything, and now I don't care what I do.'

The officer said, 'Well, I fancy you are just my man. I am trying to pick up a crew for a gunboat, and I should think you and I might strike up some kind of a bargain. You can fight, I suppose?'

'Well, sir, I don't know about fighting, but I never saw anything in my life that I was frightened of; I can say that much, if you won't fancy I am bragging.'

'All right, then; now, look here, these affairs are managed very informally. I want to get together a lot of desperadoes, and it strikes me you are the kind of fellow I could trust. Will you ship?'

Tom's heart bounded as he said, 'Like a shot, sir! I will stand to you as long as the life is in me.'

And so for many months Tom Hardy was engaged among the wild crew of reckless and forlorn blackguards who formed the ship's company of the gunboat *Mandarin*. Even amongst that dare-devil lot he was conspicuous from his absolute insensibility to danger, and his prodigious strength.

His chief one day said to him, 'By Gad! Hardy, I wish you

and I had lived in the old times. I guess that we and our boys would have taken the starch out of the Frenchmen.'

Tom laughed with a burly roar at the notion, and said: 'We certainly are giving Johnny Chinaman fits. I hear that some of the beggars pray to us. They call me the "big devil" and you the "little devil".'

From this fragment of conversation it will be seen in what kind of enterprise our sailor was engaged.

Shortly afterwards the *Mandarin* was sent out to punish a set of scoundrels who had lately massacred the entire population of a village.

At nightfall the gunboat lay at anchor in a very awkward part of a deep sluggish channel. The flats to right and left were covered with tall, rank reeds, which grew to a great height, and completely obscured the view from the vessel.

Towards midnight the captain went forward. On his return Hardy said, 'I heard a frog just now. Damned funny kind of frog. He croaked three or four times, and he was answered by another round the bend of the river. If you will excuse me, sir, I should say we had better strengthen the watch.'

'Oh, I don't think it is necessary,' answered the captain; 'the marshes are swarming with frogs.'

About an hour afterwards a Yankee sailor sang out, 'Stand by, all of you; we are going to get sky-blue fits in half a minute.'

The captain rushed to the bows and looked anxiously into the murky darkness; there was a flash, a sound of confused yelling, and before Tom Hardy had time to collect himself a perfect horde of men jumped over the bows of the gunboat and swarmed aft.

Tom didn't depend upon a sword; he picked up an enormous handspike, and dashed into the crowd just in time to find the captain in extremity. With crashing blow, right and left, he cleared a lane amongst the marauders; then with a hoarse roar like that of a wild beast he yelled, 'Come on, *Mandarins*, murder the lot!'

His tremendous figure, and the fearful power of the blows he delivered, fairly scared the pirates. The gunboat's crew rallied, and in five minutes not a pirate was left on board, excepting five who had been struck down by Tom Hardy's club.

The captain was wounded, but not seriously, and he said,

'You shall have the command of a boat for yourself, my boy, after this job is over.'

And sure enough Tom Hardy was promoted to high rank in the Chinese service.

Ralph and Jenny were chatting over their supper and speaking many kind words of poor Tom, when a knock came to the door.

Jenny shrieked, 'Oh, it's him, it's him! I knew that God would not let us lose him. Run, Nance, to the door; I can't trust myself on my feet.'

Then entered a jolly, broad-shouldered fellow, whose face was burnt almost to blackness by the tropical sun.

The boom of his deep voice sounded tremulously in the kitchen as he said, 'Well, old girl, you thought I was behaving badly; but I will make up for it now, and never go away from you any more.'

Jenny tottered to her giant, and the tears ran down his rough face as he strained her hard in his mighty arms.

Tom had been very lucky in the service, and he did not need to go to sea any more. He bought a few houses, and eked out his little income by acting as ship's husband for a small private company.

He is now a temperance lecturer, and it is worth going a long way to see strong men fall sobbing under the thrill of his great voice and his rude eloquence.

W. Clark Russell

CAN THESE DRY BONES LIVE?

William Clark Russell had the sea in his blood when he was born – his father, Henry Russell, was an old salt who commemorated his love of the nautical life by writing that famous song 'A Life on the Ocean Wave'. The younger Russell (1844–1911) followed in his footsteps by serving an apprenticeship at sea, but quit in 1874 to devote his time to writing. In the years that followed, he became by far the most prolific writer of sea stories and at the turn of the century Algernon Swinburne unhesitatingly called him 'the greatest master of the sea, living or dead'. Such praise may have been a little overblown, but Clark Russell's popularity was certainly undeniable, and he also had the distinction of being featured in the Sherlock Holmes stories – as Doctor Watson's favourite reading material!

In a number of his books, Clark Russell showed a particular fascination with the supernatural and the superstitions of seamen. The legend of the Flying Dutchman, for instance, inspired his very successful book, The Death Ship (1888), while the power of nautical omens was very much in evidence in his collection, The Mystery of the Ocean Star, published the following year. Not a few of his stories are actually narrated by old sea captains, and one of the most memorable of these, I think, is 'Can These Dry Bones Live?', which mingles fear of the unknown with a fair measure of salty logic.

'Well, sir,' said the old captain to me – a retired shipmaster, with the gaze of a vulture under the apparently sleepy lid, and a face full of lines and discoloration like the wrinkling of currents in the glassy swathes of a dead calm on some dingy spread of water off the West African coast – 'I had been always a bit superstitious up to then, but I own that that job cured me. But it made me see also that it isn't reasonable to be too contemptuous of one's fellow-creatures who believe in spirits and manifestations, of which there is no organ, sense, or quality in the human body to take notice of, saving credulity. It comes to this, sir: human nature never gets beyond a certain pass. We sail to that point, and then the wind shifts, and we drop astern. From time to time it is put into us to think foolishly, that the thoughtful amongst us may understand how little ahead of the old folks we are, spite of all our discoveries. I've watched this fad of ghosts amongst us of late; the growth of societies which aim to enlarge men's knowledge of what doesn't exist; and it takes me back to the days when I was a young 'un, when there were still witches in the country, and old women were ducked and drowned for sailing athwart the moonlight on broomsticks. We were a bit coarser then in our superstitions than now, made our ghosts hags instead of spirits of beauty, fled from candles in turnips, and reckoned that when old Bogey wanted us he arrived down the chimney. But the quality remains the same. It is only brightened in these times, polished up, and made to look in other ways finer. Now, however, to give you my yarn.

'I was master of a ship of eight hundred tons. We were loaded with a general cargo, bound to the East Indies. It is many years ago, when ship's companies were numerous, partly through the compulsion of the navigation laws, partly because owners wanted their ships to keep afloat, partly because you wouldn't have got sailors to ship if there had not been hands to do the work; and my complement numbered between forty and forty-five men. In a crowd of this kind one doesn't take particular notice. When the crew are few, you come to know your Jims, and Joes, and Toms, as you come to know your dogs at home, or as a man who is worth only a few shillings is not only conscious of what he has in his pocket, but can tell you the character of the coins also. We were without passengers, simply a well-manned cargo vessel, all of the olden time, though a handsome boat in our way, frigate-built, painted ports, wide channels, great black tops, the yards square enough to serve a line of battle-ship, and the royals, when mast-headed, sitting close against the trucks – the properest topping off, to my taste, to the fabric of a full-rigged ship.

'We had been out a fortnight, when in the afternoon there came on a sudden squall. The fore and mizen topgallant sails were clewed up, with a hand standing by at the main topgallant halliards. I noticed some figures in the forerigging going aloft to roll up the sail there, and then on a sudden there was a commotion, a running of men forward, and a gathering of them into a heap around something. I told the mate to go and see what was the matter. He returned with the news that a man in the act of going aloft had fallen dead on deck off the rail. We were without a doctor, and all hands looked to me in a case of this kind. I walked to where the man lay, and found him to be an able seaman; an old yellow-haired man, whose face I had before taken notice of for the ghastly complexion of it; a sort of dusky, parchment-like hue, the colour of sailor's duff that's been too long in the coppers. The lids were half closed, nothing but the whites showing; the lips set hard in a sort of half grin, without froth, and the arms outstretched in the posture of a crucified person. Short of a skeleton, to my notion, one ought never to be able to say cocksurely, pointing to a body, '*this* is Death'. The fellow might be in a faint, or in a fit, or a cataleptic; his body in death's strait jacket, and the mind within all alive and wondering what the deuce has gone wrong outside. I ordered him to be carried to his bunk and rubbed, and to be treated as if he was to be brought to, and if that failed, then to be stowed away out of the sight of the men; but not to be stitched up for a bit, so that if there was any spark of life in him it might have a chance. The fact is, I wanted to make sure that he was a dead man before he was tossed overboard, a very proper feeling in me, no doubt, though there was a touch of morbidity in it, too; for, to tell the truth, the one quiet horror of my life in those days was the thought of being buried alive, and what I feared for myself I was not the sort of man to put upon another.

'Well, after two days we were all agreed that he was dead, so I gave orders for him to be stitched up and brought to the gangway, and next morning after breakfast we held the service. It was always my desire that matters of this kind should be carried out with proper solemnity. I considered it worked as a wholesome influence amongst the sailors, who were made to understand that a dead seaman on the ocean was not to be treated as if he were a dead pauper out of a workhouse; that a show of respect and regret, at all events, should go to his funeral, since a shipmate is a shipmate the wide world over. The body, stitched in its hammock, with a sinker stowed away in the clews, was placed upon a grating and covered with the ensign. Then the grating was lifted by four men and brought to the rail, one end of it resting there, the other end supported by two men, who stood ready to whip off the ensign and let the body slide when the time should come for so doing.

'All hands gathered around, washed and clean. It was a quiet morning, a light breeze of wind blowing, the ship under all plain sail, everything silent aloft, the deck heaving slightly to the small beam sea. I came out of the cabin with my prayer-book in my hand and started to read, the men baring their heads, with the grinding here and there of a jaw upon a hunk of tobacco standing high in the cheek-bone, and much wistful and inquisitive peering at poor Jack's outline by eyes bleared by the gales of wind into which they had stared.

'I was proceeding, reading with great emphasis and solemnity, when there rose from under the ensign a short muffled, groaning sort of cry of *For God's sake cut me adrift, mates! I'm suffocating!*'

'The prayer-book fell from my hand; the two fellows who were holding the grating let go of it and shot forward, whereupon off rolled the body on to the deck amongst the feet of the sailors, who, letting fly a volley of curses in their alarm, bolted in all directions, some of them even jumping into the rigging. Had a bombshell exploded amongst us the clearance effected could not have been more complete.

'The mates had run away as well as the seamen, and the cowardice of all hands put temper enough into me to rally my nerves.

' "Quick," I bawled; "cut the poor wretch adrift, or he'll be

109

suffocated in good earnest, and it will be a worse murder done than had we buried him."

'On this the chief mate and some others came to the body, shouldering one another, and ripped open the hammock. Well, dead or alive, 'twould have been better to have given the thing its last toss than have witnessed such a sight. You see it was warmish weather, and the body besides had been – but I'll say no more on *that*; only that such an apparition rising before the stoutest army that ever took the field would have sent it flying without waiting for the buglers to sound. But he'd called out that he was suffocating, and we looked to see him move, all hands coming up in bunches at a time, till there we were all of a heaving and squirming muddle, with this horror in the midst of us, and the men squirting juice in all directions through sheer loathing.

' "If that man ben't dead," said the bo'sun, "my eyes ain't mates."

' "Did he wriggle at all?" said I, addressing one of the fellows who held the grating, "before you let go and run away?"

'The man aswered he hadn't noticed any movement.

' "He spoke, anyway," said the mate.

' "Well, pickle my eyes for onions if there was ever a rummier start than this," cried the carpenter, stooping to look close at the man, and then recoiling with a heave of the breast and a long wipe of his mouth down the length of his hairy arm.

'I ordered the body to be carried to a cabin, and put the second mate along with a seaman to watch it; but their report to me was that if the fellow was alive he gave no signs of it, but that, on the contrary, he was imitating death so incomparably as to oblige them to beg me to allow some others to relieve them, as they did not feel strong enough to go on. I then viewed the body myself, and no longer having a doubt gave orders that it should be stitched up afresh and once again brought to the gangway.

'It was now eight bells in the afternoon. Of course it was right that this old Jack should be buried decently, and I resolved to go through with the funeral service, but I let it be known that there was no obligation upon the men to attend outside the few who were needed to do the work. Nevertheless all hands turned up as before. Well, I started to read as I had in the morning, but at the very moment, of my pronouncing the same words I was delivering when the interruption happened, there came a most audible but half-choking and half-smothered groan or grunt of "*Oh, Lord, they mean to drown me after all!*" from under the ensign.

'The fellow that held the right corner of the grating let go, and went backing amongst his mates with a cry of dismay; but the other man, bawling out with a face darkened by passion, "You old villain! how many burials d'ye expect, and be d——d to you!" tilted the grating and away flashed the hammock overboard.

'We all stood looking on like idiots. For my part, captain as I was, I hadn't a word to say for the moment. In fact, I was thunderstruck. The groan of the corpse was scarce off the ear before the body was gone, and yet you couldn't think of us as having drowned him either, for nothing could have seemed deader than did this old Jack when I took my last view of him. However, no purpose could be served by making a fuss; it was one of those breaches of discipline that defy your cool reason though you may handle them as you will in a passion. Besides, a moment or two's reflection, coupled with a look round, satisfied me that the men would be easier in their minds for being quit of the body, and so, telling the mate to send the hands forward, I went to my cabin; but more mystified, under a livelier consternation of mind, in short, than it would suit me to admit to everybody. It was idle to talk of tricks. I might have reconciled myself to some notion of that kind had I made one of two or three spectators; but here had been forty or fifty of us all lumped together, and the reality of the thing came out in the sincerity of the fright, for the morning panic was much greater than I have put it, whilst the terror in the afternoon might have shown as wild, had the fellows at the grating let fall the body again amongst the men.

'Well, at ten o'clock that night I left the deck to lie down. All was quiet. The influence of that day's work was expressed in the manner of the men, who had moved and talked very soberly, with subdued gestures and tones, and in the dog-watches I had noticed them hanging together in knots, conversing like people fresh from an execution. I was aroused from my sleep by the second mate, who had charge of the deck.

' "There's the whole watch below, sir, come aft to complain that they can't get any rest."

' "What's the matter?" said I, starting up.

' "Why, they say they can hear old Jack's voice calling to them down in the forepeak."

' "Old Jack's voice?" I cried, and with that I followed him on deck, where, sure enough, I found all hands massed together on the quarter-deck.

' "What's the matter, men?" I called out, leaning over the rail at the break of the poop to speak to them.

'The carpenter spoke up, "There's old Jack hailing us in the forepeak, sir."

' "Nonsense, man."

' "Smite me, sir, if it ain't the blooming truth; not only hailing but a-cussing us for having drowned him."

' "But you must know that that can't be," said I, "he's leagues astern and fathoms deep."

'A voice answered, "He's cussing us all the same. He swears he'll haunt us all overboard."

'I told the second mate to go forward and report if he could hear anything of this strange voice. A shadowy group of men went with him; indeed, I doubt if he would have had heart to drop into the forecastle alone. Presently he returned, coming aft with a run and speaking with a broken breath.

' "It's true, sir," he gasped, "if it isn't old Jack, it's the devil. I heard him say, '*I'll punish all of ye for drowning of me. Head as you will, 'tis old Jack as is at the hellumm now, and so stand by!*' "

' "But, good thunder!" cried I, "how is a man's voice going to sound in the forecastle out of the forepeak? Answer me that, you fool."

' "Well, come forrards and hear it yourself, sir," he exclaimed sullenly.

'I instantly assented, and walked forward, followed by all hands; and not without a beating heart, I admit, but with a good air of carelessness upon me, I stepped into the forecastle. It was a topgallant forecastle, entered by doors abreast of the windlass ends; a slush lamp swung under the beam, and the light was very weak. I entered with the second mate, and stood listening. For some minutes nothing sounded but the hard breathing of the seamen, who filled the doorways, squeezing the foremost in, though these pressed back like a wall, making such a jam as might account for louder snorings. Queer creakings and groanings arose out of the slightly swaying hull into the silence, with the faint sound of the bow wave softly washing from the cutwater. Then, on a sudden, I heard a dim hoarse voice – weakened as it were by the thickness of the deck between, with a note of rage in it as though the fellow could barely articulate for his teeth being fixed – exclaim, "*Curse the ship, I says! Curse all hands in her, says I. I'm a murdered man, and I'll haunt ye all.*"

'"There, sir," cried the second mate, backing to the men, whose breathing was now stormy with emotion.

'Scarce was this said, when one of the seamen, who had apparently been forced forwards by the pressure of the others, was run almost up to me by the long arm of the chief mate, who, unperceived by me, had worked his way into the crowd to learn what was going on. This mate stood over six feet high, and was a giant in strength, and the head of the fellow whom his shoulder-of-mutton fist grasped by the scruff of the neck was on a level with his chin.

'"Here's the ghost, sir," said he.

'The sailors now came bundling in in a swarm.

'"This is the ghost," repeated the mate, giving the fellow a shake which threatened to throw his head off his neck. "'Tis deuced clever, my lad, but it's a joke that wants sea room," another shake. "Own to it, own to it!" he cried, "before I screw your neck off."

'"I own to it," said the man.

'"Own to what?" I asked.

'"Why sir," answered the mate, "he has the trick of throwing his voice, and wonderfully well he does it too. I had my eye on him this afternoon and suspected him. I'm sure of it now, for he didn't know I stood close behind him."

'Some of the men muttered. I perceived that they looked upon this as a conspiracy between me and the mate to allay their fears, and clearly seeing that it must be as the mate said, and heartily despising myself for the alarm I had felt throughout the day, I immediately formed a resolution.

'"Your name's Andover?" said I to the man.

' "Yes, sir," he answered.

' "You confess that it was you who made old Jack talk on the grating and down here?"

' "I do, sir," he answered, with a writhe, for the shoulder of mutton clung to him as a vice.

' "Prove it to the men," said I, "and I'll forgive you. You can let go of him, Mr Moore."

'The man coughed; a moment after we heard old Jack cursing us all in the forepeak. The deception was exquisite; in sober truth, my admiration of the skill of the fellow would have been altogether too great to suffer me to punish him, even had I not promised him forgiveness. A few further examples of his genius sufficed to reassure the sailors, and I went aft, leaving them to deal with him as they chose. However, he managed to make his peace by entertaining them with his art as a ventriloquist. Indeed, after the first spasm of temper, they were too well pleased to believe that old Jack was really dead and gone, and too much astonished by Andover's cleverness to feel much resentment.

'I often had this man in the cabin afterwards to amuse me. He had the face of a born comedian, and I strongly advised him to start as a ventriloquist ashore, where, I don't doubt, under proper training, he might have proved a fortune for himself or for an employer. But, unhappily, he got into some scrape at our first port of call; and I had to leave him behind me; and when, long afterwards, I inquired after him, I gathered that he had taken to drink and died in a hospital. Yet I recall him with gratitude, for he quite cured me of my superstitions.'

Frank T. Bullen

THE DEBT OF THE WHALE

Apart from Herman Melville, no other author has written more vividly and authentically of the whaling industry than Frank Thomas Bullen. His book, The Cruise of the Cachelot (1898), has been an indispensable companion on many voyages, and I have read and re-read its engrossing pages times without number. Bullen (1857–1915) was born in the most abject poverty in the mean streets of Paddington in London. His father was a drunkard and a gambler, and by the time he was nine, Frank was living by his wits on the streets. Three years later, he had hardened himself enough to be taken on as a cabin boy on the ship Arabella. After several long voyages, he landed up in America at New Bedford, Massachusetts, and got himself a berth on the whaling ship, Cachelot. Such was the impact of his cruises on board this vessel that, on his return to London, he dashed off his impressions in a fever of excitement. The book was a sensation, and Rudyard Kipling lead the cheers of the critics by declaring, 'I've never read anything that equals it in its deep-sea wonder and mystery.' The dark-haired, handsome Bullen (whose features were strikingly similar to those of Joseph Conrad – who was also born the same year) became something of a literary lion, much in demand to give lectures on life at sea. He also poured his experiences and those of other seamen he had met into a series of popular collections, such as Deep-Sea Plunderings (1901), Our Heritage the Sea (1906) and Fighting the Icebergs (1910). For this collection, it has seemed only right to pick one of his stories about the whaling industry, and in 'The Debt of The Whale' you will

*meet Captain Elisha Cushing, a man cast in the same redoubt-
able mould as the immortal Captain Ahab . . .*

Elisha Cushing, skipper of the *Beluga*, South Seaman, of
Martha's Vineyard, was a hard-bitten Yankee of the toughest
of that tough race. Even in the sternest of mankind there is
usually to be found some soft spot, some deeply hidden well of
feeling that at the touch of the right hand will bubble up in a
kindly stream, even though it be hermetically sealed to all the
world beside. But those who knew Captain Cushing best were
wont to say that he must have been cradled on an iceberg,
spent his childhood in a whaler's fo'c'sle, hardened himself by
the constant contemplation and practice of cruelty, until,
having arrived at the supreme position of master of his own
ship, he was less of a man than a pitiless automaton who
regarded neither God nor devil, and only looked upon other
men as an engineer might upon the cogs of a machine. Few,
indeed, are the men who, throughout a voyage lasting from
three to four years, shut up within the narrow bounds of a
small ship, could entirely do without human companionship,
could abstain from some friendly intercourse, however infre-
quent, with those around them. Yet Captain Cushing was even
such a man. No one knew how he passed his abundant leisure.
He was never seen reading, he did not smoke, no intoxicating
drink was ever allowed on board his ship; in fact, at all times,
except when whale-fishing was being carried on, he was to all
appearance a body without a mind, a figure of a man who
moved and ate and slept mechanically, yet whom to offend
was to court nothing less than torture. Those unspeculating
eyes missed nothing; not a member of the crew but felt that in
some not-to-be-explained fashion all his doings, almost his
very thoughts, were known to the grim commander, and hard,
indeed, was the lot of any unfortunate who in any way came
athwart the stern code of rules that appeared to govern
Captain Cushing's command. Nevertheless he had one virtue—
he did not interfere. So long as the business of the ship went on

as goes a good clock, there was peace. The discipline was perfect; it reduced the human items that composed the *Beluga*'s crew to something very nearly resembling a piece of carefully constructed mechanism, for Captain Cushing's genius lay that way. Out of the many crews that he had commanded during his thirty years' exercise of absolute power he was wont to winnow officers that were a reflex of his own mind, and it mattered not how raw were the recruits bundled on board his ship at the last moment before leaving home, the Cushing system speedily reduced them to a condition of absolute mindlessness as far as any wish of their own was concerned. They became simply parts of the engine whereby Captain Cushing's huge store of dollars was augmented.

It was an article of religion among the afterguard of the *Beluga*, handed on to each new-comer by some unspoken code of communication, that the 'old man's' being and doing might never be discussed. The subject was 'tabu', not to be approached upon any pretext, although nothing could be more certain than that it lay uppermost in every officer's mind. Among the crew, in that stifling den forrard where thirty men of almost as many differing nationalities lived and sometimes died, the mystery of the grim skipper's ways, coupled with queer yarns about his antecedents, was occasionally commented upon with bated breath in strange mixtures of language. But somehow it always happened that, closely following upon any conversation of the kind, the injudicious talkers ran butt up against serious trouble. No charges were made, no definite punishments were awarded; but loss of rest, danger-ous and unnecessary tasks, kickings and stripes exhibited casually, were their portion for a season. These things had the effect of exciting an almost superstitious reverence for the captain's powers of knowing what was going on, coupled with a profound distrust of each other among the fore-mast hands, that made for their subjection perhaps more potently than even the physical embarrassments which formed so liberal a part of their daily lot. And yet, such is the perversity of human nature, whenever the *Beluga* gammed another whaler, and the wretched crowd got a chance to talk to strangers, they actually indulged in tall talk, 'gas' about their skipper's smartness as a whaleman, his ability as a seaman, and, strangest of all, his eminence as a hard citizen who would 'jes' soon killer man's look at 'im'. Every fresh device of his for screwing extra work out of his galley-slaves, every mean and low-down trick played upon them for the lessening of their scanty food or robbing them of their hard-earned lay, only seemed to increase their admiration for him, as if his diabolical personality had actually inverted all their ideas of right and wrong.

The man himself, the centre of this little cosmos of whose dreary round pleasure formed not the minutest part, was apparently about fifty-five years of age. He had been tall, above the average, but a persistent stoop had modified that particular considerably. The great peculiarity about his appearance was his head, which was shaped much like a fir-cone. From the apex of it fell a few straggling wisps of hay-coloured hair that did not look as if they belonged there, but had been blown against the scalp and stuck there accidentally. Wide, outstanding ears, pointed at the top like a bat's, eyes that were just straight slits across the parchment face, from between whose bare edges two inscrutable pupils of different but unnameable colours looked out, a straight, per-fectly shaped nose, so finely finished that it looked artificial, and another straight lipless slit for a mouth completes his facial portrait. His arms were abnormally long, and his legs short, while his gait, from long walking upon greasy decks, was a bear-like shuffle. It was whispered in the fo'c'sle that his strength was gigantic, and there was a tradition extant of his having wrung a recalcitrant harpooner's neck with his bare hands as one would a fowl's; but none of his present crew had seen him exert himself at all. What impressed them most, however, was his voice. Ordinarily he spoke in almost a faint whisper, such as a dying man might be supposed to utter, but it must have been very distinct in articulation, as he was never known to speak twice. Yet, if at any time it became necessary for him to hail a boat or a passing ship, that strange opening in his head would unclose, and forth from it would issue a strident sound that carried farther than the bellow of any angry bull.

His 'luck' was proverbial. None of his officers ever knew, any more than did the meanest member of the ship's company, whither he was bound, nor in what unfrequented areas of ocean he sought the valuable creatures from which he was amassing so much wealth. Of course, they knew, as all sailors do from close observation of courses made, land seen, weather, etc., within a few hundred miles or so, but their knowledge was never ample enough to have enabled them afterwards to take another ship along the same tracks that the *Beluga* had found so richly frequented by payable whales. But Elisha Cushing added to his so-called luck almost superhuman energy. If he did not spare his unhappy slaves, he was no more merciful to himself. Never a boat was lowered after whales, no matter what the weather or how few the prey, but he was foremost; as if he loved (if it be admissible to mention love in connection with this emotionless man) the chase for its own sake, or, knowing that he carried a charmed life, dared to take risks that no ordinary man would do except under compulsion. There was one marked feature of his whaling, however, that was noticed by all his crew, if, owing to the difficulties hinted at before, it was seldom discussed. Whenever the boats approached either a single whale or a whale school, Captain Cushing would surely be seen standing high on the two quarter-cleats in the stern-sheets of his boat, searching with sparkling, almost glaring eyes among them for *something*. It was believed that the boats never 'went on a whale' until the skipper had first passed them (the whales) all in review, and fully satisfied himself that the object of his search, whatever it might be, was not there. His scrutiny over, the game commenced, and surely never, since the bold Biscayan fisherman first attacked the questing rorquals that visited their shores, with bone and flint pointed lances, was there ever seen such whale-hunting as that carried on by Elisha Cushing. Without changing colour, or raising his voice above its usual low murmur, he would haul his boat up alongside of the mountainous mammal, order her to be held there, and then, disregarding the writhings and wallowing of the great creature, he would calmly feel for the ribs or the shoulder-blades with the lance point. And having found an interspace, the long arms would straighten out, and four feet of the lance would glide like a slender bright snake into the mighty vitals, only to be withdrawn on the instant and plunged home again and again and again, each thrust taking a new turn within, and causing the black, hot blood to burst from the wound as from the nozzle of a fire-hose. Or, quietly seated on the gunwale, he would select his spot, and probe with the lance as a surgeon might seek for a bullet in the body of an insensible patient. Should the boat swerve away from the whale ever so slightly until he gave the signal, he would look round, and on the instant five men, albeit in the very shadow of death, would feel a creeping at the pit of their stomachs, and a frantic desire to avert his anger; for he had been known to reach across the boat and snatch a man from his thwart with one hand, flinging him, a limp, ragged bundle, far out of the boat, and not caring where. The only signs that he ever showed of anything unusual being toward, was a faint blue patch that appeared in the middle of his otherwise yellow cheeks, and a reddish glint in his eyes. In spite of his peculiarities, his men were proud to be members of his boat's crew, for his skill was of so high an order that his apparent recklessness never got him a boat stove or lost him a man; while his officers, though the pick and flower of whalemen, had their usual share of casualties.

About two years of the cruise had gone by, and the *Beluga*'s hold was already more than two-thirds full of oil, in spite of the fact that several shipments home had been made during the voyage. After a season on the Vasquez ground in the South Pacific, where she had averaged two whales a week, she was now steering an easterly course with a little south in it – not cruising, but making a passage apparently for the 'off-shore grounds', on the coast of Chili. One morning at daybreak the cry of 'Sail-ho!' from the crow's-nest reached Captain Cushing in his cabin, and before the officer on deck had time to answer, his deep-breathed tones were heard welling up from below in reply, 'Where away?' The stranger was a whaling barque also, lying hove-to right ahead, as if expecting and waiting for the *Beluga*. When the two vessels were within three miles of each other, Captain Cushing ordered his boat away, and with an order to the mate to 'keep her jes 's she is', he departed. No sooner had his crew put him alongside than he climbed on board, and, contrary to the usual practice, ordered them away from the stranger, telling them to lie on their oars at a little distance until he should call them. The skipper of the stranger (still an unknown ship to the *Beluga*'s crew, as she had no name visible) met Captain Cushing at the gangway, presenting as complete a contrast to that inscrutable man as could well be imagined. A dumpy, apple-faced little fellow, with a lurking smile in every dimple, and a mat of bright red curls covering his round head. Snatching the languidly offered paw of his visitor, he burst forth, 'Wall, ef this ent grate! I be tarnally ding-busted ef I wa'nt a talkin' 'bout ye las' night; talkin' t' meself that is,' he hastily interjected, upon seeing the look that Cushing turned upon him. 'But kem along daown b'low n'hev – wall, I wonder wut y' *will* hev. Don' seem sif y' ever hev anythin'. Nev' mine, less git b'low anyhaow.' And together they descended.

For a long time the little man did all the talking – after the manner of a trusted manager of a thriving business making his report to his principal. He told of whales caught, of boats stove, of gear carried away – quite the usual routine – while Cushing listened with his impenetrable mask, through which it was impossible to see whether he was interested or not. It was like talking to a graven image. But still, as the tale went on, and it appeared that the little talker had been fairly successful, there was a slight relaxing of the rigid pose, which to the eye of the initiate spelt satisfaction. For all unknown to any one except the ruddy skipper talking to him, Cushing was really the owner of this unnamed ship – a vessel that he had stolen from an anchorage in the Pelew Islands, while all her crew were ashore on a furious debauch which had lasted for several weeks, and had ever since been running her in this mysterious fashion by the aid of the one man in the wide world in whom he could be said to repose any confidence. That story is, however, too long to be told here.

The recital was apparently finished, when suddenly, as if he had just remembered an important part of his report, the narrator resumed, his jolly red face assuming an air of gravity that was strangely out of harmony with it. 'An' cap',' said he. 'I'd eenamost fergot – I met up with the spotted whale of the Bonins las' cruise. I –'

But there was a sudden change, an unearthly brightening into copper colour of Cushing's face, as he sprang to his feet, and, with his long fingers working convulsively, gurgled out,

' 'R ye sure? Don't ye mislead me, Silas, 'r ye'd be better dead every time. Naow yew jest gi' me th' hull hang o' this thing 'fore y' say 'nother word 'bout anythin'!'

There was no mask of indifference now. The man was transformed into a living embodiment of eager desire, and bold indeed would any have been that would have dared to thwart him. No such idea was in his hearer's thoughts, at any rate, for no sooner had he done speaking than Silas leaned forward and said –

'Yes, cap', I *am* sure, not thet it's hardly wuth while sayin' so, fur yew couldn't imagine me bein' mistook over a critter like thet. 'Twas this way. Ev' sence *thet* affair I've scurcely ever fergot yew're orders – t' look eout fer Spotty an' let ye' know fust chance whar he uz usin' roun', but at this perticler lowerin' we jest had all eour soup ladled eout fer us an' no mistake. Ther'd ben a matter o' a dozen ships ov us in comp'ny, 'n I wuz bizzy figgerin' haow t' git rid'r some ov 'em befo' we struck whale. I noo they wuz abaout; the air wuz jest thick up with whale smell, 'n every one ov my boys wuz all alive. Wall, we hove to thet night 's ushal till midnight, 'n then I sez t' myself, sez I, ef I don't up-stick 'n run south I'm a horse. Fur, ye see, 'twuz born in 'pon me thet whales wuz comin' up from the line away, 'n a big school too. I doan' know why, ov course not, but thar twuz – y' know how 'tis yerself.

'Sure 'nough by daypring they wa'nt a ship in sight of us, but at seven bells we raised whale, 'n b' gosh I reckon they was mos' a thousan' of 'em spread all out to looard of us more like a school o' porps than hunderd bar'l whales – which they wuz every last one ov 'em, cep them thet wuz bigger. They wa'nt much wind, 'n we lowered five boats 'n put f'r them whales all we knew. Tell y' wut, cap', I've seen some tall spoutin', but that mornin's work jest laid raight over all I ever heer tell ov, much less see. We all got fas' on the jump, 'n then we cut loose agen. Reason why, we couldn't move fur 'em. They jest crowded in on us, quite quiet; they wa'nt a bit er fight in one ov 'em, and we handled the lances on the nearest. That patch o' sea wuz jest a saladero now I'm tellin' ye. We never chipped a splinter ner used ten fathom o' tow-line, 'n be *my* recknin we killed twenty whales. Gradjully the crowd drawed off, leavin' us with all that plunder lyin' roun' loose, an I wuz beginnin' t' wish I hadn't run so fur away from the fleet. Fur I knew we couldn' handle sech a haul's thet — more'n haef ov em 'd be rotten 'fore we c'd cut in ef we'd worked f'r a week on eend 'thout a minnit's rest.

'While we wuz jest drawin' breth like after th' war, and the shipkeepers 'uz a workin' her daown t' us, my harponeer sings out 'sif he'd a ben snake bit, "Blow-w-s 'n breaches! Ee'r sh' white waterrs. Madre di Gloria, Capena, lookee what come." 'N thar shore nuff he uz comin'; Spotty fur true. I know, cap. I never see him afore. All I knoo 'bout him uz wut ye told me, an' I doan mine ownin' up naow at I thought y' mout ha ben a bit loony on thet subjec, but I tek it all back, 'n 'umbly axes yer pardin.

'Yaas, sir, he come; like all hell let loose. He jes flung himself along the top er th' sea like a dolphin, 'n I reckin we all felt kiender par'litic. Soon's I got me breath I sings out t' cut adrif', fur we'd all got tow-lines fast to flukes ready to pass abroad, and handle bomb-guns quick. Then when he come within range t' let him have 'em full butt 'n put f'r th' ship. Don't say I felt very brash 'baout it, but twuz the best I c'd think ov. He kem, oh yes, sir, he kem, 'n the sight of his charge brung a verse of th' Bible (hain't looked inside one f'r twenty years) into my mind. Goes suthin like this, "The mountings skipped like rams, th' little hills like young sheep." We done all we knoo, we twisted and tarned an' pulled an' starned; but you know, cap, better'n any of us, thet the boat never was built thet c'd git out of th' way ov a spalmacitty whale when he'd made up his mine fur mischief. 'N we wa'nt no excepshin. We weakened at las', 'n took th' water, whar we knoo he wouldn't tech us, 'n b' gosh he didn' leave a plank o' one o' them thar boats whole. I doan know why he didn' foller it up or go fur th' ship. Ef he hed thar'd a ben an eend of the story, sure. But no, he just disappeared quiet 's death, 'n we all gut picked up in time. Yes, 'n we managed to rig up our spare boat 'n git five of them whales cut in too, though I'm free t' confess the last of 'em wuz middlin' gamey by th' time they got t' th' try pots. The rest jest floated erroun 'n stunk up th' North Persific Ocean till twuz like a graveyard struck be 'n erthquake. But we got six hunderd barl out of th' catch, anyway.'

While the recital was proceeding, Cushing's face was a

study. He listened without moving a muscle, but rage, hope, and joy chased one another over that usually expressionless mask like waves raised by sudden squalls over the calm surface of a sheltered lake. And when it was over he rose wearily, saying –

'All right, Jacob; when ye're through put fur the old rondy-voos an' discharge. I'll be long 'bout March an' range fur next cruise. So long. I'm off t' th' Bonins full pelt.'

'But, Cap'n Cushing, is ut worth huntin' up that gauldern spotty beast 'n gettin' 'tarnally smashed up fur an' idee? Why cain't y' leave 'im alone? Sure's deeth he'll do ye a hurt. Take a fool's advice, cap'n, 'n let him die ov ole age or accident.'

'Jacob, my man, y' fergit yerself. When I want yew're advice I'll seek it. Till then don't ye offer it. Tain't t' my likin', fur I'm accustomed to take no man as my counsellor. So long once more, 'n don't fergit y'r orders.'

In two strides he reached the top of the companion-ladder, and with that wide-breathed cry of his that we knew so well had summoned his boat. She sprang to the nameless barque's side like a living thing, Captain Cushing stepped into her, and the queer gam was over. Back alongside he came, standing erect as a monolith in the stern-sheets, and, hardly allowing time for the boat to be hooked on, issued rapid orders for all sail to be made; the helm was put hard up, and away we went NW. No one ventured an opinion upon this sudden change, but every one looked volumes of inquiry. And no one dared even hint to his fellow the wonder, the painful curiosity, he felt as, day after day, before a strong south-east trade, the *Beluga* did her steady seven knots an hour, nor stayed for anything. Again and again the cry of 'blow' came ringing down from the crows'-nests, and as often as it was heard the old man mounted aloft with his glasses, and stayed until he had apparently satisfied himself of something. But never a halt did we make. No, and as if the very whales themselves knew of our pre-occupation, a school actually rose near and accompanied us for a whole watch, gambolling along massively within gun-shot on either side. They might as well have been a thousand miles away for all the notice the old man took of them. He just leaned upon the weather-rail, gazing with expressionless face at the unchanging ring of the horizon – a fathomless enigma to all of us. The proximity of those whales, however, troubled the officers more than anything else had done, and it took all their inbred terror of the old man to keep them from breaking into open mutiny. Even among us, who had little interest in the voyage from a monetary point of view, and to whom the capture of whales only meant a furious outburst of the hardest work, the feeling of indignation at the loss of so grand an opportunity was exceedingly hard to bear.

Onward we sped until we got among the islands, but no slackening of haste, except when the wind lulled, was indulged in. By day or by night we threaded those mazy archipelagos as if the whole intricate navigation was as familiar to the skipper as the rooms of his cabin. Such ship-handling surely never was seen. Perched upon the fore-yard, the only light visible being the blazing foam spreading widely out on either bow and ahead where the staunch old ship plunged through those phosphorescent waters, the glowing patches cropping up hither and thither all around as the indolent Pacific swell broke irritably over some up-cropping coral patch, and the steely sparkles of the stars in the blue-black sky above, Captain Cushing conned the ship as easily and confidently as a pilot entering New York harbour on midsummer day, his quiet voice sounding down from where he crouched invisible as if we were being celestially directed. There was no feeling of apprehension among us, for our confidence in his genius was perfect, making us sure that whatever of skill in navigation was required he surely possessed it.

Nevertheless, the mystery of our haste across the whole vast breadth of the Pacific fretted every man, even the dullest. It was outside all our previous experience. Perhaps the only thing that made it bearable was the knowledge that not one of the officers was any better informed than we were. Foremast hands are always jealous of the information obtainable in the cuddy, and even though it may not be of the slightest use to them, any scrap they may obtain gives to the lucky eavesdropper a sort of brevet-rank for the time being. Here, however, all that was to be known as to our movements, the reason for them, and the ultimate object of our long passage, with its unprecedented haste, was locked up in one man's mind and that man a graven image for secretiveness.

Such was the expeditiousness of our passage that seven weeks after gamming the nameless whaler on the 'off-shore' ground, we sighted one of the Volcano group of islands which lie near the Bonins in the great eddy of the Kuro Siwo or Japanese current, and form one of the landmarks of what was once the busiest sperm whaling-ground on the globe. The shape of the island, more like the comb of a cock than anything else, was familiar to many of us, and gave us for the first time for months a clear idea of our position. So we were on the Japan ground. It was a relief to know that much, certainly; but why – why had we, contrary to all whaling precedent, made a passage of several thousand miles in such haste? No answer. But having arrived, our usual whaling tactics were immediately resumed. With a difference. Instead of being kept hard at work during all the hours of daylight scrubbing, polishing, cleaning, until the old oil-barrel of a ship was as spick and span as a man-o'-war, the word was passed that the watch on deck were to keep a look-out for whale – every man of them except him at the wheel. And the watchers in the crow's-nest were provided each with a pair of binoculars – a thing unheard of before. So the ship became a veritable argus. It is safe to say that nothing, not even a frond of seaweed, or a wandering sea-bird, ever passed within range of sight without being seen and noted. After a few days of this most keen outlook came another surprise in the shape of a speech from the old man.

Calling all hands aft, he faced us for a minute in silence, while every heart beat a trifle quicker as if we were on the threshold of a mystery deeper than any that had yet worried us. He spoke quietly, dispassionately, yet with that blue patch in the middle of each yellow cheek that was to us the symbol of his most intense excitement. 'I've kem up hyar aefter *one* whale, 'n ef I git him the' v'yge is over. He's big, bigger'n enny man here's ever seen, I guess, an' he's spotted with white on brown like a pieball horse. Yew kain't mistake him. I'll give five hundred dollars t' th' man that raises him first, 'n I'll divide five thousand among ye 'cordin t' grade ef I kill him. An' when we've cut him in we'll up-stick f'r Noo Bedford. Naow, ef this is enny indoocement t' ye, keep y'r eyes skinned by day and night. Moreover, I warn ye thet this ship doan't see civilization agen until I git wut I'm after, 'r I go under. Thet'll do, all haends.'

In any other ship this harangue would have been succeeded by a buzz of chat as soon as the fellows got forward, but here not a word was spoken. Thenceforward, though it was evident that not a thought could be spared, not a look wasted from scanning the wide circle of blue around, by night and by day the watch never slackened, and men would hardly sleep for eagerness to be the first to claim the prize. Yet, as so often happens, it fell to one who had the least opportunity of obtaining it, the mulatto steward whose duties kept him below most of the time. About ten days after the skipper's offer the steward crept on deck one evening about eight bells, his long day's work just over, and slouching forward into the waist leaned over the side and began to fill his pipe. It was a heavenly evening, hardly a breath of air breaking the sleekiness of the sea-surface, the slightest perceptible swell giving us a gentle undulatory motion, and overhead the full moon hung in the cloudless dome like an immense globe glowing with electric light. The steward had finished filling his pipe, and was just feeling for a match when he stopped suddenly and said to his nearest neighbour, 'Oliver, what in thunder's thet right in the moon-glade?' The whisper ran round the ship as if on a telephone, and in less than a minute all the night-glasses were on the spot. The skipper's voice broke the silence – hardly broke it – so quiet yet audible was it. ' 'Way boats. Th' first man thet makes a noise, I'll cripple him f'r life. Stoord, g'lang b'low 'n git y'r money; ye'll find it on my bunk-shelf.'

Like a crew of ghosts, we sped to our stations, hanging over side and booming the boats off as they were lowered with the utmost caution lest there should be a rattle of a patent block or a splash as they took the water. In five minutes we were all away, five boats, the skipper leading and every man, except the officers steering, wielding an Indian paddle as if his life depended upon utter silence. As we sat facing forrard every eye was strained for a glimpse of the enemy, but at that low level and in the peculiar glare of a moonlit tropical night we could see nothing. Moreover, we were paddling along the glittering path cast upon the sea by the moon, and a few minutes' steady gaze upon that stretch of molten silver made the eyes burn and throb, so that it was an intense relief to close them for a while. At every dip of the paddles there was an additional flash in the water, behind each boat and far beneath myriads of dancing gleams disported themselves, while in ever-accumulating numbers wide bands of pale fire radiating from opaque bodies keeping company with us told us of the shark hosts mustering for the fight wherein they, at any rate, were likely to fall heirs to goodly spoil.

Without a pause for rest, and in the same utter stillness, we toiled on for at least two hours. It was back-breaking work, and but for the splendid training we were in we could not possibly have held out. Then suddenly from ahead came a yell of wild laughter, the most blood-chilling sound surely ever heard. Immediately following it we saw a veritable hill of light upraise itself out of the sea ahead, and realized that at last our quarry was brought to bay. 'In paddles, out oars!' yelled the officers, and as we obeyed we were aware that a terrific commotion was in progress ahead. The greenish-glaring spray ascended in long jets, and the dull boom of mighty blows reverberated over the hitherto quiet sea. Pulling till our sinews cracked, we reached the storm-centre, and, by what seemed a miracle, actually succeeded in getting fast to the whale – every boat did that, although it seemed to many of us a suicidal policy under the circumstances. Shouts and curses resounded until a voice was heard that enforced silence, the far-reaching tones of Captain Cushing, who was nearest to the foe, but for all his ability was unable to do more once he had got fast. For now the whale had settled down into a steady straightforward rush at the rate of about fourteen knots an hour, the five boats sweeping along in his wake like meteors glancing across the deep darkness of the night. The whale could not be seen. Only at long intervals did he slant upwards and, with a roar like the lifting of an overloaded safety-valve, disappear again.

So on we went through the warm quiet night without the slightest sign of slackening until the gladsome light of dawn quickened on the sea-rim, and showed us that we were alone – there was no sign of the ship. A gaunt and haggard crew we looked, anxiety scoring deep furrows in our wan faces. And as the sun sprang into the sky we suddenly came to a dead stop. The strain on the line compelled us to pay out, and thus we hovered in a circle, bows awash, and awaited the pleasure of our foe. There was a sudden upspringing of all boats, a hasty manoeuvring to clear one another as far as might be, and, before any of us could have imagined it possible, high into our midst leaped the spotted whale, his awful jaws agape, and his whole body writhing in its evolution. Straight for the skipper's boat he came, taking it diagonally, and, with a crash that set all our teeth on edge, she disappeared. A mist arose before our sight, the spray of the conflict filling the air, but, fired beyond fear by the wholesale tragedy we believed had taken place, we bent to our oars till they cracked, thirsting for that monster's blood. As we came bounding to the spot he disappeared, and, to our unspeakable amazement (though we had no time to show it), all the destroyed boat's crew reappeared. But if Captain Cushing had looked dangerous before, his appearance now was that of a demoniac. His cap was gone, so that the yellow dome of his head loomed strangely in the early morning light, his clothing hung from him in ribbons, and his right arm dangled as if only held by a few sinews. He had come right out of the whale's jaws. All the others were scatheless.

To all offers of help he turned a savage scowl, and seizing a bomb-gun in his uninjured hand, he jammed himself in the boat's bows, his voice, unaltered save for being a little higher in pitch, being heard and obeyed among the other boats on the instant. The whale returned. At the captain's orders all cut their lines, and the real fight began. Truly Captain Cushing was fit to be a leader of men, for his eyes missed nothing. At his orders all four boats advanced, retreated, backed, circled, stopped dead. He seemed able to penetrate the misleading medium of the water, where a whale at twenty fathoms' depth looks like a salmon, and whatever move the monster made, his counter-move baffled the savage intent. Yet all the time we were strictly on the defensive. Our long night's tow, want of food and drink, and since daylight the tremendous strain upon our nerves, was surely telling against us, and our adversary was apparently tireless. Not only so, but his ingenuity never flagged. Ruse after ruse was tried by him, but no two were alike. And without a doubt our hopes of coming alive out of this battle were growing fainter and fainter every moment.

Things were in this gloomy stage when, with a most appalling roar, the whale suddenly broke water on his back, and launched himself at the captain's boat. The wide sea boiled like a pot as he came, but, to our horror, the boat lay still, as if anchored to the spot. The crash came, and amidst its uproar we heard the sharp report of a gun. Like a great whirlpool the waters foamed and rose, nothing being distinguishable in the midst of the vortex until it gradually subsided, and we saw the fragments of the boat idly tossing upon the crimson foam. Hastening to the rescue, we found six men still alive, but all sadly hurt. The seventh was gone. At last Captain Cushing had paid in full the debt that had been owing. We were now completely overborne with fatigue as well as overloaded with helpless men – utterly unfit to compete any further with so fearful a foe. While we lay thus helplessly awaiting what all felt must be the end, the whale again broke water about twenty yards away. Up, up, up into the air he rose, effortless, majestically; and as he soared aloft every heart stood still to see the body of our late commander hanging limply at the angle of that yawning mouth. The yellow visage was toward us, the same savage grin frozen upon it, but the will against which everything had shivered was now but the will of the drift-weed round about; that clammy piece of clay was tenantless.

Down came the gigantic form, tearing up the sea into foam and disappeared from our sight, to be seen no more. Long and wearily we waited, hungry and thirsty, and some in agony from their injuries, until twenty-four hours later the *Beluga* found us, and all were safely taken on board. Strangely transformed the old ship appeared. At first we went about as we had been wont, not daring to exchange thoughts with one another. But gradually the blessed truth soaked in. We were freed from a tyranny more dire than any of us had realized – a tyranny over mind as well as body. Officers and men rejoiced together, for all had suffered. And it was at once decided to return home in leisurely fashion, calling at well-known ports on the way, and endeavouring to make up by a little joy of life for past miseries.

What the true inwardness of Captain Cushing's desire of revenge on the spotted whale was we never rightly knew, but many rumours were current among ships that we gammed that he had, with his own hand many years before, killed the whale of a small pod, or company of whales, of which the spotted whale was the leader, and that they had met on several occasions afterwards, their meeting always being attended by some grave disaster to Cushing's ship and crew. This had wrought upon his mind until it had become a mania, and he was willing to risk all for the chance of slaying his redoubtable foe. But we had no doubt that the whale was merely the instrument chosen by Providence for meting out to him a death he richly deserved for his many crimes.

Jack London

MAKE WESTING

No reader who enjoys the tales of a master storyteller can possibly ignore the work of Jack London (1876–1916), a man who was as big and vital and adventurous in his life as he was in his writings. His influence has, of course, been enormous, but he in turn had been influenced by his fellow countryman, Herman Melville, and this influence is there for all to see in his two great sea novels, The Sea-Wolf *(1904) and* The Mutiny on the Elsinore *(1914). London was also writing from experience, for he had sailed before the mast in the last sealer out of his hometown of San Francisco, had been an oyster pirate and a tramp sailor in the South Seas, and even attempted a lone, round-the-world voyage in a small ketch long before such activities became fashionable.*

There was something of the Viking in Jack London, and certainly his big frame, blond hair and engaging personality made him as formidable in an argument (he was a dedicated opponent of capitalism) as he was when skippering a sailing ship. Indeed, he was never happier than when afloat, a feeling that creeps through in all his maritime stories. 'Make Westing', which happens to be a favourite of mine, well exemplifies this, especially in its graphic description of Captain Dan Cullen's epic battle with the elements around Cape Horn – surely one of the most feared stretches of ocean in the world.

> 'Whatever you do, make westing! make westing!'
>   — *Sailing directions for Cape Horn*

For seven weeks the *Mary Rogers* had been between 50° south in the Atlantic and 50° south in the Pacific, which meant that for seven weeks she had been struggling to round Cape Horn. For seven weeks she had been either in dirt, or close to dirt, save once, and then, following upon six days of excessive dirt, which she had ridden out under the shelter of the redoubtable Tierra del Fuego coast, she had almost gone ashore during a heavy swell in the dead calm that had suddenly fallen. For seven weeks she had wrestled with the Cape Horn greybeards, and in return been buffeted and smashed by them. She was a wooden ship, and her ceaseless straining had opened her seams, so that twice a day the watch took its turn at the pumps.

The *Mary Rogers* was strained, the crew was strained, and big Dan Cullen, master, was likewise strained. Perhaps he was strained most of all, for upon him rested the responsiblity of that titanic struggle. He slept most of the time in his clothes, though he rarely slept. He haunted the deck at night, a great, burly, robust ghost, black with the sunburn of thirty years of sea and hairy as an orang-outang. He, in turn, was haunted by one thought of action, a sailing direction for the Horn: *Whatever you do, make westing! make westing!* It was an obsession. He thought of nothing else, except, at times, to blaspheme God for sending such bitter weather.

Make westing! He hugged the Horn, and a dozen times lay hove to with the iron Cape bearing east-by-north, or north-north-east, a score of miles away. And each time the eternal west wind smote him back and he made easting. He fought gale after gale, south to 64°, inside the antarctic drift-ice, and pledged his immortal soul to the Powers of Darkness, for a bit of westing, for a slant to take him around. And he made easting. In despair, he had tried to make the passage through the Straits of Le Maire. Halfway through, the wind hauled to the north'ard of north-west, the glass dropped to 28.88, and he turned and ran before a gale of cyclonic fury, missing, by a hair's breadth, piling up the *Mary Rogers* on the black-toothed rocks. Twice he had made west to the Diego Ramirez Rocks, one of the times saved between two snow-squalls by sighting the gravestones of ships a quarter of a mile dead ahead.

Blow! Captain Dan Cullen instanced all his thirty years at sea to prove that never had it blown so before. The *Mary Rogers* was hove to at the time he gave the evidence, and, to clinch it, inside half an hour the *Mary Rogers* was hove down to the hatches. Her now maintopsail and brand new spencer were blown away like tissue paper; and five sails, furled and fast under double gaskets, were blown loose and stripped from the yards. And before morning the *Mary Rogers* was hove down twice again, and holes were knocked in her bulwarks to ease her decks from the weight of ocean that pressed her down.

On an average of once a week Captain Dan Cullen caught glimpses of the sun. Once, for ten minutes, the sun shone at midday, and ten minutes afterwards a new gale was piping up, both watches were shortening sail, and all was buried in the obscurity of a driving snow-squall. For a fortnight, once, Captain Dan Cullen was without a meridian or a chronometer sight. Rarely did he know his position within half of a degree, except when in sight of land; for sun and stars remained hidden behind the sky, and it was so gloomy that even at the best the horizons were poor for accurate observations. A grey gloom shrouded the world. The clouds were grey; the great driving seas were leaden grey; the smoking crests were a grey churning; even the occasional albatrosses were grey, while the snow-flurries were not white, but grey, under the sombre pall of the heavens.

Life on board the *Mary Rogers* was grey – grey and gloomy. The faces of the sailors were blue grey; they were afflicted with sea-cuts and sea-boils, and suffered exquisitely. They were shadows of men. For seven weeks, in the forecastle or on deck, they had not known what it was to be dry. They had forgotten what it was to sleep out a watch, and all watches it was, 'All hands on deck!' They caught the snatches of agonized sleep, and they slept in their oil-skins ready for the everlasting call. So weak and worn were they that it took both watches to do the work of one. That was why both watches were on deck so much of the time. And no shadow of a man could shirk duty. Nothing less than a broken leg could enable a man to knock off work; and there were two such, who had been mauled and pulped by the seas that broke aboard.

One other man who was the shadow of a man was George Dorety. He was the only passenger on board, a friend of the firm, and he had elected to make the voyage for his health. But seven weeks off Cape Horn had not bettered his health. He gasped and panted in his bunk through the long, heaving nights; and when on deck he was so bundled up for warmth that he resembled a peripatetic old-clothes shop. At midday, eating at the cabin table in a gloom so deep that the swinging sea-lamps burned always, he looked as blue-grey as the sickest, saddest man for'ard. Nor did gazing across the table at Captain Dan Cullen have any cheering effect upon him. Captain Cullen chewed and scowled and kept silent. The scowls were for God, and with every chew he reiterated the sole thought of his existence, which was *make westing*. He was a big, hairy brute, and the sight of him was not stimulating to the other's appetite. He looked upon George Dorety as a Jonah, and told him so once each meal savagely transferring the scowl from God to the passenger and back again.

Nor did the mate prove a first aid to a languid appetite. Joshua Higgins by name, a seaman by profession and pull, but a pot-walloper by capacity, he was a loose-jointed, sniffling creature, heartless and selfish and cowardly, without a soul, in fear of his life of Dan Cullen, and a bully over the sailors, who knew that behind the mate was Captain Cullen, and law-giver and compeller, the driver and the destroyer, the incarnation of a dozen bucko mates. In that wild weather at the southern end of the earth, Joshua Higgins ceased washing. His grimy face usually robbed George Dorety of what little appetite he managed to accumulate. Ordinarily this lavatorial dereliction would have caught Captain Cullen's eye and vocabulary, but in the present his mind was filled with making westing, to the exclusion of all other things not contributory thereto. Whether the mate's face was clean or dirty had no bearing upon westing. Later on, when 50° south in the Pacific had been reached, Joshua Higgins would wash his face very abruptly. In the meantime, at the cabin table, where grey twilight alternated with lamplight while the lamps were being filled, George Dorety sat between the two men, one a tiger and the other a hyena, and wondered why God had made them. The second mate, Matthew Turner, was a true sailor and a man, but George Dorety did not have the solace of his company, for he ate by himself, solitary, when they had finished.

On Saturday morning, July 24, George Dorety awoke to a feeling of life and headlong movement. On deck he found the *Mary Rogers* running off before a howling south-easter. Nothing was set but the lower topsails and the foresail. It was all she could stand, yet she was making fourteen knots, as Mr Turner shouted in Dorety's ear when he came on deck. And it was all westing. She was going round the Horn at last . . . if the wind held. Mr Turner looked happy. The end of the struggle was in sight. But Captain Cullen did not look happy. He scowled at Dorety in passing. Captain Cullen did not want God to know that he was pleased with that wind. He had a conception of a malicious God, and believed in his secret soul that if God knew it was a desirable wind, God would promptly efface it and send a snorter from the west. So he walked softly before God, smothering his joy down under scowls and muttered curses, and, so, fooling God, for God was the only thing in the universe of which Dan Cullen was afraid.

All Saturday and Saturday night the *Mary Rogers* raced her westing. Persistently she logged her fourteen knots, so that by Sunday morning she had covered three hundred and fifty miles. If the wind held, she would make around. If it failed, and the snorter came from anywhere between south-west and north, back the *Mary Rogers* would be hurled and be no better off than she had been seven weeks before. And on Sunday morning the wind *was* failing. The big sea was going down and running smooth. Both watches were on deck setting sail after sail as fast as the ship could stand it. And now Captain Cullen went around brazenly before God, smoking a big cigar, smiling jubilantly, as if the failing wind delighted him, while down underneath he was raging against God for taking the life out of the blessed wind. *Make westing!* So he would, if God would only leave him alone. Secretly, he pledged himself anew to the Powers of Darkness, if they would let him make westing. He pledged himself so easily because he did not believe in the Powers of Darkness. He really believed only in God, though he did not know it. And in his inverted theology God was really the Prince of Darkness. Captain Cullen was a devil-worshipper, but he called the devil by another name, that was all.

At midday, after calling eight bells, Captain Cullen ordered the royals on. The men went aloft faster than they had gone in weeks. Not alone were they nimble because of the westing, but a benignant sun was shining down and limbering their stiff bodies. George Dorety stood aft, near Captain Cullen, less bundled in clothes than usual, soaking in the grateful warmth as he watched the scene. Swiftly and abruptly the incident occurred. There was a cry from the foreroyal-yard of 'Man overboard!' Somebody threw a life-buoy over the side, and at the same instant the second mate's voice came aft, ringing and peremptory —

'Hard down your helm!'

The man at the wheel never moved a spoke. He knew better, for Captain Dan Cullen was standing alongside of him. He wanted to move a spoke, to move all the spokes, to grind the wheel down, hard down, for his comrade drowning in the sea. He glanced at Captain Dan Cullen, and Captain Dan Cullen gave no sign.

'Down! Hard down!' the second mate roared, as he sprang aft.

But he ceased springing and commanding, and stood still, when he saw Dan Cullen by the wheel. And big Dan Cullen puffed at his cigar and said nothing. Astern, and going astern fast, could be seen the sailor. He had caught the life-buoy and was clinging to it. Nobody spoke. Nobody moved. The men aloft clung to the royal yards and watched with terror-stricken faces. And the *Mary Rogers* raced on, making her westing. A long, silent minute passed.

'Who was it?' Captain Cullen demanded.

'Mops, sir,' eagerly answered the sailor at the wheel.

Mops topped a wave astern and disappeared temporarily in the trough. It was a large wave, but it was no greybeard. A small boat could live easily in such a sea, and in such a sea the *Mary Rogers* could easily come to. But she could not come to and make westing at the same time.

For the first time in all his years, George Dorety was seeing a real drama of life and death — a sordid little drama in which the scales balanced an unknown sailor named Mops against a few miles of longitude. At first he had watched the man astern, but now he watched big Dan Cullen, hairy and black, vested with power of life and death, smoking a cigar.

Captain Dan Cullen smoked another long, silent minute. Then he removed the cigar from his mouth. He glanced aloft at the spars of the *Mary Rogers*, and overside at the sea.

'Sheet home the royals!' he cried.

Fifteen minutes later they sat at table, in the cabin, with food served before them. On one side of George Dorety sat Dan Cullen, the tiger, on the other side, Joshua Higgins, the hyena. Nobody spoke. On deck the men were sheeting home the skysails. George Dorety could hear their cries, while a persistent vision haunted him of a man called Mops, alive and well, clinging to a life-buoy miles astern in that lonely ocean. He glanced at Captain Cullen, and experienced a feeling of nausea, for the man was eating his food with relish, almost bolting it.

'Captain Cullen,' Dorety said, 'you are in command of this ship, and it is not proper for me to comment now upon what you do. But I wish to say one thing. There is a hereafter, and yours will be a hot one.'

Captain Cullen did not even scowl. In his voice was regret as he said —

'It was blowing a living gale. It was impossible to save the man.'

'He fell from the royal-yard,' Dorety cried hotly. 'You were setting the royals at the time. Fifteen minutes afterwards you were setting the skysails.'

'It was a living gale, wasn't it, Mr Higgins?' Captain Cullen said, turning to the mate.

'If you'd brought her to, it'd have taken the sticks out of her,' was the mate's answer. 'You did the proper thing, Captain Cullen. The man hadn't a ghost of a show.'

George Dorety made no answer, and to the meal's end no one spoke. After that, Dorety had his meals served in his state-room. Captain Cullen scowled at him no longer, though no speech was exchanged between them, while the *Mary Rogers* sped north towards warmer latitudes. At the end of the week, Dan Cullen cornered Dorety on deck.

'What are you going to do when we get to 'Frisco?' he demanded bluntly.

'I am going to swear out a warrant for your arrest,' Dorety answered quietly. 'I am going to charge you with murder, and I am going to see you hanged for it.'

'You're almighty sure of yourself,' Captain Cullen sneered, turning on his heel.

A second week passed, and one morning found George Dorety standing in the coach-house companionway at the for'ard end of the long poop, taking his first gaze around the deck. The *Mary Rogers* was reaching full-and-by, in a stiff breeze. Every sail was set and drawing, including the staysails. Captain Cullen strolled for'ard along the poop. He strolled carelessly, glancing at the passenger out of the corner of his eye. Dorety was looking the other way, standing with head and shoulders outside the companionway, and only the back of his head was to be seen. Captain Cullen, with swift eye, embraced the mainstaysail-block and the head and estimated the distance. He glanced about him. Nobody was looking. Aft, Joshua Higgins, pacing up and down, had just turned his back and was going the other way. Captain Cullen bent over suddenly and cast the staysail-sheet off from its pin. The heavy block hurtled through the air, smashing Dorety's head like an egg-shell and hurtling on and back and forth as the staysail whipped and slatted in the wind. Joshua Higgins turned around to see what had carried away, and met the full blast of the vilest portion of Captain Cullen's profanity.

'I made the sheet fast myself,' whimpered the mate in the first lull, 'with an extra turn to make sure. I remember it distinctly.'

'Made fast?' the Captain snarled back, for the benefit of the watch as it struggled to capture the flying sail before it tore to ribbons. 'You couldn't make your grandmother fast, you useless hell's scullion. If you made that sheet fast with an extra turn, why in hell didn't it stay fast? That's what I want to know. Why in hell didn't it stay fast?'

The mate whined inarticulately.

'Oh, shut up!' was the final word of Captain Cullen.

Half an hour later he was as surprised as any when the body of George Dorety was found inside the companionway on the floor. In the afternoon, alone in his room, he doctored up the log.

'*Ordinary seaman, Karl Brun,*' he wrote, '*lost overboard from foreroyal-yard in a gale of wind. Was running at the time, and for the safety of the ship did not dare to come up the wind. Nor could a boat have lived in the sea that was running.*'

On another page he wrote:

'*Had often warned Mr Dorety about the danger he ran because of his carelesssness on deck. I told him, once, that some day he would get his head knocked off by a block. A carelessly fastened mainstaysail sheet was the cause of the accident, which was deeply to be regretted because Mr Dorety was a favourite with all of us.*'

Captain Dan Cullen read over his literary effort with admiration, blotted the page, and closed the log. He lighted a cigar and stared before him. He felt the *Mary Rogers* lift, and heel, and surge along, and knew that she was making nine knots. A smile of satisfaction slowly dawned on his black and hairy face. Well, anyway, he had made his westing and fooled God.

Joseph Conrad

TYPHOON

A captain pitting all his skill against the might of the ocean – surely the ultimate test of the seaman – is also the theme of this next tale by another of the greats of maritime fiction, Joseph Conrad (1857–1924). Although he was born in the Polish Ukraine, Conrad went to sea in an English merchant ship in 1878, and developed such an affection for Britain that in 1886, when he gained his ticket as a master, he also applied for citizenship. He was not yet ready to settle down, however, and spent some years in the Far East where he gained an intimate knowledge of the seas and waterways of such places as Singapore and Borneo. His years afloat also gave him a deep insight into the 'brotherhood of the sea', which he used to such great effect in the book that made his reputation as a writer, Lord Jim, published in 1900.

When Conrad settled permanently in England in 1896, he chose to lead a rather reclusive life, yet quickly established an unrivalled reputation as a writer of perceptive tales about the sea and those who go upon it. Collections of his short stories such as Tales of Unrest (1898) and Twixt Land and Sea (1912) brilliantly underlined this ability. Among his tales I think 'Typhoon' is one of the very best, and few sea captains have ever been so vividly portrayed as Captain MacWhirr. This is perhaps not surprising when one learns that the Captain was based on the author himself, for as Conrad wrote in 1919, 'McWhirr is not an acquaintance of a few hours, or a few weeks, or a few months. He is the product of twenty years of life. My own life.' He also admitted that every aspect of the story was also authentic — both statements making what follows doubly fascinating . . .

I

Captain MacWhirr, of the steamer *Nan-Shan*, had a physiognomy that, in the order of material appearances, was the exact counterpart of his mind: it presented no marked characteristics of firmness or stupidity; it had no pronounced characteristics whatever; it was simply ordinary, irresponsive, and unruffled.

The only thing his aspect might have been said to suggest, at times, was bashfulness; because he would sit, in business offices ashore, sunburnt and smiling faintly, with downcast eyes. When he raised them, they were perceived to be direct in their glance and of blue colour. His hair was fair and extremely fine, clasping from temple to temple the bald dome of his skull in a clamp as of fluffy silk. The hair of his face, on the contrary, carroty and flaming, resembled a growth of copper wire clipped short to the line of the lip; while, no matter how close he shaved, fiery metallic gleams passed, when he moved his head, over the surface of his cheeks. He was rather below the medium height, a bit round-shouldered, and so sturdy of limb that his clothes always looked a shade too tight for his arms and legs. As if unable to grasp what is due to the difference of latitudes, he wore a brown bowler hat, a complete suit of a brownish hue, and clumsy black boots. These harbour togs gave to his thick figure an air of stiff and uncouth smartness. A thin silver watch-chain looped his waistcoat, and he never left his ship for the shore without clutching in his powerful, hairy fist an elegant umbrella of the very best quality, but generally unrolled. Young Jukes, the chief mate, attending his commander to the gangway, would sometimes venture to say, with the greatest gentleness, 'Allow me, sir' — and possessing himself of the umbrella deferentially, would elevate the ferrule, shake the folds, twirl a neat furl in a jiffy, and hand it back; going through the performance with a face of such portentous gravity, that Mr Solomon Rout, the chief engineer, smoking his morning cigar over the skylight, would turn away his head in order to hide a smile. 'Oh! aye! The blessed gamp . . . Thank 'ee, Jukes, thank 'ee,' would mutter Captain MacWhirr, heartily, without looking up.

Having just enough imagination to carry him through each successive day, and no more, he was tranquilly sure of himself; and from the very same cause he was not in the least conceited. It is your imaginative superior who is touchy, overbearing, and difficult to please; but every ship Captain MacWhirr commanded was the floating abode of harmony and peace. It was, in truth, as impossible for him to take a flight of fancy as it would be for a watchmaker to put together a chronometer with nothing except a two-pound hammer and a whip-saw in the way of tools. Yet the uninteresting lives of men so entirely given to the actuality of the bare existence have their mysterious side. It was impossible in Captain MacWhirr's case, for instance, to understand what under heaven could have induced that perfectly satisfactory son of a petty grocer in Belfast to run away to sea. And yet he had done that very thing at the age of fifteen. It was enough, when you thought it over, to give you the idea of an immense, potent, and invisible hand thrust into the ant-heap of the earth, laying hold of shoulders, knocking heads together, and setting the unconscious faces of the multitude towards inconceivable goals and in undreamt-of directions.

His father never really forgave him for this undutiful stupidity. 'We could have got on without him,' he used to say later on, 'but there's the business. And he an only son, too!' His mother wept very much after his disappearance. As it had never occurred to him to leave word behind, he was mourned over for dead till, after eight months, his first letter arrived from Talcahuano. It was short, and contained the statement: 'We had very fine weather on our passage out.' But evidently, in the writer's mind, the only important intelligence was to the effect that his captain had, on the very day of writing, entered him regularly on the ship's articles as Ordinary Seaman. 'Because I can do the work,' he explained. The mother again wept copiously, while the remark, 'Tom's an ass,' expressed the emotions of the father. He was a corpulent man, with a gift for sly chaffing, which to the end of his life he exercised in his intercourse with his son, a little pityingly, as if upon a half-witted person.

MacWhirr's visits to his home were necessarily rare, and in the course of years he despatched other letters to his parents, informing them of his successive promotions and of his movements upon the vast earth. In these missives could be found sentences like this: 'The heat here is very great.' Or: 'On Christmas Day at 4 p.m. we fell in with some icebergs.' The old people ultimately became acquainted with a good many names of ships, and with the names of the skippers who commanded them – with the names of Scots and English shipowners – with the names of seas, oceans, straits, promontories – with outlandish names of lumber-ports, of rice-ports, of cotton-ports – with the names of islands – with the name of their son's young woman. She was called Lucy. It did not suggest itself to him to mention whether he thought the name pretty. And then they died.

The great day of MacWhirr's marriage came in due course, following shortly upon the great day when he got his first command.

All these events had taken place many years before the morning when, in the chart-room of the steamer *Nan-Shan*, he stood confronted by the fall of a barometer he had no reason to distrust. The fall – taking into account the excellence of the instrument, the time of the year, and the ship's position on the terrestrial globe – was of a nature ominously prophetic; but the red face of the man betrayed no sort of inward disturbance. Omens were as nothing to him, and he was unable to discover the message of a prophecy till the fulfilment had brought it home to his very door. 'That's a fall, and no mistake,' he thought. 'There must be some uncommonly dirty weather knocking about.'

The *Nan-Shan* was on her way from the southward to the treaty port of Fu-chau, with some cargo in her lower holds, and two hundred Chinese coolies returning to their village homes in the province of Fo-kien, after a few years of work in various tropical colonies. The morning was fine, the oily sea heaved without a sparkle, and there was a queer white misty patch in the sky like a halo of the sun. The fore-deck, packed with Chinamen, was full of sombre clothing, yellow faces, and pigtails, sprinkled over with a good many naked shoulders, for there was no wind, and the heat was close. The coolies lounged, talked, smoked, or stared over the rail; some, drawing water over the side, sluiced each other; a few slept on hatches, while several small parties of six sat on their heels surrounding iron trays with plates of rice and tiny teacups; and every single Celestial of them was carrying with him all he had in the world – a wooden chest with a ringing lock and brass on the corners, containing the savings of his labours: some clothes of ceremony, sticks of incense, a little opium maybe, bits of nameless rubbish of conventional value, and a small hoard of silver dollars, toiled for in coal lighters, won in gambling-houses or in petty trading, grubbed out of earth, sweated out in mines, on railway lines, in deadly jungle, under heavy burdens – amassed patiently, guarded with care, cherished fiercely.

A cross swell had set in from the direction of Formosa Channel about ten o'clock, without disturbing these passengers much, because the *Nan-Shan*, with her flat bottom, rolling chocks on bilges, and great breadth of beam, had the reputation of an exceptionally steady ship in a sea-way. Mr Jukes, in moments of expansion on shore, would proclaim loudly that the 'old girl was as good as she was pretty'. It would never have occurred to Captain MacWhirr to express his favourable opinion so loud or in terms so fanciful.

She was a good ship, undoubtedly, and not old either. She had been built in Dumbarton less than three years before, to the order of a firm of merchants in Siam – Messrs Sigg and Son. When she lay afloat, finished in every detail and ready to take up the work of her life, the builders contemplated her with pride.

'Sigg has asked us for a reliable skipper to take her out,' remarked one of the partners; and the other, after reflecting for a while, said: 'I think MacWhirr is ashore just at present.' 'Is he? Then wire him at once. He's the very man,' declared the senior, without a moment's hesitation.

Next morning MacWhirr stood before them unperturbed, having travelled from London by the midnight express after a sudden but undemonstrative parting with his wife. She was the daughter of a superior couple who had seen better days.

'We had better be going together over the ship, Captain,' said the senior partner; and the three men started to view the perfections of the *Nan-Shan* from stem to stern, and from her keelson to the trucks of her two stumpy pole-masts.

Captain MacWhirr had begun by taking off his coat, which he hung on the end of a steam windlass embodying all the latest improvements.

'My uncle wrote of you favourably by yesterday's mail to our good friends – Messrs Sigg, you know – and doubtless they'll continue you out there in command,' said the junior partner. 'You'll be able to boast of being in charge of the handiest boat of her size on the coast of China, Captain,' he added.

'Have you? Thank 'ee,' mumbled vaguely MacWhirr, to whom the view of a distant eventuality could appeal no more than the beauty of a wide landscape to a purblind tourist; and his eyes happening at the moment to be at rest upon the lock of the cabin door, he walked up to it, full of purpose, and began to rattle the handle vigorously, while he observed, in his low, earnest voice, 'You can't trust the workmen nowadays. A brand-new lock, and it won't act at all. Stuck fast. See? See?'

As soon as they found themselves alone in their office across the yard: 'You praised that fellow up to Sigg. What is it you see in him?' asked the nephew, with faint contempt.

'I admit he has nothing of your fancy skipper about him, if that's what you mean,' said the elder man, curtly. 'Is the foreman of the joiners on the *Nan-Shan* outside? . . . Come in, Bates. How is it that you let Tait's people put us off with a defective lock on the cabin door? The Captain could see directly he set eye on it. Have it replaced at once. The little straws, Bates . . . the little straws . . .'

The lock was replaced accordingly, and a few days afterwards the *Nan-Shan* steamed out to the East, without Mac-Whirr having offered any further remark as to her fittings, or having been heard to utter a single word hinting at pride in his ship, gratitude for his appointment, or satisfaction at his prospects.

With a temperament neither loquacious nor taciturn he

found very little occasion to talk. There were matters of duty, of course – directions, orders, and so on; but the past being to his mind done with, and the future not there yet, the more general actualities of the day required no comment – because facts can speak for themselves with overwhelming precision.

Old Mr Sigg liked a man of few words, and one that 'you could be sure would not try to improve upon his instructions'. MacWhirr, satisfying these requirements, was continued in command of the *Nan-Shan*, and applied himself to the careful navigation of his ship in the China seas. She had come out on a British register, but after some time Messrs Sigg judged it expedient to transfer her to the Siamese flag.

At the news of the contemplated transfer Jukes grew restless, as if under a sense of personal affront. He went about grumbling to himself, and uttering short scornful laughs. 'Fancy having a ridiculous Noah's Ark elephant in the ensign of one's ship,' he said once at the engine-room door. 'Dash me if I can stand it: I'll throw up the billet. Don't it make *you* sick, Mr Rout?' The chief engineer only cleared his throat with the air of a man who knows the value of a good billet.

The first morning the new flag floated over the stern of the *Nan-Shan* Jukes stood looking at it bitterly from the bridge. He struggled with his feelings for a while, and then remarked, 'Queer flag for a man to sail under, sir.'

'What's the matter with the flag?' inquired Captain MacWhirr. 'Seems all right to me.' And he walked across to the end of the bridge to have a good look.

'Well, it looks queer to me,' burst out Jukes, greatly exasperated, and flung off the bridge.

Captain MacWhirr was amazed at these manners. After a while he stepped quietly into the chart-room, and opened his International Signal Code-book at the plate where the flags of all the nations are correctly figured in gaudy rows. He ran his finger over them, and when he came to Siam he contemplated with great attention the red field and the white elephant. Nothing could be more simple; but to make sure he brought the book out on the bridge for the purpose of comparing the coloured drawing with the real thing at the flagstaff astern. When next Jukes, who was carrying on the duty that day with a sort of suppressed fierceness, happened on the bridge, his commander observed:

'There's nothing amiss with that flag.'

'Isn't there?' mumbled Jukes, falling on his knees before a deck-locker and jerking therefrom viciously a spare lead-line.

'No. I looked up the book. Length twice the breadth and the elephant exactly in the middle. I thought the people ashore would know how to make the local flag. Stands to reason. You were wrong, Jukes . . .'

'Well, sir,' began Jukes, getting up excitedly, 'all I can say —' He fumbled for the end of the coil of line with trembling hands.

'That's all right.' Captain MacWhirr soothed him, sitting heavily on a little canvas folding-stool he greatly affected. 'All you have to do is to take care they don't hoist the elephant upside-down before they get quite used to it.'

Jukes flung the new lead-line over on the fore-deck with a loud 'Here you are, bo'ss'en — don't forget to wet it thoroughly', and turned with immense resolution towards his commander; but Captain MacWhirr spread his elbows on the bridge-rail comfortably.

'Because it would be, I suppose, understood as a signal of distress,' he went on. 'What do you think? That elephant there, I take it, stands for something in the nature of the Union Jack in the flag . . .'

'Does it!' yelled Jukes, so that every head on the *Nan-Shan's* decks looked towards the bridge. Then he sighed, and with sudden resignation: 'It would certainly be a dam' distressful sight,' he said, meekly.

Later in the day he accosted the chief engineer with a confidential, 'Here, let me tell you the old man's latest.'

Mr Solomon Rout (frequently alluded to as Long Sol, Old Sol, or Father Rout), from finding himself almost invariably the tallest man on board every ship he joined, had acquired the habit of a stooping, leisurely condescension. His hair was scant and sandy, his flat cheeks were pale, his bony wrists and long scholarly hands were pale, too, as though he had lived all his life in the shade.

He smiled from on high at Jukes, and went on smoking and glancing about quietly, in the manner of a kind uncle lending

148

an ear to the tale of an excited schoolboy. Then, greatly amused but impassive, he asked:

'And did you throw up the billet?'

'No,' cried Jukes, raising a weary, discouraged voice above the harsh buzz of the *Nan-Shan*'s friction winches. All of them were hard at work, snatching slings of cargo, high up, to the end of long derricks, only, as it seemed, to let them rip down recklessly by the run. The cargo chains groaned in the gins, clinked on coamings, rattled over the side; and the whole ship quivered, with her long grey flanks smoking in wreaths of steam. 'No,' cried Jukes, 'I didn't. What's the good? I might just as well fling my resignation at this bulkhead. I don't believe you can make a man like that understand anything. He simply knocks me over.'

At that moment Captain MacWhirr, back from the shore, crossed the deck, umbrella in hand, escorted by a mournful, self-possessed Chinaman, walking behind in paper-soled silk shoes, and who also carried an umbrella.

The master of the *Nan-Shan*, speaking just audibly and gazing at his boots as his manner was, remarked that it would be necessary to call at Fu-chau this trip, and desired Mr Rout to have steam up to-morrow afternoon at one o'clock sharp. He pushed back his hat to wipe his forehead, observing at the time that he hated going ashore anyhow; while overtopping him Mr Rout, without deigning a word, smoked austerely, nursing his right elbow in the palm of his left hand. Then Jukes was directed in the same subdued voice to keep the forward 'tween-deck clear of cargo. Two hundred coolies were going to be put down there. The Bun Hin Company were sending that lot home. Twenty-five bags of rice would be coming off in a sampan directly, for stores. All seven-years'-men they were, said Captain MacWhirr, with a camphor-wood chest to every man. The carpenter should be set to work nailing three-inch battens along the deck below, fore and aft, to keep these boxes from shifting in a sea-way. Jukes had better look to it at once. 'D'ye hear, Jukes?' This Chinaman here was coming with the ship as far as Fu-chau – a sort of interpreter he would be. Bun Hin's clerk he was, and wanted to have a look at the space. Jukes had better take him forward. 'D'ye hear, Jukes?'

Jukes took care to punctuate these instructions in proper

149

places with the obligatory 'Yes, sir,' ejaculated without enthusiasm. His brusque 'Come along, John; make look see' set the Chinaman in motion at his heels.

'Wanchee look see, all same look see can do,' said Jukes, who having no talent for foreign languages mangled the very pidgin-English cruelly. He pointed at the open hatch. 'Catchee number one piecie place to sleep in. Eh?'

He was gruff, as became his racial superiority, but not unfriendly. The Chinaman, gazing sad and speechless into the darkness of the hatchway, seemed to stand at the head of a yawning grave.

'No catchee rain down there — savee?' pointed out Jukes. 'Suppose all'ee same fine weather, one piecie coolie-man come top-side,' he pursued, warming up imaginatively. 'Make so — Phooooo!' He expanded his chest and blew out his cheeks. 'Savee, John? Breathe — fresh air. Good. Eh? Washee him piecie pants, chow-chow top-side — see, John?'

With his mouth and hands he made exuberant motions of eating rice and washing clothes; and the Chinaman, who concealed his distrust of this pantomime under a collected demeanour tinged by a gentle and refined melancholy, glanced out of his almond eyes from Jukes to the hatch and back again. 'Velly good,' he murmured, in a disconsolate undertone, and hastened smoothly along the decks, dodging obstacles in his course. He disappeared, ducking low under a sling of ten dirty gunny-bags full of some costly merchandise and exhaling a repulsive smell.

Captain MacWhirr meantime had gone on the bridge, and into the chart-room, where a letter, commenced two days before, awaited termination. These long letters began with the words, 'My darling wife', and the steward, between the scrubbing of the floors and the dusting of chronometer-boxes, snatched at every opportunity to read them. They interested him much more than they possibly could the woman for whose eye they were intended; and this for the reason that they related in minute detail each successive trip of the *Nan-Shan*.

Her master, faithful to facts, which alone his consciousness reflected, would set them down with painstaking care upon many pages. The house in a northern suburb to which these pages were addressed had a bit of garden before the bow-windows, a deep porch of good appearance, coloured glass with imitation lead frame in the front door. He paid five-and-forty pounds a year for it, and did not think the rent too high, because Mrs MacWhirr (a pretentious person with a scraggy neck and a disdainful manner) was admittedly ladylike, and in the neighbourhood considered as 'quite superior'. The only secret of her life was her abject terror of the time when her husband would come home to stay for good. Under the same roof there dwelt also a daughter called Lydia and a son, Tom. These two were but slightly acquainted with their father. Mainly, they knew him as a rare but privileged visitor, who of an evening smoked his pipe in the dining-room and slept in the house. The lanky girl, upon the whole, was rather ashamed of him; the boy was frankly and utterly indifferent in a straightforward, delightful, unaffected way manly boys have.

And Captain MacWhirr wrote home from the coast of China twelve times every year, desiring quaintly to be 'remembered to the children', and subscribing himself 'your loving husband', as calmly as if the words so long used by so many men were, apart from their shape, worn-out things, and of a faded meaning.

The China seas north and south are narrow seas. They are seas full of every-day, eloquent facts, such as islands, sandbanks, reefs, swift and changeable currents – tangled facts that nevertheless speak to a seaman in clear and definite language. Their speech appealed to Captain MacWhirr's sense of realities so forcibly that he had given up his state-room below and practically lived all his days on the bridge of the ship, often having his meals sent up, and sleeping at night in the chartroom. And he indited there his home letters. Each of them, without exception, contained the phrase, 'The weather has been very fine this trip', or some other form of a statement to that effect. And this statement, too, in its wonderful persistence, was of the same perfect accuracy as all the others they contained.

Mr Rout likewise wrote letters; only no one on board knew how chatty he could be, pen in hand, because the chief engineer had enough imagination to keep his desk locked. His wife relished his style greatly. They were a childless couple, and Mrs Rout, a big, high-bosomed, jolly woman of forty, shared with

Mr Rout's toothless and venerable mother a little cottage near Teddington. She would run over her correspondence, at breakfast, with lively eyes, and scream out interesting passages in a joyous voice at the deaf old lady, prefacing each extract by the warning shout, 'Solomon says!' She had the trick of firing off Solomon's utterances also upon strangers, astonishing them easily by the unfamiliar text and the unexpectedly jocular vein of these quotations. On the day the new curate called for the first time at the cottage, she found occasion to remark, 'As Solomon says: "the engineers that go down to the sea in ships behold the wonders of sailor nature";' when a change in the visitor's countenance made her stop and stare.

'Solomon . . . Oh! . . . Mrs Rout,' stuttered the young man, very red in the face, 'I must say . . . I don't . . .'

'He's my husband,' she announced in a great shout, throwing herself back in the chair. Perceiving the joke, she laughed immoderately with a handkerchief to her eyes, while he sat wearing a forced smile, and, from his inexperience of jolly women, fully persuaded that she must be deplorably insane. They were excellent friends afterwards; for, absolving her from irreverent intention, he came to think she was a very worthy person indeed; and he learned in time to receive without flinching other scraps of Solomon's wisdom.

'For my part,' Solomon was reported by his wife to have said once, 'give me the dullest ass for a skipper before a rogue. There is a way to take a fool; but a rogue is smart and slippery.' This was an airy generalization drawn from the particular case of Captain MacWhirr's honesty, which, in itself, had the heavy obviousness of a lump of clay. On the other hand, Mr Jukes, unable to generalize, unmarried, and unengaged, was in the habit of opening his heart after another fashion to an old chum and former shipmate, actually serving as second officer on board an Atlantic liner.

First of all he would insist upon the advantages of the Eastern trade, hinting at its superiority to the Western Ocean service. He extolled the sky, the seas, the ships, and the easy life of the Far East. The *Nan-Shan*, he affirmed, was second to none as a sea-boat.

'We have no brass-bound uniforms, but then we are like brothers here,' he wrote. 'We all mess together and live like fighting-cocks ... All the chaps of the black-squad are as decent as they made that kind, and old Sol, the Chief, is a dry stick. We are good friends. As to our old man, you could not find a quieter skipper. Sometimes you would think he hadn't sense enough to see anything wrong. And yet it isn't that. Can't be. He has been in command for a good few years now. He doesn't do anything actually foolish, and gets his ship along all right without worrying anybody. I believe he hasn't brains enough to enjoy kicking up a row. I don't take advantage of him. I would scorn it. Outside the routine of duty he doesn't seem to understand more than half of what you tell him. We get a laugh out of this at times; but it is dull, too, to be with a man like this — in the long-run. Old Sol says he hasn't much conversation. Conversation! O Lord! He never talks. The other day I had been yarning under the bridge with one of the engineers, and he must have heard us. When I came up to take my watch, he steps out of the chart-room and has a good look all round, peeps over at the sidelights, glances at the compass, squints upwards at the stars. That's his regular performance. By-and-by he says: "Was that you talking just now in the port alleyway?" "Yes, sir." "With the third engineer?" "Yes, sir." He walks off to starboard, and sits under the dodger on a little campstool of his, and for half an hour perhaps he makes no sound, except that I heard him sneeze once. Then after a while I hear him getting up over there, and he strolls across to port, where I was. "I can't understand what you can find to talk about," says he. "Two solid hours. I am not blaming you. I see people ashore at it all day long, and then in the evening they sit down and keep at it over the drinks. Must be saying the same things over and over again. I can't understand."

'Did you ever hear anything like that? And he was so patient about it. It made me quite sorry for him. But he is exasperating, too, sometimes. Of course one would not do anything to vex him even if it were worth while. But it isn't. He's so jolly innocent that if you were to put your thumb to your nose and wave your fingers at him he would only wonder gravely to himself what got into you. He told me once quite simply that he found it very difficult to make out what made people always act so queerly. He's too dense to trouble about, and that's the truth.'

Thus wrote Mr Jukes to his chum in the Western Ocean trade, out of the fulness of his heart and the liveliness of his fancy.

He had expressed his honest opinion. It was not worth while trying to impress a man of that sort. If the world had been full of such men, life would have probably appeared to Jukes an unentertaining and unprofitable business. He was not alone in his opinion. The sea itself, as if sharing Mr Jukes's good-natured forbearance, had never put itself out to startle the silent man, who seldom looked up, and wandered innocently over the waters with the only visible purpose of getting food, raiment, and house-room for three people ashore. Dirty weather he had known, of course. He had been made wet, uncomfortable, tired in the usual way, felt at the time and presently forgotten. So that upon the whole he had been justified in reporting fine weather at home. But he had never been given a glimpse of immeasurable strength and of immoderate wrath, the wrath that passes exhausted but never appeased – the wrath and fury of the passionate sea. He knew it existed, as we know that crime and abominations exist; he had heard of it as a peaceable citizen in a town hears of battles, famines, and floods, and yet knows nothing of what these things mean – though, indeed, he may have been mixed up in a street row, have gone without his dinner once, or been soaked to the skin in a shower. Captain MacWhirr had sailed over the surface of the oceans as some men go skimming over the years of existence to sink gently into a placid grave, ignorant of life to the last, without ever having been made to see all it may contain of perfidy, of violence, and of terror. There are on sea and land such men thus fortunate – or thus disdained by destiny or by the sea.

II

Observing the steady fall of the barometer, Captain MacWhirr thought, 'There's some dirty weather knocking about.' This is precisely what he thought. He had had an experience of moderately dirty weather – the term dirty as applied to the weather implying only moderate discomfort to the seaman. Had he been informed by an indisputable authority that the end of the world was to be finally accomplished by a catastrophic disturbance of the atmosphere, he would have assimilated the information under the simple idea of dirty weather, and no other, because he had no experience of cataclysms, and belief does not necessarily imply comprehension. The wisdom of his country had pronounced by means of an Act of Parliament that before he could be considered as fit to take charge of a ship he should be able to answer certain simple questions on the subject of circular storms such as hurricanes, cyclones, typhoons; and apparently he had answered them, since he was now in command of the *Nan-Shan* in the China seas during the season of typhoons. But if he had answered he remembered nothing of it. He was, however, conscious of being made uncomfortable by the clammy heat. He came out on the bridge, and found no relief to this oppression. The air seemed thick. He gasped like a fish, and began to believe himself greatly out of sorts.

The *Nan-Shan* was ploughing a vanishing furrow upon the circle of the sea that had the surface and the shimmer of an undulating piece of grey silk. The sun, pale and without rays, poured down leaden heat in a strangely indecisive light, and the Chinamen were lying prostrate about the decks. Their bloodless, pinched, yellow faces were like the faces of bilious invalids. Captain MacWhirr noticed two of them expecially, stretched out on their backs below the bridge. As soon as they had closed their eyes they seemed dead. Three others, however, were quarrelling barbarously away forward; and one big fellow, half naked, with herculean shoulders, was hanging limply over a winch; another, sitting on the deck, his knees up and his head drooping sideways in a girlish attitude, was plaiting his pigtail with infinite languor depicted in his whole person and in the very movement of his fingers. The smoke struggled with difficulty out of the funnel, and instead of streaming away spread itself out like an infernal sort of cloud, smelling of sulphur and raining soot all over the decks.

'What the devil are you doing there, Mr Jukes?' asked Captain MacWhirr.

This unusual form of address, though mumbled rather than spoken, caused the body of Mr Jukes to start as though it had been probed under the fifth rib. He had had a low bench brought on the bridge, and sitting on it, with a length of rope curled about his feet and a piece of canvas stretched over his knees, was pushing a sail-needle vigorously. He looked up, and his surprise gave to his eyes an expression of innocence and candour.

'I am only roping some of that new set of bags we made last trip for whipping up coals,' he remonstrated, gently. 'We shall want them for the next coaling, sir.'

'What became of the others?'

'Why, worn out, of course sir.'

Captain MacWhirr, after glaring down irresolutely at his chief mate, disclosed the gloomy and cynical conviction that more than half of them had been lost overboard, 'if only the truth was known', and retired to the other end of the bridge. Jukes, exasperated by this unprovoked attack, broke the needle at the second stitch, and dropping his work got up and cursed the heat in a violent undertone.

The propeller thumped, the three Chinamen forward had given up squabbling very suddenly, and the one who had been plaiting his tail clasped his legs and stared dejectedly over his knees. The lurid sunshine cast faint and sickly shadows. The swell ran higher and swifter every moment, and the ship lurched heavily in the smooth, deep hollows of the sea.

'I wonder where that beastly swell comes from,' said Jukes aloud, recovering himself after a stagger.

'North-east,' grunted the literal MacWhirr, from his side of the bridge. 'There's some dirty weather knocking about. Go and look at the glass.'

When Jukes came out of the chart-room, the cast of his countenance had changed to thoughtfulness and concern. He caught hold of the bridge-rail and stared ahead.

The temperature in the engine-room had gone up to a hundred and seventeen degrees. Irritated voices were ascending through the skylight and through the fiddle of the stokehold in a harsh and resonant uproar, mingled with angry clangs and scrapes of metal, as if men with limbs of iron and throats of bronze had been quarrelling down there. The second engineer was falling foul of the stokers for letting the steam go down. He was a man with arms like a blacksmith, and generally feared; but that afternoon the stokers were answering him back recklessly, and slammed the furnace doors with the fury of despair. Then the noise ceased suddenly, and the second engineer appeared, emerging out of the stokehold streaked with grime and soaking wet like a chimney-sweep coming out of a well. As soon as his head was clear of the fiddle he began to scold Jukes for not trimming properly the stokehold ventilators; and in answer Jukes made with his hands deprecatory soothing signs meaning: No wind—can't be helped—you can see for yourself. But the other wouldn't hear reason. His teeth flashed angrily in his dirty face. He didn't mind, he said, the trouble of punching their blanked heads down there, blank his soul, but did the condemned sailors think you could keep steam up in the God-forsaken boilers simply by knocking the blanked stokers about? No, by George! You had to get some draught, too — may he be everlastingly blanked for a swab-headed deck-hand if you didn't! And the chief, too, rampaging before the steam-gauge and carrying on like a lunatic up and down the engine-room ever since noon. What did Jukes think he was stuck up there for, if he couldn't get one of his decayed, good-for-nothing deck-cripples to turn the ventilators to the wind?

The relations of the 'engine-room' and the 'deck' of the *Nan-Shan* were, as is known, of a brotherly nature; therefore Jukes leaned over and begged the other in a restrained tone not to make a disgusting ass of himself; the skipper was on the other side of the bridge. But the second declared mutinously that he didn't care a rap who was on the other side of the bridge, and Jukes, passing in a flash from lofty disapproval into a state of exaltation, invited him in unflattering terms to come up and twist the beastly things to please himself, and catch such wind as a donkey of his sort could find. The second rushed up to the fray. He flung himself at the port ventilator as though he meant to tear it out bodily and toss it overboard. All he did was to move the cowl round a few inches, with an enormous expenditure of force, and seemed spent in the effort. He leaned against the back of the wheel-house, and Jukes walked up to him.

'Oh, Heavens!' ejaculated the engineer in a feeble voice. He lifted his eyes to the sky, and then let his glassy stare descend to meet the horizon that, tilting up to an angle of forty degrees, seemed to hang on a slant for a while and settled down slowly. 'Heavens! Phew! What's up, anyhow?'

Jukes, straddling his long legs like a pair of compasses, put on an air of superiority. 'We're going to catch it this time,' he said. 'The barometer is tumbling down like anything, Harry. And you trying to kick up that silly row . . .'

The word 'barometer' seemed to revive the second engineer's mad animosity. Collecting afresh all his energies, he directed Jukes in a low and brutal tone to shove the unmentionable instument down his gory throat. Who cared for his crimson barometer? It was the steam — the steam — that was going down; and what between the firemen going faint and the chief going silly, it was worse than a dog's life for him; he didn't care a tinker's curse how soon the whole show was blown out of the water. He seemed on the point of having a cry, but after regaining his breath he muttered darkly, 'I'll faint them,' and dashed off. He stopped upon the fiddle long enough to shake his fist at the unnatural daylight, and dropped into the dark hole with a whoop.

When Jukes turned, his eyes fell upon the rounded back and the big red ears of Captain MacWhirr, who had come across. He did not look at his chief officer, but said at once, 'That's a very violent man, that second engineer.'

'Jolly good second, anyhow,' grunted Jukes. 'They can't keep up steam,' he added, rapidly, and made a grab at the rail against the coming lurch.

Captain MacWhirr, unprepared, took a run and brought himself up with a jerk by an awning stanchion.

'A profane man,' he said, obstinately. 'If this goes on, I'll have to get rid of him the first chance.'

'It's the heat,' said Jukes. 'The weather's awful. It would make a saint swear. Even up here I feel exactly as if I had my head tied up in a woollen blanket.'

Captain MacWhirr looked up. 'D'ye mean to say, Mr Jukes, you ever had your head tied up in a blanket? What was that for?'

'It's a manner of speaking, sir,' said Jukes, stolidly.

'Some of you fellows do go on! What's that about saints swearing? I wish you wouldn't talk so wild. What sort of saint would that be that would swear? No more saint than yourself,

I expect. And what's a blanket got to do with it — or the weather either . . . The heat does not make me swear — does it? It's filthy bad temper. That's what it is. And what's the good of your talking like this?'

Thus Captain MacWhirr expostulated against the use of images in speech, and at the end electrified Jukes by a contemptuous snort, followed by words of passion and resentment: 'Damme! I'll fire him out of the ship if he don't look out.'

And Jukes, incorrigible, thought: 'Goodness me! Somebody's put a new inside to my old man. Here's temper, if you like. Of course it's the weather; what else? It would make an angel quarrelsome — let alone a saint.'

All the Chinamen on deck appeared at their last gasp.

At its setting the sun had a diminished diameter and an expiring brown, rayless glow, as if millions of centuries elapsing since the morning had brought it near its end. A dense bank of cloud became visible to the northward; it had a sinister dark olive tint, and lay low and motionless upon the sea, resembling a solid obstacle in the path of the ship. She went floundering towards it like an exhausted creature driven to its death. The coppery twilight retired slowly, and the darkness brought out overhead a swarm of unsteady, big stars, that, as if blown upon, flickered exceedingly and seemed to hang very near the earth. At eight o'clock Jukes went into the chart-room to write up the ship's log.

He copied neatly out of the rough-book the number of miles, the course of the ship, and in the column for 'wind' scrawled the word 'calm' from top to bottom of the eight hours since noon. He was exasperated by the continuous, monotonous rolling of the ship. The heavy inkstand would slide away in a manner that suggested perverse intelligence in dodging the pen. Having written in the large space under the head of 'Remarks' 'Heat very oppressive', he stuck the end of the pen-holder in his teeth, pipe fashion, and mopped his face carefully.

'Ship rolling heavily in a high cross swell,' he began again, and commented to himself, 'Heavily is no word for it.' Then he wrote: 'Sunset threatening, with a low bank of clouds to N and E. Sky clear overhead.'

Sprawling over the table with arrested pen, he glanced out of the door, and in that frame of his vision he saw all the stars flying upwards between the teakwood jambs on a black sky. The whole lot took flight together and disappeared, leaving only a blackness flecked with white flashes, for the sea was as black as the sky and speckled with foam afar. The stars that had flown to the roll came back on the return swing of the ship, rushing downwards in their glittering multitude, not of fiery points, but enlarged to tiny discs brilliant with a clear wet sheen.

Jukes watched the flying big stars for a moment, and then wrote: '8 p.m. Swell increasing. Ship labouring and taking water on her decks. Battened down the coolies for the night. Barometer still falling.' He paused, and thought to himself, 'Perhaps nothing whatever'll come of it.' And then he closed resolutely his entries: 'Every appearance of a typhoon coming on.'

On going out he had to stand aside, and Captain MacWhirr strode over the doorstep without saying a word or making a sign.

'Shut the door, Mr Jukes, will you?' he cried from within.

Jukes turned back to do so, muttering ironically: 'Afraid to catch cold, I suppose.' It was his watch below, but he yearned for communion with his kind; and he remarked cheerily to the second mate: 'Doesn't look so bad, after all – does it?'

The second mate was marching to and fro on the bridge, tripping down with small steps one moment, and the next climbing with difficulty the shifting slope of the deck. At the sound of Juke's voice he stood still, facing forward, but made no reply.

'Hallo! That's a heavy one,' said Jukes, swaying to meet the long roll till his lowered head touched the planks. This time the second mate made in his throat a noise of an unfriendly nature.

He was an oldish, shabby little fellow, with bad teeth and no hair on his face. He had been shipped in a hurry in Shanghai that trip when the second officer brought from home had delayed the ship three hours in port by contriving (in some manner Captain MacWhirr could never understand) to fall overboard into an empty coal-lighter lying alongside, and had to be sent ashore to the hospital with concussion of the brain and a broken limb or two.

Jukes was not discouraged by the unsympathetic sound. 'The Chinamen must be having a lovely time of it down there,' he said. 'It's lucky for them the old girl has the easiest roll of any ship I've ever been in. There now! This one wasn't so bad.'

'You wait,' snarled the second mate.

With his sharp nose, red at the tip, and his thin pinched lips he always looked as though he were raging inwardly; and he was concise in his speech to the point of rudeness. All his time off duty he spent in his cabin with the door shut, keeping so still in there that he was supposed to fall asleep as soon as he had disappeared; but the man who came in to wake him for his watch on deck would invariably find him with his eyes wide open, flat on his back in the bunk, and glaring irritably from a soiled pillow. He never wrote any letters, did not seem to hope for news from anywhere; and though he had been heard once to mention West Hartlepool, it was with extreme bitterness, and only in connection with the extortionate charges of a boarding-house. He was one of those men who are picked up at need in the ports of the world. They are competent enough, appear hopelessly hard up, show no evidence of any sort of vice, and carry about them all the signs of manifest failure. They come aboard on an emergency, care for no ship afloat, live in their own atmosphere of casual connection amongst their shipmates who know nothing of them, and make up their minds to leave at inconvenient times. They clear out with no words of leave-taking in some God-forsaken port other men would fear to be stranded in, and go ashore in company of a shabby sea-chest, corded like a treasure-box, and with an air of shaking the ship's dust off their feet.

'You wait,' he repeated, balanced in great swings with his back to Jukes, motionless and implacable.

'Do you mean to say we are going to catch it hot?' asked Jukes with boyish interest.

'Say? . . . I say nothing. You don't catch me,' snapped the little second mate, with a mixture of pride, scorn, and cunning, as if Jukes's question had been a trap cleverly detected. 'Oh, no! None of you here shall make a fool of me if I know it,' he mumbled to himself.

Jukes reflected rapidly that this second mate was a mean little beast, and in his heart he wished poor Jack Allen had never smashed himself up in the coal-lighter. The far-off blackness ahead of the ship was like another night seen through the starry night of the earth – the starless night of the immensities beyond the created universe, revealed in its appalling stillness through a low fissure in the glittering sphere of which the earth is the kernel.

'Whatever there might be about,' said Jukes, 'we are steaming straight into it.'

'*You've* said it,' caught up the second mate, always with his back to Jukes. 'You've said it, mind – not I.'

'Oh, go to Jericho!' said Jukes, frankly; and the other emitted a triumphant little chuckle.

'You've said it,' he repeated.

'And what of that?'

'I've known some real good men get into trouble with their skippers for saying a dam' sight less,' answered the second mate feverishly. 'Oh, no! You don't catch me.'

'You seem deucedly anxious not to give yourself away,' said Jukes, completely soured by such absurdity. 'I wouldn't be afraid to say what I think.'

'Aye, to me. That's no great trick. I am nobody, and well I know it.'

The ship, after a pause of comparative steadiness started upon a series of rolls, one worse than the other, and for a time Jukes, preserving his equilibrium, was too busy to open his mouth. As soon as the violent swinging had quieted down somewhat, he said: 'This is a bit too much of a good thing. Whether anything is coming or not I think she ought to be put head on to that swell. The old man is just gone in to lie down. Hang me if I don't speak to him.'

But when he opened the door of the chart-room he saw his captain reading a book. Captain MacWhirr was not lying down: he was standing up with one hand grasping the edge of the bookshelf and the other holding open before his face a thick volume. The lamp wriggled in the gimbals, the loosened books toppled from side to side on the shelf, the long barometer swung in jerky circles, the table altered its slant every moment. In the midst of all this stir and movement Captain MacWhirr, holding on, showed his eyes above the upper edge, and asked, 'What's the matter?'

'Swell getting worse, sir.'

'Noticed that in here,' muttered Captain MacWhirr. 'Anything wrong?'

Jukes, inwardly disconcerted by the seriousness of the eyes looking at him over the top of the book, produce an embarrassed grin.

'Rolling like old boots,' he said, sheepishly.

'Aye! Very heavy – very heavy. What do you want?'

At this Jukes lost his footing and began to flounder.

'I was thinking of our passengers,' he said, in the manner of a man clutching at a straw.

'Passengers?' wondered the Captain, gravely. 'What passengers?'

'Why, the Chinamen, sir,' explained Jukes, very sick of this conversation.

'The Chinamen! Why don't you speak plainly? Couldn't tell what you meant. Never heard a lot of coolies spoken of as passengers before. Passengers, indeed! What's come to you?'

Captain MacWhirr, closing the book on his forefinger, lowered his arm and looked completely mystified. 'Why are you thinking of the Chinamen, Mr Jukes?' he inquired.

Jukes took a plunge, like a man driven to it. 'She's rolling her decks full of water, sir. Thought you might put her head on perhaps – for a while. Till this goes down a bit – very soon, I dare say. Head to the eastward. I never knew a ship roll like this.'

He held on in the doorway, and Captain MacWhirr, feeling his grip on the shelf inadequate, made up his mind to let go in a hurry, and fell heavily on the couch.

'Head to the eastward?' he said, struggling to sit up. 'That's more than four points off her course.'

'Yes, sir. Fifty degrees . . . Would just bring her head far enough round to meet this . . .'

Captain MacWhirr was now sitting up. He had not dropped the book, and he had not lost his place.

'To the eastward?' he repeated, with dawning astonishment. 'To the . . . Where do you think we are bound to? You want me to haul a full-powered steamship four points off her course to make the Chinamen comfortable! Now, I've heard more than enough of mad things done in the world – but this . . . If I didn't know you, Jukes, I would think you were in liquor. Steer four points off . . . And what afterwards? Steer four points over the other way, I suppose, to make the course good. What put it into your head that I would start to tack a steamer as if she were a sailing-ship?'

'Jolly good thing she isn't,' threw in Jukes, with bitter readiness. 'She would have rolled every blessed stick out of her this afternoon.'

'Aye! And you just would have had to stand and see them go,' said Captain MacWhirr, showing a certain animation. 'It's a dead calm, isn't it?'

'It is, sir. But there's something out of the common coming, for sure.'

'Maybe. I suppose you have a notion I should be getting out of the way of that dirt,' said Captain MacWhirr, speaking with the utmost simplicity of manner and tone, and fixing the oilcloth on the floor with a heavy stare. Thus he noticed neither Juke's discomfiture nor the mixture of vexation and astonished respect on his face.

'Now, here's this book,' he continued with deliberation, slapping his thigh with the closed volume. 'I've been reading the chapter on the storms there.'

This was true. He had been reading the chapter on the storms. When he had entered the chart-room, it was with no intention of taking the book down. Some influence in the air – the same influence, probably, that caused the steward to bring without orders the Captain's sea-boots and oilskin coat up to the chart-room – had as it were guided his hand to the shelf; and without taking the time to sit down he had waded with a conscious effort into the terminology of the subject. He lost himself amongst advancing semi-circles, left- and right-hand quadrants, the curves of the tracks, the probable bearing of the centre, the shifts of wind and the readings of barometer. He tried to bring all these things into a definite relation to himself, and ended by becoming contemptuously angry with such a lot of words and with so much advice, all head-work and supposition, without a glimmer of certitude.

'It's the damnedest thing, Jukes,' he said. 'If a fellow was to believe all that's in there, he would be running most of his time all over the sea trying to get behind the weather.'

Again he slapped his leg with the book; and Jukes opened his mouth, but said nothing.

'Running to get behind the weather! Do you understand that, Mr Jukes? It's the maddest thing!' ejaculated Captain MacWhirr, with pauses, gazing at the floor profoundly. 'You would think an old woman had been writing this. It passes me. If that thing means anything useful, then it means that I should at once alter the course away, away to the devil somewhere, and come booming down on Fu-chau from the northward at the tail of this dirty weather that's supposed to be knocking about in our way. From the north! Do you understand, Mr Jukes? Three hundred extra miles to the distance, and a pretty coal bill to show. I couldn't bring myself to do that if every word in there was gospel truth, Mr Jukes. Don't you expect me . . .'

And Jukes, silent, marvelled at this display of feeling and loquacity.

'But the truth is that you don't know if the fellow it right, anyhow. How can you tell what a gale is made of till you get it? He isn't aboard here, is he? Very well. Here he says that the centre of them things bears eight points off the wind; but we haven't got any wind, for all the barometer falling. Where's his centre now?'

'We will get the wind presently,' mumbled Jukes.

'Let it come, then,' said Captain MacWhirr, with dignified indignation. 'It's only to let you see, Mr Jukes, that you don't find everything in books. All these rules for dodging breezes and circumventing the winds of heaven, Mr Jukes, seem to me the maddest thing, when you come to look at it sensibly.'

He raised his eyes, saw Jukes gazing at him dubiously, and tried to illustrate his meaning.

'About as queer as your extraordinary notion of dodging the ship head to sea, for I don't know how long, to make the Chinamen comfortable; whereas all we've got to do is to take them to Fu-chau, being timed to get there before noon on Friday. If the weather delays me — very well. There's your log-book to talk straight about the weather. But suppose I went swinging off my course and came in two days late, and they asked me: "Where have you been all that time, Captain?" What could I say to that? "Went around to dodge the bad weather," I would say. "It must've been dam' bad," they would say. "Don't know," I would have to say; "I've dodged clear of it." See that, Jukes? I have been thinking it all out this afternoon.'

He looked up again in his unseeing, unimaginative way. No one had ever heard him say so much at one time. Jukes, with his arms open in the doorway, was like a man invited to behold a miracle. Unbounded wonder was the intellectual meaning of his eye, while incredulity was seated in his whole countenance.

'A gale is a gale, Mr Jukes,' resumed the Captain, 'and a full-powered steamship has got to face it. There's just so much dirty weather knocking about the world, and the proper thing is to go through it with none of what old Captain Wilson of the *Melita* calls "storm strategy". The other day ashore I heard him hold forth about it to a lot of shipmasters who came in and sat at a table next to mine. It seemed to me the greatest nonsense. He was telling them how he out-manoeuvred, I think he said, a terrific gale, so that it never came nearer than fifty miles to him. A neat piece of head-work he called it. How he knew there was a terrific gale fifty miles off beats me altogether. It was like listening to a crazy man. I would have thought Captain Wilson was old enough to know better.'

Captain MacWhirr ceased for a moment, then said, 'It's your watch below, Mr Jukes?'

Jukes came to himself with a start. 'Yes, sir.'

'Leave orders to call me at the slightest change,' said the Captain. He reached up to put the book away, and tucked his legs upon the couch. 'Shut the door so that it don't fly open, will you? I can't stand a door banging. They've put a lot of rubbishy locks into this ship, I must say.'

Captain MacWhirr closed his eyes.

He did so to rest himself. He was tired, and he experienced that state of mental vacuity which comes at the end of an exhaustive discussion that had liberated some belief matured in the course of meditative years. He had indeed been making his confession of faith, had he only known it; and its effect was to make Jukes, on the other side of the door, stand scratching his head for a good while.

Captain MacWhirr opened his eyes.

He thought he must have been asleep. What was that loud

166

noise? Wind? Why had he not been called? The lamp wriggled in its gimbals, the barometer swung in circles, the table altered its slant every moment; a pair of limp sea-boots with collapsed tops went sliding past the couch. He put out his hand instantly, and captured one.

Jukes's face appeared in a crack of the door: only his face, very red, with staring eyes. The flame of the lamp leaped, a piece of paper flew up, a rush of air enveloped Captain MacWhirr. Beginning to draw on the boot, he directed an expectant gaze at Jukes's swollen, excited features.

'Came on like this,' shouted Jukes, 'five minutes ago . . . all of a sudden.'

The head disappeared with a bang, and a heavy splash and patter of drops swept past the closed door as if a pailful of melted lead had been flung against the house. A whistling could be heard now upon the deep vibrating noise outside. The stuffy chart-room seemed as full of draughts as a shed. Captain MacWhirr collared the other sea-boot on its violent passage along the floor. He was not flustered, but he could not find at once the opening for inserting his foot. The shoes he had flung off were scurrying from end to end of the cabin, gambolling playfully over each other like puppies. As soon as he stood up he kicked at them viciously, but without effect.

He threw himself into the attitude of a lunging fencer, to reach after his oilskin coat; and afterwards he staggered all over the confined space while he jerked himself into it. Very grave, straddling his legs far apart, and stretching his neck, he started to tie deliberately the strings of his sou'-wester under his chin, with thick fingers that trembled slightly. He went through all the movements of a woman putting on her bonnet before a glass, with a strained, listening attention, as though he had expected every moment to hear the shout of his name in the confused clamour that had suddenly beset his ship. Its increase filled his ears while he was getting ready to go out and confront whatever it might mean. It was tumultuous and very loud – made up of the rush of the wind, the crashes of the sea, with that prolonged deep vibration of the air, like the roll of an immense and remote drum beating the charge of the gale.

He stood for a moment in the light of the lamp, thick,

clumsy, shapeless in his panoply of combat, vigilant and red-faced.

'There's a lot of weight in this,' he muttered.

As soon as he attempted to open the door the wind caught it. Clinging to the handle, he was dragged out over the doorstep, and at once found himself engaged with the wind in a sort of personal scuffle whose object was the shutting of that door. At the last moment a tongue of air scurried in and licked out the flame of the lamp.

Ahead of the ship he perceived a great darkness lying upon a multitude of white flashes; on the starboard beam a few amazing stars drooped, dim and fitful, above an immense waste of broken seas, as if seen through a mad drift of smoke.

On the bridge a knot of men, indistinct and toiling, were making great efforts in the light of the wheel-house windows that shone mistily on their heads and backs. Suddenly darkness closed upon one pane, then on another. The voices of the lost group reached him after the manner of men's voices in a gale, in shreds and fragments of forlorn shouting snatched past the ear. All at once Jukes appeared at his side, yelling, with his head down.

'Watch – put in – wheelhouse shutters – glass – afraid – blow in.'

Jukes heard his commander upbraiding.

'This – come – anything – warning – call me.'

He tried to explain, with the uproar pressing on his lips.

'Light air – remained – bridge – sudden – north-east – could turn – though – you – sure – hear.'

They had gained the shelter of the weather-cloth, and could converse with raised voices, as people quarrel.

'I got the hands along to cover up all the ventilators. Good job I had remained on deck. I didn't think you would be asleep, and so . . . What did you say, sir? What?'

'Nothing,' cried Captain MacWhirr. 'I said – all right.'

'By all the powers! We've got it this time,' observed Jukes in a howl.

'You haven't altered her course?' inquired Captain Mac-Whirr, straining his voice.

'No, sir. Certainly not. Wind came out right ahead. And here comes the head sea.'

A plunge of the ship ended in a shock as if she had landed her forefoot upon something solid. After a moment of stillness a lofty flight of sprays drove hard with the wind upon their faces.

'Keep her at it as long as we can,' shouted Captain Mac-Whirr.

Before Jukes had squeezed the salt water out of his eyes all the stars had disappeared.

III

Jukes was as ready a man as any half-dozen young mates that may be caught by casting a net upon the waters; and though he had been somewhat taken aback by the startling viciousness of the first squall, he had pulled himself together on the instant, had called out the hands and had rushed them along to secure such openings about the deck as had not been already battened down earlier in the evening. Shouting in his fresh, stentorian voice, 'Jump, boys, and bear a hand!' he led in the work, telling himself the while that he had 'just expected this'.

But at the same time he was growing aware that this was rather more than he had expected. From the first stir of the air felt on his cheek the gale seemed to take upon itself the accumulated impetus of an avalanche. Heavy sprays enveloped the *Nan-Shan* from stem to stern, and instantly in the midst of her regular rolling she began to jerk and plunge as though she had gone mad with fright.

Jukes thought, 'This is no joke.' While he was exchanging explanatory yells with his captain, a sudden lowering of the darkness came upon the night, falling before their vision like something palpable. It was as if the masked lights of the world had been turned down. Jukes was uncritically glad to have his captain at hand. It relieved him as though that man had, by simply coming on deck, taken most of the gale's weight upon his shoulders. Such is the prestige, the privilege, and the burden of command.

Captain MacWhirr could expect no relief of that sort from any one on earth. Such is the loneliness of command. He was trying to see, with that watchful manner of a seaman who stares into the wind's eye as if into the eye of an adversary, to penetrate the hidden intention and guess the aim and force of the thrust. The strong wind swept at him out of a vast obscurity; he felt under his feet the uneasiness of his ship, and he could not even discern the shadow of her shape. He wished it were not so; and very still he waited, feeling stricken by a blind man's helplessness.

To be silent was natural to him, dark or shine. Jukes, at his elbow, made himself heard yelling cheerily in the gusts, 'We must have got the worst of it at once, sir.' A faint burst of lightning quivered all round, as if flashed into a cavern – into a black and secret chamber of the sea, with a floor of foaming crests.

It unveiled for a sinister, fluttering moment a ragged mass of clouds hanging low, the lurch of the long outlines of the ship, the black figures of men caught on the bridge, heads forward, as if petrified in the act of butting. The darkness palpitated down upon all this, and then the real thing came at last.

It was something formidable and swift, like the sudden smashing of a vial of wrath. It seemed to explode all round the ship with an overpowering concussion and a rush of great waters, as if an immense dam had been blown up to windward. In an instant the men lost touch of each other. This is the disintegrating power of a great wind: it isolates one from one's kind. An earthquake, a landslip, an avalanche, overtake a man incidentally, as it were – without passion. A furious gale attacks him like a personal enemy, tries to grasp his limbs, fastens upon his mind, seeks to rout his very spirit out of him.

Jukes was driven away from his commander. He fancied himself whirled a great distance through the air. Everything disappeared – even, for a moment, his power of thinking; but his hand had found one of the rail-stanchions. His distress was by no means alleviated by an inclination to disbelieve the reality of this experience. Though young, he had seen some bad weather, and had never doubted his ability to imagine the worst; but this was so much beyond his powers of fancy that it appeared incompatible with the existence of any ship what-ever. He would have been incredulous about himself in the same way, perhaps, had he not been so harassed by the necessity of exerting a wrestling effort against a force trying to tear him away from his hold. Moreover, the conviction of not being utterly destroyed returned to him through the sensations of being half-drowned, bestially shaken, and partly choked.

It seemed to him he remained there precariously alone with the stanchion for a long, long time. The rain poured on him, flowed, drove in sheets. He breathed in gasps; and sometimes the water he swallowed was fresh and sometimes it was salt. For the most part he kept his eyes shut tight, as if suspecting his sight might be destroyed in the immense flurry of the elements. When he ventured to blink hastily, he derived some moral support from the green gleam on the starboard light shining feebly upon the flight of rain and sprays. He was actually looking at it when its ray fell upon the uprearing sea which put it out. He saw the head of the wave topple over, adding the mite of its crash to the tremendous uproar raging around him, and almost at the same instant the stanchion was wrenched away from his embracing arms. After a crushing thump on his back he found himself suddenly afloat and borne upwards. His first irresistible notion was that the whole China Sea had climbed on the bridge. Then more sanely, he concluded himself gone overboard. All the time he was being tossed, flung, and rolled in great volumes of water, he kept on repeating mentally, with the utmost precipitation, the words: 'My God! My God! My God! My God!'

All at once, in a revolt of misery and despair, he formed the crazy resolution to get out of that. And he began to thresh about with his arms and legs. But as soon as he commenced his wretched struggles he discovered that he had becomed somehow mixed up with a face, and oilskin coat, somebody's boots. He clawed ferociously all these things in turn, lost them, found them again, lost them once more, and finally was himself caught in the firm clasp of a pair of stout arms. He returned the embrace closely round a thick solid body. He had found his captain.

They tumbled over and over, tightening their hug. Suddenly the water let them down with a brutal bang; and, stranded against the side of the wheelhouse, out of breath and bruised, they were left to stagger up in the wind and hold on where they could.

Jukes came out of it rather horrified, as though he had escaped some unparalleled outrage directed at his feelings. It weakened his faith in himself. He started shouting aimlessly to the man he could feel near him in the fiendish blackness, 'Is it you, sir? Is it you, sir?' till his temples seemed ready to burst. And he heard in answer a voice, as if crying far away, as if screaming to him fretfully from a very great distance, the one word 'Yes!' Other seas swept again over the bridge. He received them defencelessly right over his bare head, with both his hands engaged in holding.

The motion of the ship was extravagant. Her lurches had an appalling helplessness: she pitched as if taking a header into a void, and seemed to find a wall to hit every time. When she rolled she fell on her side headlong, and she would be righted back by such a demolishing blow that Jukes felt her reeling as a clubbed man reels before he collapses. The gale howled and scuffled about gigantically in the darkness, as though the entire world were one black gully. At certain moments the air streamed against the ship as if sucked through a tunnel with a concentrated solid force of impact that seemed to lift her clean out of the water and keep her up for an instant with only a quiver running through her from end to end. And then she would begin her tumbling again as if dropped back into a boiling cauldron. Jukes tried hard to compose his mind and judge things coolly.

The sea, flattened down in the heavier gust, would uprise and overwhelm both ends of the *Nan-Shan* in snowy rushes of foam, expanding wide, beyond both rails, into the night. And on this dazzling sheet, spread under the blackness of the clouds and emitting a bluish glow, Captain MacWhirr could catch a desolate glimpse of a few tiny specks black as ebony, the tops of the hatches, the battened campanions, the heads of the covered winches, the foot of a mast. This was all he could see of his ship. Her middle structure, covered by the bridge which bore him, his mate, the closed wheelhouse where a man was steering shut up with the fear of being swept overboard together with the whole thing in one great crash – her middle structure was like a half-tide rock awash upon a coast. It was like an outlying rock with the water boiling up, streaming over, pouring off, beating round – like a rock in the surf to which shipwrecked people cling before they let go – only it rose, it sank, it rolled continuously, without respite and rest, like a rock that should have miraculously struck adrift from a coast and gone wallowing upon the sea.

The *Nan-Shan* was being looted by the storm with a senseless, destructive fury: trysails torn out of the extra gaskets, double-lashed awnings blown away, bridge swept clean, weather-cloths burst, rails twisted, light-screens smashed — and two of the boats had gone already. They had gone unheard and unseen, melting, as it were, in the shock and smother of the wave. It was only later, when upon the white flash of another high sea hurling itself amidships, Jukes had a vision· of two pairs of davits leaping black and empty out of the solid blackness, with one overhauled fall flying and an iron-bound block capering in the air, that he became aware of what had happened within about three yards of his back.

He poked his head forward, groping for the ear of his commander. His lips touched it — big, fleshy, very wet. He cried in an agitated tone, 'Our boats are going now, sir.'

And again he heard that voice, forced and ringing feebly, but with a penetrating effect of quietness in the enormous discord of noises, as if sent out from some remote spot of peace beyond the black wastes of the gale; again he heard a man's voice — the frail and indomitable sound that can be made to carry an infinity of thought, resolution and purpose, that shall be pronouncing confident words on the last day, when heavens fall, and justice is done — again he heard it, and it was crying to him, as if from very, very far — 'All right.'

He thought he had not managed to make himself understood. 'Our boats — I say boats — the boats, sir! Two gone!'

The same voice, within a foot of him and yet so remote, yelled sensibly, 'Can't be helped.'

Captain MacWhirr had never turned his face, but Jukes caught some more words on the wind.

'What can — expect — when hammering through — such — Bound to leave — something behind — stands to reason.'

Watchfully Jukes listened for more. No more came. This was all Captain MacWhirr had to say; and Jukes could picture to himself rather than see the broad squat back before him. An impenetrable obscurity pressed down upon the ghostly glimmers of the sea. A dull conviction seized upon Jukes that there was nothing to be done.

If the steering-gear did not give way, if the immense volumes of water did not burst the deck in or smash one of the hatches, if the engines did not give up, if way could be kept on the ship against this terrific wind, and she did not bury herself in one of these awful seas, of whose white crest alone, topping high above her bows, he could now and then get a sickening glimpse – then there was a chance of her coming out of it. Something within him seemed to turn over, bringing uppermost the feeling that the *Nan-Shan* was lost.

'She's done for,' he said to himself, with a surprising mental agitation, as though he had discovered an unexpected meaning in this thought. One of these things was bound to happen. Nothing could be prevented now, and nothing could be remedied. The men on board did not count, and the ship could not last. This weather was too impossible.

Jukes felt an arm thrown heavily over his shoulders; and to this overture he responded with great intelligence by catching hold of his captain round the waist.

They stood clasped thus in the blind night, bracing each other against the wind, cheek to cheek and lip to ear, in the manner of two hulks lashed stem to stern together.

And Jukes heard the voice of his commander hardly any louder than before, but nearer, as though, starting to march athwart the prodigious rush of the hurricane, it had approached him, bearing that strange effect of quietness like the serene glow of a halo.

'D'ye know where the hands got to?' it asked, vigorous and evanescent at the same time, overcoming the strength of the wind, and swept away from Jukes instantly.

Jukes didn't know. They were all on the bridge when the real force of the hurricane struck the ship. He had no idea where they had crawled to. Under the circumstances they were nowhere, for all the use that could be made of them. Somehow the Captain's wish to know distressed Jukes.

'Want the hands, sir?' he cried, apprehensively.

'Ought to know,' asserted Captain MacWhirr. 'Hold hard.'

They held hard. An outburst of unchained fury, a vicious rush of the wind absolutely steadied the ship; she rocked only, quick and light like a child's cradle, for a terrific moment of suspense, while the whole atmosphere, as it seemed, streamed furiously past her, roaring away from the tenebrous earth.

It suffocated them, and with eyes shut they tightened their grasp. What from the magnitude of the shock might have been a column of water running upright in the dark, butted against the ship, broke short, and fell, on her bridge, crushingly, from on high, with a dead burying weight.

A flying fragment of that collapse, a mere splash, enveloped them in one swirl from their feet over their heads, filling violently their ears, mouths and nostrils with salt water. It knocked out their legs, wrenched in haste at their arms, seethed away swiftly under their chins; and opening their eyes, they saw the piled-up masses of foam dashing to and fro amongst what looked like the fragments of a ship. She had given way as if driven straight in. Their panting hearts yielded, too, before the tremendous blow; and all at once she sprang up again to her desperate plunging, as if trying to scramble out from under the ruins.

The seas in the dark seemed to rush from all sides to keep her back where she might perish. There was hate in the way she was handled, and a ferocity in the blows that fell. She was like a living creature thrown to the rage of a mob: hustled terribly, struck at, borne up, flung down, leaped upon. Captain Mac-Whirr and Jukes kept hold of each other, deafened by the noise, gagged by the wind; and the great physical tumult beating about their bodies, brought, like an unbridled display of passion, a profound trouble to their souls. One of those wild and appalling shrieks that are heard at times passing mysteriously overhead in the steady roar of a hurricane, swooped, as if borne on wings, upon the ship, and Jukes tried to outscream it.

'Will she live through this?'

The cry was wrenched out of his breast. It was as unintentional as the birth of a thought in the head, and he heard nothing of it himself. It all became extinct at once – thought, intention, effort – and of his cry the inaudible vibration added to the tempest waves of the air.

He expected nothing from it. Nothing at all. For indeed what answer could be made? But after a while he heard with amazement the frail and resisting voice in his ear, the dwarf sound, unconquered in the giant tumult.

'She may!'

It was a dull yell, more difficult to seize than a whisper. And presently the voice returned again, half submerged in the vast crashes, like a ship battling against the waves of an ocean.

'Let's hope so!' it cried – small, lonely and unmoved, a stranger to the visions of hope or fear; and it flickered into disconnected words: 'Ship . . . This . . . Never – Anyhow . . . for the best.' Jukes gave it up.

Then, as if it had come suddenly upon the one thing fit to withstand the power of a storm, it seemed to gain force and firmness for the last broken shouts:

'Keep on hammering . . . builders . . . good men . . . And chance it . . . engines . . . Rout . . . good man.'

Captain MacWhirr removed his arm from Jukes's shoulders, and thereby ceased to exist for his mate, so dark it was; Jukes, after a tense stiffening of every muscle, would let himself go limp all over. The gnawing of profound discomfort existed side by side with an incredible disposition to somnolence, as though he had been buffeted and worried into drowsiness. The wind would get hold of his head and try to shake it off his shoulders; his clothes, full of water, were as heavy as lead, cold and dripping like an armour of melting ice: he shivered – it lasted a long time; and with his hands closed hard on his hold, he was letting himself sink slowly into the depths of bodily misery. His mind became concentrated upon himself in an aimless, idle way, and when something pushed lightly at the back of his knees he nearly, as the saying is, jumped out of his skin.

In the start forward he bumped the back of Captain Mac-Whirr, who didn't move; and then a hand gripped his thigh. A lull had come, a menacing lull of the wind, the holding of a stormy breath – and he felt himself pawed all over. It was the boatswain. Jukes recognized these hands, so thick and enormous that they seemed to belong to some new species of man.

The boatswain had arrived on the bridge, crawling on all fours against the wind, and had found the chief mate's legs with the top of his head. Immediately he crouched and began to explore Jukes's person upwards with prudent, apologetic touches, as became an inferior.

He was an ill-favoured, undersized, gruff sailor of fifty, coarsely hairy, short-legged, long-armed, resembling an elderly ape. His strength was immense; and in his great lumpy paws, bulging like brown boxing-gloves on the end of furry fore-arms, the heaviest objects were handled like playthings. Apart from the grizzled pelt on his chest, the menacing demeanour and the hoarse voice, he had none of the classical attributes of his rating. His good nature almost amounted to imbecility: the men did what they liked with him, and he had not an ounce of initiative in his character, which was easy-going and talkative. For these reasons Jukes disliked him; but Captain MacWhirr, to Jukes's scornful disgust, seemed to regard him as a first-rate petty officer.

He pulled himself up by Jukes's coat, taking that liberty with the greatest moderation, and only so far as it was forced upon him by the hurricane.

'What is it, boss'n, what is it?' yelled Jukes, impatiently. What could that fraud of a boss'n want on the bridge? The typhoon had got on Jukes's nerves. The husky bellowings of the other, though unintelligible, seemed to suggest a state of lively satisfaction. There could be no mistake. The old fool was pleased with something.

The boatswain's other hand had found some other body, for in a changed tone he began to inquire: 'Is it you, sir? Is it you, sir?' The wind strangled his howls.

'Yes!' cried Captain MacWhirr.

IV

All that the boatswain, out of a superabundance of yells, could make clear to Captain MacWhirr was the bizarre intelligence that 'All them Chinamen in the fore 'tween deck have fetched away, sir.'

Jukes to leeward could hear these two shouting within six inches of his face, as you may hear on a still night half a mile away two men conversing across a field. He heard Captain MacWhirr's exasperated 'What? What?' and the strained pitch of the other's hoarseness. 'In a lump . . . seen them myself . . . Awful sight, sir . . . thought . . . tell you.'

Jukes remained indifferent, as if rendered irresponsible by

the force of the hurricane, which made the very thought of action utterly vain. Besides, being very young, he had found the occupation of keeping his heart completely steeled against the worst so engrossing that he had come to feel an overpowering dislike towards any other form of activity whatever. He was not scared; he knew this because, firmly believing he would never see another sunrise, he remained calm in that belief.

These are the moments of do-nothing heroics to which even good men surrender at times. Many officers of ships can no doubt recall a case in their experience when just such a trance of confounded stoicism would come all at once over a whole ship's company. Jukes, however, had no wide experience of men or storms. He conceived himself to be calm – inexorably calm; but as a matter of fact he was daunted; not abjectly, but only so far as a decent man may, without becoming loathsome to himself.

It was rather like a forced-on numbness of spirit. The long, long stress of a gale does it; the suspense of the interminably culminating catastrophe; and there is a bodily fatigue in the mere holding on to existence within the excessive tumult; a searching and insidious fatigue that penetrates deep into a man's breast to cast down and sadden his heart, which is incorrigible, and of all the gifts of the earth – even before life itself – aspires to peace.

Jukes was benumbed much more than he supposed. He held on – very wet, very cold, stiff in every limb; and in a momentary hallucination of swift visions (it is said that a drowning man thus reviews all his life) he beheld all sorts of memories altogether unconnected with his present situation. He remembered his father, for instance: a worthy business man, who at an unfortunate crisis in his affairs went quietly to bed and died forthwith in a state of resignation. Jukes did not recall these circumstances, of course, but remaining otherwise unconcerned he seemed to see distinctly the poor man's face; a certain game of nap played when quite a boy in Table Bay on board a ship, since lost with all hands; the thick eyebrows of his first skipper; and without any emotion, as he might years ago have walked listlessly into her room and found her sitting there with a book, he remembered his mother – dead, too, now

– the resolute woman, left badly off, who had been very firm in his bringing up.

It could not have lasted more than a second, perhaps not so much. A heavy arm had fallen about his shoulders; Captain MacWhirr's voice was speaking his name into his ear.

'Jukes! Jukes!'

He detected the tone of deep concern. The wind had thrown its weight on the ship, trying to pin her down amongst the seas. They made a clean breach over her, as over a deep-swimming log; and the gathered weight of crashes menaced monstrously from afar. The breakers flung out of the night with a ghostly light on their crests – the light of sea-foam that in a ferocious, boiling-up pale flash showed upon the slender body of the ship the toppling rush, the downfall, and the seething mad scurry of each wave. Never for a moment could she shake herself clear of the water; Jukes, rigid, perceived in her motion the ominous sign of haphazard floundering. She was no longer struggling intelligently. It was the beginning of the end; and the note of busy concern in Captain MacWhirr's voice sickened him like an exhibition of blind and pernicious folly.

The spell of the storm had fallen upon Jukes. He was penetrated by it, absorbed by it; he was rooted in it with a rigour of dumb attention. Captain MacWhirr persisted in his cries, but the wind got between them like a solid wedge. He hung round Jukes's neck as heavy as a millstone, and suddenly the sides of their heads knocked together.

'Jukes! Mr Jukes, I say!'

He had to answer that voice that would not be silenced. He answered in the customary manner: '. . . Yes, sir.'

And directly, his heart, corrupted by the storm that breeds a craving for peace, rebelled against the tyranny of training and command.

Captain MacWhirr had his mate's head fixed firm in the crook of his elbow, and pressed it to his yelling lips mysteriously. Sometimes Jukes would break in, admonishing hastily: 'Look out, sir!' or Captain MacWhirr would bawl an earnest exhortation to 'Hold hard, there!' and the whole black universe seemed to reel together with the ship. They paused. She floated yet. And Captain MacWhirr would resume his shouts.

'. . . Says . . . whole lot . . . fetched away . . . Ought to see . . . what's the matter.'

Directly the full force of the hurricane had struck the ship, every part of her deck became untenable; and the sailors, dazed and dismayed, took shelter in the port alleyway under the bridge. It had a door aft, which they shut; it was very black, cold, and dismal. At each heavy fling of the ship they would groan all together in the dark, and tons of water could be heard scuttling about as if trying to get at them from above. The boatswain had been keeping up a gruff talk, but a more unreasonable lot of men, he said afterwards, he had never been with. They were snug enough there, out of harm's way, and not wanted to do anything, either; and yet they did nothing but grumble and complain peevishly like so many sick kids. Finally, one of them said that if there had been at least some light to see each other's noses by, it wouldn't be so bad. It was making him crazy, he declared, to lie there in the dark waiting for the blamed hooker to sink.

'Why don't you step outside, then, and be done with it at once?' the boatswain turned on him.

This called up a shout of execration. The boatswain found himself overwhelmed with reproaches of all sorts. They seemed to take it ill that a lamp was not instantly created for them out of nothing. They would whine after a light to get drowned by – anyhow! And though the unreason of their revilings was patent – since no one could hope to reach the lamp-room, which was forward – he became greatly distressed. He did not think it was decent of them to be nagging at him like this. He told them so, and was met by general contumely. He sought refuge, therefore, in an embittered silence. At the same time their grumbling and sighing and muttering worried him greatly, but by-and-by it occurred to him that there were six globe lamps hung in the 'tween-deck, and that there could be no harm in depriving the coolies of one of them.

The *Nan-Shan* had an athwartship coal-bunker, which being at times used as cargo space, communicated by an iron door with the fore 'tween-deck. It was empty then, and its manhole was the foremost one in the alleyway. The boatswain could get in, therefore, without coming out on deck at all; but to his great surprise he found he could induce no one to help him in taking off the manhole cover. He groped for it all the same, but one of the crew lying in his way refused to budge.

'Why, I only want to get you that blamed light you are crying for,' he expostulated, almost pitifully.

Somebody told him to go and put his head in a bag. He regretted he could not recognize the voice, and that it was too dark to see, otherwise, as he said, he would have put a head on *that* son of a sea-cook, anyway, sink or swim. Nevertheless, he had made up his mind to show them he could get a light, if he were to die for it.

Through the violence of the ship's rolling, every movement was dangerous. To be lying down seemed labour enough. He nearly broke his neck dropping into the bunker. He fell on his back, and was sent shooting helplessly from side to side in the dangerous company of a heavy iron bar — a coal-trimmer's slice probably — left down there by somebody. This thing made him as nervous as though it had been a wild beast. He could not see it, the inside of the bunker coated with coal-dust being perfectly and impenetrably black; but he heard it sliding and clattering, and striking here and there, always in the neighbourhood of his head. It seemed to make an extraordinary noise, too — to give heavy thumps as though it had been as big as a bridge girder. This was remarkable enough for him to notice while he was flung from port to starboard and back again, and clawing desperately the smooth sides of the bunker in the endeavour to stop himself. The door into the 'tween-deck not fitting quite true, he saw a thread of dim light at the bottom.

Being a sailor, and a still active man, he did not want much of a chance to regain his feet; and as luck would have it, in scrambling up he put his hand on the iron slice, picking it up as he rose. Otherwise he would have been afraid of the thing breaking his legs, or at least knocking him down again. At first he stood still. He felt unsafe in this darkness that seemed to make the ship's motion unfamiliar, unforeseen, and difficult to counteract. He felt so much shaken for a moment that he dared not move for fear of 'taking charge again'. He had no mind to get battered to pieces in that bunker.

He had struck his head twice; he was dazed a little. He seemed to hear yet so plainly the clatter and bangs of the iron slice flying about his ears that he tightened his grip to prove to himself he had it there safely in his hand. He was vaguely amazed at the plainness with which down there he could hear the gale raging. Its howls and shrieks seemed to take on, in the emptiness of the bunker, something of the human character, of human rage and pain – being not vast but infinitely poignant. And there were, with every roll, thumps, too – profound, ponderous thumps, as if a bulk object of five-ton weight or so had got play in the hold. But there was no such thing in the cargo. Something on deck? Impossible. Or alongside? Couldn't be.

He thought all this quickly, clearly, competently, like a seaman, and in the end remained puzzled. This noise, though, came deadened from outside, together with the washing and pouring of water on deck above his head. Was it the wind? Must be. It made down there a row like the shouting of a big lot of crazed men. And he discovered in himself a desire for a light, too – if only to get drowned by – and a nervous anxiety to get out of that bunker as quickly as possible.

He pulled back the bolt: the heavy iron plate turned on its hinges; and it was though he had opened the door to the sounds of the tempest. A gust of hoarse yelling met him: the air was still; and the rushing of water overhead was covered by a tumult of strangled, throaty shrieks that produced an effect of desperate confusion. He straddled his legs the whole width of the doorway and stretched his neck. And at first he perceived only what he had come to seek: six small yellow flames swinging violently on the great body of the dusk.

It was stayed like the gallery of a mine, with a row of stanchions in the middle, and cross beams overhead, penetrating into the gloom ahead – indefinitely. And to port there loomed, like the caving in of one of the sides, a bulky mass with a slanting outline. The whole place, with the shadows and the shapes, moved all the time. The boatswain glared: the ship lurched to starboard, and a great howl came from that mass that had the slant of fallen earth.

Pieces of wood whizzed past. Planks, he thought, inexpressibly startled, and flinging back his head. At his feet a man went sliding over, open-eyed, on his back, straining with uplifted arms for nothing: and another came bounding like a detached stone with his head between his legs and his hands clenched. His pigtail whipped in the air; he made a grab at the boatswain's legs, and from his opened hand a bright white disc rolled against the boatswain's foot. He recognized a silver dollar, and yelled at it with astonishment. With a precipitated sound of trampling and shuffling of bare feet, and with guttural cries, the mound of writhing bodies piled up to port detached itself from the ship's side and sliding, inert and struggling, shifted to starboard, with a dull, brutal thump. The cries ceased. The boatswain heard a long moan through the roar and whistling of the wind; he saw an inextricable confusion of heads and shoulders, naked soles kicking upwards, fists raised, tumbling backs, legs, pigtails, faces.

'Good Lord!' he cried, horrified, and banged-to the iron door upon this vision.

This was what he had come on the bridge to tell. He could not keep it to himself; and on board ship there is only one man to whom it is worth while to unburden yourself. On his passage back the hands in the alleyway swore at him for a fool. Why didn't he bring that lamp? What the devil did the coolies matter to anybody? And when he came out, the extremity of the ship made what went on inside of her appear of little moment.

At first he thought he had left the alleyway in the very moment of her sinking. The bridge ladders had been washed away, but an enormous sea filling the after-deck floated him up. After that he had to lie on his stomach for some time, holding to a ring-bolt, getting his breath now and then, and swallowing salt water. He struggled farther on his hands and knees, too frightened and distracted to turn back. In this way he reached the after part of the wheelhouse. In that comparatively sheltered spot he found the second mate. The boatswain was pleasantly surprised—his impression being that everybody on deck must have been washed away a long time ago. He asked eagerly where the captain was.

The second mate was lying low, like a malignant little animal under a hedge.

'Captain? Gone overboard, after getting us into this mess.'

The mate, too, for all he knew or cared. Another fool. Didn't matter. Everybody was going by-and-by.

The boatswain crawled out again into the strength of the wind; not because he much expected to find anybody, he said, but just to get away from 'that man'. He crawled out as outcasts go to face an inclement world. Hence his great joy at finding Jukes and the Captain. But what was going on in the 'tween-deck was to him a minor matter by that time. Besides, it was difficult to make yourself heard. But he managed to convey the idea that the Chinamen had broken adrift together with their boxes, and that he had come up on purpose to report this. As to the hands, they were all right. Then, appeased, he subsided on the deck in a sitting posture, hugging with his arms and legs the stand of the engine-room telegraph – an iron casting as thick as a post. When that went, why, he expected he would go, too. He gave no more thought to the coolies.

Captain MacWhirr had made Jukes understand that he wanted him to go down below – to see.

'What am I to do then, sir?' And the trembling of his whole wet body caused Jukes's voice to sound like bleating.

'See first . . . Boss'n . . . says . . . adrift.'

'That boss'n is a confounded fool,' howled Jukes, shakily.

The absurdity of the demand made upon him revolted Jukes. He was as unwilling to go as if the moment he had left the deck the ship were sure to sink.

'I must know . . . can't leave . . .'

'They'll settle, sir.'

'Fight . . . boss'n says they fight . . . Why? Can't have . . . fighting . . . board ship . . . Much rather keep you here . . . case . . . I should . . . washed overboard myself . . . Stop it . . . some way. You see and tell me . . . through engine-room tube. Don't want you . . . come up here . . . too often. Dangerous . . . moving about . . . deck.'

Jukes, held with his head in chancery, had to listen to what seemed horrible suggestions.

'Don't want . . . you get lost . . . so long . . . ship isn't . . . Rout . . . Good man . . . Ship . . . may . . . through this . . . all right yet.'

All at once Jukes understood he would have to go.

'Do you think she may?' he screamed.

But the wind devoured the reply, out of which Jukes heard only the one word, pronounced with great energy '. . . Always . . .'

Captain MacWhirr released Jukes, and bending over the boatswain, yelled 'Get back with the mate.' Jukes only knew that the arm was gone off his shoulders. He was dismissed with his orders – to do what? He was exasperated into letting go his hold carelessly, and on the instant was blown away. It seemed to him that nothing could stop him from being blown right over the stern. He flung himself down hastily, and the boatswain, who was following, fell on him.

'Don't you get up yet, sir,' cried the boatswain. 'No hurry!'

A sea swept over. Jukes understood the boatswain to splutter that the bridge ladders were gone. 'I'll lower you down, sir, by your hands,' he screamed. He shouted also something about the smoke-stack being as likely to go overboard as not. Jukes thought it very possible, and imagined the fires were out, the ship helpless . . . The boatswain by his side kept on yelling. 'What? What is it?' Jukes cried distressfully; and the other repeated, 'What would my old woman say if she saw me now?'

In the alleyway, where a lot of water had got in and splashed in the dark, the men were still as death, till Jukes stumbled against one of them and cursed him savagely for being in the way. Two or three voices then asked, eager and weak, 'Any chance for us, sir?'

'What's the matter with you fools?' he said, brutally. He felt as though he could throw himself down amongst them and never move any more. But they seemed cheered; and in the midst of obsequious warnings, 'Look out! Mind that manhole lid, sir,' they lowered him into the bunker. The boatswain tumbled down after him, and as soon as he had picked himself up he remarked, 'She would say, "Serve you right, you old fool, for going to sea."'

The boatswain had some means, and made a point of alluding to them frequently. His wife – a fat woman – and two grown-up daughters kept a greengrocer's shop in the East-end of London.

In the dark, Jukes, unsteady on his legs, listened to a faint thunderous patter. A deadened screaming went on steadily at his elbow, as it were; and from above the louder tumult of the storm descended upon these near sounds. His head swam. To him, too, in that bunker, the motion of the ship seemed novel and menacing, sapping his resolution as though he had never been afloat before.

He had half a mind to scramble out again; but the remembrance of Captain MacWhirr's voice made this impossible. His orders were to go and see. What was the good of it? he wanted to know. Enraged, he told himself he would see – of course. But the boatswain, staggering clumsily, warned him to be careful how he opened that door; there was a blamed fight going on. And Jukes, as if in great bodily pain, desired irritably to know what the devil they were fighting for.

'Dollars! Dollars, sir. All their rotten chests got burst open. Blamed money skipping all over the place, and they are tumbling after it head over heels – tearing and biting like anything. A regular little hell in there.'

Jukes convulsively opened the door. The short boatswain peered under his arm.

One of the lamps had gone out, broken perhaps. Rancorous, guttural cries burst out loudly on their ears, and a strange panting sound, the working of all these straining breasts. A hard blow hit the side of the ship: water fell above with a stunning shock, and in the forefront of the gloom, where the air was reddish and thick, Jukes saw a head bang the deck violently, two thick calves waving on high, muscular arms twined round a naked body, a yellow-face, open-mouthed and with a set wild stare, look up and slide away. An empty chest clattered turning over; a man fell head first with a jump, as if lifted by a kick; and farther off, indistinct, others streamed like a mass of rolling stones down a bank, thumping the deck with their feet and flourishing their arms wildly. The hatchway ladder was loaded with coolies swarming on it like bees on a branch. They hung on the steps in a crawling, stirring cluster, beating madly with their fists the underside of the battened hatch, and the headlong rush of the water above was heard in the intervals of their yelling. The ship heeled over more, and they began to drop off: first one, then two, then all the rest went away together, falling straight off with a great cry.

Jukes was confounded. The boatswain, with gruff anxiety, begged him, 'Don't you go in there, sir.'

The whole place seemed to twist upon itself, jumping incessantly the while; and when the ship rose to a sea Jukes fancied that all these men would be shot upon him in a body. He backed out, swung the door to, and with trembling hands pushed at the bolt . . .

As soon as his mate had gone Captain MacWhirr, left alone on the bridge, sidled and staggered as far as the wheelhouse. Its door being hinged forward, he had to fight the gale for admittance, and when at last he managed to enter, it was with an instantaneous clatter and a bang, as though he had been fired through the wood. He stood within, holding on to the handle.

The steering-gear leaked steam, and in the confined space the glass of the binnacle made a shiny oval of light in a thin white fog. The wind howled, hummed, whistled, with sudden booming gusts that rattled the doors and shutters in the vicious patter of sprays. Two coils of lead-line and a small canvas bag hung on a long lanyard, swung wide off, and came back clinging to the bulkheads. The gratings underfoot were nearly afloat; with every sweeping blow of a sea, water squirted violently through the cracks all round the door, and the man at the helm had flung down his cap, his coat, and stood propped against the gear-casing in a striped cotton shirt open on his breast. The little brass wheel in his hands had the appearance of a bright and fragile toy. The cords of his neck stood hard and lean, a dark patch lay in the hollow of his throat, and his face was still and sunken as in death.

Captain MacWhirr wiped his eyes. The sea that had nearly taken him overboard had, to his great annoyance, washed his sou'-wester hat off his bald head. The fluffy, fair hair, soaked and darkened, resembled a mean skein of cotton threads festooned round his bare skull. His face, glistening with sea-water, bad been made crimson with the wind, with the sting of sprays. He looked as though he had come off sweating from before a furnace.

'You here?' he muttered, heavily.

The second mate had found his way into the wheelhouse some time before. He had fixed himself in a corner with his knees up, a fist pressed against each temple; and this attitude suggested rage, sorrow, resignation, surrender, with a sort of concentrated unforgiveness. He said mournfully and defiantly, 'Well, it's my watch below now: ain't it?'

The steam gear clattered, stopped, clattered again; and the helmsman's eyeballs seemed to project out of a hungry face as if the compass-card behind the binnacle glass had been meat. God knows how long he had been left there to steer, as if forgotten by all his shipmates. The bells had not been struck; there had been no reliefs; the ship's routine had gone down wind; but he was trying to keep her head north-north-east. The rudder might have been gone for all he knew, the fires out, the engines broken down, the ship ready to roll over like a corpse. He was anxious not to get muddled and lose control of her head because the compass-card swung far both ways, wriggling on the pivot, and sometimes seemed to whirl right round. He suffered from mental stress. He was horribly afraid, also, of the wheelhouse going. Mountains of water kept on tumbling against it. When the ship took one of her desperate dives the corners of his lips twitched.

Captain MacWhirr looked up at the wheelhouse clock. Screwed to the bulk-head, it had a white face on which the black hands appeared to stand quite still. It was half-past one in the morning.

'Another day,' he muttered to himself.

The second mate heard him, and lifting his head as one grieving amongst ruins, 'You won't see it break,' he exclaimed. His wrists and his knees could be seen to shake violently. 'No, by God! You won't . . .'

He took his face again between his fists.

The body of the helmsman had moved slightly, but his head didn't budge on his neck – like a stone head fixed to look one way from a column. During a roll that all but took his booted legs from under him, and in the very stagger to save himself, Captain MacWhirr said austerely, 'Don't you pay any attention to what that man says.' And then with an indefinable change of tone, very grave, he added, 'He isn't on duty.'

The sailor said nothing.

The hurricane boomed, shaking the little place, which

seemed air-tight; and the light of the binnacle flickered all the time.

'You haven't been relieved,' Captain MacWhirr went on, looking down. 'I want you to stick to the helm, though, as long as you can. You've got the hang of her. Another man coming here might make a mess of it. Wouldn't do. No child's play. And the hands are probably busy with a job down below . . . Think you can?'

The steering-gear leaped into an abrupt short clatter, stopped smouldering like an ember; and the still man, with a motionless gaze, burst out, as if all the passion in him had gone into his lips: 'By Heavens, sir! I can steer for ever if nobody talks to me.'

'Oh! aye! All right . . .' The Captain lifted his eyes for the first time to the man, '. . . Hackett.'

And he seemed to dismiss this matter from his mind. He stooped to the engine-room speaking-tube, blew in, and bent his head. Mr Rout below answered, and at once Captain MacWhirr put his lips to the mouthpiece.

With the uproar of the gale around him he applied alternately his lips and his ear, and the engineer's voice mounted to him, harsh and as if out of the heat of an engagement. One of the stokers was disabled, the others had given in, the second engineer and the donkey-man were firing-up. The third engineer was standing by the steam-valve. The engines were being tended by hand. How was it above?

'Bad enough. It mostly rests with you,' said Captain MacWhirr. Was the mate down there yet? No? Well, he would be presently. Would Mr Rout let him talk through the speaking-tube? – through the deck speaking-tube, because he – the Captain – was going out on the bridge directly. There was some trouble among the Chinamen. They were fighting, it seemed. Couldn't allow fighting anyhow . . .

Mr Rout had gone away, and Captain MacWhirr could feel against his ear the pulsation of the engines, like the beat of the ship's heart. Mr Rout's voice down there shouted something distantly. The ship pitched headlong, the pulsation leaped with a hissing tumult, and stopped dead. Captain MacWhirr's face was impassive, and his eyes were fixed aimlessly on the crouching shape of the second mate. Again Mr Rout's voice cried out in the depths, and the pulsating beats recommenced, with slow strokes – growing swifter.

Mr Rout had returned to the tube. 'It don't matter much what they do,' he said, hastily; and then, with irritation, 'She takes these dives as if she never meant to come up again.'

'Awful sea,' said the Captain's voice from above.

'Don't let me drive her under,' barked Solomon Rout up the pipe.

'Dark and rain. Can't see what's coming,' uttered the voice. 'Must – keep – her – moving – enough to steer – and chance it,' it went on to state distinctly.

'I am doing as much as I dare.'

'We are – getting – smashed up – a good deal up here,' proceeded the voice mildly. 'Doing – fairly well – though. Of course, if the wheelhouse should go . . .'

Mr Rout, bending an attentive ear, muttered peevishly something under his breath.

But the deliberate voice up there became animated to ask: 'Jukes turned up yet?' Then, after a short wait, 'I wish he would bear a hand. I want him to be done and come up here in case of anything. To look after the ship. I am all alone. The second mate's lost . . .'

'What?' shouted Mr Rout into the engine-room, taking his head away. Then up the tube he cried, 'Gone overboard?' and clapped his ear to.

'Lost his nerve,' the voice from above continued in a matter-of-fact tone. 'Damned awkward circumstance.'

Mr Rout, listening with bowed neck, opened his eyes wide at this. However, he heard something like the sounds of a scuffle and broken exclamations coming down to him. He strained his hearing; and all the time Beale, the third engineer, with his arms uplifted, held between the palms of his hands the rim of a little black wheel projecting at the side of a big copper pipe. He seemed to be poising it above his head, as though it were a correct attitude in some sort of game.

To steady himself, he pressed his shoulder against the white bulkhead, one knee bent, and a sweat-rag tucked in his belt hanging on his hip. His smooth cheek was begrimed and flushed, and the coal dust on his eyelids, like the black pencilling of a make-up, enhanced the liquid brilliance of the whites, giving to his youthful face something of a feminine, exotic and fascinating aspect. When the ship pitched he would with hasty movements of his hands screw hard at the little wheel.

'Gone crazy,' began the Captain's voice suddenly in the tube. 'Rushed at me .. Just now. Had to knock him down . . . This minute. You heard, Mr Rout?'

'The devil!' muttered Mr Rout. 'Look out, Beale!'

His shout rang out like the blast of a warning trumpet, between the iron walls of the engine-room. Painted white, they rose high into the dusk of the skylight, sloping like a roof; and the whole lofty space resembled the interior of a monument, divided by floors of iron grating, with lights flickering at different levels, and a mass of gloom lingering in the middle, within the columnar stir of machinery under the motionless swelling of the cylinders. A loud and wild resonance, made up of all the noises of the hurricane, dwelt in the still warmth of the air. There was in it the smell of hot metal, of oil, and a slight mist of steam. The blows of the sea seemed to traverse it in an unringing, stunning shock, from side to side.

Gleams, like pale long flames, trembled upon the polish of metal; from the flooring below the enormous crank-heads emerged in their turns with a flash of brass and steel — going over; while the connecting-rods, big-jointed, like skeleton limbs, seemed to thrust them down and pull them up again with an irresistible precision. And deep in the half-light other rods dodged deliberately to and fro, crossheads nodded, discs of metal rubbed smoothly against each other, slow and gentle, in a commingling of shadows and gleams.

Sometimes all those powerful and unerring movements would slow down simultaneously, as if they had been the functions of a living organism, stricken suddenly by the blight of languor; and Mr Rout's eye would blaze darker in his long sallow face. He was fighting this fight in a pair of carpet slippers. A short shiny jacket barely covered his loins, and his white wrists protruded far out of the tight sleeves, as though the emergency had added to his stature, had lengthened his limbs, augmented his pallor, hollowed his eyes.

He moved, climbing high up, disappearing low down, with a restless, purposeful industry, and when he stood still, holding the guard-rail in front of the starting-gear, he would keep glancing to the right at the steam-gauge, at the water-gauge, fixed upon the white wall in the light of a swaying lamp. The mouths of two speaking-tubes gaped stupidly at his elbow, and the dial of the engine-room telegraph resembled a clock of large diameter, bearing on its face curt words instead of figures. The grouped letters stood out heavily black, around the pivot-head of the indicator, emphatically symbolic of loud exclamations: AHEAD, ASTERN, SLOW, HALF, STAND BY; and the fat black hand pointed downwards to the word FULL, which, thus singled out, captured the eye as a sharp cry secures attention.

The wood-encased bulk of the low-pressure cylinder, frowning portly from above, emitted a faint wheeze at every thrust, and except for that low hiss the engines worked their steel limbs headlong or slow with a silent, determined smoothness. And all this, the white walls, the moving steel, the floor plates under Solomon Rout's feet, the floors of iron grating above his head, the dusk and the gleams, uprose and sank continuously, with one accord, upon the harsh wash of the waves against the ship's side. The whole loftiness of the place, booming hollow to the great voice of the wind, swayed at the top like a tree, would go over bodily, as if borne down this way and that by the tremendous blasts.

'You've got to hurry up,' shouted Mr Rout, as soon as he saw Jukes appear in the stokehold doorway.

Jukes's glance was wandering and tipsy; his red face was puffy, as though he had overslept himself. He had had an arduous road, and had travelled over it with immense vivacity, the agitation of his mind corresponding to the exertions of his body. He had rushed up out of the bunker, stumbling in the dark alleyway amongst a lot of bewildered men who, trod upon, asked 'What's up, sir?' in awed mutters all round him — down the stokehold ladder, missing many iron rungs in his hurry, down into a place deep as a well, black as Tophet, tipping over back and forth like a see-saw. The water in the bilges thundered at each roll, and lumps of coal skipped to and fro, from end to end, rattling like an avalanche of pebbles on a slope of iron.

Somebody in there moaned with pain, and somebody else could be seen crouching over what seemed the prone body of a

dead man; a lusty voice blasphemed; and the glow under each
fire-door was like a pool of flaming blood radiating quietly in
a velvety blackness.

A gust of wind struck upon the nape of Jukes's neck and next
moment he felt it streaming about his wet ankles. The
stokehold ventilators hummed: in front of the six fire-doors
two wild figures, stripped to the waist, staggered and stooped,
wrestling with two shovels.

'Hallo! Plenty of draught now,' yelled the second engineer at
once, as though he had been all the time looking out for Jukes.
The donkeyman, a dapper little chap with a dazzling fair skin
and a tiny, gingery moustache, worked in a sort of mute
transport. They were keeping a full head of steam, and a
profound rumbling, as of an empty furniture van trotting over
a bridge, made a sustained bass to all the other noises of the
place.

'Blowing off all the time,' went on yelling the second. With a
sound as of a hundred scoured saucepans, the orifice of a
ventilator spat upon his shoulder a sudden gush of salt water,
and he volleyed a stream of curses upon all things on earth
including his own soul, ripping and raving, and all the time
attending to his business. With a sharp clash of metal the
ardent pale glare of the fire opened upon his bullet head,
showing his spluttering lips, his insolent face, and with another
clang closed like the white-hot wink of an iron eye.

Where's the blooming ship? Can you tell me? blast my eyes!
Under water – or what? It's coming down here in tons. Are the
condemned cowls gone to Hades? Hey? Don't you know
anything – you jolly sailor-man you . . . ?'

Jukes, after a bewildered moment, had been helped by a roll
to dart through; and as soon as his eyes took in the comparative vastness, peace and brilliance of the engine-room, the ship,
setting her stern heavily in the water, sent him charging head
down upon Mr Rout.

The chief's arm, long like a tentacle, and straightening as if
worked by a spring, went out to meet him, and deflected his
rush into a spin towards the speaking-tubes. At the same time
Mr Rout repeated earnestly:

'You've got to hurry up, whatever it is.'

Jukes yelled 'Are you there, sir?' and listened. Nothing.

Suddenly the roar of the wind fell straight into his ear, but presently a small voice shoved aside the shouting hurricane quietly.

'You, Jukes? – Well?'

Jukes was ready to talk: it was only time that seemed to be wanting. It was easy enough to account for everything. He could perfectly imagine the coolies battened down in the reeking 'tween-deck, lying sick and scared between the rows of chests. Then one of these chests – or perhaps several at once – breaking loose in a roll, knocking out others, sides splitting, lids flying open, and all these clumsy Chinamen rising up in a body to save their property. Afterwards every fling of the ship would hurl that tramping, yelling mob here and there, from side to side, in a whirl of smashed wood, torn clothing, rolling dollars. A struggle once started, they would be unable to stop themselves. Nothing could stop them now except main force. It was a disaster. He had seen it, and that was all he could say. Some of them must be dead, he believed. The rest would go on fighting . . .

He sent up his words, tripping over each other, crowding the narrow tube. They mounted as if into a silence of an enlightened comprehension dwelling alone up there with a storm. And Jukes wanted to be dismissed from the face of that odious trouble intruding on the great need of the ship.

V

He waited. Before his eyes the engines turned with slow labour, that in the moment of going off into a mad fling would stop dead at Mr Rout's shout, 'Look out, Beale!' They paused in an intelligent immobility, stilled in mid-stroke, a heavy crank arrested on the cant, as if conscious of danger and the passage of time. Then, with a 'Now, then!' from the chief, and the sound of a breath expelled through clenched teeth, they would accomplish the interrupted revolution and begin another.

There was the purdent sagacity of wisdom and the deliberation of enormous strength in their movements. This was their work – this patient coaxing of a distracted ship over the fury of the waves and into the very eye of the wind. At times Mr Rout's chin would sink on his breast, and he watched them with knitted eyebrows as if lost in thought.

The voice that kept the hurricane out of Jukes's ear began: 'Take the hands with you . . .' and left off unexpectedly.

'What could I do with them, sir?'

A harsh, abrupt, imperious clang exploded suddenly. The three pairs of eyes flew up to the telegraph dial to see the hand jump from FULL to STOP, as if snatched by a devil. And then these three men in the engine-room had the intimate sensation of a check upon the ship, of a strange shrinking, as if she had gathered herself for a desperate leap.

'Stop her!' bellowed Mr Rout.

Nobody – not even Captain MacWhirr, who alone on deck had caught sight of a white line of foam coming on at such a height that he couldn't believe his eyes – nobody was to know the steepness of that sea and the awful depth of the hollow the hurricane had scooped out behind the running wall of water.

It raced to meet the ship, and, with a pause, as of girding the loins, the *Nan-Shan* lifted her bows and leaped. The flames in all the lamps sank, darkening the engine-room. One went out. With a tearing crash and a swirling, raving tumult, tons of water fell upon the deck, as though the ship had darted under the foot of a cataract.

Down there they looked at each other, stunned.

'Swept from end to end, by God!' bawled Jukes.

She dipped into the hollow straight down, as if going over the edge of the world. The engine-room toppled forward menacingly, like the inside of a tower nodding in an earthquake. An awful racket, of iron things falling, came from the stokehold. She hung on this appalling slant long enough for Beale to drop on his hands and knees and begin to crawl as if he meant to fly on all fours out of the engine-room, and for Mr Rout to turn his head slowly, rigid, cavernous, with the lower jaw dropping. Jukes had shut his eyes, and his face in a moment became hopelessly blank and gentle, like the face of a blind man.

At last she rose slowly, staggering, as if she had to lift a mountain with her bows.

Mr Rout shut his mouth; Jukes blinked; and little Beale stood up hastily.

'Another one like this, and that's the last of her,' cried the chief.

He and Jukes looked at each other, and the same thought came into their heads. The Captain! Everything must have been swept away. Steering-gear gone – ship like a log. All over directly.

'Rush!' ejaculated Mr Rout thickly, glaring with enlarged, doubtful eyes at Jukes, who answered him by an irresolute glance.

The clang of the telegraph gong soothed them instantly. The black hand dropped in a flash from STOP to FULL.

'Now then, Beale!' cried Mr Rout.

The steam hissed low. The piston-rods slid in and out. Jukes put his ear to the tube. The voice was ready for him. It said: 'Pick up all the money. Bear a hand now. I'll want you up here.' And that was all.

'Sir?' called up Jukes. There was no answer.

He staggered away like a defeated man from the field of battle. He had got, in some way or other, a cut above his left eyebrow – a cut to the bone. He was not aware of it in the least: quantities of the China Sea, large enough to break his neck for him, had gone over his head, had cleaned, washed, and salted that wound. It did not bleed, but only gaped red: and this gash over the eye, his dishevelled hair, the disorder of his clothes, gave him the aspect of a man worsted in a fight with fists.

'Got to pick up the dollars.' He appealed to Mr Rout, smiling pitifully at random.

'What's that?' asked Mr Rout, wildly. 'Pick up . . . ? I don't care . . .' Then, quivering in every muscle, but with an exaggeration of paternal tone, 'Go away now, for God's sake. You deck people'll drive me silly. There's that second mate been going for the old man. Don't you know? You fellows are going wrong for want of something to do . . .'

At these words Jukes discovered in himself the beginnings of anger. Want of something to do – indeed . . . Full of hot scorn against the chief, he turned to go the way he had come. In the stokehold the plump donkeyman toiled with his shovel mutely, as if his tongue had been cut out; but the second was carrying on like a noisy, undaunted maniac, who had preserved his skill in the art of stoking under a marine boiler.

196

'Hallo, you wandering officer! Hey! Can't you get some of your slush-slingers to wind up a few of them ashes? I am getting choked with them there. Curse it! Hallo! Hey! Remember the articles: *Sailors and firemen to assist each other*. Hey! D'ye hear?'

Jukes was climbing out frantically, and the other, lifting up his face after him, howled, 'Can't you speak? What are you poking about here for? What's your game, anyhow?'

A frenzy possessed Jukes. By the time he was back amongst the men in the darkness of the alleyway, he felt ready to wring all their necks at the slightest sign of hanging back. The very thought of it exasperated him. *He* couldn't hang back. They shouldn't.

The impetuosity with which he came amongst them carried them along. They had already been excited and startled at all his comings and goings — by the fierceness and rapidity of his movements; and more felt than seen in his rushes, he appeared formidable — busied with matters of life and death that brooked no delay. At the first word he heard them drop into the bunker one after another obediently, with heavy thumps.

They were not clear as to what would have to be done. 'What is it? What is it?' they were asking each other. The boatswain tried to explain; the sounds of a great scuffle surprised them: and the mighty shocks, reverberating awfully in the black bunker, kept them in mind of their danger. When the boatswain threw open the door it seemed that an eddy of the hurricane, stealing through the iron sides of the ship, had set all these bodies whirling like dust: there came to them a confused uproar, a tempestuous tumult, a fierce mutter, gusts of screams dying away, and the tramping of feet mingling with the blows of the sea.

For a moment they glared amazed, blocking the doorway. Jukes pushed through them brutally. He said nothing, and simply darted in. Another lot of coolies on the ladder, struggling suicidally to break through the battened hatch to a swamped deck, fell off as before, and he disappeared under them like a man overtaken by a landslide.

The boatswain yelled excitedly: 'Come along. Get the mate out. He'll be trampled to death. Come on.'

They charged in, stamping on breasts, on fingers, on faces, catching their feet in heaps of clothing, kicking broken wood; but before they could get hold of him Jukes emerged waist deep in a multitude of clawing hands. In the instant he had been lost to view, all the buttons of his jacket had gone, its back had got split up to the collar, his waistcoat had been torn open. The central struggling mass of Chinamen went over to the roll, dark, indistinct, helpless, with a wild gleam of many eyes in the dim light of the lamps.

'Leave me alone — damm you. I am all right,' screeched Jukes. 'Drive them forward. Watch your chance when she pitches. Forward with 'em. Drive them against the bulkhead. Jam 'em up.'

The rush of the sailors into the seething 'tween-deck was like a splash of cold water into a boiling cauldron. The commotion sank for a moment.

The bulk of Chinamen were locked in such a compact scrimmage that, linking their arms and aided by an appalling dive of the ship, the seamen sent it forward in one great shove, like a solid block. Behind their backs small clusters and loose bodies tumbled from side to side.

The boatswain performed prodigious feats of strength. With his long arms open, and each great paw clutching at a stanchion, he stopped the rush of seven entwined Chinamen rolling like a boulder. His joints cracked; he said, 'Ha!' and they flew apart. But the carpenter showed the greater intelligence. Without saying a word to anybody he went back into the alleyway, to fetch several coils of cargo gear he had seen there — chain and rope. With these life-lines were rigged.

There was really no resistance. The struggle, however it began, had turned into a scramble of blind panic. If the coolies had started up after their scattered dollars they were by that time fighting only for their footing. They took each other by the throat merely to save themselves from being hurled about. Whoever got a hold anywhere would kick at the others who caught at his legs and hung on, till a roll sent them flying together across the deck.

The coming of the white devils was a terror. Had they come to kill? The individuals torn out of the ruck became very limp in the seamen's hands: some, dragged aside by the heels, were passive, like dead bodies, with open, fixed eyes. Here and there a coolie would fall on his knees as if begging for mercy; several, whom the excess of fear made unruly, were hit with hard fists between the eyes, and cowered; while those who were hurt submitted to rough handling, blinking rapidly without a plaint. Faces streamed with blood; there were raw places on the shaven heads, scratches, bruises, torn wounds, gashes. The broken porcelain out of the chests was mostly responsible for the latter. Here and there a Chinaman, wild-eyed, with his tail unplaited, nursed a bleeding sole.

They had been ranged closely, after having been shaken into submission, cuffed a little to allay excitement, addressed in gruff words of encouragement that sounded like promises of evil. They sat on the deck in ghastly, drooping rows, and at the end the carpenter, with two hands to help him, moved busily from place to place, setting taut and hitching the life-lines. The boatswain, with one leg and one arm embracing a stanchion, struggled with a lamp pressed to his breast, trying to get a light, and growling all the time like an industrious gorilla. The figures of seamen stooped repeatedly, with the movements of gleaners, and everything was being flung into the bunker: clothing, smashed wood, broken china, and the dollars, too, gathered up in men's jackets. Now and then a sailor would stagger towards the doorway with his arms full of rubbish; and dolorous, slanting eyes followed his movements.

With every roll of the ship the long rows of sitting Celestials would sway forward brokenly, and her headlong dives knocked together the line of shaven polls from end to end. When the wash of water rolling on the deck died away for a moment, it seemed to Jukes, yet quivering from his exertions, that in his mad struggle down there he had overcome the wind somehow: that a silence had fallen upon the ship, a silence in which the sea struck thunderously at her sides.

Everything had been cleared out of the 'tween-deck — all the wreckage, as the men said. They stood erect and tottering above the level of heads and drooping shoulders. Here and there a coolie sobbed for his breath. Where the high light fell, Jukes could see the salient ribs of one, the yellow, wistful face of another; bowed necks; or would meet a dull stare directed at his face. He was amazed that there had been no corpses; but the lot of them seemed at their last gasp, and they appeared to him more pitiful than if they had been all dead.

Suddenly one of the coolies began to speak. The light came and went on his lean, straining face; he threw his head up like a baying hound. From the bunker came the sounds of knocking and the tinkle of some dollars rolling loose; he stretched out his arm, his mouth yawned black, and the incomprehensible guttural hooting sounds, that did not seem to belong to a human language, penetrated Jukes with a strange emotion as if a brute had tried to be eloquent.

Two more started mouthing what seemed to Jukes fierce denunciations; the others stirred with grunts and growls. Jukes ordered the hands out of the 'tween-decks hurriedly. He left last himself, backing through the door, while the grunts rose to a loud murmur and hands were extended after him as after a malefactor. The boatswain shot the bolt, and remarked uneasily, 'Seems as if the wind had dropped, Sir.'

The seamen were glad to get back into the alleyway. Secretly each of them thought that at the last moment he could rush out on deck – and that was a comfort. There is something horribly repugnant in the idea of being drowned under a deck. Now they had done with the Chinamen, they again became conscious of the ship's position.

Jukes on coming out of the alleyway found himself up to the neck in the noisy water. He gained the bridge, and discovered he could detect obscure shapes as if his sight had become preternaturally acute. He saw faint outlines. They recalled not the familiar aspect of the *Nan-Shan*, but something remembered – an old dismantled steamer he had seen years ago rotting on a mudbank. She recalled that wreck.

There was no wind, not a breath, except the faint currents created by the lurches of the ship. The smoke tossed out of the funnel was settling down upon her deck. He breathed it as he passed forward. He felt the deliberate throb of the engines, and heard small sounds that seemed to have survived the great uproar: the knocking of broken fittings, the rapid tumbling of some piece of wreckage on the bridge. He perceived dimly the squat shape of his captain holding on to a twisted bridge-rail, motionless and swaying as if rooted to the planks. The unexpected stillness of the air oppressed Jukes.

'We have done it, sir,' he gasped.

'Thought you would,' said Captain MacWhirr.

'Did you?' murmured Jukes to himself.

'Wind fell all at once,' went on the Captain.

Jukes burst out: 'If you think it was an easy job —'

But the captain, clinging to the rail, paid no attention. 'According to the books the worst is not over yet.'

'If most of them hadn't been half dead with sea-sickness and fright, not one of us would have come out that 'tween-deck alive,' said Jukes.

'Had to do what's fair by them,' mumbled MacWhirr, stolidly. 'You don't find everything in books.'

'Why, I believe they would have risen on us if I hadn't ordered the hands out of that pretty quick,' continued Jukes with warmth.

After the whisper of their shouts, their ordinary tones, so distinct, rang out very loud to their ears in the amazing stillness of the air. It seemed to them they were talking in a dark and echoing vault.

Through a jagged aperture in the dome of clouds the light of a few stars fell upon the black sea, rising and falling confusedly. Sometimes the head of a watery cone would topple on board and mingle with the rolling flurry of foam on the swamped deck; and the *Nan-Shan* wallowed heavily at the bottom of a circular cistern of clouds. This ring of dense vapours, gyrating madly round the calm of the centre, encompassed the ship like a motionless and unbroken wall of an aspect inconceivably sinister. Within, the sea, as if agitated by an internal commotion, leaped in peaked mounds that jostled each other, slapping heavily against her sides; and a low moaning sound, the infinite plaint of the storm's fury, came from beyond the limits of the menacing calm. Captain Mac-Whirr remained silent, and Jukes's ready ear caught suddenly the faint, long-drawn roar of some immense wave rushing unseen under that thick blackness, which made the appalling boundary of his vision.

'Of course,' he started resentfully, 'they thought we had caught at the chance to plunder them. Of course! You said — pick up the money. Easier said than done. They couldn't tell what was in our heads. We came in, smash — right into the middle of them. Had to do it by a rush.'

'As long as it's done . . .' mumbled the Captain, without attempting to look at Jukes. 'Had to do what's fair.'

'We shall find yet there's the devil to pay when this is over,' said Jukes, feeling very sore. 'Let them only recover a bit, and you'll see. They will fly at our throats, sir. Don't forget, sir, she isn't a British ship now. These brutes know it well, too. The damned Siamese flag.'

'We are on board, all the same,' remarked Captain MacWhirr.

'The trouble's not over yet,' insisted Jukes, prophetically, reeling and catching on. 'She's a wreck,' he added, faintly.

'The trouble's not over yet,' assented Captain MacWhirr, half aloud . . . 'Look out for her a minute.'

'Are you going off the deck, sir?' asked Jukes, hurriedly, as if the storm were sure to pounce upon him as soon as he had been left alone with the ship.

He watched her, battered and solitary, labouring heavily in a wild scene of mountainous black waters lit by the gleams of distant worlds. She moved slowly, breathing into the still core of the hurricane the excess of her strength in a white cloud of steam — and the deep-toned vibration of the escape was like the defiant trumpeting of a living creature of the sea impatient for the renewal of the contest. It ceased suddenly. The still air moaned. Above Jukes's head a few stars shone into a pit of black vapours. The inky edge of the cloud-disc frowned upon the ship under the patch of glittering sky. The stars, too, seemed to look at her intently, as if for the last time, and the cluster of their splendour sat like a diadem on a lowering brow.

Captain MacWhirr had gone into the chart-room. There was no light there; but he could feel the disorder of that place where he used to live tidily. His armchair was upset. The books had tumbled out on the floor: he scrunched a piece of glass under his boot. He groped for the matches, and found a box on a shelf with a deep ledge. He struck one, and puckering the corners of his eyes, held out the little flame towards the barometer whose glittering top of glass and metals nodded at him continuously.

It stood very low — incredibly low, so low that Captain

MacWhirr grunted. The match went out, and hurriedly he extracted another, with thick, stiff fingers.

Again a little flame flared up before the nodding glass and metal of the top. His eyes looked at it narrowed with attention, as if expecting an imperceptible sign. With his grave face he resembled a booted and misshapen pagan burning incense before the oracle of a Joss. There was no mistake. It was the lowest reading he had ever seen in his life.

Captain MacWhirr emitted a low whistle. He forgot himself till the flame diminished to a blue spark, burnt his fingers and vanished. Perhaps something had gone wrong with the thing!

There was an aneroid glass screwed above the couch. He turned that way, struck another match, and discovered the white face of the other instrument looking at him from the bulkhead, meaningly, not to be gainsaid, as though the wisdom of men were made unerring by the indifference of matter. There was no room for doubt now. Captain MacWhirr pshawed at it, and threw the match down.

The worst was to come, then – and if the books were right this worst would be very bad. The experience of the last six hours had enlarged his conception of what heavy weather could be like. 'It'll be terrific,' he pronounced, metally. He had not consciously looked at anything by the light of the matches except at the barometer; and yet somehow he had seen that his water-bottle and the two tumblers had been flung out of their stand. It seemed to give him a more intimate knowledge of the tossing the ship had gone through. 'I wouldn't have believed it,' he thought. And his table had been cleared, too; his rulers, his pencils, the inkstand – all the things that had their safe appointed places – they were gone, as if a mischievous hand had plucked them out one by one and flung them on the wet floor. The hurricane had broken in upon the orderly arrangements of his privacy. This had never happened before, and the feeling of dismay reached the very seat of his composure. And the worst was to come yet! He was glad the trouble in the 'tween-deck had been discovered in time. If the ship had to go after all, then, at least, she wouldn't be going to the bottom with a lot of people in her fighting teeth and claw. That would have been odious. And in that feeling there was a humane intention and a vague sense of the fitness of things.

These instantaneous thoughts were yet in their essence heavy and slow, partaking of the nature of the man. He extended his hand to put back the matchbox in its corner of the shelf. There were always matches there – by his order. The steward had his instructions impressed upon him long before. 'A box . . . just there, see? Not so very full . . . where I can put my hand on it, steward. Might want a light in a hurry. Can't tell on board ship *what* you might want in a hurry. Mind, now.'

And of course on his side he would be careful to put it back in its place scrupulously. He did so now, but before he removed his hand it occurred to him that perhaps he would never have occasion to use that box any more. The vividness of the thought checked him and for an infinitesimal fraction of a second his fingers closed again on the small object as though it had been the symbol of all these little habits that chain us to the weary round of life. He released it at last, and letting himself fall on the settee, listened for the first sounds of returning wind.

Not yet. He heard only the wash of water, the heavy splashes, the dull shocks of the confused seas boarding his ship from all sides. She would never have a chance to clear her decks.

But the quietude of the air was startlingly tense and unsafe, like a slender hair holding a sword suspended over his head. By this awful pause the storm penetrated the defences of the man and unsealed his lips. He spoke out in the solitude and the pitch darkness of the cabin, as if addressing another being awakened within his breast.

'I shouldn't like to lose her,' he said half aloud.

He sat unseen, apart from the sea, from his ship, isolated, as if withdrawn from the very current of his own existence, where such freaks as talking to himself surely had no place. His palms reposed on his knees, he bowed his short neck and puffed heavily, surrendering to a strange sensation of weariness he was not enlightened enough to recognize for the fatigue of mental stress.

From where he sat he could reach the door of a washstand locker. There should have been a towel there. There was. Good. . . . He took it out, wiped his face, and afterwards went on rubbing his wet head. He towelled himself with energy in the dark, and then remained motionless with the towel on his knees. A moment passed, of a stillness so profound that no one could have guessed there was a man sitting in that cabin. Then a murmur arose.

'She may come out of it yet.'

When Captain MacWhirr came out on deck, which he did brusquely, as though he had suddenly become conscious of having stayed away too long, the calm had lasted already more than fifteen minutes – long enough to make itself intolerable even to his imagination. Jukes, motionless on the forepart of the bridge, began to speak at once. His voice, blank and forced as though he were talking through hard-set teeth, seemed to flow away on all sides into the darkness, deepening again upon the sea.

'I had the wheel relieved. Hackett began to sing out that he was done. He's lying in there alongside the steering-gear with a face like death. At first I couldn't get anybody to crawl out and relieve the poor devil. That boss'en's worse than no good, I always said. Thought I would have had to go myself and haul out one of them by the neck.'

'Ah, well,' muttered the Captain. He stood watchful by Jukes's side.

'The second mate's in there, too, holding his head. Is he hurt, sir?'

'No – crazy,' said Captain MacWhirr, curtly.

'Looks as if he had a tumble, though.'

'I had to give him a push,' explained the Captain.

Jukes gave an impatient sigh.

'It will come very sudden,' said Captain MacWhirr, 'and from over there, I fancy. God only knows though. These books are only good to muddle your head and make you jumpy. It will be bad, and there's an end. If we only can steam her round in time to meet it . . .'

A minute passed. Some of the stars winked rapidly and vanished.

'You left them pretty safe?' began the Captain abruptly, as though the silence were unbearable.

'Are you thinking of the coolies, sir? I rigged life-lines all ways across that 'tween-deck.'

'Did you? Good idea, Mr Jukes.'

'I didn't . . . think you cared to . . . know,' said Jukes – the lurching of the ship cut his speech as though somebody had been jerking him around while he talked – 'how I got on with . . . that infernal job. We did it. And it may not matter in the end.'

'Had to do what's fair, for all – they are only Chinamen. Give them the same chance with ourselves – hang it all. She isn't lost yet. Bad enough to be shut up below in a gale –'

'That's what I thought when you gave me the job, sir,' interjected Jukes, moodily.

'– without being battered to pieces,' pursued Captain Mac-Whirr with rising vehemence. 'Couldn't let that go on in my ship, if I knew she hadn't five minutes to live. Couldn't bear it, Mr Jukes.'

A hollow echoing noise, like that of a shout rolling in a rocky chasm, approached the ship and went away again. The last star, blurred, enlarged, as if returning to the fiery mist of its beginning, struggled with the colossal depth of blackness hanging over the ship – and went out.

'Now for it!' muttered Captain MacWhirr. 'Mr Jukes.'

'Here, sir.'

The two men were growing indistinct to each other.

'We must trust her to go through it and come out on the other side. That's plain and straight. There's no room for Captain Wilson's storm-strategy here.'

'No, sir.'

'She will be smothered and swept again for hours,' mumbled the Captain. 'There's not much left by this time above deck for the sea to take away – unless you or me.'

'Both, sir,' whispered Jukes, breathlessly.

'You are always meeting trouble half way, Jukes,' Captain MacWhirr remonstrated quaintly. 'Though it's a fact that the second mate is no good. D'ye hear, Mr Jukes? You would be left alone if . . .'

Captain MacWhirr interrupted himself, and Jukes, glancing on all sides, remained silent.

'Don't you be put out by anything,' the Captain continued, mumbling rather fast. 'Keep her facing it. They may say what they like, but the heaviest seas run with the wind. Facing it –

always facing it – that's the way to get through. You are a young sailor. Face it. That's enough for any man. Keep a cool head.'

'Yes, sir,' said Jukes, with a flutter of the heart.

In the next few seconds the Captain spoke to the engine-room and got an answer.

For some reason Jukes experienced an access of confidence, a sensation that came from outside like a warm breath, and made him feel equal to every demand. The distant muttering of the darkness stole into his ears. He noted it unmoved, out of that sudden belief in himself, as a man safe in a shirt of mail would watch a point.

The ship laboured without intermission amongst the black hills of water, paying with this hard tumbling the price of her life. She rumbled in her depths, shaking a white plummet of steam into the night, and Jukes's thought skimmed like a bird through the engine-room, where Mr Rout – good man – was ready. When the rumbling ceased it seemed to him that there was a pause of every sound, a dead pause in which Captain MacWhirr's voice rang out startlingly.

'What's that? A puff of wind?' – it spoke much louder than Jukes had ever heard it before – 'On the bow. That's right. She may come out of it yet.'

The mutter of the winds drew near apace. In the forefront could be distinguished a drowsy waking plaint passing on, and far off the growth of a multiple clamour, marching and expanding. There was the throb as of many drums in it, a vicious rushing note, and like the chant of a tramping multitude.

Jukes could no longer see his captain distinctly. The dark-ness was absolutely piling itself upon the ship. At most he made out movements, a hint of elbows spread out, of a head thrown up.

Captain MacWhirr was trying to do up the top button of his oilskin coat with unwonted haste. The hurricane, with its power to madden the seas, to sink ships, to uproot trees, to overturn strong walls and dash the very birds of the air to the ground, had found this taciturn man in its path, and, doing its utmost, had managed to wring out a few words. Before the renewed wrath of winds swooped on his ship, Captain Mac-

Whirr was moved to declare, in a tone of vexation, as it were: 'I wouldn't like to lose her.'

He was spared that annoyance.

<h1 style="text-align:center">VI</h1>

On a bright sunshiny day, with the breeze chasing her smoke far ahead, the *Nan-Shan* came into Fu-chau. Her arrival was at once noticed on shore, and the seamen in harbour said: 'Look! Look at that steamer. What's that? Siamese – isn't she? Just look at her!'

She seemed, indeed, to have been used as a running target for the secondary batteries of a cruiser. A hail of minor shells could not have given her upper works a more broken, torn, and devastated aspect: and she had about her the worn, weary air of ships coming from the far ends of the world – and indeed with truth, for in her short passage she had been very far; sighting, verily, even the coast of the Great Beyond, whence no ship ever returns to give up her crew to the dust of the earth. She was incrusted and grey with salt to the trucks of her masts and to the top of her funnel; as though (as some facetious seaman said) 'the crowd on board had fished her out somewhere from the bottom of the sea and brought her in here for salvage'. And further, excited by the felicity of his own wit, he offered to give five pounds for her – 'as she stands'.

Before she had been quite an hour at rest, a meagre little man, with a red-tipped nose and a face cast in an angry mould, landed from a sampan on the quay of the Foreign Concession, and incontinently turned to shake his fist at her.

A tall individual, with legs much too thin for a rotund stomach, and with watery eyes, strolled up and remarked, 'Just left her – eh? Quick work.'

He wore a soiled suit of blue flannel with a pair of dirty cricketing shoes; a dingy grey moustache drooped from his lip, and daylight could be seen in two places between the rim and the crown of his hat.

'Hallo! what are you doing here?' asked the ex-second mate of the *Nan-Shan*, shaking hands hurriedly.

'Standing by for a job – chance worth taking – got a quiet

hint,' explained the man with the broken hat, in jerky, apathetic wheezes.

The second shook his fist again at the *Nan-Shan*. 'There's a fellow there that ain't fit to have the command of a scow,' he declared, quivering with passion, while the other looked about listlessly.

'Is there?'

But he caught sight on the quay of a heavy seaman's chest, painted brown under a fringed sailcloth cover, and lashed with new manila line. He eyed it with awakened interest.

'I would talk and raise trouble if it wasn't for that damned Siamese flag. Nobody to go to – or I would make it hot for him. The fraud! Told his chief engineer – that's another fraud for you – I had lost my nerve. The greatest lot of ignorant fools that ever sailed the seas. No! You can't think . . .'

'Got your money all right?' inquired his seedy acquaintance suddenly.

'Yes. Paid me off on board,' raged the second mate. ' "Get your breakfast on shore," says he.'

'Mean skunk!' commented the tall man, vaguely, and passed his tongue on his lips. 'What about having a drink of some sort?'

'He struck me,' hissed the second mate.

'No! Struck! You don't say?' The man in blue began to bustle about sympathetically. 'Can't possibly talk here. I want to know all about it. Struck – eh? Let's get a fellow to carry your chest. I know a quiet place where they have some bottled beer . . .'

Mr Jukes, who had been scanning the shore through a pair of glasses, informed the chief engineer afterwards that 'our late second mate hasn't been long in finding a friend. A chap looking uncommonly like a bummer. I saw them walk away together from the quay.'

The hammering and banging of the needful repairs did not disturb Captain MacWhirr. The steward found in the letter he wrote, in a tidy chart-room, passages of such absorbing interest that twice he was nearly caught in the act. But Mrs MacWhirr, in the drawing-room of the forty-pound house, stifled a yawn – perhaps out of self-respect – for she was alone.

She reclined in a plush-bottomed and gilt hammock-chair

near a tiled fireplace, with Japanese fans on the mantel and a glow of coals in the grate. Lifting her hands, she glanced wearily here and there into the many pages. It was not her fault they were so prosy, so completely uninteresting – from 'My darling wife' at the beginning, to 'Your loving husband' at the end. She couldn't be really expected to understand all these ship affairs. She was glad, of course, to hear from him, but she had never asked herself why, precisely.

'. . . They are called typhoons . . . The mate did not seem to like it . . . Not in books . . . Couldn't think of letting it go on . . .'

The paper rustled sharply. '. . . A calm that lasted more than twenty minutes,' she read perfunctorily; and the next words her thoughtless eyes caught, on the top of another page, were: 'see you and the children again . . .' She had a movement of impatience. He was always thinking of coming home. He had never had such a good salary before. What was the matter now?

It did not occur to her to turn back overleaf to look. She would have found it recorded there that betweeen 4 and 6 a.m. on December 25th, Captain MacWhirr did actually think that his ship could not possibly live another hour in such a sea, and that he would never see his wife and children again. Nobody was to know this (his letters got mislaid so quickly) – nobody whatever but the steward, who had been greatly impressed by that disclosure. So much so, that he tried to give the cook some idea of the 'narrow squeak we all had' by saying solemnly, 'The old man himself had a dam' poor opinion of our chance.'

'How do you know?' asked, contemptuously, the cook, an old soldier. 'He hasn't told you, maybe?'

'Well, he did give me a hint to that effect,' the steward brazened it out.

'Get along with you! He will be coming to tell *me* next,' jeered the old cook, over his shoulder.

Mrs MacWhirr glanced farther, on the alert. '. . . Do what's fair . . . Miserable objects . . . Only three, with a broken leg each, and one . . . Thought had better keep the matter quiet . . . hope to have done the fair thing . . .'

She let fall her hands. No: there was nothing more about coming home. Must have been merely expressing a pious wish.

Mrs MacWhirr's mind was set at ease, and a black marble clock, priced by the local jeweller at £3 18s. 6d., had a discreet stealthy tick.

The door flew open, and a girl in the long-legged, short-frocked period of existence flung into the room. A lot of colourless, rather lanky hair was scattered over her shoulders. Seeing her mother, she stood still, and directed her pale prying eyes upon the letter.

'From father,' murmured Mrs MacWhirr. 'What have you done with your ribbon?'

The girl put her hands up to her head and pouted.

'He's well,' continued Mrs MacWhirr, languidly. 'At least I think so. He never says.' She had a little laugh. The girl's face expressed a wandering indifference, and Mrs MacWhirr surveyed her with fond pride.

'Go and get your hat,' she said after a while. 'I am going out to do some shopping. There is a sale at Linom's.'

'Oh, how jolly!' uttered the child, impressively, in unexpectedly grave vibrating tones, and bounded out of the room.

It was a fine afternoon, with a grey sky and dry sidewalks. Outside the draper's Mrs MacWhirr smiled upon a woman in a black mantle of generous proportions armoured in jet and crowned with flowers blooming falsely above a bilious matronly countenance. They broke into a swift little babble of greetings and exclamations both together, very hurried, as if the street were ready to yawn open and swallow all that pleasure before it could be expressed.

Behind them the high glass doors were kept on the swing. People couldn't pass, men stood aside waiting patiently, and Lydia was absorbed in poking the end of her parasol between the stone flags. Mrs MacWhirr talked rapidly.

'Thank you very much. He's not coming home yet. Of course it's very sad to have him away, but it's such a comfort to know he keeps so well.' Mrs MacWhirr drew breath. 'The climate there agrees with him,' she added, beamingly, as if poor MacWhirr had been away touring in China for the sake of his health.

Neither was the chief engineer coming home yet. Mr Rout knew too well the value of a good billet.

'Solomon says wonders will never cease,' cried Mrs Rout

joyously at the old lady in her armchair by the fire. Mr Rout's mother moved slightly, her withered hands lying in black half-mittens on her lap.

The eyes of the engineer's wife fairly danced on the paper. 'That captain of the ship he is in – a rather simple man, you remember, mother? – has done something rather clever, Solomon says.'

'Yes, my dear,' said the old woman meekly, sitting with bowed silvery head, and that air of inward stillness characteristic of very old people who seem lost in watching the last flickers of life. 'I think I remember.'

Solomon Rout, Old Sol, Father Sol, the Chief, 'Rout, good man' – Mr Rout, the condescending and paternal friend of youth, had been the baby of her many children – all dead by this time. And she remembered him best as a boy of ten – long before he went away to serve his apprenticeship in some great engineering works in the North. She had seen so little of him since, she had gone through so many years, that she had now to retrace her steps very far back to recognize him plainly in the mist of time. Sometimes it seemed that her daughter-in-law was talking of some strange man.

Mrs Rout junior was disappointed. 'H'm. H'm.' She turned the page. 'How provoking! He doesn't say what it is. Says I couldn't understand how much there was in it. Fancy! What could it be so very clever? What a wretched man not to tell us!'

She read on without further remark soberly, and at last sat looking into the fire. The chief wrote just a word or two of the typhoon; but something had moved him to express an increased longing for the companionship of the jolly woman. 'If it hadn't been that mother must be looked after, I would send you your passage-money to-day. You could set up a small house out here. I would have a chance to see you sometimes then. We are not growing younger . . .'

'He's well, mother,' sighed Mrs Rout, rousing herself.

'He always was a strong healthy boy,' said the old woman, placidly.

But Mr Jukes's account was really animated and very full. His friend in the Western Ocean trade imparted it freely to the other officers of his liner. 'A chap I know writes to me about an extraordinary affair that happened on board his ship in that typhoon – you know – that we read of in the papers two months ago. It's the funniest thing! Just see for yourself what he says. I'll show you his letter.'

There were phrases in it calculated to give the impression of light-hearted, indomitable resolution. Jukes had written them in good faith, for he felt thus when he wrote. He described with lurid effect the scenes in the 'tween-deck. '. . . It struck me in a flash that those confounded Chinamen couldn't tell we weren't a desperate kind of robbers. 'Tisn't good to part the Chinaman from his money if he is the stronger party. We need have been desperate indeed to go thieving in such weather, but what could these beggars know of us? So, without thinking of it twice, I got the hands away in a jiffy. Our work was done – that the old man had set his heart on. We cleared out without staying to inquire how they felt. I am convinced that if they had not been so unmercifully shaken, and afraid – each individual one of them – to stand up, we would have been torn to pieces. Oh! It was pretty complete, I can tell you; and you may run to and fro across the Pond to the end of time before you find yourself with such a job on your hands.'

After this he alluded professionally to the damage done to the ship, and went on thus:

'It was when the weather quieted down that the situation became confoundedly delicate. It wasn't made any better by us having been lately transferred to the Siamese flag; though the skipper can't see that it makes any difference – "as long as *we* are on board" – he says. There are feelings that this man simply hasn't got – and there's an end of it. You might just as well try to make a bedpost understand. But apart from this it is an infernally lonely state for a ship to be going about the China seas with no proper consuls, not even a gunboat of her own anywhere, nor a body to go to in case of some trouble.

'My notion was to keep these Johnnies under hatches for another fifteen hours or so; as we weren't much farther than that from Fu-chau. We would find there, most likely, some sort of a man-of-war, and once under her guns we were safe enough; for surely any skipper of a man-of-war – English, French or Dutch – would see white men through as far as row on board goes. We could get rid of them and their money afterwards by delivering them to their Mandarin or Taotai, or whatever they call these chaps in goggles you see being carried about in sedan-chairs through their stinking streets.

'The old man wouldn't see it somehow. He wanted to keep the matter quiet. He got that notion into his head, and a steam windlass couldn't drag it out of him. He wanted as little fuss made as possible, for the sake of the ship's name and for the sake of the owners – "for the sake of all concerned", says he, looking at me very hard. It made me angry hot. Of course you couldn't keep a thing like that quiet; but the chests had been secured in the usual manner and were safe enough for any earthly gale, while this had been an altogether fiendish business I couldn't give you even an idea of.

'Meantime, I could hardly keep on my feet. None of us had a spell of any sort for nearly thirty hours, and there the old man sat rubbing his chin, rubbing the top of his head, and so bothered he didn't even think of pulling his long boots off.

' "I hope, sir," says I, "you won't be letting them out on deck before we make ready for them in some shape or other." Not, mind you, that I felt very sanguine about controlling these beggars if they meant to take charge. A trouble with a cargo of Chinamen is no child's play. I was dam' tired, too. "I wish," said I, "you would let us throw the whole lot of these dollars down to them and leave them to fight it out amongst themselves, while we get a rest."

' "Now you talk wild, Jukes," says he, looking up in his slow way that makes you ache all over, somehow. "We must plan out something that would be fair to all parties."

'I had no end of work on hand, as you may imagine, so I set the hands going, and then I thought I would turn in a bit. I hadn't been asleep in my bunk ten minutes when in rushes the steward and begins to pull at my leg.

' "For God's sake, Mr Jukes, come out! Come on deck quick, sir. Oh, do come out!"

'The fellow scared all the sense out of me. I didn't know what had happened: another hurricane – or what. Could hear no wind.

' "The Captain's letting them out. Oh, he is letting them out! Jump on deck, sir, and save us. The chief engineer has just run below for his revolver."

'That's what I understood the fool to say. However, Father Rout swears he went in there only to get a clean pocket-handkerchief. Anyhow, I made one jump into my trousers and flew on deck aft. There was certainly a good deal of noise going on forward of the bridge. Four of the hands with the boss'en were at work abaft. I passed up to them some of the rifles all the ships on the China coast carry in the cabin and led them on the bridge. On the way I ran against Old Sol, looking startled and sucking at an unlighted cigar.

' "Come along," I shouted to him.

'We charged, the seven of us, up to the chart-room. All was over. There stood the old man with his sea-boots still drawn up to the hips and in shirt-sleeves — got warm thinking it out, I suppose. Bun-hin's dandy clerk at his elbow as dirty as a sweep, was still green in the face. I could see directly I was in for something.

' "What the devil are these monkey tricks, Mr Jukes?" asks the old man, as angry as ever he could be. I tell you frankly it made me lose my tongue. "For God's sake, Mr Jukes," says he, "do take away these rifles from the men. Somebody's sure to get hurt before long if you don't. Damme, if this ship isn't worse than Bedlam! Look sharp now. I want you up here to help me and Bun-hin's Chinaman to count that money. You wouldn't mind lending a hand, too, Mr Rout, now you are here. The more of us the better."

'He had settled it all in his mind while I was having a snooze. Had we been an English ship, or only going to land our cargo of coolies in an English port, like Hong-Kong, for instance, there would have been no end of inquiries and bother, claims for damages and so on. But these Chinamen know their officials better than we do.

'The hatches had been taken off already, and they were all on deck after a night and a day down below. It made you feel queer to see so many gaunt, wild faces together. The beggars stared about at the sky, at the sea, at the ship, as though they had expected the whole thing to have been blown to pieces. And no wonder! They had had a doing that would have shaken the soul out of a white man. But then they say a Chinaman has no soul. He has, though, something about him that is deuced tough. There was a fellow (amongst others of the badly hurt) who had had his eye all but knocked out. It stood out of his head the size of half a hen's egg. This would have laid out a white man on his back for a month: and yet there was that chap elbowing here and there in the crowd and talking to the others as if nothing had been the matter. They made a great hubbub amongst themselves, and whenever the old man showed his bald head on the foreside of the bridge, they would all leave off jawing and look at him from below.

'It seems that after he had done his thinking he made that Bun-hin's fellow go down and explain to them the only way they could get their money back. He told me afterwards that, all the coolies having worked in the same place and for the same length of time, he reckoned he would be doing the fair thing by them as near as possible if he shared all the cash we had picked up equally among the lot. You couldn't tell one man's dollars from another's, he said, and if you asked each man how much money he brought on board he was afraid they would lie, and he would find himself a long way short. I think he was right there. As to giving up the money to any Chinese official he could scare up in Fu-chau, he said he might just as well put the lot in his own pocket at once for all the good it would be to them. I suppose they thought so, too.

'We finished the distribution before dark. It was rather a sight: the sea running high, the ship a wreck to look at, these Chinamen staggering up on the bridge one by one for their share, and the old man still booted, and in his shirt-sleeves, busy paying out at the chart-room door, perspiring like anything, and now and then coming down sharp on myself or Father Rout about one thing or another not quite to his mind. He took the share of those who were disabled himself to them on the No. 2 hatch. There were three dollars left over, and these went to the three most damaged coolies, one to each. We turned-to afterwards, and shovelled out on deck heaps of wet rags, all sorts of fragments of things without shape, and that you couldn't give a name to, and let them settle the ownership themselves.

'This certainly is coming as near as can be to keeping the thing quiet for the benefit of all concerned. What's your opinion, you pampered mail-boat swell? The old chief says that this was plainly the only thing that could be done. The skipper remarked to me the other day, "There are things you find nothing about in books." I think that he got out of it very well for such a stupid man.'

W. W. Jacobs

OUTSAILED

If ever I have needed cheering up at sea, the one writer I have always been able to rely on for a laugh has been William Wymark Jacobs (1863–1943). Ever since I was young and first discovered his collections of short stories about the sea, they have proved a never-failing source of amusement, portraying the lighter and occasionally hilarious side of life on the ocean waves. Some of the best known of his tales are yarns spun by an old man referred to simply as the 'night watchman' who lives in Wapping – the district of London from which Jacobs himself originated. Others feature a trio of accident-prone seafarers called Ginger Dick, Sam Small and Peter Russet. To any reader who has yet to discover the pleasure of reading W. W. Jacobs, I can do no better than recommend such collections as Many Cargoes (1897), The Lady of the Barge (1902) and Night Watches (1914).

As you may have gathered from these remarks, choosing a W. W. Jacobs story for this book has not been an easy task for me. There are so many about the captains of sailing barges or the skippers of small yachts that I would have liked to include. In the end, I have settled for one that is typical of many others, both in terms of its humour and the characters of its central figures. Everyone who has ever been to sea will know about the rivalry that can exist between captains about the respective merits of their vessels – but I doubt if any dispute has ever been settled in quite the same way as you are now about to discover in 'Outsailed' . . .

It was a momentous occasion. The two skippers sat in the private bar of the 'Old Ship', in High Street, Wapping, solemnly sipping cold gin and smoking cigars, whose sole merit consisted in the fact that they had been smuggled. It is well known all along the waterside that this greatly improves their flavour.

'Draw all right?' queried Captain Berrow — a short, fat man of few ideas, who was the exulting owner of a bundle of them.

'Beautiful,' replied Captain Tucker, who had just made an excursion into the interior of his with the small blade of his penknife. 'Why don't you keep smokes like these, landlord?'

'He can't,' chuckled Captain Berrow fatuously. 'They're not to be 'ad — money couldn't buy 'em.'

The landlord grunted. 'Why don't you settle about that race o' yours an' ha' done with it,' he cried, as he wiped down his counter. 'Seems to me, Cap'n Tucker's hanging fire.'

'I'm ready when he is,' said Tucker, somewhat shortly.

'It's taking your money,' said Berrow slowly; 'the *Thistle* can't hold a candle to the *Good Intent*, and you know it. Many a time that little schooner o' mine has kept up with a steamer.'

'Wher'd you ha' been if the tow rope had parted, though?' said the master of the *Thistle*, with a wink at the landlord.

At this remark Captain Berrow took fire, and, with his temper rapidly rising to fever heat, wrathfully repelled the scurvy insinuation in language which compelled the respectful attention of all the other customers and the hasty intervention of the landlord.

'Put up the stakes,' he cried impatiently. 'Put up the stakes, and don't have so much jaw about it.'

'Here's mine,' said Berrow, sturdily handing over a greasy fiver. 'Now, Cap'n Tucker, cover that.'

'Come on,' said the landlord encouragingly; 'don't let him take the wind out of your sails like that.'

Tucker handed over five sovereigns.

'High water's at 12.13,' said the landlord, pocketing the stakes. 'You understand the conditions — each of you does the best he can for hisself after eleven, an' the one what gets to Poole first has the ten quid. Understand?'

Both gamblers breathed hard, and, fully realising the desperate nature of the enterprise upon which they had embarked, ordered some more gin. A rivalry of long standing as to the merits of their respective schooners had led to them calling in the landlord to arbitrate, and this was the result. Berrow, vaguely feeling that it would be advisable to keep on good terms with the stakeholder, offered him one of the famous cigars. The stakeholder, anxious to keep on good terms with his stomach, declined it.

'You've both got your moorings up, I s'pose?' he inquired.

'Got 'em up this evening,' replied Tucker. 'We're just made fast one on each side of the *Dolphin* now.'

'The wind's light, but it's from the right quarter,' said Captain Berrow, 'an' I only hope as 'ow the best ship'll win. I'd like to win myself, but, if not, I can only say as there's no man breathing I'd sooner have lick me than Cap'n Tucker. He's as smart a seaman as ever comes into the London river, an' he's got a schooner angels would be proud of.'

'Glasses o' gin round,' said Tucker promptly. 'Cap'n Berrow, here's your very good health, an' a fair field an' no favour.'

With these praiseworthy sentiments the master of the *Thistle* finished his liquor, and, wiping his mouth on the back of his hand, nodded farewell to the twain and departed. Once in the High Street he walked slowly, as one in deep thought, then, with a sudden resolution, turned up Nightingale Lane, and made for a small, unsavoury thoroughfare leading out of Ratcliff Highway. A quarter of an hour later he emerged into that famous thoroughfare again, smiling incoherently, and, retracing his steps to the waterside, jumped into a boat, and was pulled off to his ship.

'Comes off to-night, Joe,' said he, as he descended to the cabin, 'an' it's arf a quid to you if the old gal wins.'

'What's the bet?' inquired the mate, looking up from his task of shredding tobacco.

'Five quid,' replied the skipper.

'Well, we ought to do it,' said the mate slowly; ' 't wont be my fault if we don't.'

'Mine neither,' said the skipper. 'As a matter o' fact, Joe, I reckon I've about made sure of it. All's fair in love and war and racing, Joe.'

'Ay, ay,' said the mate, more slowly than before, as he revolved this addition to the proverb.

'I just nipped round and saw a chap I used to know named Dibbs,' said the skipper. 'Keeps a boarding-house for sailors. Wonderful sharp little chap he is. Needles ain't nothing to him. There's heaps of needles, but only one Dibbs. He's going to make old Berrow's chaps as drunk as lords.'

'Does he know 'em?' inquired the mate.

'He knows where to find 'em,' said the other. 'I told him they'd either be in the "Duke's Head" or the "Town o' Berwick". But he'd find 'em wherever they was. Ah, even if they was in a coffee pallis, I b'leeve that man 'ud find 'em.'

'They're steady chaps,' objected the mate, but in a weak fashion, being somewhat staggered by this tribute to Mr Dibbs' remarkable powers.

'My lad,' said the skipper, 'it's Dibbs' business to mix sailors' liquors so's they don't know whether they're standing on their heads or their heels. He's the most wonderful mixer in Christendom; takes a reg'lar pride in it. Many a sailorman has got up a ship's side, thinking it was stairs, and gone off half acrost the world instead of going to bed, through him.'

'We'll have a easy job of it, then,' said the mate. 'I b'leeve we could ha' managed it without that, though. 'Tain't quite what you'd call sport, is it?'

'There's nothing like making sure of a thing,' said the skipper placidly. 'What time's our chaps coming aboard?'

'Ten thirty, the latest,' replied the mate. 'Old Sam's with 'em, so they'll be all right.'

'I'll turn in for a couple of hours,' said the skipper, going towards his berth. 'Lord! I'd give something to see old Berrow's face as his chaps come up the side.'

'P'raps they won't git as far as that,' remarked the mate.

'Oh, yes they will,' said the skipper. 'Dibbs is going to see to that. I don't want any chance of the race being scratched. Turn me out in a couple of hours.'

He closed the door behind him, and the mate, having stuffed his clay with the coarse tobacco, took some pink note-paper with scalloped edges from his drawer, and, placing the paper at his right side, and squaring his shoulders, began some private correspondence.

For some time he smoked and wrote in silence, until the increasing darkness warned him to finish his task. He signed the note, and, having put a few marks of a tender nature below his signature, sealed it ready for the post, and sat with half-closed eyes, finishing his pipe. Then his head nodded, and, placing his arms on the table, he too slept.

It seemed but a minute since he had closed his eyes when he was awakened by the entrance of the skipper, who came blundering into the darkness from his stateroom, vociferating loudly and nervously.

'Ay, ay!' said Joe, starting up.

'Where's the lights?' said the skipper. 'What's the time? I dreamt I'd overslept myself. What's the time?'

'Plenty o' time,' said the mate vaguely, as he stifled a yawn.

'Ha'-past ten,' said the skipper, as he struck a match. 'You've been asleep,' he added severely.

'I ain't,' said the mate stoutly, as he followed the other on deck. 'I've been thinking. I think better in the dark.'

'It's about time our chaps was aboard,' said the skipper, as he looked round the deserted deck. 'I hope they won't be late.'

'Sam's with 'em,' said the mate confidently, as he went on to the side; 'there ain't no festivities going on aboard the *Good Intent*, neither.'

'There will be,' said his worthy skipper, with a grin, as he looked across the intervening brig at the rival craft; 'there will be.'

He walked round the deck to see that everything was snug and ship-shape, and got back to the mate just as a howl of surprising weirdness was heard proceeding from the neigh-bouring stairs.

'I'm s'prised at Berrow allowing his men to make that noise,' said the skipper waggishly. 'Our chaps are there too, I think. I can hear Sam's voice.'

'So can I,' said the mate, with emphasis.

'Seems to be talking rather loud,' said the master of the *Thistle*, knitting his brows.

'Sounds as though he's trying to sing,' said the mate, as, after some delay, a heavily-laden boat put off from the stairs and made slowly for them. 'No, he ain't; he's screaming.'

There was no longer any doubt about it. The respectable and

greatly trusted Sam was letting off a series of wild howls which would have done credit to a penny-gaff Zulu, and was evidently very much out of temper about something.

'Ahoy, *Thistle*! Ahoy!' bellowed the waterman, as he neared the schooner. 'Chuck us a rope – quick!'

The mate threw him one, and the boat came alongside. It was then seen that another waterman, using impatient and deplorable language, was forcibly holding Sam down in the boat.

'What's he done? What's the row?' demanded the mate.

'Done?' said the waterman, in disgust. 'Done? He's 'ad a small lemon, an' it's got into his silly old head. He's making all this fuss 'cos he wanted to set the pub on fire, an' they wouldn't let him. Man ashore told us they belonged to the *Good Intent*, but I know they're your men.'

'Sam!' roared the skipper, with a sinking heart, as his glance fell on the recumbent figures in the boat; 'come aboard at once, you drunken disgrace! D'ye hear?'

'I can't leave him,' said Sam, whimpering.

'Leave who?' growled the skipper.

'Him,' said Sam, placing his arms round the waterman's neck. 'Him an' me's like brothers.'

'Get up, you old loonatic!' snarled the waterman, extricating himself with difficulty, and forcing the other towards the side. 'Now, up you go!'

Aided by the shoulders of the waterman and the hands of his superior officers, Sam went up, and then the waterman turned his attention to the remainder of his fares, who were snoring contentedly in the bottom of the boat.

'Now, then!' he cried; 'look alive with you! D'ye hear? Wake up! wake up! Kick 'em, Bill!'

'I can't kick no 'arder,' grumbled the other waterman.

'What the devil's the matter with 'em?' stormed the master of the *Thistle*. 'Chuck a pail of water over 'em, Joe!'

Joe obeyed with gusto; and, as he never had much of a head for details, bestowed most of it upon the watermen. Through the row which ensued the *Thistle*'s crew snored peacefully, and at last were handed up over the sides like sacks of potatoes, and the indignant watermen pulled back to the stairs.

'Here's a nice crew to win a race with!' wailed the skipper, almost crying with rage. 'Chuck the water over 'em, Joe! Chuck the water over 'em!'

Joe obeyed willingly, until at length, to the skipper's great relief, one man stirred, and, sitting up on the deck, sleepily expressed his firm conviction that it was raining. For a moment they both had hopes of him, but as Joe went to the side for another bucketful, he evidently came to the conclusion that he had been dreaming, and, lying down again, resumed his nap. As he did so the first stroke of Big Ben came booming down the river.

'Eleven o'clock!' shouted the excited skipper.

It was too true. Before Big Ben had finished, the neighbouring church clocks commenced striking with feverish haste, and hurrying feet and hoarse cries were heard proceeding from the deck of the *Good Intent*.

'Loose the sails!' yelled the furious Tucker. 'Loose the sails! Damme, we'll get under way by ourselves!'

He ran forward, and, assisted by the mate, hoisted the jibs, and then, running back, cast off from the brig, and began to hoist the mainsail. As they disengaged themselves from the pier, there was just sufficient sail for them to advance against the tide; while in front of them the *Good Intent*, shaking out sail after sail, stood boldly down the river.

'This was the way of it,' said Sam, as he stood before the grim Tucker at six o'clock the next morning, surrounded by his mates. 'He came into the "Town o' Berwick", where we was, as nice a spoken little chap as ever you'd wish to see. He said he'd been a-looking at the *Good Intent*, and he thought it was the prettiest little craft 'e ever seed, and the exact image of one his dear brother, which was a missionary, 'ad, and he'd like to stand a drink to every man of her crew. Of course, we all said we was the crew direckly, an' all I can remember arter that is two coppers an' a little boy trying to giv' me the frog's march, an' somebody chucking pails o' water over me. It's crool 'ard losing a race, what we didn't know nothink about, in this way; but it warn't our fault — it warn't, indeed. It's my belief that the little man was a missionary of some sort hisself, and wanted to convert us, an' that was his way of starting on the job. It's all very well for the mate to have highstirriks; but it's quite true, every word of it, an' if you go an' ask at the pub they'll tell you the same.'

C. J. Cutcliffe Hyne

THE LINER AND THE ICEBERG

A Captain Kettle Adventure

No discussion about humorous sea stories could possibly fail to overlook the irrascible Captain Owen Kettle, a tough and occasionally ruthless master mariner who somehow always manages to inject a laugh or two into even the most impossible situation. The Captain is a unique figure in nautical fiction, and it surprises me that the books of his adventures are not made more readily available. Let me try and remedy that by including one of his adventures in these pages. The creator of the wiry little captain was Charles John Cutcliffe Hyne (1865–1944), a Cambridge-educated northerner bitten by wanderlust, who sailed and travelled about the world for many years before settling in Yorkshire to transform his experiences into tales of high adventure.

Captain Kettle, who is actually based on a real Scottish seaman whom Cutcliffe Hyne met in South America, first appeared in the weekly Pearson's Magazine *in 1897 and proved so popular with readers that the author was forced to continue what he had originally planned to be just enough episodes to fill one book. In the years that followed, he expounded the Captain's many and varied adventures in places all over the globe, building up a total of over a dozen collections. From among these, I have picked the story of what happened when the Captain found himself in charge of an ocean-going liner instead of his usual cargo-ship, and how he became involved with a Fenian plot and an iceberg. And if that hasn't wetted your appetite, I can't imagine what will!*

Captain Kettle had been thanking Carnforth for getting him command of the Atlantic liner *Armenia*. 'But,' he went on, 'qualifications, sir, are all my eye. Interest's the thing that shoves a shipmaster along. Yes, Mr Carnforth, interest and luck. I've got qualifications by the fathom, and you know pretty well what they've ever done for me. But you're a rich man and an MP; you've got interest; you come up and give me a good word with an owner, and look, the thing's done.'

'Well, I sincerely wish you a long reign,' said Carnforth. 'The *Armenia*'s the slowest and oldest ship on the line, but she was the best I could get the firm to give you. It's seldom they change their captains, and they promote from the bottom, upwards. You've got all the line before you, Kettle, and the rest must depend on yourself. I'd sincerely like to see you commodore of the firm's fleet, but you'll have to do the climbing to that berth by your own wit. I've done all I can.'

'You've done more for me, sir, than any other creature living's done, and believe me, I'm a very grateful fellow. And you can bet I shall do my best to stick to a snug berth now I've got it. I'm a married man, Mr Carnforth, with children; I've them always at the back of my memory; and I've known what it is to try all the wretched jobs that the knockabout shipmaster's put to if he doesn't choose his belongings to starve. The only thing I've got to be frightened of now is luck, and that's a thing which is outside my hands, and outside yours, and outside the hands of everyone else on this earth. I guess that God above keeps the engineering of luck as His own private department; and He deals it out according to His good pleasure; and we get what's best for us.'

Now the SS *Armenia*, or the old *Atrocity*, as she was more familiarly named, with other qualifying adjectives according to taste, was more known than respected in the Western Ocean passenger trade. In her day she had been a flier, and had cut a record; but her day was past. Ship-building and engine-building are forever on the improve, and with competition, and the rush of trade, the older vessels are constantly getting outclassed in speed and economy.

So heavy stoke-hold crews and extravagant coal consumption no longer made the *Armenia* tremble along at her topmost speed. The firm had built newer and faster boats to do the showy trips which got spoken about in the newspapers; and in these they carried the actresses, and the drummers, and the other people who run up heavy wine bills and insist on expensive state-rooms; and they had lengthened the *Armenia*'s scheduled time of passage beween ports to what was most economical for coal consumption, and made her other arrangements to match. They advertised first-class bookings from Liverpool to New York for £11 and upwards, and passengers who economised and bought £11 tickets, fondly imagining that they were going to cross in one of the show boats, were wont to find themselves consigned to berths in inside cabins on the *Armenia*.

The present writer (before Captain Kettle took over command) knew the *Armenia* well. A certain class of passenger had grown native to her. On outward trips she was a favourite boat for Mormon missionaries and their converts. The saints themselves voyaged first class, and made a very nasty exhibition of manners; their wives were in the second cabin; and the ruck of the converts – Poles, Slavs, Armenians, and other noisome riff-raff – reposed in stuffy barracks far below the water-line, and got the best that could be given them for their contract transport price of three-pound-ten a head. Besides the Mormons (and shunning them as oil does water) there were civilised passengers who shipped by the *Armenia* either because the cheap tariff suited their purses, or because an extra couple of days at sea did not matter to them, and they preferred her quiet *régime* to the hurry, and noise, and dazzle, and vibration of the crowded and more popular greyhounds.

On to the head of this queer family party, then, Captain Owen Kettle was pitchforked by the Fates and Mr Carnforth, and at first he found the position bewilderingly strange. He was thirty-seven years of age, and it was his *début* as an officer on a passenger boat. The whole routine was new to him. Even the deckhands were of a class strange to his experience, and did as they were bidden smartly and efficiently, and showed no disposition to simmer to a state of constant mutiny. But newest of all, he came for the first time in contact with an official called a Purser (in the person of one Mr Reginald Horrocks) at whose powers and position he was inclined to look very much askance.

It was Mr Horrocks who welcomed him on board, and the pair of them sized one another up with diligence. Kettle was suspicious, brusque, and inclined to assert his position. But the Purser was more a man of the world, and, besides, he was by profession urbane, and a cultivator of other people's likings. He made it his boast that he could in ten minutes get on terms of civility with the sourest passenger who was ever put into an undesirable room; and he was resolved to get on a footing of geniality with the new skipper if his art could manage it. Mr Horrocks had sailed on bad terms with a captain once in the days of his novitiate, and he did not wish to repeat the experience.

But Kettle was by nature an autocrat, and could not shake down into the new order of things all at once. The *Armenia* was in dock, noisy with stevedores working cargo, when the new Captain paid his first preliminary visit of inspection. Horrocks was in attendance, voluble and friendly, and they went through every part of her, from the sodden shaft-tunnel, to the glory-hole where the stewards live. The Purser was all affability, but Kettle resented his tone, and at last, when they had ended their excursion, and walked together into the chart-house on the lower bridge, the little sailor turned round and faced the other, and put the case to him significantly.

'You will kindly remember that I am Captain of this ferry,' he said.

'You're Captain all the way, sir,' said Horrocks genially. 'My department is the care of the passengers as your deputy, and the receiving in of stores from the superintendent purser ashore; and I wish to handle them all according to your orders.'

'Oh,' said Kettle, 'you'll have a pretty free hand here. I don't mind telling you I'm new to this hotel-keeping business. I've been in cargo boats up to now.'

'Well, of course, Captain, a Purser's work is a profession to itself, and the details are not likely to have come in your way. I suppose I'd better run things on much as before to start with, and when you see a detail you want changed, you tell me, and I'll see it changed right away. That's where I come in; I'm a very capable man at carrying out orders. And there's another thing, Captain; I know my place: I'm just your assistant.'

Captain Kettle pressed the bell. 'Purser,' said he, 'I believe we shall get on well. I hope we shall; it's most comfortable that way.' A bare-headed man in a short jacket knocked, and came in through the chart-house door. 'Steward, bring a bottle of whisky, and put my name on it, and keep it in the rack yonder; and bring some fresh water and two glasses – Purser, you'll have a drink with me?'

'Well, here's plenty of cargo,' said Kettle, when the whisky came.

'Here's plenty of passengers and a popular ship,' said the Purser.

But if Mr Horrocks was civil and submissive in words on the *Armenia*, it was because he had mastered the art of only saying those things which are profitable, and keeping his private thoughts for disclosure on more fitting occasions. When he sat at tea that night with his wife across in their little house in New Brighton, he mentioned that the new captain did not altogether meet with his august approval. 'He's a queer savage they've got hold of, and no mistake this time,' said he; 'a fellow that's lived on cargo boats all his life, and never seen a serviette, and doesn't know what to do with his entertainment money.'

'Tell the firm,' suggested Mrs Horrocks.

'Not much. At least, not yet. He's new, and so naturally they think he's a jewel. I'm not going to make myself unpopular by complaining too soon. Give this new old man string enough, and he'll hang himself neatly without my help.'

'Like the last?'

'Oh, this one's worse than him. In fact I'm beginning to be sorry I ever did get our last old man the push. He was all right so long as I didn't make my perquisites too big. But as for this one, I don't suppose he'll understand I've a right to perquisites at all.'

'But,' said Mrs Horrocks, 'you're Purser. What does he suppose you live on? He must know that the pay don't go far.'

'Well he didn't seem to know what a Purser was, and when I tried to hint it to him, he just snapped out that he was Captain of this blooming ship.'

'And then?'

Mr Horrocks shrugged his shoulders. 'Oh, I agreed right away. May as well tickle a fool as tease him, my dear. He thinks because he's a splendid seaman – and he may be that, I'll admit – he's fit to skipper a Western Ocean passenger boat. He's a lot to learn yet, and I'm the man that's going to educate him.'

Now the exasperating part of it was, that not only did this process of 'education' promptly begin, but Captain Kettle knew it. Never before had he had any one beneath him on board ship who had dared to dispute his imperial will, and done it successfully. There was no holding this affable purser, no pinning him down to a specific offence. If he mapped out a plan of action, and Captain Kettle objected to it, he was all civility, and would give it up without argument. 'Certainly, sir,' he would say. 'You're Captain on this boat, as you say, and I'm Purser, and I just know my place.' And then afterwards would invariably come a back thrust which Captain Kettle could never parry.

There were three long tables in the saloon, headed by the Captain, the Purser, and the Doctor; and when the passengers came on board at Liverpool or New York, it was Mr Horrocks who arranged their meal places. He had a nice discrimination, this Purser, and from long habit could sum up a passenger's general conversational qualities at a glance. He knew also Captain Kettle's tastes and limitations, and when that redoubtable mariner had been making things unpleasant, he rewarded him with dinner companions for the next run who kept him in a state of subdued frenzy. It was quite an easy thing to do, and, managed craftily, it was a species of torture impossible to resent.

In fact it may be owned at once that as a conversational head to a liner's table, Captain Kettle did not shine. The situation was new and strange to him. Up till then he had fought his way about the seas in cargo tramps, with only here and there a stray passenger, and, at table, professional topics had made up the talk, or, what was more common, glum, scowling silence had prevailed.

Here, on this steam hotel, he suddenly found himself looked up to as a head of society. His own real reminiscences of the sea he kept back: he felt them to be vastly impolite; he never dreamed that they might be interesting.

His power of extracting sweet music from the accordion he kept rigidly in the background. Accordions seemed out of place somehow with these finicking passengers. He felt that his one genteel taste was for poetry, but only once did he let it slip out. It was half-way across the Atlantic on a homeward trip, and conversation had lagged. The Purser's and the Doctor's tables were in a rattle of cheerful talk: Kettle's was in a state of boredom. In desperation he brought out his sacred topic.

At once every ear within range started to listen: he saw that at once. But he mistook the motive. The men around him — they were mostly American — thought that the whole thing was an effort of humour. It never occurred to them that this vinegary-faced little sailor actually himself made the sentimental rhymes he quoted to them: and when it dawned upon them that this was no joke, and the man was speaking in sober, solemn earnest, the funniness of it swept over them like a wave. The table yelped with inextinguishable laughter.

Of a sudden Captain Kettle realised that he was his passengers' butt, and sat back in his chair as though he was getting ready for a spring.

In his first torrent of rage he could with gusto have shot the lot of them; but to begin with he was unarmed, and, in the second place, passengers are not crew; and moreover, after the first explosion, the laughter began to die away. One by one the diners looked at the grim, savage, little face glaring at them from the end of the table, and their mirth seemed to chill. The laughter ended, and an uncomfortable silence grew, and remained to the finish of the meal.

During the succeeding meals, moreover, up till the end of the voyage, that silence was very little encroached upon at the Captain's end of the middle table. Anyone who ventured to speak, had the benefit of Captain Kettle's full gaze, and found it disconcerting. Even to passengers on a modern steam ferry the Captain is a person of some majesty, and this one had a look about him that did not invite further liberties.

That batch of passengers dispersed to the four corners of the earth from Queenstown and Liverpool, and the *Armenia* saw them no more; but news of the fracas somehow or another reached the headquarters' office, and a kindly hint was given to Captain Kettle that such scenes would be better avoided for the future.

'I quite know that passengers are awkward cattle to deal with,' said the partner who put it to him, 'but you see, Captain, we make our living by carrying them, and we can't afford to have our boats made unpopular. You should use more tact, my dear skipper. Tact; that's what you want. Stand 'em champagne out of your entertainment allowance, and they'll stand it back, and run up bigger bills with the wine steward. It all means profit, Captain, and those are the ways you must get it for us. We aren't asking you to drum round for cargo now. Your game is to make the boat cheery and comfortable for passengers, so that they'll spend a lot of money on board, and like it, and come again and spend some more. Tumble?'

The captain of the *Armenia* heard, and intended to conform. But, admirer of his though I must conscientiously write myself, I cannot even hope that in time he would have shaken down fitly into the berth; for to tell the truth, I do not think a more unsuitable man to govern one of these modern steam hotels could be found on the seas of either hemisphere. However, as it happened, the concession was not demanded of him. His luck, that cruel, evil fortune, got up and hit him again, and his ship was cast away, and he saw himself once more that painful thing, a shipmaster without employ. More cruel still, he found himself at the same time in intimate touch with a great temptation.

The fatal voyage was from New York home, and it was in the cold, raw springtime when passenger lists are thin. The day before sailing a letter addressed 'Captain Kettle, SS *Armenia*' made its appearance on the chart-house table. How it got there no one seemed to know, but with the crowd of stevedores and others working cargo, it would have been very easy for a messenger from the wharf to slip it on board unobserved. The letter was typewritten, and carried the address of an obscure saloon in the Bowery. It said:

There is a matter of $50,000 (£10,000) waiting for you to earn with a little pluck and exertion. You can either take the game or leave it, but if you conclude to hear more, come here and ask the barman for a five-dollar cocktail, and he will show you right inside. If you are frightened, don't come. We've got no use for frightened men. We can easy find a man with more sand in him somewhere else.

The little sailor considered over this precious document for the full of an hour. 'Some smuggling lay,' was his first conclusion, but the sum of money appeared too big for this; then he was half-minded to put down the whole thing as a joke; then as a lure to rob him. The final paragraph and the address given, which was in the worst part of New York city, seemed to point shrewdly to this last. And I believe the prospect of a scrimmage was really the thing that in the end sent him off. But anyway, that evening he went, and after some difficulty found the ruffianly drinking shop to which he had been directed.

He went inside and looked inquiringly across the bar.

The shirt-sleeved barman shifted his cigar. 'Well, mister, what can I fix up for you?'

'You're a bit proud of your five-dollar cocktails here, aren't you?'

The man lowered his voice. 'Say, are you Captain Cuttle?'

'Kettle! confound you.'

'Same thing, I guess. Walk right through that door yonder, and up the stair.'

Captain Kettle patted a jacket pocket that bulged with the outline of a revolver. 'If anyone thinks they are going to play larks on me here, I pity 'em.'

The barman shrugged his shoulders. 'Don't blame you for coming "heeled", boss. Guess a gun sometimes chips in handy round here. But I think the gents upstairs mean square biz.'

'Well,' said Kettle, 'I'm going to see,' and opened the door and stumped briskly up the stairway.

He stepped into a room, barely furnished, and lit by one grimy window. There was no one to receive him, so he drummed the table to make his presence known.

Promptly a voice said to him: 'Howdy, Captain? Will ye mind shuttin' the door?'

Now Kettle was not a man given to starting, but he started then. The place was in the worst slum of New York. Except for a flimsy table and two battered chairs, the room was stark empty, and this voice seemed to come from close beside him. Instinctively his fingers gripped on the weapon in his jacket pocket.

He slewed sharply round to make sure he was alone, and even kicked his foot under the table to see that there was no jugglery about that, and then the voice spoke to him again, with Irish brogue and Yankee idiom quaintly intermingled.

'Sure, Captain, I have to ask yer pardon for keepin' a brick wall right here between us. But I've me health to consider, an' I reckon our biz will be safest done this way.'

The little sailor's grim face relaxed into a smile. His eye had caught the end of a funnel which lay flush with the wall.

'Ho?' he said. 'That's your game, is it? A speaking-tube. Then I suppose you've got something to say you are ashamed of?'

'Faith, I'm proud of it. A patriot is never ashamed of his cause.'

'Get to business,' said Kettle. 'My time's short, and this waiting-room of yours is not over savoury.'

'It's just a little removal we wish you to undertake for us, Captain. You have gotten a Mr Grimshaw on your passenger list for this run to Liverpool?'

'Have I?'

'It's so. He's one of the big bosses of your British Government.'

'Well, supposing I have?'

'He's been out here as a sort of commission, and he's found out more than is good for him. He sails by the *Armenia* to-morrow, and if you can – well – so contrive that he doesn't land at the other side, it means you are set up for life.'

Captain Kettle's face stiffened, and he was about to break out with something sharp. But he restrained himself and asked instead: 'What's the figure?'

'$50,000 – say 10,000 of your English sovereigns.'

'And how do I know that I should get paid?'

The answer was somewhat astounding. 'You can pocket the money here, right now,' said the voice.

'And once I got paid, what hold would you have on me? How do you know I'd shove this Grimshaw over the side? That I suppose is what you want?'

The voice chuckled. 'We've agents everywhere, Captain. We'd have you removed pretty sharp if you tried to diddle us.'

'Oh, would you?' snapped Kettle. 'I've bucked against some tolerably ugly toughs in my time and come out top side, and shouldn't mind tackling your crowd for the sheer sport of the thing. But look here, Mr Paddy Fenian, you've got hold of the wrong man when you came to me. By James! yes, you skulking, cowardly swine! You face behind a wall! Come out here and talk. I won't lift my hands. I'll use my feet to you and kick your backbone through your hat. You'd dare to ask me to murder a man, would you?'

Captain Kettle's eloquence had an unlooked-for effect. The voice from the speaking-tube laughed.

The sailor went on afresh, and spoke of the unseen one's ancestors on both sides of the house, his personal habits, and probable future. He had acquired a goodly flow of this kind of vituperation during his professional career, and had been compelled to keep it bottled up before the passengers on the liner. He felt a kind of gusto in letting his tongue run loose again, and had the proud consciousness that each of his phrases would cut like the lash of a whip.

But the unseen man apparently heard him unruffled. 'Blow off steam, skipper,' said he; 'don't mind me.'

Kettle looked round the empty room dejectedly. 'You thing!' he said. 'I could make a man with more spirit than you out of putty.'

'Of course you could, skipper,' said the voice with the brogue; 'of course you could. I don't really exist. I'm only a name, as your beastly Saxon papers say when they abuse me. But I can hit, as they know, and I can draw cheques as you can find out if you choose. You can have your pay yet if you see fit to change your mind, and "remove" spy Grimshaw between here and Liverpool. We've plenty of money, and you may as well have it as anyone else. It's got to be spent somehow.'

'I'd give a lot to wring your neck,' said Kettle. He tapped the wall to test its thickness.

'You tire me,' said the voice. 'Why can't you drop that? You can't get at me; and if you go outside and set on all the police in New York city, you'll do no good. The police in this city know which side their bread's margarined. I'm the man with the cheque-book, sonny, and you bet they're not the sample of fools that'd go and try to snuff me out.'

'This is no place for me,' said Kettle. 'It seems I can't lug you out of the drain where you live, and if I stay in touch of your breath any longer, I shall be poisoned. I've told you who I consider your mother to be. Don't forget.' And the little bearded sailor strode off down the stair again and into the street. He had no inclination to go to the police, having a pious horror of the law, and so he got a trolley car which took him down to the East River, and a ferry which carried him across to his ship.

The time was 2 a.m., and the glow of the arc lamps and the rattle of winch chains, and the roar of working cargo, went up far into the night. But noise made little difference to him, and even the episode he had just gone through was not sufficient to keep him awake.

The master of a Western Ocean ferry gets little enough of sleep when he is on the voyage, and so on the night before sailing he stores up as much as may be.

As it chanced Mr Grimshaw took steps to impress himself on Captain Kettle's notice at an early stage of the next day's proceedings. The ship was warping out of dock with the help of a walking-beam tug, and a passenger attempted to pass the quartermaster at the foot of the upper bridge ladder. The sailor was stubborn, but the passenger was imperative, and at last pushed his way up, and was met by Kettle himself at the head of the ladder.

'Well, sir?' said that official.

'I've come to see you take your steamer out into New York Bay, Captain.'

'Oh, have you?' said Kettle. 'Are you the Emperor of Germany by any chance?'

'I am Mr Robert Grimshaw.'

'Same thing. Neither you nor he is Captain here. I am. So I'll trouble you to get to Halifax out of this before you're put. Quartermaster, I'll log you for neglect of duty.'

Grimshaw turned and went down the ladder with a flushed cheek. 'Thank you, Captain,' he said, over his shoulder. 'I've got influence with your owners. I'll not neglect to use it.'

It chanced also that Captain Kettle had been cutting down

his Purser's perquisites more ruthlessly than usual in New York, and that worthy man thirsted for revenge. He had taken Mr Grimshaw's measure pretty accurately at first sight, and was tolerably sure that eight days of his conversation would irritate his skipper into a state approaching frenzy. So he portioned off the commissioner to the end right-hand chair at the Captain's table, and promised himself pleasant revenge in overlooking the result.

Captain Kettle worked the *Armenia* outside the bar and came down to dinner. Horrocks whispered in his ear as he came down the companion. 'Mr Grimshaw's the man on your right, sir. Had to give him to you. He's some sort of a big bug in the government at home, been over in New York inquiring into the organisation of those Patlander rebels.'

Kettle nodded curtly and went on to his seat. The meal began, and went on. Mr Grimshaw made no allusion to the previous encounter. He had made up his mind to exact retaliation in full, and started at once to procure it. He had the reputation in London of being a 'most superior person', and he possessed in a high degree the art of being courteously offensive. He was a clever man with his tongue, and never overstepped the bounds of suavity.

How the wretched Kettle sat through that meal he did not know. Under this polished attack he was impotent of defence. Not a chance was given him for retort, and all the thrusts went home. He retired from the dinner table with a moist perspiration on his face, and an earnest prayer that the *Armenia* would carry foul weather with her all the way up to Prince's landing stage, so that he might be forced to spend the next seven or eight days on the chilly eminence of the upper bridge.

And now we come to the story of how Captain Owen Kettle's luck again buffeted him.

The *Armenia* was steaming along through the night, to the accompaniment of deep and dismal hootings from the siren. A fog spread over the Atlantic, and the bridge telegraph pointed to 'Half speed ahead', as the Board of Trade directs. The engine-room, however, had private instructions as usual, and kept up the normal speed.

On the forecastle head four look-out men peered solemnly into the fog, and knew that for all the practical good they were doing they might just as well be in their bunks.

On the bridge, in glistening oilskins, Kettle and two mates stared before them into the thickness, but could not see as far as the foremast. And the *Armenia* surged along at her comfortable fourteen knots, with five hundred people asleep beneath her deck. The landsman fancies that on these occasions steamships slow down or stop; the liner captain knows that if once he did so, he would have little chance of taking his ship across the Atlantic again. A day lost to one of these ocean ferries means in coal, and food, and wages, and so on, a matter of £1,000 or so out of the pockets of her owners, and this is a little sum they do not care to forfeit without strong reason. They expect their Captains to drive the boats along as usual, and make up for the added risk by increased watchfulness and precaution, and a keen noting of the thermometer for any sudden fall which should foretell the neighbourhood of ice.

Now the *Armenia* was skirting the edge of the Banks, on the recognised steam-lane to the Eastward, which differs from that leading West; and by all the laws of navigation there should have been nothing in the way. Nothing, that is, except fishing schooners, which do not matter, as they are the only sufferers if they haven't the sense to get out of the way.

But, suddenly, through the fog ahead there loomed out a vast shape, and almost before the telegraph rung its message to the engine-room, and certainly before steam could be shut off, the *Armenia*'s bow was clashing and clanging and ripping and buckling as though it had charged full tilt against a solid cliff.

The engines stopped, and the awful tearing noises ceased, save for a tinkling rattle as of a cascade of glass, and: 'There goes my blooming ticket,' said Kettle bitterly. 'Who'd have thought of an iceberg as far south as here this time of year.' But he was prompt to act on the emergency.

'Now, Mr Mate, away forward with you, and get the carpenter, and go down and find out how big the damage is.' The crew were crowding out on deck. 'All hands to boat stations. See all clear for lowering away, and then hold on all. Now, keep your heads, men. There's no damage, and if there was damage there's no hurry. Put a couple of hands at each of the companion-ways, and keep all passengers below. We can't have them messing round here yet awhile.'

The Purser was standing at the bottom of the upper bridge ladder half-clad, cool, and expectant. 'Ah, Mr Horrocks, come here.'

The *Armenia* had slipped back from the berg by this time and lay still, with the fog dense all around her. 'Now it's all up with the old *Atrocity*, Purser: look how she's by the head already. Get your crew of stewards together, and victual the boats. Keep 'em in hand well, or else we shall have a stampede and a lot of drowning. I'll have the boats in the water by the time you're ready, and then you must hand up the passengers, women first.'

'Aye, aye, sir.'

'Wait a minute. If anyone won't do as he's bid, shoot. We must keep order.'

The Purser showed a pistol. 'I put that in my pocket,' said he, 'when I heard her hit. Goodbye, skipper, I'm sorry I haven't been a better shipmate to you.'

'Goodbye, Purser,' said Kettle, 'you aren't a bad sort.'

Mr Horrocks ran off below, and the chief officer came back with his report, which he whispered quietly in the shipmaster's ear. 'It's fairly scratched the bottom off her. There's sixty feet gone, clean. Collision bulkhead's nowhere. There's half the Atlantic on board already.'

'How long will she swim?'

'The carpenter said twenty minutes, but I doubt it.'

'Well, away with you, Mr Mate, and stand by your boat. Take plenty of rockets and distress lights, and if the fog lifts we ought to get picked up by the *Georgic* before morning. She's close on our heels somewhere. If you miss her and get separated, make for St John's.'

'Aye, aye, sir.'

'So long, Mr Mate. Good luck to you.'

'Goodbye, skipper. Get to the inquiry if you can. I'll swear till all's blue that it wasn't your fault, and you may save your ticket yet.'

'All right, Matey, I see what you mean. But I'm not going to shoot myself this journey. I've got the missis and the kids to think about.'

240

The Mate ran off down the ladder, and Kettle had the upper bridge to himself. The decks of the steamer glowed with flares and blue lights. A continuous stream of rockets spouted from her superstructure far into the inky sky. The main fore-deck was already flush with the water, and on the hurricane deck aft, thrust up high into the air, frightened human beings bustled about like the inhabitants of some disturbed ant-hill.

Pair by pair the davit tackles screamed out, and the liner's boats kissed the water, rode there for a minute to their painters as they were loaded with the dense human freight, and then pushed off out of suction reach, and lay to. Dozen by dozen the passengers left the luxurious steam hotel, and got into the frail open craft which danced so dangerously in the clammy fog of that Atlantic night. Deeper the *Armenia*'s fore part sank beneath the cold waters as her forward compartments swamped.

From far beneath him in the hull, Kettle could hear the hum of the bilge pumps as they fought the incoming sluices; and then at last those stopped, and a gush of steam burred from the twin funnels to tell that the engineers had been forced to blow off their boilers to save an explosion.

A knot of three men stood at the head of port gangway ladder shouting for Kettle. He went gloomily down and joined them. They were the purser, the second mate, and Mr Grimshaw.

Kettle turned with a blaze of fury on his suave tormentor. 'Into the boat with you, sir. How do you dare to disobey my orders and stay behind when the passengers were ordered to go? Into the boat with you, or by James! I'll throw you there.'

Mr Robert Grimshaw opened his lips for speech.

'If you answer me back,' said Kettle, 'I'll shoot you dead.'

Mr Grimshaw went. He had a tolerable knowledge of men, and he understood that this ruined shipmaster would be as good as his word. He picked his way down the swaying ladder to where the white-painted lifeboat plunged beneath, finding footsteps with clumsy landsman's diffidence. He reached the grating at the foot of the ladder, and paused. The lifeboat surged up violently towards him over a sea, and then swooped down again in the trough.

'Jump, you blame' fool,' the second mate yelled in his ear,

'or the steamer will be down under us.' And Grimshaw jumped, cannoned heavily against the boat's white gunwale, and sank like a stone into the black water.

At a gallop there flashed through Captain Kettle's brain a string of facts. He was offered £10,000 if this man did not reach Liverpool; he himself would be out of employ, and back on the streets again; his wife and children would go hungry. Moreover, he had endured cruel humiliation from this man, and hated him poisonously. Even by letting him passively drown he would procure revenge and future financial easement. But then the memory of that Irish-American at the speaking-tube in the Bowery came back to him, and the thought of obliging a cowardly assassin like that drove all other thoughts from his mind. He thrust Horrocks and the second mate aside, and dived into the waters after this passenger.

It is no easy thing to find a man in a rough sea and an inky night like that, and for long enough neither returned to the surface. The man in the lifeboat, fearing that the *Armenia* would founder and drag them down in her wash, were beginning to shove off, when the two bodies showed on the waves, and were dragged on board with boat-hooks.

Both were insensible, and in the press of the moment were allowed to remain so on the bottom gratings of the boat. Oars straggled out from her sides, frantically labouring, and the boat fled over the seas like some uncouth insect.

But they were not without a mark to steer for rockets were streaming up out of another part of the night, and presently, as they rowed on over that bleak watery desert, the outline of a great steamer shone out, lit up like some vast stage picture. The other boats had delivered up their freights, and been sent adrift. The second mate's boat rowed to the foot of her gangway ladder.

'This is the *Georgic*,' said a smart officer, who received them. 'You are the last boat. We've got all your other people unless you've lost any.'

'No,' said the second mate. 'We're all right. That's the Old Man down there with his fingers in that passenger's hair.'

'Dead?'

'No, I saw 'em both move as we came alongside.'

'Well pass 'em up and let's get 'em down to our doctor. Hurry now. We wanted to break the record this passage, and we've lost a lot of time already over you.'

'Right-o,' said the *Armenia*'s second mate drearily, 'though I don't suppose our poor old skipper will thank us for keeping him alive. After piling up the old *Atrocity*, he isn't likely to ever get another berth.'

'Man has to take luck as he finds it at sea,' said the *Georgic*'s officer, and shouted to the rail above him 'All aboard, sir.'

'Cast off that boat!' 'Up gangway,' came the orders, and the *Georgic* continued her race to the East.

Morley Roberts

THE INGENUITY OF CAPTAIN SPINK

Though he is far less well-known than Captain Kettle, there was a time when Captain Harry Sharpness Spink of Glo'ster was almost as popular with British magazine readers. Created by the ingeniously inventive writer, Morley Roberts, Captain Spink was also initially intended to appear in just a single story, but so caught the public imagination that Roberts was forced to put him to sea time and time again, and then assemble the best of his adventures in book form.

The similarity between the two captains was also matched by their two authors, for Morley Roberts (1857–1942) had also received a first-class education but then set off to travel the world before settling down to earn his living from writing. He, too, found the inspiration for his captain from a gnarled old merchantman he befriended in America. 'The Ingenuity of Captain Spink' presents the sea dog at his most amusing, and the resolution of this story is every bit as clever as the title suggests.

'Six-penn'orth of ease is worth a shilling, or, on a stretch, half-a-dollar,' said Spink, 'but if you interfere with me much more, Ward, I shall arise in my might and lay you out cold and paralytic.'

'Oh, have your own way,' said Ward, 'not that you can paralyse me with anything but your tongue.'

The tramp steamer *Swan of Avon* was just entering the western channel of the Korean Strait, and right ahead of her lay a thick fog which stood like a cliff. Ward, the chief officer, Day, the second officer, and Captain Harry Sharpness Spink of Glo'ster, who commanded, were on the bridge together, while the Malay serang and some of the deck hands stood in number two hatch and stared eastwards towards Japan. The setting sun gleamed like hot, polished copper over China, and its reflections lipped with blood and fire the diverging and transverse wave pattern made by the bluff entrance of the *Swan*.

'She's after us,' said Spink.

'And will catch us, too,' said Ward.

Along the wall of fog which hid Tsushima Island came a third-class Japanese cruiser with a bone in her teeth, that is to say, with a white bow wave which flamed and glittered in the sun.

'I'd stop and let her overhaul us,' said Ward. 'Why not?'

The *Swan* was bound for Vladivostok with coal, some oil on deck, and a deal of dynamite and picric acid under the coal. Over all were a thousand bags of sugar, shipped in Sourabaya. But from Sourabaya Spink had naturally cleared for Wonsan, in the north of Korea, as the war was in full swing. There was no particular need, as Ward and Day had argued all up the Celebes Sea, to fear a Japanese till they were north of Wonsan. But the little skipper scorned their arguments, and the more sound they seemed the more he scoffed at them.

'I'd rather not be searched,' said Spink, 'and, what's more, I don't mean to be. It's hard on my dignity as a British sailor to be asked questions and have my word doubted, when I know I'm lying, by any Eastern son of a gun.'

So now he turned on Ward.

'Yes, you'd stop, but Captain Harry Sharpness Spink of Glo'ster ain't the one to do any such thing. I'm going into that fog, Ward, and shall rely upon my luck and ingenuity.'

'You haven't any real ingenuity,' said Ward. And just then the cruiser fired a gun.

'That's "heave-to",' said Day, who spoke for the first time.

'Would you do it, Day?' asked Spink.

'I would,' said Day. 'I don't rely on your luck a cent, and to run is to confess you've contraband on board. They'd be justified in takin' us into Nagasaki on that alone.'

For a moment the lucky and ingenious Spink really hesitated, but just then a portion of the wall of fog bulged out and hid the cruiser. And Ward, of course, said the wrong thing.

'I suppose your ingenuity made this fog, eh?'

'I'm goin' ahead,' retorted Spink, 'and I'll trouble you to be civil for once. I'll have my own way if we're sunk, so there.'

The fog looked almost solid as a cliff as they ran for it. It was now less than half-a-mile distant, and the *Swan* was doing, under pressure, something over nine knots. But again they saw the cruiser, which saw them also, and fired a shot. They heard it scream overhead.

'Dip the Jack,' said Spink, and as Day went to do it, the skipper called out —

'Dip nothing; here's the fog coming down right on the charge.'

And indeed it moved suddenly. The *Swan*'s bows were in it while the sun still shone brightly upon her red funnel. The next minute they could hardly see their hands before their faces, and the Chinese quartermaster could not read the compass card till the binnacle lamps were lighted.

'I call this luck!' said Spink, rubbing his hands.

'I thought you called it ingeniousness,' said Ward.

'Not the fog, but usin' it is ingenious,' replied Spink. 'And you ought to be the last man to question my ingenuity, Ward. What about the Philadelphia girl I rescued you from? When I step into the breach to save you I don't turn as red as Bibby's house-flag or as yellow as the funnel of an Elder Dempster boat. I'm equal to the circumstances, and any common, ordinary, measly circumstace knocks you endways. You know it.'

'I don't,' said Ward, who couldn't bear to hear about the Philadelphia girl.

'You do,' said Spink. 'But I'm lucky, courageous and full of ingenuity.'

'You've no foresight or caution,' said Ward.

'Caution never caught ducks,' retorted Spink. 'Let this fog

last and we're all hunky. What will that cruiser do, Ward?'

'Cut us off or run us down,' said Ward sulkily.

'He'll reckon we shall alter our course,' said Spink, 'so alter nothing and keep the boilers busting. Let her scoot!'

He went into the chart-house, lighted a Java cigar and sat smoking. Ward and Day stood together on the bridge.

'Was there ever such a bull-headed blighter as our own special Spink?' asked Ward. 'We'll be copped and taken into Nagasaki and fed on a catty of rice a day.'

'You're always thinking of grub,' said Day, who had a very fair twist himself.

'All right. I'll get even with you for that,' replied Ward.

'You do – at meals,' retorted Day brightly.

'You – you alligator,' said Ward. 'Hallo, what's that?'

Day heard nothing, but Spink heard Ward's exclamation, and came on the bridge. He stood grasping the telegraph, and they all listened, hearing nothing but the thump, thump of the *Swan*'s engines.

'I hear nothing,' said Spink.

'No more do I, now,' said Ward.

But fog is as deceitful as any girl, whether from Philadelphia or London town, or as any big mate who courts one and has to be saved from her wrath by an ingenious skipper. What one hears in a fog isn't evidence, or it is the kind of evidence listened to by a sad and unbelieving judge when an arson case is being tried or a case in a divorce court. A fog says too much or too little, and is as easy to cross-examine as it is to decipher Hittite inscriptions or Greek palimpsests by the light of nature.

But presently Ward, who had flaps to his ears about the size of an engine-room ventilator, once more said he heard something.

'You ought to, with your hearing apparatus,' said Spink. 'I wonder you don't catch on to what they're sayin' ashore.'

Ward was too anxious about the general situation to resent these insults or Day's chuckles, which lasted till Spink told him to go aloft to see if he could get above the fog. When he came back to say he couldn't, the ingenious Spink had the accommodation ladder lowered till it nearly touched the water, and instructed Day to go down and look under the fog. This scheme, which is often useful at sea and too little practised, only made Day wet and cross, for the fog was as thick there as above. And just then Spink heard something himself.

'You're right, Ward. I believe it's that benighted cruiser.'

And Ward, who seldom received praise, since he was fearfully chary of bestowing it, purred like a cat and looked, as seamen say, like a dog with two tails.

Just as there are areas of silence in a fog, so are there areas where no fog is. The *Swan* now hit upon one which was roughly triangular, with each side of the triangle about two cable-lengths long. She ran right out of the fog, as one may run into the calm centre of a cyclone, and as she did so Ward and Spink saw the stern of a vessel disappearing on the other side.

'The devil!' said Spink. He rang the *Swan* down to half speed, so that her engines should make less noise, and altered her course forty-five degrees to starboard. When they were in the fog again he went full speed once more.

'On this course we shall soon be ashore,' said Ward.

Spink requested, with a good deal of ornament, to be told something he didn't know. Ward, who could do as he was requested when he found something disagreeable to say, obliged him with a few oaths translated from the worst Spanish.

'That'll do, you,' said Spink; 'if there are ears the size of yours aboard that cruiser, they'll hear you. But, all the same, I believe we've bilked the blighter.'

But he was wrong. Perhaps someone on board the cruiser had seen or heard the *Swan*, after all. For inside of ten minutes they heard her again, and presently saw a grey-black shadow on their port side. Much to Ward's astonishment, Spink yanked the lanyard of the *Swan*'s whistle and made it bellow as if with fear. And he rang her down to 'stop' and 'full speed astern'. While he did so he used some of Ward's new expressions. He was never too old to learn.

'Now you're done,' said the mate.

They were hailed in Japanese, and Ward, who was the linguist on board, said they were asking 'What ship's that?'

'Say we're the – oh, the *Annandale* from Fusan to Nagasaki in ballast,' said Spink.

'If that's your ingenuity, say it yourself,' replied Ward. 'I'll take no hand in it.'

Spink did say it himself. He also said things to Ward which are not fit for publication.

'My ingenuity has no limits,' he declared. Then he asked the cruiser who she was.

'The Japanese cruiser *Yoshino*, and we'll send a boat aboard you,' replied a voice from the cruiser.

'Where's you ingenuity now?' asked Ward bitterly. 'Why didn't you pipe out Wonsan?'

'Cruiser ahoy!' said Spink, and he was answered with the orthodox 'Hallo!'

'We've got smallpox on board, sir,' said Spink.

They heard voices speaking. The officer who hailed them evidently translated 'smallpox' into Japanese.

'Smallpox, did you say?' asked the officer.

'Yes, and two cases very bad,' said Spink mournfully.

'If you're bound for Nagasaki, why are you steering north-east?' asked the officer suspiciously.

'We altered our course for another steamer which nearly ran us down just now,' said Spink, 'a steamer bound for the nor'ard. Didn't you hear us? It was a very narrow shave.'

There was an air of simple truth about Spink at any time, and, as Ward owned afterwards, he almost swallowed what he heard, even to the smallpox.

'They believe you,' said Ward; 'they actually believe you!'

'Dry up,' said Spink; 'you leather-lunged Mick, dry up!'

'Oh, all right,' returned Ward; 'we'll see about that later.'

They heard the officers of the cruiser speaking through the fog. Its starboard side-light threw a sickly glare on the mist. And then suddenly the light disappeared.

Spink spoke through the engine-room speaking-tube and ordered them to go ahead dead slow.

'We'll send a boat aboard of you,' said the voice from the cruiser.

'Please let me have a little quinine and some salts,' roared Spink; 'if you will, I shall be much obliged, very much obliged.'

The voice that answered was lost in the fog. It was now as thick as a blanket. But Spink listened for the splash of the cruiser's boat in the water, and when he heard it he went half speed ahead and turned her to port under the cruiser's stern.

Then he let her out full speed, and as he did so he heard dim exclamations from the lost war-vessel.

'Now you've done it,' said Ward. 'If you'd said we were bound for Wonsan and showed 'em your papers we should have got off. If we're caught now your name's Dennis.'

But Spink was joyous.

'Wonsan's thin enough, and too thin,' he said cheerfully. 'I want no Jap blighter aboard me, with his "Hatches off, if you'll be so good as to be so kind". We'll lose 'em in this fog. I never thought to bless one before.'

'Wait till you're out of it,' said Ward, who saw a cruiser in every wreath of mist. But, as a matter of fact, Spink's luck served him. The cruiser had to pick up her boat again, and by that time the *Swan* was out of hearing, and might have been at the bottom of the sea for all the Japanese knew. Spink steamed round in a half-circle and then laid a course to clear the island of Tsushima, if he didn't knock a hole in it. He went north-east again an hour later.

'What did I tell you blighters about my ingenuity?' asked Spink.

'Your luck, you mean,' said Ward. 'Is there another skipper in the British merchant service that has it?'

'There isn't, I own,' said Spink; 'but my saying smallpox very near bluffed 'em. I consider it highly ingenious.'

'I don't. Do you, Day?' asked Ward.

'Certainly not,' said Day; 'far from it.'

'You're a lot of measly, unappreciative swine,' said Spink. 'If I ain't ingenious, I'm nothing. I'll show you I'm ingenious before I'm through with you. And I've got courage too, heaps of it.'

'Bull-headedness,' sniffed Ward.

'You were scared to death, Ward,' said Spink; 'but did my voice tremble when I lied? When you were lying to that Philadelphia girl, a child could have spotted it.'

'You don't know her as I did,' said Ward weakly, 'or you'd have trembled too.'

'I knew her better before I had her choked off, and I'll never help you with another unless you own I'm ingenious,' said Spink.

'I won't,' said Ward.

'I'll make you before I'm through with you,' said Spink firmly. 'There's no one equal to me for running in a bluff on a man, woman, girl, or child. Is there, Day?'

'Heaps of them,' said Day. 'You ain't half the liar that Middleshaw of the *Peruvian* is. Oh, he's a dandy at it, a real dandy.'

'Oh, very well,' said Spink; 'but I'll make you own I can lie equal to Middleshaw, or I'll bust. See if I don't. You're both ungracious swabs, and Ward's ungrateful. Didn't Philadelphia ring with what I did for him, from the Pennsylvania Railroad Depot to the Naval Asylum? But I'll take a snooze in the chart-house. Both of you are to keep a bright look-out till we're clear of this fog or till it's daylight.'

And in three minutes he was fast asleep. He looked like a hardy, innocent child, as indeed he was.

'Wonderful chap, the skipper,' said Day.

'Too bally wonderful! He *must* walk crooked. Why don't he say he's for Wonsan straight out? Why shouldn't we take coal and sugar to Wonsan, I'd like to know? Let 'em come and search. They'll not find the dynamite,' said Ward.

'It's the blighter's way. He can't let us off a piece of acting,' said Day. 'He'll prove he's ingenious enough to get out of a trap if he has to make the trap to get into. But he's an amazin' galoot.'

'He is. I own it freely,' said Ward. 'But I'd not let him know I thought so for a tank full of dollars.'

'Not for a round-bottomed chest of twenty-dollar gold pieces,' said Day.

'I suppose we'll make Vladivostok some time?' said Ward.

'He'll coax a Jap cruiser into towing us there,' said Day. 'We may lick him at scrappin', but for luck, lying and ingeniousness he lays us out cold and paralytic. Think of the time he tackled that girl of yours at Philadelphia.'

'Oh, shut it!' said Ward.

'And that other piece at Boston.'

'Oh, dry up!' said Ward.

'To say nothing of the others.'

'Oh, give us a rest, and don't make a song about my girls,' said Ward. 'I'm in a cold sweat when I think of some of them.

But I'll say this for Spink: he's a good sort. When I took that Cadiz girl from him he never bore malice.'

'You – you ass!' said Day scornfully.

'What d'ye mean?' asked the angry mate.

'Ain't you tumbled to the machine-laid fact that he wanted to get shut of that piece? Oh, you are a blighter.'

'I'm your superior officer, and you're insubordinate,' said Ward, with as much dignity as he could call up considering the conversation.

'So are you insubordinate to the skipper,' said Day. 'There never was such a ship as the *Swan* for insubordination, and it's all Spink's character that causes it. What can you do with a skipper who goes for you and gets knocked out?'

'But he always keeps up his end,' said Ward, 'so far as brains go.'

'You and I haven't the brains of a duck compared to him,' said Day. 'That's where it is. He may be crazy and unlike any skipper that ever cursed a tramp or her owners, but he has brains and we haven't.'

'Speak for yourself,' said Ward.

'Blimy, I can speak for you too.'

'I consider "blimy" a low expression,' said Ward.

'I'm a low person,' said Day, 'and the fact never fazed me. I'd be a duke if I could, but I can't.'

An hour later the *Swan* emerged from the fog as suddenly as she had entered it, and, so far as mere sight could tell, there was nothing between them and Siberia. But Ward called Spink, and the skipper, who was always considerate, said he would take Ward's watch on deck, for the mate had been up since dawn.

'I'm a very wonderful man, Ward,' he said.

'Yes,' said Ward, yawning, 'are you?'

He was too tired to contradict the skipper, and went below, leaving Spink to consider what a marvellous person he was.

'I've left that blighted Jap in the fog hunting for me,' said Spink, 'and I hope she'll go and butt Tsushima into the middle of next week. It'll be a deal handier there than in the middle of the fairway. But what shall I do if I'm pulled up again? I believe they're not half scared of smallpox. Next time I'll make it plague. Oh, I'm a wonder!'

About noon next day they saw a steamer right ahead, and made out that she was a tramp. Presently they were close alongside each other, and Ward said he knew her. She was the *Queen Victoria.*

'Her skipper's luckier even than you, Spink,' said Ward. 'She goes in and out of Port Arthur and Vladivostok as if she owned the high seas, and never gets held up.'

Spink held a short conversation through a megaphone with the luckier skipper.

'Seen any Japs about?' he asked.

'There's one somewheres about Wonsan,' bellowed the other skipper. 'But I'm that lucky I never run aboard 'em till I'm in ballast or with beans out of Wonsan, as I am now. Good luck to you.'

'Humph!' said Spink to Ward; 'I scorn pure luck. Any fool can be lucky. You might be lucky, Ward,'

'I am – to sail with you,' said Ward, sniffing.

'You mean that for satire, don't you,' said Spink, 'and for sarcasm? But I scorn it. When I get my brand of sarcasm to work you turn red and white.'

'And when I get red,' retorted Ward, 'you turn off your sarcasm quick and bring out butter.'

'Let it go at that,' said Spink. 'You can lick me with the gloves or without 'em, but my tongue is your master, Ward. You don't understand the pleasures of the intellect.'

Ward owned sulkily that he didn't.

'It ain't a pleasure to you to read poetry or to see my quickness and ingenuity in peril,' said Spink. 'Now suppose as we pass this blighted island we see a Jap cruiser lying doggo, what would you do?'

'Let him search us, and chance it,' said Ward. 'You're for Wonsan, and why not, as I keep on tellin' you?'

'I'd rather he didn't,' said Spink. 'You never know what they'll think, and if they see coal under sugar they may wonder what's under coal. I'd rather bluff them again.'

'With smallpox?' asked Ward. 'They'll be gettin' tired of that.'

'You talk as if I'd no resources, Ward,' said Spink, 'and you ought to know I'm full of 'em. Look here, get that Malay serang to do something for me.'

'What is it now?' asked Ward wearily. 'More ingeniousness?'

'I want a corpse,' said Spink, thoughtfully.

'You want what?'

'Don't you understand English?' asked Spink. 'I want a corpse.'

'You want – oh, my! here comes Day. I say, Day, he wants a corpse,' said Ward.

'Well, give it him,' said Day. 'I don't mind.'

'I want the serang to make one,' said Spink.

'Out of a Chinaman?' asked Day casually.

'No, out of anything,' said Spink. 'How would you make one, Ward?'

'The nearest I ever came to it was with a belayin' pin,' said Ward, 'but the bull-headed blighter got well.'

'Don't you see I want a dummy, not a real one. You've got the native savvy of an epileptic chicken,' said Spink.

'Oh, have I?' asked Ward. 'Well, you and Day can fix your deader. It's my watch below.'

Spink turned to Day.

'He's got a poor intellect, Day. You and the serang fix me up a kind of dummy. Make it of a donkey's breakfast and a blanket, and fix it up dandy with a couple of fire bars at its feet.'

'What's the game?' asked Day.

'Aren't you more intelligent than Ward?' asked the skipper, 'or are you an epileptic too? Don't you see already that there's a cruiser lyin' doggo behind Takashima there with her smoke over the land? Get me that corpse or I'll log you for insubordination and refusin' duty.'

So Day and the serang fixed up the dummy, while the Chinese deck-hands looked on wondering what it was all about.

'Tell 'em it's a Chinkey, and one of them,' said Spink, 'and tell 'em to look sorrowful, or I'll come down and make 'em too muchee solly faitee.'

So Day told them it was alla same one piecee dead Chinaman, and they looked solemn and wondered all the more.

'Up with the gaudy yellow and black,' said Spink, and they hoisted the black and yellow squares that mean cholera or plague.

'And half-mast the glorious flag of England,' said Spink. 'Oh, ain't we gay?'

And coming past the point of Takashima Island they saw a Jap cruiser there lying at anchor.

Spink rang the *Swan* down to slow, and Day hoisted signal flags reading D N B C, which signal equals plague.

'Get the funeral ready,' said Spink. 'Be quick but solemn, all the same.'

They saw a boat put off from the cruiser as Day, bareheaded, tipped the plank and launched a seaman's mattress, commonly known as a donkey's breakfast, into the sea. Spink and Ward took their caps off, while the Chinamen, acting under orders from the serang, raised a melancholy howl.

'Make 'em howl again, serang,' said Spink.

'Accha Tuan!' said the serang. 'Makee plopa numpa one bobbery; capitan sahib he makee play pidgin for dam Japanee.'

Whereon the Chinkies moaned again in chorus, and Spink put on his cap. He turned the telegraph to 'stop', and as the *Swan*'s screw ceased to revolve, the Japanese cruiser's boat came to within twenty fathoms and backed water.

'What's the mattah? You have plague, eh?' asked the bright little Jap lieutenant in the sternsheets.

'That's so, a Chinaman,' said Spink.

'Where you from?'

'From Singapore!'

'Where you bound for?'

'Wonsan,' said Spink.

'What with?'

'Coal and some sugar,' said Spink. 'Could you come aboard, or would you like to look at my papers where you are?'

The lieutenant, who loved plague no better than any one else, and had orders not to board this tramp if things seemed straight, said he would look at the papers where he was. He sheered in alongside, and Spink lowered him down a tin case and the official log carefully made fast to a piece of line.

'Don't drop 'em overboard,' said Spink anxiously. A ship-master's soul, if he has one or is allowed to mention it now-a-days, is wrapped up in his papers. Without them he is no better than a pirate or a person wandering about the high seas with no visible means of subsistence.

'What you think, eh?' said the Jap, as he undid the case and took out the precious documents. For the information of the unlearned in such matters, it may be mentioned that they consisted of the ship's register, the articles, the Victualling Bill from Singapore, the manifest, the Bills of Lading, the Charter Party, the Suez Canal certificate, the latest Lights Bill, the load line certificate, and, as Wonsan was in Korea, technically a Chinese port still, a consular manifest as well, all of which shows that it takes hard faking to pretend at sea to be anything but what you are.

The Japanese lieutenant went through them all as gingerly as if they were full of plague germs, and after returning them to their case, he washed his hands over the side of the boat.

'All right, Capitan,' he said, 'they're all in order, very good. What weather you have in the straits?'

'That foggy you could make bricks out of it, lieutenant,' said Spink, shaking his head.

'You see Russians?'

'Never a sight of one. We spoke your cruiser *Yoshino* in the fog.'

'I have brother in her,' said the Jap. 'Have you any more sick with plague?'

'Not yet,' said Spink, who could never resist a joke, though his face was as solemn as an owl's, 'but I think my mate's sickening for it.'

Ward turned white at the very notion, and under cover of the rail, as he stood on the main deck, shook his fist at the skipper.

'Very good,' said the Japanese. 'I think we have more fog, eh?'

It certainly looked thickish to the north, and the sun, which had been bright, was a little paler already.

'It looks like it,' said Spink. 'Good-bye, and thanks, and good luck to you. My best regards to your brother, please.'

With that he took off his cap, rang the *Swan* up to full speed ahead, and waved his hand to his visitor, who turned back to his ship. Ward came up the ladder to the bridge, where Day and Spink were.

'Why d'ye say I'm goin' to have plague?' he asked sulkily.

'I was wrong,' said Spink. 'It's I've got it, and you're it. But what do you think of my ingeniousness now?'

'Very little,' said Ward. 'They don't want to interfere with British ships if they can help it, and —'

'You're a very disappointin' beggar and hard to please,' said Spink, 'and it's only jealousy. It would have been a long time till you'd have invented such a powerful notion as mine. I believe that mournful howl of the crew worked wonders.'

'Bah!' said Ward.

'Fog's coming down,' said Day.

'It comes out of Ward's intellect,' said Spink, who had expected praise. But Ward didn't hear him. He was looking astern. Presently he gave a loud and bitter laugh.

'What's the joke now?' asked Spink.

'Joke! Well, it is a joke,' said Ward. 'Your ingeniousness has let you in this time, or I'm a Korean in a high hat. That deader of yours has come up! See!'

He handed Spink the glasses. Spink clapped them to his eyes and saw the late lamented mattress and red blanket on the surface of the sea. The boat which had visited them had nearly reached the cruiser, but they saw her turn about and row for the spot where the red blanket showed.

'Curse you, Day, that's your fault,' said Spink. 'You never made them fire bars properly fast! Did any shipmaster ever have such officers? Here's all my ingeniousness wasted, and worse than wasted. Likely they'll know it was a fake funeral and be after us!'

He swore in English, French, German, Italian, and Spanish, to say nothing of American, for though he was a poor linguist, he knew the swear-words of most languages. Even as he spoke they saw their late visitor inspecting the floating object, at first with great care, and then with none. He went round again and rowed for the cruiser. As soon as he got within hail of it, they heard the capstan going, and the cruiser got under way as they picked him up.

'Now where's you ingeniousness?' asked Ward. 'If you'd

just played no games it would have been all right. The matter with you, Spink, is that you're too ingenious.'

For once Spink felt that Ward was right. But he wouldn't own it. He hit at Ward's sore point.

'You didn't think so when that Philadelphia girl came aboard with her brother,' said Spink, 'oh no, you didn't say so or think so then! No, you came to me as if I was your father and your brother, and I saved you from death or marriage! And now you turn on me! You're the most ungrateful swab between the North and South Poles. A tame alligator is a trustworthy pet compared with you.'

'Leave me and my girls alone,' said Ward, 'and as for that Philadelphia girl –'

'Here she comes,' said Day. But he referred to the cruiser, not to the young lady from Philadelphia.

'Yes, she does,' said Spink. 'We're bound for Nagasaki after all. You and Ward will look well on a catty of rice apiece per day. Hallo!'

For the cruiser fired a gun.

'That's heave to!' said Ward.

'Is it? said Spink. 'Then I don't heave to. I'll run to the last and trust to my luck. Where's that fog? Oh, where is it?'

It was overhead if anywhere, for the sun went out and the sea turned green and grey and as desolate as poor Spink's prospects.

'Yes, I was too ingenious,' he said, 'I own it.'

The crusier fired a dumb shell from a four-inch gun over the *Swan*. It screamed mournfully, and Ward ducked his head.

'You'd better stop her and cave in,' said Ward uneasily.

'I won't,' said Spink. 'Here comes the fog!'

But it didn't come, or not their way. Yet on looking astern at the cruiser, which began to come along in a hurry, they saw her in a mist a couple of miles astern.

'I trust to my luck still,' said Spink. 'It can't, it won't desert me!'

It didn't. The next minute the clouds overhead settled down on the sea as calmly and sweetly as a thistle-down in a green pasture. Spink turned swiftly to the Chinese quartermaster at the wheel.

'Hard a-port,' he said. And the *Swan* turned to starboard.

'They'll run us down if you don't watch it,' said Ward nervously.

'Dry up,' said Spink. And Ward did dry up while the *Swan* ran north-east for half-a-mile. Then Spink stopped her. They heard the cruiser pass astern of them going full speed, but saw nothing. Spink went ahead again, turned the *Swan* another eight points to starboard, and went back south about round the island they had just left.

'Once more I'm in luck,' said Spink triumphantly, 'and I shall be glad if Mr Ward and Mr Day will apologise for doubting it.'

'I will when we get to Vladivostok,' said Ward. 'But I'd have you understand you're not there yet.'

'Who said I was?' asked Spink. 'But I suppose you own it would be cruel, right down cruel, of Providence to go back on me after all this?'

'After leadin' you on, I suppose you mean,' said Ward.

'Yes, leadin' me to suppose I was all hunky and as good as in Vladivostok,' said Spink. 'You own that would be cruel?'

'Very,' said Ward. 'And where are we now? I hope you know, for I don't.'

The fog thickened till it was like good pea-soup, as Spink presently suggested, real soup that a spoon would stand up in, not the bilge water of a vessel loaded with split peas.

'I don't know exactly where we are,' said Spink, 'but in this life, and especially in blockade running, you've got to take chances, so I'll lay her straight for Vladivostok and chance those Japanese ducks.'

After they had been running for two hours at full speed, that is to say at nine knots, Spink sighed pleasantly, or as pleasantly as a seaman can in a fog, and declared they were all right now.

'And I hope you'll own, Ward, that I've been very ingenious,' he ended up with.

'Why do you want me to own it?' asked Ward.

'Because I like praise when it's my due,' said Spink modestly, 'and I want to see a man like you, that's obstinate to a degree, give in and own it's my due.'

'I'll own you're lucky so far,' growled Ward, 'but as to the ingeniousness, I don't see it that it did more than give you another opportunity to be lucky. It looks as if you carried a fog in your pocket and let it out when you wanted it, but that's not cleverness.'

'I've been known to be clever and ingenious since I was knee-high to a grasshopper,' said Spink in an injured tone of voice, 'all Glo'ster owned it, and owned it freely. And Glo'ster is a fine place full of very clever men, especially my father. I've never told you about him, but I will some day. So when I prove I'm ingenious, I like to have it owned.'

'Well, your father may have been as clever as mud,' said Ward, 'and Glo'ster may be fair rotten with ingenuity, but I'll never own you are more than lucky. And Day won't, either.'

Spink snorted.

'Oh, Day! What's his opinion worth?' he asked. 'He ruined my plan by not fastening those fire bars in and letting up the reputed corpse. But for that you know it would have worked. My luck's not good with either of my mates that my unfortunate nature compels me to sail with. They're not respectful.'

'How can you reckon on us bein' respectful when you behave as you do?' asked Ward. 'I've sailed with a dozen worse men than you, and been as polite to 'em as if they were tin gods. You talk and brag too much to be respected, unless you can knock us about.'

Spink shook his head gloomily.

'No doubt you're right, Ward. I'm what I am, and can't help it. I've not a high and haughty nature, and I can't sit by my lonesome in my own cabin and pass the time of day with a gin-bottle, which too many skippers do. I ain't askin' you to treat me like a tin god or a brass one, but I do think I might have a little appreciation of my ingenuity. Why, I'll bet you a fiver the very Chinamen see that I'm ingenious.'

'I'll bet you ten dollars they don't and won't,' said Ward.

'I'll take that bet,' said Spink. And just then the fog began to thin perceptibly, and lift from the surface of the sea as if it were alive.

'By Gosh!' said Ward. 'Look there!'

'And when Spink looked he saw a big warship right ahead of them.

'Have you another fog in your pocket?' asked Ward sadly.

'I'll use your intellect for one if it's needed,' said Spink. 'Don't you know she's a Russian, and the *Rurik* at that?

You've no eye for the profile of a battleship or cruiser, you eminent idiot.'

And Ward was too much relieved to resent Spink's language. The *Swan* steamed close past the *Rurik*, and Spink informed her in joyous tones that he was bound for Vladivostok. Day came out on deck in his pyjamas to see what the row was. Spink called to him.

'Now ain't I ingenious? Won't you own it, Day, after lettin' me in with your cursed carelessness?'

'Luck's not ingenuity,' said Day.

'That's what I've been tellin' him,' said Ward.

'A Chinaman would see it,' said Spink. 'I've ten dollars in my pouch screaming out that a mere Chinky could see it.'

'I'll bet you haven't,' said Day, going back to his berth.

'Done with you,' said Spink.

And leaving Ward in charge of the *Swan*, he went below.

'But I'll prove it yet,' he said. And as he fell asleep he seemed to see how he could prove it. When he woke he tried it. He sent the Chinese steward for the Malay serang.

'You want five dollars, serang?' asked Spink graciously.

'Velly muchee, tuan,' said the Malay, who talked pidgin-English with every one but Ward, who, as he said, was a whale at Lascari-bât. 'Oh, Capitan sahib, I velly much likee dollah.'

'To-morrow we shall be at Vladivostok,' said Spink. 'You savvy, eh?'

'Plenty savvy,' said the serang, 'velly good, I t'ink.'

'Suppose you and the Chinamen come for'ard after we're at anchor and I'm still on the bridge, and you stand on number two hatch,' said Spink.

'Yes, tuan. What for makee so?' asked the beady-eyed Malay anxiously.

'Suppose you bow to me, makee kowtow, you savvy, and say, "Oh, Capitan sahib, you muchee clever inside,"' said Spink, nodding.

'I savvy, tuan,' said the serang, 'and you give five dollah. Accha, I makee t'at: can do!'

'All say one time, "Capitan sahib, you velly ingenious, plenty clever inside,"' insisted Spink.

'In — in — me no savvy that talkee,' said the serang.

'In-ge-ni-ous,' repeated Spink. 'All-a-same clever.'

'Ingeni-ous,' said the Malay. 'All-li, Capitan sahib, I savvy him numpa one.'

Next morning they anchored off the town in the Zolotoi Rog, and before the Customs' boat came aboard, Day and Ward were much surprised to see the whole crew, including the serang and the Chinese steward, mustering on number two hatch.

'What do the blighters want?' said Spink innocently.

'Blamed if I know,' said Day. 'Hi, serang, what for this bobbery?'

'Tuan, Chinamen wantchee makee kowtow to Capitan sahib,' replied the serang solemnly.

'Yes, what is it?' said Spink. 'Speak up, serang.'

Whereupon the entire crew bowed down before Spink and wailed unanimously –

'Capitan sahib velly, velly clever inside; he muchee in-ge-ni-ous!'

'Say it again,' said Spink, 'I no savvy!'

And again they bowed and said –

'Capitan velly, velly clever inside; he muchee in-ge-ni-ous!'

'Thank you, men,' said Spink. 'I'm much obliged to you. Steward, give them a drink. That'll do!'

And turning to Ward and Day, Spink held out his hand.

'Ten dollars each, please.'

They looked at each other and paid in silence.

'Ain't I ingenious, or am I not?' asked Spink.

'By the Lord, you are!' said Ward.

William Hope Hodgson

THE THING IN THE WEEDS

The eternal mystery of the sea has fascinated writers of sea stories for generations, and apart from Herman Melville and Joseph Conrad, I doubt if anyone has dealt with it so skilfully as my next contributor, William Hope Hodgson (1877–1918). While many writers have described the sea's beauty and wild grandeur, few have so superbly captured its brooding terror. For terror there surely is – and not just that represented by the elements, but rather the unknown that can lurk in the murky depths below or just beyond the horizon.

Hodgson was, in fact, obsessed with the sea from his childhood and actually tried to stow away aboard a cargo ship when he was a small boy. Although he was caught, he managed to convince his clergyman father that his intentions were serious, and in 1891 he was allowed to sign up. He voyaged for some eight years, travelling three times around the world, and although his life at sea was always tough, he proved himself a worthy seaman — on one occasion saving a fellow crew-member from drowning, a deed for which he was awarded the Royal Humane Society's medal for bravery. It was, however, the mystery of the sea, and in particular the legends that surrounded certain areas, that really captured his imagination. And when he returned to England, it was just such ideas that he drew upon to earn his living as a storyteller. The books that flowed from his pen, though not immediately appreciated then, have since become recognised as classics, and I might just cite as examples The Boats of the Glen Carrig (1907), The Ghost Pirates (1909) and Men of Deep Waters, published in

1914 *at the start of the war that was to take his life, in the trenches of Ypres.*

The ocean mystery that undoubtedly fascinated William Hope Hodgson more than any other was the Sargasso Sea, that weed-strewn ocean off the coast of America, which, legend maintained, was haunted by monstrous creatures waiting to pounce on any vessel and its crew foolish enough to venture too close. Indeed, he wrote a series of stories set in this locality, of which 'The Thing in the Weeds' is one of the very best, and still capable of making me shudder even after all the times I have read it. I certainly wouldn't wish anyone the creepy feeling I experienced when I first came across it on a voyage in the South Atlantic one hot summer's night. But still more, I would not like for a moment to find myself in the nightmare situation that actually faces Captain Jeldy and his men in the pages that follow . . .

I

This is an extraordinary tale. We had come up from the Cape, and owing to the Trades heading us more than usual, we had made some hundreds of miles more westing than I ever did before or since.

I remember the particular night of the happening perfectly. I suppose what occurred stamped it solid into my memory, with a thousand little details that, in the ordinary way, I should never have remembered an hour. And, of course, we talked it over so often among ourselves that this, no doubt, helped to fix it all past any forgetting.

I remember the mate and I had been pacing the weather side of the poop and discussing various old shellbacks' superstitions. I was third mate, and it was between four and five bells in the first watch, i.e. between ten and half-past. Suddenly he stopped in his walk and lifted his head and sniffed several times.

'My word, mister,' he said, 'there's a rum kind of stink somewhere about. Don't you smell it?'

I sniffed once or twice at the light airs that were coming in on the beam; then I walked to the rail and leaned over, smelling again at the slight breeze. And abruptly I got a whiff of it, faint and sickly, yet vaguely suggestive of something I had once smelt before.

'I can smell something, Mr Lammart,' I said. 'I could almost give it name; and yet somehow I can't.' I stared away into the dark to windward. 'What do you seem to smell?' I asked him.

'I can't smell anything now,' he replied, coming over and standing beside me. 'It's gone again. No! By Jove! there it is again. My goodness! Phew!'

The smell was all about us now, filling the night air. It had still that indefinable familiarity about it, and yet it was curiously strange, and, more than anything else, it was certainly simply beastly.

The stench grew stronger, and presently the mate asked me to go for'ard and see whether the look-out man noticed anything. When I reached the break of the fo'c's'le head I called up to the man, to know whether he smelled anything.

'Smell anythin', sir?' he sang out. 'Jumpin' larks! I sh'u'd think I do. I'm fair p'isoned with it.'

I ran up the weather steps and stood beside him. The smell was certainly very plain up there, and after savouring it for a few moments I asked him whether he thought it might be a dead whale. But he was very emphatic that this could not be the case, for, as he said, he had been nearly fifteen years in whaling ships, and knew the smell of a dead whale, 'like as you would the smell of bad whisky, sir', as he put it. ''Tain't no whale yon, but the Lord He knows what 'tis. I'm thinking it's Davy Jones come up for a breather.'

I stayed with him some minutes, staring out into the darkness, but could see nothing; for, even had there been something big close to us, I doubt whether I could have seen it, so black a night it was, without a visible star, and with a vague, dull haze breeding an indistinctness all about the ship.

I returned to the mate and reported that the look-out complained of the smell, but that neither he nor I had been able to see anything in the darkness to account for it.

By this time the queer, disgusting odour seemed to be in all the air about us, and the mate told me to go below and shut all the ports, so as to keep the beastly smell out of the cabins and the saloon.

When I returned he suggested that we should shut the companion doors, and after that we commenced to pace the poop again, discussing the extraordinary smell, and stopping from time to time to stare through our night-glasses out into the night about the ship.

'I'll tell you what it smells like, mister,' the mate remarked once, 'and that's like a mighty old derelict I once went aboard in the North Atlantic. She was a proper old-timer, an' she gave us all the creeps. There was just this funny, dank, rummy sort of century-old bilge-water and dead men an' seaweed. I can't stop thinkin' we're nigh some lonesome old packet out there; an' a good thing we've not much way on us!'

'Do you notice how almighty quiet everything's gone the last half-hour or so?' I said a little later. 'It must be the mist thickening down.'

'It is the mist,' said the mate, going to the rail and staring out. 'Good Lord, what's that?' he added.

Something had knocked his hat from his head, and it fell with a sharp rap at my feet. And suddenly, you know, I got a premonition of something horrid.

'Come away from the rail, sir!' I said sharply, and gave one jump and caught him by the shoulders and dragged him back. 'Come away from the side!'

'What's up, mister?' he growled at me, and twisted his shoulders free. 'What's wrong with you? Was it you knocked off my cap?' He stooped and felt around for it, and as he did so I *heard* something unmistakably fiddling away at the rail which the mate had just left.

'My God, sir!' I said, 'there's something there. Hark!'

The mate stiffened up, listening; then he heard it. It was for all the world as if something was feeling and rubbing the rail there in the darkness, not two fathoms away from us.

'Who's there?' said the mate quickly. Then, as there was no answer: 'What the devil's this hanky-panky? Who's playing the goat there?' He made a swift step through the darkness towards the rail, but I caught him by the elbow.

'Don't go, mister!' I said, hardly above a whisper. 'It's not one of the men. Let me get a light.'

'Quick, then!' he said, and I turned and ran aft to the binnacle and snatched out the lighted lamp. As I did so I heard the mate shout something out of the darkness in a strange voice. There came a sharp, loud, rattling sound, and then a crash, and immediately the mate roaring to me to hasten with the light. His voice changed even whilst he shouted, and gave out something that was nearer a scream than anything else. There came two loud, dull blows and an extraordinary gasping sound; and then, as I raced along the poop, there was a tremendous smashing of glass and an immediate silence.

'Mr Lammart!' I shouted. 'Mr Lammart!' And then I had reached the place where I had left the mate for forty seconds before; but he was not there.

'Mr Lammart!' I shouted again, holding the light high over my head and turning quickly to look behind me. As I did so my foot glided on some slippery substance, and I went headlong to the deck with a tremendous thud, smashing the lamp and putting out the light.

I was on my feet again in an instant. I groped a moment for the lamp, and as I did so I heard the men singing out from the maindeck and the noise of their feet as they came running aft. I found the broken lamp and realised it was useless; then I jumped for the companion-way, and in half a minute I was back with the big saloon lamp glaring bright in my hands.

I ran for'ard again, shielding the upper edge of the glass chimney from the draught of my running, and the blaze of the big lamp seemed to make the weather side of the poop as bright as day, except for the mist, that gave something of a vagueness to things.

Where I had left the mate there was blood upon the deck, but nowhere any signs of the man himself. I ran to the weather rail and held the lamp to it. There was blood upon it, and the rail itself seemed to have been wrenched by some huge force. I put out my hand and found that I could shake it. Then I leaned out-board and held the lamp at arm's length, staring down over the ship's side.

'Mr Lammart!' I shouted into the night and the thick mist. 'Mr Lammart! Mr Lammart!' But my voice seemed to go, lost and muffled and infinitely small, away into the billowy darkness.

I heard the men snuffling and breathing, waiting to leeward of the poop. I whirled round to them, holding the lamp high.

'We heard somethin', sir,' said Tarpley, the leading seaman in our watch. 'Is anythin' wrong, sir?'

'The mate's gone,' I said blankly. 'We heard something, and I went for the binnacle lamp. Then he shouted, and I heard a sound of things smashing, and when I got back he'd gone clean.' I turned and held the light out again over the unseen sea, and the men crowded round along the rail and stared, bewildered.

'Blood, sir,' said Tarpley, pointing. 'There's somethin' almighty queer out there.' He waved a huge hand into the darkness. 'That's what stinks –'

He never finished; for suddenly one of the men cried out something in a frightened voice: 'Look out, sir! Look out, sir!'

I saw, in one brief flash of sight, something come in with an infernal flicker of movement; and then, before I could form any notion of what I had seen, the lamp was dashed to pieces across the poop deck. In that instant my perceptions cleared, and I saw the incredible folly of what we were doing; for there we were, standing up against the blank, unknowable night, and out there in the darkness there surely lurked some thing of monstrousness; and we were at its mercy. I seemed to feel it hovering – hovering over us, so that I felt the sickening creep of gooseflesh all over me.

'Stand back from the rail!' I shouted. 'Stand back from the rail!' There was a rush of feet as the men obeyed, in sudden apprehension of their danger, and I gave back with them. Even as I did so I felt some invisible thing brush my shoulder, and an indescribable smell was in my nostrils from something that moved over me in the dark.

'Down into the saloon everyone!' I shouted. 'Down with you all! Don't wait a moment!'

There was a rush along the dark weather deck, and then the men went helter-skelter down the companion steps into the saloon, falling and cursing over one another in the darkness. I sang out to the man at the wheel to join them, and then I followed.

I came upon the men huddled at the foot of the stairs and filling up the passage, all crowding each other in the darkness. The skipper's voice was filling the saloon, and he was demanding in violent adjectives the cause of so tremendous a noise. From the steward's berth there came also a voice and the splutter of a match, and then the glow of a lamp in the saloon itself.

I pushed my way through the men and found the captain in the saloon in his sleeping gear, looking both drowsy and angry, though perhaps bewilderment topped every other feeling. He held his cabin lamp in his hand, and shone the light over the huddle of men.

I hurried to explain, and told him of the incredible disappearance of the mate, and of my conviction that some extraordinary thing was lurking near the ship out in the mist and the darkness. I mentioned the curious smell, and told how the mate had suggested that we had drifted down near some old-time, sea-rotted derelict. And, you know, even as I put it into awkward words, my imagination began to awaken to horrible discomforts; a thousand dreadful impossibilities of the sea became suddenly possible.

The captain (Jeldy was his name) did not stop to dress, but ran back into his cabin, and came out in a few moments with a couple of revolvers and a handful of cartridges. The second mate had come running out of his cabin at the noise, and had listened intensely to what I had to say; and now he jumped back into his berth and brought out his own lamp and a large Smith and Wesson, which was evidently ready loaded.

Captain Jeldy pushed one of his revolvers into my hands, with some of the cartridges, and we began hastily to load the weapons. Then the captain caught up his lamp and made for the stairway, ordering the men into the saloon out of his way.

'Shall you want them, sir?' I asked.

'No,' he said. 'It' no use their running any unnecessary risks.' He threw a word over his shoulder: 'Stay quiet here, men; if I want you I'll give you a shout; then come spry!'

'Aye, aye, sir,' said the watch in a chorus; and then I was following the captain up the stairs, with the second mate close behind.

We came up through the companion-way on to the silence of

the deserted poop. The mist had thickened up, even during the brief time that I had been below, and there was not a breath of wind. The mist was so dense that it seemed to press in upon us, and the two lamps made a kind of luminous halo in the mist, which seemed to absorb their light in a most peculiar way.

'Where was he?' the captain asked me, almost in a whisper.

'On the port side, sir,' I said, 'a little foreside the charthouse and about a dozen feet in from the rail. I'll show you the exact place.'

'We went for'ard along what had been the weather side, going quietly and watchfully, though, indeed, it was little enough that we could see, because of the mist. Once, as I led the way, I thought I heard a vague sound somewhere in the mist, but was all unsure because of the slow creak, creak of the spars and gear as the vessel rolled slightly upon an odd, oily swell. Apart from this slight sound, and the far-up rustle of the canvas slatting gently against the masts, there was no sound at all throughout the ship. I assure you the silence seemed to me to be almost menacing, in the tense, nervous state in which I was.

'Hereabouts is where I left him,' I whispered to the captain a few seconds later. 'Hold your lamp low, sir. There's blood on the deck.'

Captain Jeldy did so, and made a slight sound with his mouth at what he saw. Then, heedless of my hurried warning, he walked across to the rail, holding his lamp high up. I followed him, for I could not let him go alone; and the second mate came too, with his lamp. They leaned over the port rail and held their lamps out into the mist and the unknown darkness beyond the ship's side. I remember how the lamps made just two yellow glares in the mist, ineffectual, yet serving somehow to make extraordinarily plain the vastitude of the night and the *possibilities of the dark*. Perhaps that is a queer way to put it, but it gives you the effect of that moment upon my feelings. And all the time, you know, there was upon me the brutal, frightening expectancy of something reaching in at us from out of that everlasting darkness and mist that held all the sea and the night, so that we were just three mist-shrouded, hidden figures, peering nervously.

The mist was now so thick that we could not even see the

surface of the water overside, and fore and aft of us the rail vanished away into the fog and the dark. And then, as we stood here staring, I heard something moving down on the main-deck. I caught Captain Jeldy by the elbow.

'Come away from the rail, sir,' I said, hardly above a whisper; and he, with the swift premonition of danger, stepped back and allowed me to urge him well inboard. The second mate followed, and the three of us stood there in the mist, staring round about us and holding our revolvers handily, and the dull waves of the mist beating in slowly upon the lamps in vague wreathings and swirls of fog.

'What was it you heard, mister?' asked the captain after a few moments.

'Sst!' I muttered. 'There it is again. There's something moving down on the maindeck!'

Captain Jeldy heard it himself now, and the three of us stood listening intensely. Yet it was hard to know what to make of the sounds. And then suddenly there was the rattle of a deck ringbolt, and then again, as if something or someone were fumbling and playing with it.

'Down there on the maindeck!' shouted the captain abruptly, his voice seeming hoarse close to my ear, yet immediately smothered by the fog. 'Down there on the maindeck! Who's there?'

But there came never an answering sound. And the three of us stood there, looking quickly this way and that, and listening. Abruptly the second mate muttered something:

'The look-out, sir! The look-out!'

Captain Jeldy took the hint on the instant.

'On the look-out there!' he shouted.

And then, far away and muffled-sounding, there came the answering cry of the look-out man from the fo'c'sle head:

'Sir-r-r?' A little voice, long drawn out through unknowable alleys of fog.

'Go below into the fo'c'sle and shut both doors, an' don't stir out till you're told!' sung out Captain Jeldy, his voice going lost into the mist. And then the man's answering 'Aye, aye, sir!' coming to us faint and mournful. And directly afterwards the clang of a steel door, hollow-sounding and remote; and im-mediately the sound of another.

271

'That puts them safe for the present, anyway,' said the second mate. And even as he spoke there came again that indefinite noise down upon the maindeck of something moving with an incredible and unnatural stealthiness.

'On the maindeck there!' shouted Captain Jeldy sternly. 'If there is anyone there, answer, or I shall fire!'

The reply was both amazing and terrifying, for suddenly a tremendous blow was stricken upon the deck, and then there came the dull, rolling sound of some enormous weight going hollowly across the maindeck. And then an abominable silence.

'My God!' said Captain Jeldy in a low voice, 'what was *that*?' And he raised his pistol, but I caught him by the wrist. 'Don't shoot, sir!' I whispered. 'It'll be no good. That – that – whatever it is – I – mean it's something enormous, sir. I – I really wouldn't shoot –' I found it impossible to put my vague idea into words; but I felt there was a force aboard, down on the maindeck, that it would be futile to attack with so ineffectual a thing as a puny revolver bullet.

And then, as I held Captain Jeldy's wrist, and he hesitated, irresolute, there came a sudden bleating of sheep and the sound of lashings being burst and the cracking of wood; and the next instant a huge crash, followed by crash after crash, and the anguished ma-a-a-a-ing of sheep.

'My God!' said the second mate, 'the sheep-pen's being beaten to pieces against the deck. Good God! What sort of thing could do that?'

The tremendous beating ceased, and there was a splashing overside; and after that a silence so profound that it seemed as if the whole atmosphere of the night was full of an unbearable, tense quietness. And then the damp slatting of a sail, far up in the night, that made me start – a lonesome sound to break suddenly through that infernal silence upon my raw nerves.

'Get below, both of you. Smartly now!' muttered Captain Jeldy. 'There's something run either aboard us or alongside; and we can't do anything till daylight.'

We went below and shut the doors of the companion-way, and there we lay in the wide Atlantic, without wheel or look-out or officer in charge, and something incredible down on the dark maindeck.

For some hours we sat in the captain's cabin talking the matter over whilst the watch slept, sprawled in a dozen attitudes on the floor of the saloon. Captain Jeldy and the second mate still wore their pyjamas, and our loaded revolvers lay handy on the cabin table. And so we watched anxiously through the hours for the dawn to come in.

As the light strengthened we endeavoured to get some view of the sea from the ports, but the mist was so thick about us that it was exactly like looking out into a grey nothingness, that became presently white as the day came.

'Now,' said Captain Jeldy, 'we're going to look into this.'

He went out through the saloon to the companion stairs. At the top he opened the two doors, and the mist rolled in on us, white and impenetrable. For a little while we stood there, the three of us, absolutely silent and listening, with our revolvers handy; but never a sound came to us except the odd, vague slatting of a sail or the slight creaking of the gear as the ship lifted on some slow, invisible swell.

Presently the captain stepped cautiously out on to the deck; he was in his cabin slippers, and therefore made no sound. I was wearing gum-boots, and followed him silently, and the second mate after me in his bare feet. Captain Jeldy went a few paces along the deck, and the mist hid him utterly. 'Phew!' I heard him mutter, 'the stink's worse than ever!' His voice came odd and vague to me through the wreathing of the mist.

'The sun'll soon eat up all this fog,' said the second mate at my elbow, in a voice little above a whisper.

We stepped after the captain, and found him a couple of fathoms away, standing shrouded in the mist in an attitude of tense listening.

'Can't hear a thing!' he whispered. 'We'll go for'ard to the break, as quiet as you like. Don't make a sound.'

We went forward, like three shadows, and suddenly Captain Jeldy kicked his shin against something and pitched headlong over it, making a tremendous noise. He got up quickly, swearing grimly, and the three of us stood there in silence, waiting lest any infernal thing should come upon us out of all that white invisibility. Once I felt sure I saw something coming towards me, and I raised my revolver, but saw in a moment that there was nothing. The tension of imminent, nervous expectancy eased from us, and Captian Jeldy stooped over the object on the deck.

'The port hencoop's been shifted out here!' he muttered. 'It's all stove!'

'That must be what I heard last night when the mate went, I whispered. 'There was a loud crash just before he sang out to me to hurry with the lamp.'

Captain Jeldy left the smashed hencoop, and the three of us tiptoed silently to the rail across the break of the poop. Here we leaned over and stared down into the blank whiteness of the mist that hid everything.

'Can't see a thing,' whispered the second mate; yet as he spoke I could fancy that I heard a slight, indefinite, slurring noise somewhere below us; and I caught them each by an arm to draw them back.

'There's something down there,' I muttered. 'For goodness' sake, come back from the rail.'

We gave back a step or two, and then stopped to listen; and even as we did so there came a slight air playing through the mist.

'The breeze is coming,' said the second mate. 'Look, the mist is clearing already.'

He was right. Already the look of white impenetrability had gone, and suddenly we could see the corner of the after-hatch coamings through the thinning fog. Within a minute we could see as far for'ard as the mainmast, and then the stuff blew away from us, clear of the vessel, like a great wall of whiteness, that dissipated as it went.

'*Look!*' we all exclaimed together. The whole of the vessel was now clear to our sight; but it was not at the ship herself that we looked, for, after one quick glance along the empty maindeck, we had seen something beyond the ship's side. All around the vessel there lay a submerged spread of weed, for, maybe, a good quarter of a mile upon every side.

'Weed!' sang out Captain Jeldy in a voice of comprehension. 'Weed! Look! By Jove, I guess I know now what got the mate!'

He turned and ran to the port side and looked over. And suddenly he stiffened and beckoned silently over his shoulder to us to come and see. We had followed, and now we stood, one on each side of him, staring.

'Look!' whispered the captain, pointing. 'See the great brute! Do you see it? There! Look!'

At first I could see nothing except the submerged spread of the weed, into which we had evidently run after dark. Then, as I stared intently, my gaze began to separate from the surrounding weed a leathery-looking something that was somewhat darker in hue than the weed itself.

'My God!' said Captain Jeldy. 'What a monster! What a monster! Just look at the brute! Look at the thing's eyes! That's what got the mate. What a creature out of hell itself!'

I saw it plainly now; three of the massive feelers lay twined in and out among the clumpings of the weed; and then, abruptly, I realised that the two extraordinary round discs, motionless and inscrutable, were the creature's eyes, just below the surface of the water. It appeared to be staring, expressionless, up at the steel side of the vessel. I traced, vaguely, the shapeless monstrosity of what must be termed its head. 'My God!' I muttered. 'It's an enormous squid of some kind! What an awful brute! What –'

The sharp report of the captain's revolver came at that moment. He had fired at the thing, and instantly there was a most awful commotion alongside. The weed was hove upward, literally in tons. An enormous quantity was thrown aboard us by the thrashing of the monster's great feelers. The sea seemed almost to boil, in one great cauldron of weed and water, all about the brute, and the steel side of the ship resounded with the dull, tremendous blows that the creature gave in its struggle. And into all that whirling boil of tentacles, weed, and seawater the three of us emptied our revolvers as fast as we could fire and reload. I remember the feeling of fierce satisfaction I had in thus aiding to avenge the death of the mate.

Suddenly the captain roared out to us to jump back, and we obeyed on the instant. As we did so the weed rose up into a great mound over twenty feet in height, and more than a ton of it slopped aboard. The next instant three of the monstrous tentacles came in over the side, and the vessel gave a slow, sullen roll to port as the weight came upon her, for the monster had literally hove itself almost free of the sea against our port side, in one vast, leathery shape, all wreathed with weed-fronds, and seeming drenched with blood and curious black liquid.

The feelers that had come inboard thrashed round here and there, and suddenly one of them curled in the most hideous, snake-like fashion around the base of the mainmast. This seemed to attract it, for immediately it curled the two others about the mast, and forthwith wrenched upon it with such hideous violence that the whole towering length of spars, through all their height of a hundred and fifty feet, were shaken visibly, whilst the vessel herself vibrated with the stupendous efforts of the brute.

'It'll have the mast down, sir!' said the second mate, with a gasp. 'My God! It'll strain her side open! My —'

'One of those blasting cartridges!' I said to Jeldy almost in a shout, as the inspiration took me. 'Blow the brute to pieces!'

'Get one, quick!' said the captain, jerking his thumb towards the companion. 'You know where they are.'

In thirty seconds I was back with the cartridge. Captain Jeldy took out his knife and cut the fuse dead short; then, with a steady hand, he lit the fuse, and calmly held it, until I backed away, shouting to him to throw it, for I knew it must explode in another couple of seconds.

Captain Jeldy threw the thing like one throws a quoit, so that it fell into the sea just on the outward side of the vast bulk of the monster. So well had he timed it that it burst, with a stunning report, just as it struck the water. The effect upon the squid was amazing. It seemed literally to collapse. The enormous tentacles released themselves from the mast and curled across the deck helplessly, and were drawn inertly over the rail, as the enormous bulk sank away from the ship's side, out of sight, into the weed. The ship rolled slowly to starboard, then steadied. 'Thank God!' I muttered, and looked at the two others. They were pallid and sweating, and I must have been the same.

'Here's the breeze again,' said the second mate, a minute later. 'We're moving.' He turned, without another word, and raced aft to the wheel, whilst the vessel slid over and through the weed-field.

'Look where that brute broke up the sheep-pen!' cried Jeldy, pointing. 'And here's the skylight of the sail-locker smashed to bits!'

He walked across to it, and glanced down. And suddenly he let out a tremendous shout of astonishment:

'Here's the mate down here!' he shouted. 'He's not overboard at all! He's *here*!'

He dropped himself down through the skylight on to the sails, and I after him; and, surely, there was the mate, lying all huddled and insensible on a hummock of spare sails. In his right hand he held a drawn sheath-knife, which he was in the habit of carrying, A.B. fashion, whilst his left hand was all caked with dried blood, where he had been badly cut. Afterwards, we concluded he had cut himself in slashing at one of the tentacles of the squid, which had caught him round the left wrist, the tip of the tentacle being still curled tight about his arm, just as it had been when he hacked it through. For the rest, he was not seriously damaged, the creature having obviously flung him violently away through the framework of the skylight, so that he had fallen in a stunned condition on to the pile of sails.

We got him on deck, and down into his bunk, where we left the steward to attend to him. When we returned to the poop the vessel had drawn clear of the weed-field, and the captain and I stopped for a few moments to stare astern over the taffrail.

As we stood and looked, something wavered up out of the heart of the weed – a long, tapering, sinuous thing, that curled and wavered against the dawn-light, and presently sank back again into the demure weed – a veritable spider of the deep, waiting in the great web that Dame Nature had spun for it in the eddy of her tides and currents.

And we sailed away northwards, with strengthening 'trades', and left that patch of monstrousness to the loneliness of the sea.

John Masefield

DON ALFONSO'S TREASURE HUNT

Any collection of sea stories must, of course, find a place for a
tale or two of pirates – and because I've always enjoyed a
rousing story about buccaneers, I've found space for two here:
both by very well-known writers. The first is by John Masefield
(1878–1967), the distinguished man of English letters who
was the Poet Laureate from 1930 until his death. Masefield
was also a superb writer of sea stories in his earlier days – a fact
that some people tend to forget. Indeed, he looked set to have a
career at sea when he was schooled for the merchant service on
the training ship HMS Conway. Following this, he served his
apprenticeship on a windjammer during which time he assimilated all the knowledge of the sea that he later crafted into both
poetry and prose. It was ill-health that caused Masefield to give
up the sea, but the effect it had had upon him was there for all
to see in his first poetical work, Salt-Water Ballads, published
in 1902. This was followed by collections of short stories and
factual items about great seamen and the lore of the oceans.
From one of these volumes, A Mainsail Haul (1905), I have
picked the colourful yarn of Don Alfonso and how he com-
mandeered a ship and crew to go searching for every pirate's
dream – a hoard of buried treasure!

Now in the old days, before steam, there was a young Spanish buck who lived in Trinidad, and his name was Don Alfonso. Now Trinidad is known, in a way of speaking, among sailor-men, as Hell's Lid, or Number One Hatch, by reason of its being very hot there. They've a great place there, which they show to folk, where it's like a cauldron of pitch. It bubbles pitch out of the earth, all black and hot, and you see great slimy workings, all across, like ropes being coiled inside. And talk about smell there! — talk of brimstone! — why, it's like a cattle-ship gone derelict, that's what that place is like.

Now by reason of the heat there, the folk of those parts — a lot of Spaniards mostly, Dagoes and that — they don't do nothing but just sit around. When they turn out of a morning they get some yellow paper and some leaf tobacco, and they rolls what they calls cigarellers and sticks them in their ears like pens. That's their day's work, that is — rolling them yellow cigarellers. Well, then, they set around and they smokes — big men, too, most of them — and they put flowers in their hats — red roses and that — and that's how they pass their time.

Now this Don Alfonso he was a terror, he was; for they've got a licker in those parts. If you put some of it on a piece of paint-work — and this is gospel that I'm giving you — that paint it comes off like you was using turps. Now Don Alfonso he was a terror at that licker — and that's the sort of Dago-boy Alfonso was.

Now Alfonso's mother was a widow, and he was her only child, like in the play.

Now one time, when Don Alfonso was in the pulperia (that's Spanish for grog-shop), he was a-bluin' down that licker the same as you or I would be bluin' beer. And there was a gang of Dagoes there, and all of them chewing the rag, and all of them going for the vino — that's the Spanish name for wine — v-i-n-o. It's red wine, vino is; they give it you in port to save water.

Now among them fancy Dagoes there was a young Eye-talian who'd been treasure-hunting, looking for buried treasure, in that Blue Nose ship which went among the islands. Looking for gold, he'd been, gold that was buried by the pirates. They're a gay crew, them Blue Nose fellers. What'd the pirates bury treasure for? Not them. It stands to reason. Did

279

you ever see a shellback go reeving his dollars down a rabbit-warren? It stands to reason. Golden dollar coins indeed. Bury them customs fellers if you like. Now this young Dago, he was coming it proud about that treasure. In one of them Tortugas, he was saying, or off of the Chagres, or if not there among them smelly Samballs, there's tons of it lying in a foot of sand with a skellinton on the top. They used to kill a nigger, he was saying, when they buried their blunt, so's his ghost would keep away thieves. There's a sight of thieves, ain't there, in them smelly Samballs? An' niggers ain't got no ghosts, not that I ever heard.

Oh, he was getting gay about that buried treasure. Gold there was, and silver dollars and golden jewels, and I don't know what all. 'And I knows the place,' he says, 'where it's all lying,' and out he pulls a chart with a red crost on it, like in them Deadwood Dicky books. And what with the vino and that there licker, he got them Dagoes strung on a line. So the end of it was that Don Alfonso he came down with the blunt. And that gang of Dagoes they charters a brigantine – she'd a Bible name to her, as is these Dagoes' way – and off they sails a galley-vaunting looking for gold with a skellinton on the top. Now one dusk, just as they was getting out the lamps and going forward with the kettle, they spies a land ahead and sings out 'Land, O!' By dark they was within a mile of shore, hove-to off of a lighthouse that was burning a red flare. Now the old man he comes to Alfonso, and he says, 'I dunno what land this may be. There's no land due to us this week by my account. And that red flare there; there's no light burning a flare nearer here than Sydney.' 'Let go your anchor,' says Don Alfonso, 'for land there is, and where there's land there's rum. And lower away your dinghy, for I'm going in for a drink. You can take her in, mister, with two of the hands, and then lay aboard till I whistle.' So they lower the dinghy, and Don Alfonso takes some cigarellers, and ashore he goes for that there licker.

Now when he sets foot ashore, and the boat was gone off, Don Alfonso he walked up the quay in search of a pulperia. And it was a strange land he was in, and that's the truth. Quiet it was, and the little white houses still as corfins, and only a lamp or two burning, and never a sound nor a song. Oh, a glad lad was Don Alfonso when he sees a nice little calaboosa lying to leeward, with a red lamp burning in the stoop. So in he goes for a dram – into the grog-house, into a little room with a fire lit and a little red man behind the bar. Now it was a caution was that there room, for instead of there bein' casks like beer or vino casks, there was only corfins. And the little red man he gives a grin, and he gives the glad hand to Don Alfonso, and he sets them up along the bar, and Alfonso lights a cigareller. So then the Don drinks, and the little red man says, 'Salue.' And the little red man drinks, and Alfonso says, 'Drink hearty.' And then they drinks two and two together. Then Alfonso sings some sort of a Dago song, and the little red man he plays a tune on the bones, and then they sets them up again and has more bones and more singing. Then Alfonso says, 'It's time I was gettin' aboard'; but the little man says, 'Oh, it's early days yet – the licker lies with you.' So every time Alfonso tries to go, the little red man says that. Till at last, at dawn, the little red man turned into a little red cock and crowed like a cock in the ox yard. And immejitly the corfins all burst into skellintons, and the bar broke into bits, and the licker blew up like corpse-lights – like blue fire, the same as in the scripters. And the next thing Don Alfonso knowed he was lying on the beach with a head on him full of mill-wheels and the mill working overtime.

So he gets up and sticks his head in the surf, and blows his whistle for the boat to come. But not a sign of a boat puts in, and not a sign of a hand shows aboard, neither smoke nor nothing'. So when he'd blew for maybe an hour he sees a old skellinton of a boat lying bilged on the sand. And he went off in her, paddling with the rudder, and he got alongside before she actually sank.

Now, when he gets alongside, that there brigantine was all rusty and rotted and all grown green with grass. And flowers were growing on the deck, and barnacles were a foot thick below the water. The gulls had nested in her sails, and the ropes drifted in the wind like flags, and a big red rose-bush was twisted up the tiller. And there in the grass, with daisies and such, were the lanky white bones of all them Dagoes. They lay where they'd died, with the vino casks near by and a pannikin of tin that they'd been using as a dice-box. They was dead white bones, the whole crew – dead of waiting for Don Alfonso while he was drinking with the little red man.

So Don Alfonso he kneels and he prays, and 'Oh,' he says, 'that I might die too, and me the cause of these here whited bones, and all from my love of licker! Never again will I touch rum,' he says. 'If I reach home,' he says — he was praying, you must mind — 'you'll see I never will.' And he hacks through the cable with an axe and runs up the rotten jib by pully-hauly.

Long he was sailing, living on dew and gulls' eggs, sailing with them white bones in that there blossoming old hulk. But at long last he comes to Port of Spain and signals for a pilot, and brings up just as sun was sinking. Thirty long years had he been gone, and he was an old man when he brought the whited bones home. But his old mother was alive, and they lived happily ever after. But never any licker would he drink, except only dew or milk — he was that changed from what he was.

Rafael Sabatini

THE BLANK SHOT

A Captain Blood Story

There is no more famous buccaneer in maritime literature than Captain Peter Blood who, having trained as a doctor, is wrongly sentenced into slavery by the infamous Judge Jeffreys and escapes to go pirating out of a rankling sense of injustice. The stories about Blood are all infused with a great sense of the atmosphere of the seventeenth century, and the characters seem to leap from the pages of the books. It was no doubt due as much to the romantic background from which Blood's creator, Rafael Sabatini, came as from his incredible imagination and deep knowledge of the sea, that the tales were so popular when they were first published in the Twenties and Thirties, and why they are still so readable today. Sabatini (1875–1950), a member of a noble family, was born in the picturesque and historic little Italian city of Jesi, and in such surroundings could hardly fail to become fascinated by both history and romance. His love of the sea was early revealed when he published The Sea Hawk *in 1915: this was later made into two films, the first in 1924 with Milton Sills, and the second with the great swashbuckler, Errol Flynn, in 1940.*

It was Sabatini's creation of Captain Blood in 1922 that made his name, however, and earned him a huge success both in terms of book sales and the 1925 and 1935 film versions, the latter also starring Errol Flynn. The initial group of stories were followed by The Chronicles of Captain Blood *in 1931 and* The Fortunes of Captain Blood *in 1936. Among the various yarns about Blood, I have always particularly enjoyed those in which he matches his wits and cunning against his great adversary, the unscrupulous Captain Easterling. So for this book I have selected one of their most desperate duels as described in 'The Blank Shot' . . .*

The story of the long duel between Peter Blood and Captain Easterling, pirate, finds an important place in the chronicles which Jeremy Pitt has left us, and is of importance to the serious student of Blood's curious career. Indeed, but for Easterling, it may well be that there would have been no chronicles, since but for his intervention in the fortunes of Peter Blood the latter might never have become a buccaneer.

A man's destiny may be shaped by the set of the wind at a given moment. And Peter Blood's was certainly shaped, at a time when it was still fluid, by the October hurricane which blew Captain Easterling's ten-gun sloop into Cayona Bay. This Easterling – as nasty a scoundrel as ever sailed the Caribbean – carried under hatches some tons of cacao of which he had lightened a Dutch merchantman homing from the Antilles. Had he suspected the Dutchman of being no more richly laden, he would have let her pass unchallenged. That she should have carried nothing of more value than cacao was a contingency for which he blamed the evil fortune which, of late, had dogged him, an evil fortune which was making it increasingly difficult for him to find men to sail with him.

Considering these things and dreaming of great enterprises, he brought his sloop, the *Bonaventure*, into the shelter of the rock-bound harbour of Tortuga, and there dismissed his dreams to gaze upon a curious reality. It took the shape of a great red-hulled ship that rode proudly at anchor among the lesser craft, like a swan amid a gaggle of geese.

When he had come near enough to read the name, *Cinco Llagas*, boldly painted in letters of gold above her counter, and under this the port of origin, Cadiz, he rubbed his eyes so that he might read again. Thereafter, he sought in conjecture an explanation of the presence of that magnificent ship of Spain in this pirates' nest of Tortuga. A thing of beauty she was, from gilded beak-head, above which the brass cannons glinted in the morning sun, to towering sterncastle, and a thing of power, as announced by the forty guns which Easterling's practised eye computed her to carry behind her closed ports.

The *Bonaventure* cast anchor within a cable's length of the great ship, in ten fathoms, close under the shadow of the Mountain Fort, which crowned the great rock on the harbour's western side, and Easterling went ashore to discover the explanation of this mystery.

In the market-place beyond the mole, amid the crowd of seamen, beachcombers, negroes and Indians who loafed or trafficked there, the Captain found a couple of rascals very ready with the singular tale of how that noble vessel out of Cadiz came to ride so peacefully at anchor in Cayona Bay.

She had belonged to a great Spanish admiral, who by way of reprisals for the injury done to Spanish settlements by English adventurers and privateers, had made a raid upon Barbados, paralysed the garrison at Bridgetown, seized the Governor and held the place to ransom. But that night, while he was ashore with all his force, a party of wretched slaves from the plantations had crept aboard his ship, surprised and overpowered the inadequate watch, and in the morning had turned her guns upon the boats in which the victorious Spaniards were returning to her. Thereafter they had sailed away with their prize to freedom.

It was an amusing tale and an impressive one to such a man as Easterling. He desired more particular knowledge of the men who had engaged in such an enterprise. He learnt that they numbered not above a score, and that they were all political offenders, rebels who, in England, had been out with Monmouth, preserved from the gallows because of the need of slaves in the West Indian plantations. They had been led by a man named Peter Blood, who, because of his skill as a physician, and so that he might practise it to the profit of his owner, had been emancipated from the ordinary labour of a slave. Thus he had enjoyed a certain measure of personal freedom which had enabled him to seize the opportunity when it presented itself. With his fellow-convicts he had come for shelter to Tortuga, and here they had been abiding for the past month. It was thought that Blood desired to take ship for France, and that most of his followers would accompany him. But one or two wilder spirits, men who had been trained to the sea, were likely to remain behind and join the Brotherhood of the Coast, as the buccaneering fraternity called itself.

All this Easterling learnt in the market-place behind the mole, whence his narrow, close-set eyes continued to con the great red ship.

With such a vessel as that under his feet there was no limit to the things he might achieve. The fame of Henry Morgan, with whom once he had sailed and under whom he had served his apprenticeship to piracy, should become a pale thing beside his own. Those poor escaped convicts should be ready enough to sell a ship which had served its purpose by them, and they should not be exorbitant in their notions of her value. The cacao aboard the *Bonaventure* should more than suffice to pay for her.

Captain Easterling smiled as he stroked his crisp black beard.

He made his way through the rudely built little town by the road white with coral dust. He went so purposefully that he disregarded the hails that greeted him from the tavern of The King of France, nor paused to crush a cup with the gaudy buccaneers who filled the place with their noisy mirth. The Captain had business that morning with Monsieur d'Ogeron, the courtly middle-aged Governor of Tortuga, who, in representing the French West India Company, seemed to represent France herself.

In the fair, white, green-shuttered house, pleasantly set amid fragrant pimento trees and other aromatic shrubs, Captain Easterling was received with dignified friendliness by the slight, elegant Frenchman who brought to the wilds of Tortuga a faint perfume of the elegances of Versailles.

The Governor offered him a chair, and gave him his attention. In the matter of the cacao there was no difficulty. Monsieur d'Ogeron cared not whence it came. That he had no illusions on the subject was shown by the price per quintal at which he announced himself prepared to purchase. It was a price representing rather less than half the value of the merchandise. Monsieur d'Ogeron was a diligent servant of the French West India Company.

Easterling haggled vainly, grumbled, accepted and passed to the major matter. He desired to acquire the Spanish ship in the bay. Would Monsieur d'Ogeron undertake the purchase for him from the fugitive convicts who, he understood, were in possession of her.

Monsieur d'Ogeron took time to reply.

'It is possible,' he said at last, 'that they may not wish to sell.'

'Not sell? In God's name what use is the ship to those poor ragamuffins?'

'Come to me this evening,' said Monsieur d'Ogeron, 'and you shall have your answer.'

When Easterling returned as bidden, Monsieur d'Ogeron was not alone. As the Governor rose to receive his visitor, there rose with him a tall, spare man in his early thirties from whose shaven face, swarthy as a gipsy's, looked out a pair of eyes that were startlingly blue, level and penetrating. If Monsieur d'Ogeron in dress and air suggested Versailles, his companion as markedly suggested the Alameda. He was very richly dressed in black, in the Spanish fashion, with an abundance of silver lace and a foam of fine point at throat and wrists, and he wore a heavy black periwig whose curls descended to his shoulders.

Monsieur d'Ogeron presented him:

'Here, Captain, is Mr Peter Blood to answer you in person.'

Easterling was almost disconcerted, so different was the man's appearance from anything that he could have imagined.

Mr Blood began to speak. He had a pleasant voice whose metallic quality was softened by a drawling Irish accent. But what he said made Captain Easterling impatient. It was not his intention to sell the Cinco Llagas.

Aggressively before the elegant Mr Blood, stood now the buccaneer, a huge, hairy, dangerous-looking man, in coarse shirt and leather breeches, his cropped head swathed in a red-and-yellow kerchief. Aggressively he demanded Blood's reasons for retaining a ship that could be of no use to him and his fellow-convicts.

Blood's voice was softly courteous in reply, which but increased Easterling's contempt of him. Captain Easterling was assured that he was mistaken in his assumptions. It was probable that the fugitives from Barbados would employ the vessel to return to Europe, so as to make their way to France or Holland.

'Maybe we're not quite as ye're supposing us, Captain. One of my companions is a shipmaster, and three others have served, in various ways, in the King's Navy.'

'Bah!' Easterling's contempt exploded loudly. 'And what of the perils of the sea? Perils of capture? How will you face those with your paltry crew?'

Still Captain Blood preserved his pleasant temper.

'What we lack in men we make up in weight of metal. While I may not be able to navigate a ship across the ocean, I can certainly fight a ship at need. I learnt it under de Ruyter.'

The famous name gave pause to Easterling's scorn.

'Under de Ruyter?'

'I held a commission with him some years ago.'

Easterling was plainly dumbfounded.

'I thought it's a doctor ye was.'

'I am that, too,' said the Irishman simply.

The buccaneer expressed disgusted amazement in a speech liberally festooned with oaths. And then Monsieur d'Ogeron made an end of the interview.

'So that, you see, Captain Easterling, there is no more to be said in the matter.'

On his disgruntled way back to the mole, Easterling thought that although there was no more to be said there was a good deal to be done. Having already looked upon the majestic *Cinco Llagas* as his own, he was by no means disposed to forego the prospect of possession.

Monsieur d'Ogeron also appeared to think that there was still at least a word to be added, and he added it after Easterling's departure.

'That,' he said quietly, 'is a nasty and a dangerous man. You will do well to bear it in mind, Monsieur Blood.'

Blood treated the matter lightly.

'The warning was hardly necessary. His person would have announced the blackguard to me even if I had not known him for a pirate.'

A shadow that was almost suggestive of annoyance flitted across the delicate features of the Governor of Tortuga.

'Oh, but a filibuster is not of necessity a blackguard, nor is the career of a filibuster one for your contempt, Monsieur Blood. There are those among the buccaneers who do good service to your country and to mine by setting a restraint upon the rapacity of Spain, a rapacity which is responsible for their existence. But for the buccaneers, in these waters, where neither France nor England can maintain a fleet, the Spanish dominion would be as absolute as it is inhuman. You will remember that your country honoured Henry Morgan with a knighthood and the deputy-governorship of Jamaica. And he was an even worse pirate, if it is possible, than your Sir Francis Drake, or Hawkins, or Frobisher, or several others I could name, whose memory your country also honours.'

Followed upon this from Monsieur d'Ogeron, who derived considerable revenues from the percentages he levied by way of harbour dues on all prizes brought into Tortuga, solemn counsels that Mr Blood should follow in the footsteps of those heroes. Being outlawed as he was, in possession of a fine ship and the nucleus of an able following, and being, as he had shown, a man of unusual resource, Monsieur d'Ogeron did not doubt that he would prosper finely as a filibuster.

Mr Blood didn't doubt it himself. He never doubted himself. But he did not on that account incline to the notion. Nor, probably, would he ever have so inclined but for that which ensued, however much the majority of his followers might have sought to persuade him.

Among these there were two, Hagthorpe and Pitt, who were perhaps the most persistent. It was all very well for Blood, they told him, to plan a return to Europe. He was master of a peaceful art, in the pursuit of which he might earn a livelihood in France or Flanders. But they were men of the sea, and knew no other trade. Dyke, who had been a petty officer in the Navy before he embarked on politics and rebellion, held similar views, and Ogle, the gunner, demanded to know of heaven and hell and Mr Blood what guns they thought the British Admiralty would entrust to a man who had been out with Monmouth.

Things were reaching a stage in which Peter Blood could see no alternative to that of parting from these men whom a common misfortune had endeared to him. It was in this pass that Fate intervened in the shape of Captain Easterling.

One morning, three days after his interview with Mr Blood at the Governor's house, the Captain came alongside the *Cinco Llagas* in the cock-boat from his sloop. As he heaved his massive bulk into the waist of the ship, his small, narrow eyes were everywhere at once. The *Cinco Llagas* was not only well-found, but irreproachably kept. Her decks were scoured, her cordage stowed, and everything in place. The muskets in the rack about the mainmast, and the brasswork on the scuttle-butts shone like gold in the bright sunshine.

And there was Mr Blood himself, in black and silver, looking like a Grandee of Spain, doffing a black hat with a sweep of claret ostrich plume about it, and bowing until the wings of his periwig met across his face like the pendulous ears of a spaniel. With him stood Nathaniel Hagthorpe, a pleasant gentleman of Mr Blood's own age, whose steady eye and clear-cut face announced the man of breeding; Jeremy Pitt, the flaxen-haired young Somerset shipmaster; and the short, sturdy Nicholas Dyke, who had been a petty officer and had served under King James when he was Duke of York. There was nothing of the ragamuffin about these, as Easterling had so readily imagined.

Having presented them, Mr Blood invited the Captain of the *Bonaventure* to the great cabin in the stern, which for spaciousness and richness of furniture surpassed any cabin Captain Easterling had ever entered.

A negro servant in a white jacket brought, besides the usual rum and sugar and fresh limes, a bottle of golden Canary which had been in the ship's original equipment and which Mr Blood recommended with solicitude to his unbidden guest.

They occupied the elegantly cushioned seats about the table of black oak, and Captain Easterling praised the Canary liberally, to justify the liberality with which he consumed it. Thereafter, he came to business by asking if Mr Blood, upon reflection, had not perhaps changed his mind about selling the ship.

'In that case,' he added, with a glance at Blood's three companions, 'considering among how many the purchase money will be divided, you will find me generous.'

If by this he had hoped to make an impression upon those three, their stolid countenances disappointed him.

Mr Blood shook his head.

'It's wasting your time, ye are, Captain. Whatever else we decide, we keep the *Cinco Llagas*.'

'Whatever you decide?' The great black brows went up on that shallow brow. 'Ye're none so decided then as ye was about this voyage to Europe? Why, then, I'll come at once to the business I'd propose if ye wouldn't sell. It is that with this ship ye join the *Bonaventure* in a venture – a bonaventure.' And he laughed noisily at his own jest with a flash of white teeth behind the great black beard.

'You honour us. But we haven't a mind to piracy.'

Easterling gave no sign of offence. He waved a great ham of a hand as if to dismiss the notion.

'It ain't piracy I'm proposing.'

'What then?'

'I can trust ye?' Easterling asked, and his eyes included the four of them.

'Ye're not obliged to. And it's odds ye'll waste your time in any case.'

It was not encouraging. Nevertheless, Easterling proceeded. It might be known to them that he had sailed with Morgan. He had been with Morgan in the great march across the Isthmus of Panama. Now it was well known that when the spoil came to be divided after the sack of that Spanish city, it was found to be far below the reasonable expectations of the buccaneers. There were murmurs that Morgan had not dealt fairly with his men. Those murmurs, Easterling could tell them, were well-founded. There were pearls and jewels from San Felipe of fabulous value, which Morgan had secretly appropriated for himself. But as the rumours grew and reached his ears, he became afraid of a search that should convict him. And so, midway on the journey across the Isthmus, he one night buried the treasure he had filched.

'Only one man knew this,' said Captain Easterling to his attentive listeners. 'The man who helped him in a labour he couldn't ha' done alone. I am that man.'

He paused a moment to let the impressive fact sink home, and then resumed.

The business he proposed was that the fugitives on the *Cinco Llagas* should join him in an expedition to Darien to recover the treasure, sharing equally in it with his own men and on the scale usual among the Brethren of the Coast.

'If I put the value of what Morgan buried at five hundred thousand pieces of eight, I am being modest.'

It was a sum to set his audience staring. Even Blood stared, but not quite with the expression of the others.

'Sure now, it's very odd,' said he thoughtfully.

'What is odd, Mr Blood?'

Mr Blood's answer took the form of another question.

'How many do you number aboard the *Bonaventure*?'

'Something less than two hundred men.'

'And the twenty men who are with me make such a difference that you deem it worth while to bring us this proposal!'

Easterling laughed outright, a deep, guttural laugh.

'I see that you don't understand at all.' His voice bore a familiar echo of Mr Blood's Irish intonation. 'It's not the men I lack so much as a stout ship in which to guard the treasure when we have it. In a bottom such as this we'd be as snug as in a fort, and I'd defy any Spanish galleon to molest me.'

'Faith now, I understand,' said Hagthorpe, and Pitt and Dyke nodded with him. But the glittering blue eye of Peter Blood continued to stare unwinkingly upon the bulky pirate.

'As Hagthorpe says, it's understandable. But a tenth of the prize which, by heads, is all that would come to the *Cinco Llagas*, is far from adequate in the circumstances.'

Easterling blew out his cheeks and waved his great hand in a gesture of bonhomie.

'What share would you propose?'

'That's to be considered. But it would be not less than one fifth.'

The buccaneer's face remained impassive. He bowed his gaudily swathed head.

'Bring these friends of yours to dine to-morrow aboard the *Bonaventure*, and we'll draw up the articles.'

For a moment Blood seemed to hesitate. Then in courteous terms he accepted the invitation.

But when the buccaneer had departed, he checked the satisfaction of his three followers.

'I was warned that Captain Easterling is a dangerous man. That's to flatter him. For to be dangerous a man must be clever, and Captain Easterling is not clever.'

'What maggot's burrowing under your periwig, Peter?' wondered Hagthorpe.

'I'm thinking of the reason he gave for desiring our association. It was the best he could do when bluntly asked the question.'

'It could not have been more reasonable,' said Hagthorpe, who was finding Blood unnecessarily difficult.

'Reasonable!' Blood laughed. 'Specious, if you will. Specious until you come to examine it. A ship as strong as a fort in which to stow a half-million pieces of eight, and this fortress ship in the hands of ourselves. A trusting fellow this Easterling for a scoundrel.'

They thought it out, and their eyes grew round. Pitt, however, was not yet persuaded.

'In his need he'll trust our honour.'

Blood looked at him with scorn.

'I never knew a man with eyes like Easterling's to trust to anything but possession. If he means to stow that treasure aboard this ship, it is because he means to be in possession of this ship by the time he does so. Honour! Bah! could such a man believe that honour would prevent us from giving him the slip one night, once we had the treasure aboard, or even of bringing our weight of metal to bear upon his sloop and sinking her? It's fatuous you are, Jeremy, with your talk of honour.'

Still, the thing was not quite clear to Hagthorpe.

'What, then, do you suppose to be his reason for inviting us to join him?'

'The reason that he gave. He wants our ship, be it for the conveyance of his treasure, if it exists, be it for other reasons. Didn't he first seek to buy the *Cinco Llagas*? Oh, he wants her, naturally enough; but he wants not us, nor would he keep us long, be sure of that.'

And yet, perhaps because the prospect of a share in Morgan's treasure was a glittering one, they were reluctant to abandon it. So now Hagthorpe, Pitt and Dyke opined that Blood was leaping to conclusions from a prejudice sown in him by Monsieur d'Ogeron, who may have had reasons of his own to serve. Let them at least dine to-morrow with Easterling, and hear what articles he proposed.

'Can you be sure that we shall not be poisoned?' wondered Blood.

But this was pushing prejudice too far. They mocked him freely. How could they be poisoned by meat and drink that Easterling must share with them? And what end would thus be served? How would that give Easterling possession of the *Cinco Llagas*?

'By swarming aboard her with a couple of score of his ruffians and taking the men here unawares, at a time when there would be none to lead them.'

'What?' cried Hagthorpe. 'Here in Tortuga? In this haven of the buccaneers? Come, come, Peter! I must suppose there is some honour among thieves.'

'You may suppose it. I prefer to suppose otherwise. I hope no man will call me timid; and yet I'd as soon be called that as rash.'

The weight of opinion, however, was against him. Every man of the crew of the *Cinco Llagas* was as eager for the enterprise, when it came to be disclosed, as were the three leaders.

And so, despite himself, at eight bells on the morrow, Captain Blood went over with Hagthorpe, Pitt and Dyke, to dine aboard the *Bonaventure*.

Easterling welcomed them boisterously, supported by his entire crew of ruffians. Some eight score of them swarmed in the waist, on the forecastle, and even on the poop, and all were

294

armed. Their presence and the leering mockery stamped upon their villainous countenances, made Blood's three followers ask themselves at last if they had walked into a trap.

It was too late to retreat. By the break of the poop, at the entrance of the gangway leading to the cabin, stood Captain Easterling waiting to conduct them.

Blood paused there a moment to look up into the pellucid sky above the rigging about which the gulls were circling. He looked towards the mole, forsaken now in the noontide heat, and then across the crystalline sparkling waters towards the great red *Cinco Llagas*, where she rode in majesty and strength. To his uneasy companions it seemed as if he were wondering from what quarter help might come if it were needed. Then, responding to Easterling's inviting gesture, he passed into the gloom of the gangway, followed by the others.

Like the rest of the ship, which the first glance had revealed for dishevelled and unclean, the cabin was in no way comparable with that of the stately *Cinco Llagas*. It was so low that there was barely headroom for tall men like Blood and Hagthorpe. It was ill-furnished, containing little more than the cushioned lockers set about a deal table that was stained and hacked.

The dinner proved to be much as the surroundings promised. The fresh pork and fresh vegetables had been befouled in cooking, so that, in forcing himself to eat, the fastidious stomach of Mr Blood was almost turned. The company provided by Easterling matched the rest. A half-dozen of his fellows served him as a guard of honour. They had been elected, he announced, by the men, so that they might agree the articles on behalf of all. To these had been added a young Frenchman named Joinville, who was secretary to Monsieur d'Ogeron, and stood there to represent the Governor and to lend, as it were, a legal sanction to what was to be done. If the presence of this rather vacuous, pale-eyed gentleman served to reassure Mr Blood a little, it served to intrigue him more.

Amongst them they crowded the narrow confines of the cabin, and Easterling's fellows were so placed along the two sides of the table that no two of the men from the *Cinco Llagas* sat together, and so that Blood and the Captain of the *Bonaventure* immediately faced each other across the board.

Business was left until dinner was over. Until then the men of the *Bonaventure* kept things gay with the heavily salted talk that passed for wit amongst them. At last, the table cleared of all save bottles, and pens and ink being furnished together with a sheet of paper each to Easterling and Blood, the Captain of the *Bonaventure* opened the matter of the terms, and Peter Blood heard himself for the first time addressed as Captain. Easterling shortly informed him that the one-fifth share he had demanded was by the men of the *Bonaventure* accounted excessive.

Momentarily, Captain Blood's hopes rose.

'Shall we deal in plain terms now, Captain? Do you mean that they'll not consent to them?'

'What else should I mean?'

'In that case, Captain, it only remains for us to take our leave, in your debt for this liberal entertainment and the richer for the improvement in our acquaintance.'

The elaborate courtesy of those grossly inaccurate terms did not seem to touch the ponderous Easterling. His little, close-set eyes stared blankly from his great red face.

'You'll take your leave?' There was a sneering undertone to his guttural voice. 'I'll trouble you in turn to be plain with me. D'ye mean that ye'll quit from the business?' Two or three of his followers made a rumbling, challenging echo to his question.

Captain Blood — to give him now the title Easterling had bestowed upon him — had the air of being intimidated. He hesitated, looking as if for guidance to his companions, who returned him only uneasy glances.

'If,' he said at length, 'you find our terms unreasonable, I must assume ye'll not be wishing to go further, and it only remains for us to withdraw.'

He spoke with a diffidence which amazed his own followers, who had never known him other than bold in the face of any odds. It provoked a sneer from Easterling.

'Faith, doctor,' said he, 'ye were best to return to cupping and bleeding, and leave ships to men who can handle them.'

There was a lightning flash from those blue eyes, as vivid as it was transient. The swarthy countenance never lost its faint air of diffidence. Meanwhile Easterling had swung to the

296

Governor's representative, who sat on his immediate right.

'What do you think of that, Mossoo Joinville?'

The fair, flabby young Frenchman smiled amiably upon Blood's diffidence.

'Would it not be wise and proper, sir, to hear what terms Captain Easterling now proposes?'

'I'll hear them. But —'

'Leave the buts till afterwards, doctor,' Easterling cut in. 'The terms we'll grant are the terms I told ye. Your men share equally with mine.'

'But that means no more than a tenth for the *Cinco Llagas*.' And Blood, too, now appealed to M. Joinville. 'Do you, sir, account that fair? I have explained to Captain Easterling that for what we lack in men we more than make up in weight of metal, and our guns are handled by a gunner such as I dare swear has no compeer in the Caribbean. A remarkable gunner is Ned Ogle. The very devil of a gunner, as you'd believe if you'd seen him pick those Spanish boats off the water in Bridgetown Harbour.'

He would have continued upon the subject of Ned Ogle, but that Easterling interrupted him.

'Hell, man! What's a gunner more or less.'

'Oh, an ordinary gunner, maybe. But this is no ordinary gunner. An eye he has. Gunners like Ogle are like poets; they are born, so they are. He'll put you a shot between wind and water, will Ogle, as neatly as you can pick your teeth.'

Easterling banged the table.

'What's all this to the point?'

'It may be something. And, meanwhile, it shows you the valuable ally ye're acquiring.' And he was off again on the subject of his gunner. 'He was trained in the King's Navy, was Ned Ogle, and a bad day for the King's Navy it was when Ogle took to politics and followed the Protestant champion to Sedgemoor.'

'Leave that,' growled one of the officers of the *Bonaventure*, a ruffian who answered to the name of Chard. 'Leave it, I say, or we'll waste the day in talk.'

Easterling confirmed this with a coarse oath. Captain Blood observed that they did not mean to spare offensiveness, and his speculations on their aims, starting from that, took a fresh turn.

Joinville intervened.

'Could you not compromise with Captain Blood? After all, there is some reason on his side. He might reasonably claim to put a hundred men aboard his ship, and in that case he would naturally take a heavier share.'

'In that case he might be worth it,' was the truculent answer.

'I am worth it as it is,' Blood insisted.

'Ah, bah!' he was answered, with a flick of finger and thumb under his very nose.

He began to suspect that Easterling sought to entice him into an act of rashness, in reply to which he and his followers would probably be butchered where they sat, and M. Joinville would afterwards be constrained to bear witness to the Governor that the provocation had proceeded from the guests. He perceived at last the probable reason for the Frenchman's presence.

But at the moment Joinville was remonstrating.

'Come, come, Captain Easterling! Thus you will never reach agreement. Captain Blood's ship is of advantage to you, and we have to pay for what is advantageous. Could you not offer him an eighth or even a seventh share?'

Easterling silenced the growl of disagreement from Chard and became almost suave.

'What would Captain Blood say to that?'

Captain Blood considered for a long moment. Then he shrugged.

'I say what you know I must say; that I can say nothing until I have taken the wishes of my followers. We'll resume the discussion when I have done so – another day.'

'Oh, s'death!' roared Easterling. 'Do you play with us? Haven't you brought your officers with you, and ain't they empowered to speak for your men, same as mine? Whatever we settles here, my men abides by. That's the custom of the Brethren of the Coast. And I expect the same from you. And I've the right to expect it, as you can tell him, Mossoo Joinville.'

The Frenchman nodded gloomily, and Easterling roared on.

'We are not children! And we're not here to play, but to agree terms. And, by God, we'll agree them before you leave!'

'Or not, as the case may be,' said Blood quietly. It was to be remarked that he had lost his diffidence by now.

'Or not? What the devil do you mean with your "or not"?' Easterling came to his feet in a vehemence that Peter Blood believed assumed, as the proper note at this stage of the comedy he was playing.

'I mean or not, quite simply.' He accounted that the time had come to compel the buccaneers to show their hand. 'If we fail to agree terms, why, that's the end of the matter.'

'Oho! The end of the matter, eh? Stab me, but it may prove the beginning of it.'

Blood smiled up into his face, and cool as ice he commented:

'That's what I was supposing. But the beginning of what, if you please, Captain Easterling?'

'Indeed, indeed, Captain!' cried Joinville. 'What can you mean?'

'Mean?' Captain Easterling glared at the Frenchman. He appeared to be extremely angry. 'Mean?' he repeated. 'Look you, mossoo, this fellow here, this Blood, this doctor, this escaped convict, made believe that he would enter into articles with us so as to get from me the secret of Morgan's treasure. Now that he's got it, he makes difficulties about the articles. He no longer wants to join us, it seems. He proposes to withdraw. It'll be plain to you why he proposes to withdraw, Mossoo Joinville; just as it'll be plain to you why I can't permit it.'

'Why, here's paltry invention!' sneered Blood. 'What do I know of his secret beyond his tale of a treasure buried somewhere.'

'Not somewhere. You know where. For I've been fool enough to tell you.'

Blood actually laughed, and by his laughter scared his companions, to whom the danger of their situation was now clear enough.

'Somewhere on the Isthmus of Darien. There's precision, on my soul! With that information, I can go straight to the spot, and set my hand on it. As for the rest, M. Joinville, I invite you to observe it's not myself is making difficulties about the articles. On the one-fifth share which I asked from the outset, I was prepared to join Captain Easterling. But now that I'm confirmed in all that I suspected of him and more, why, I wouldn't join him for a half share in this treasure, supposing it to exist at all, which I do not.'

That brought every man of the *Bonaventure* to his feet as if it had been a signal, and they were clamorous, too, until Easterling waved them into silence. Upon that silence cut the tenor voice of M. Joinville.

'You are a singularly rash man, Captain Blood.'

'Maybe, maybe,' says Blood, light and airily. 'Time will show. The last word's not yet been said.'

'Then here's to say it,' quoth Easterling, quietly sinister on a sudden. 'I was about to warn you that ye'll not be allowed to leave this ship with the information ye possess until the articles is signed. But since ye so clearly show your intentions, why, things have gone beyond warnings.'

From his seat at the table, which he retained, Captain Blood looked up at the sinister bulk of the Captain of the *Bonaventure*, and the three men from the *Cinco Llagas* observed with mingled amazement and dismay that he was smiling. At first so unusually diffident and timid; now so deliberately and recklessly provoking. He was beyond understanding. It was Hagthorpe who spoke for them.

'What do you mean, Captain? What do you intend by us?'

'Why, to clap you into irons, and stow you under hatches, where you can do no harm.'

'My God, sir . . .' Hagthorpe was beginning, when Captain Blood's crisp, pleasant voice cut across his speech.

'And you, M. Joinville, will permit this without protest?'

Joinville spread his hands, thrust out a nether lip, and shrugged.

'You have brought it on yourself, Captain Blood.'

'So that is what you are here to report to Monsieur d'Ogeron! Well, well!' He laughed with a touch of bitterness.

And then, abruptly, on the noontide stillness outside came the thunder of a gun to shake them all. Followed the screaming of startled gulls, and then, a shade uneasily, came the question from Easterling, addressed to no one in particular:

'What the devil's that?'

It was Blood who answered him pleasantly.

'Now don't let it alarm ye, Captain, darling. It's just a salute fired in your honour by Ogle, the gunner – the highly skilled gunner – of the *Cinco Llagas*. Have I told you about him yet?' His eyes embraced the company in the question.

'A salute?' quoth Easterling. 'What do you mean? A salute?'

'Why, just a courtesy, as a reminder to us and a warning to you. It's a reminder to us that we've taken up an hour of your time, and that we must put no further strain upon your hospitality.' He got to his feet and stood, easy and elegant in his Spanish suit of black and silver. 'It's a very good day we'll be wishing you, Captain.'

Inflamed of countenance, Easterling plucked a pistol from his belt.

'You play-acting buffoon! Ye don't leave this ship!'

But Captain Blood continued to smile.

'Faith, that will be very bad for the ship, and for all aboard her, including this ingenuous Monsieur Joinville, who really believes you'll pay him the promised share of your phantom treasure for bearing false witness against me, so as to justify you in the eyes of the Governor for seizing the *Cinco Llagas*. Ye see, I am under no delusions concerning you, my dear Captain. For a rogue ye're a thought too transparent.'

Easterling loosed a volley of minatory obscenity, waving his pistol. He was restrained from using it only by an indefinable uneasiness aroused by his guest's bantering manner.

'We are wasting time,' Blood interrupted him, 'and the moments, believe me, are growing singularly precious. You'd best know where you stand. My orders to Ogle were that if within ten minutes of his firing that salute I and my friends here were not over the side of the *Bonaventure*, he was to put a round shot into your forecastle along the water-line, and as many more after that as may be necessary to sink you by the head. I do not think that many will be necessary. Ogle is a singularly skilful marksman.'

It was Joinville who broke the moment's silence that followed.

'God of my life!' he bleated, bounding to his feet. 'Let me out of this!'

'Oh, stow your squealing, you French rat!' snarled the infuriated and baffled Easterling.

Then he turned his fury upon Blood, balancing the pistol ominously. 'You sneaking leech, you college offal! You'd ha' done better to ha' stuck to your cupping and bleedings, as I told you.'

His murderous intention was plain. But Blood was too swift for him. Before any could so much as guess his purpose, he had snatched up by its neck the flagon of Canary that stood before him and crashed it across Captain Easterling's left temple.

As the captain of the *Bonaventure* reeled back against the cabin bulkhead, Peter Blood bowed slightly to him.

'I regret,' said he, 'that I have no cup; but, as you see, I can practise phlebotomy with a bottle.'

Easterling sagged down in a limp, unconscious mass at the foot of the bulkhead. The spectacle stirred his officers. There was a movement towards Captain Blood, and a din of raucous voices, and someone laid hands upon him. But above the uproar rang his vibrant voice.

'Be warned! The moments are speeding. The ten minutes have all but fled, and either I and my friends depart, or we all sink together in this bottom.'

'In God's name, bethink you of it!' cried Joinville, and started for the door.

A buccaneer who did bethink him of it and who was of a practical turn of mind, seized him about the body and flung him back.

'You, there!' he shouted to Captain Blood. 'You and your men go first. And bestir yourselves! We've no mind to drown like rats.'

They went as they were bidden, curses following them and threats of a reckoning to follow with Captain Easterling.

Either the ruffians aswarm on the deck above were not in the secret of Easterling's intentions, or else a voice of authority forbade them to hinder the departure of Captain Blood and his companions.

In the cock-boat, midway between the two vessels, Hagthorpe found his voice at last.

'On my soul's salvation, Peter, there was a moment when I thought our sands were run.'

'Ay, ay,' said Pitt with fervour. 'And even as it was they might have been.' He swung to Peter Blood, where he sat in the sternsheets. 'Suppose that for one reason or another we had not got out in those ten minutes, and Ogle had opened fire in earnest. What then?'

'Ah!' said Blood. 'Our real danger lay in that he wasn't like to do it.'

'But if you so ordered him?'

'Nay, that's just what I forgot to do. All I told him was to loose a blank shot when we had been gone an hour. I thought that, however things went, it might prove useful. And, on my soul, I believe it did. Lord!' He took off his hat and mopped his brow under the staring eyes of his companions.

'I wonder now if it's the heat that's making me sweat like this.'

'Taffrail'

THE LUCK OF THE *TAVY*

Few authors have written more dramatically and authentically about war at sea this century than the man who called himself 'Taffrail'. My friend Douglas Reeman has admitted the debt he owes to 'Taffrail', and I too am a keen reader of 'Taffrail's' books myself – two very good reasons for including one of his stories here. 'Taffrail's' real name was Captain Henry Tapprell Dorling (1883–1968) and the reason why he brought such conviction to his work was quite simple – he had been at sea since his youth and experienced a great deal of naval action at first hand.

Captain Dorling was apprenticed on HMS Britannia, *and thereafter served on the appropriately named HMS* Terrible *based in South Africa and China, taking part in the relief of Peking in 1900. During World War I he commanded several destroyers and was awarded the Gold Medal by the Swedish Government for saving a life at sea in 1917. The British Government also recognised his skill and bravery, and as well as being mentioned in dispatches, he was awarded a DSO. He retired from the Navy in 1929 to write, but he was recalled in 1939 and again went to sea, though this time in several different kinds of ships. From 1942 to 1945, he was on the staff of the Commander-in-Chief Mediterranean. After the war, Captain Dorling regularly broadcast on naval matters as well as serving as naval correspondent on* The Observer *newspaper and writing his books under the pseudonym of 'Taffrail'. Among the most popular of these were* Sea, Spray and Spindrift *(1917),* Men o' War *(1929),* The Navy in Action

(1940) and Battle of the Atlantic *(1946). From among this rich store, I have selected 'The Luck of the Tavy' because it is representative of the life of a sea captain during World War I, and also because there is undoubtedly something of Captain Dorling himself in the story's central character.*

It was a dirty night; there was no possible mistake about that, and Sub-Lieutenant Patrick Munro, RN, of HM TBD *Tavy*, crouching for shelter behind the canvas weather screens on the bridge, felt supremely miserable.

For one thing, he was rather seasick, for the destroyer, well out in mid-Channel, was punching her way westward in the teeth of a rapidly rising south-westerly gale. No sailor likes a gale; those in destroyers hate them.

The sea was big, and every now and then as the *Tavy* plunged her nose into the heart of an advancing wave, masses of solid water came pouring over the forecastle and sheets of spray went flying over the bridge.

The night was very dark and the sky overcast. The wind cut like a knife, and in spite of his oilskins, sou'-wester, sea-boots, and a profusion of woollen mufflers, the sub was nearly wet through and chilled to the very marrow.

He was keeping the middle watch — midnight till 4 a.m., and now, at 1.30, he had still another two and a half hours before he would be relieved by the gunner and could retire to the warm bunk in his cabin.

Even then it seemed doubtful if he would get any sleep, for the *Tavy* rolled and pitched abominably. Moreover, at odd moments she had a playful habit of throwing her stern high into the air on top of a wave and of shaking it like a dog's tail. It was disconcerting, to say the least of it.

The destroyer was by herself, and not a solitary gleam of light was in sight anywhere. Somewhere over the horizon to the northward lay the south coast of England; but as it was war time all shore lights had long since been extinguished. They afforded too good a guide to hostile submarines.

The war had been in progress for well over eighteen months at the time of which we write, and neither the *Tavy* nor her sub-lieutenant had seen a shot fired in anger. They had come across plenty of mines, floating and otherwise, and on one occasion had seen a merchant ship blown up and sunk and had rescued her crew.

Once they had sighted a Zeppelin, miles away on the horizon until it looked like an overgrown, animated sausage; while many, many times they had been sent to sea to assist in 'strafing' hostile submarines. But they had never 'strafed' any, had never fired a gun or a torpedo in real earnest; whereat the hearts of all the officers and men had grown sick, and they envied those of their comrades who had been lucky enough to be in action in the Dardanelles or North Sea.

The weather had grown steadily worse as the night wore on. They had been steaming twenty knots to start with, but on account of the sea, had had to ease down first to fifteen, and then to twelve, lest the masses of heavy water coming over the bows should strain the ship and carry things away.

The lieutenant in command, Travers, was vainly endeavouring to get a little sleep on the cushioned locker in the chart-house underneath the bridge. He had been on deck till 12.30 a.m., and his last orders to Munro were to the effect that he was to be called at four o'clock or if any lights were sighted.

The time wore on, and towards two o'clock, as the sub was beginning to feel a little better and was wondering whether he were bold enough to manage some cocoa from his vacuum flask, he heard the signalman on watch utter a sudden exclamation.

'What's the matter?' he asked.

'I thought I saw a flash o' some kind on the 'orizon a little on the port bow, sir!' the man replied excitedly, peering in the direction named.

'What sort of flash?'

'It looked like a gun, sir.'

They both gazed anxiously out over the water, dodging the sheets of spray as they came flying over the bows, but not a thing was visible.

'If it had been a gun,' the sub pointed out at last, 'surely we should have heard it? The place where you thought you saw the flash is almost dead to wind'ard.'

'I don't rightly know, sir,' the signalman answered. 'Maybe we'd not hear it if it was a small gun.'

Hardly had he spoken when a sharp spurt of ruby flame broke out from the darkness right ahead. It was unmistakably the flash of a gun, apparently about five miles away, and the sub strained his ears for the report. He heard nothing except the wash of the breaking seas.

But an instant later the fiery trail of a rocket cleft the air in exactly the same spot. It rose in a curve, and finally burst in a shower of stars which seemed to illuminate the sea for miles round.

The glare died away, but not before he had caught a fleeting glimpse of the dark shape of a vessel. She carried no lights of any kind, so far as he could see, and what sort of craft she was he could not determine. But she was a ship of some kind, he could swear to that.

'Signalman, go and tell the captain!' he ordered excitedly. 'Messenger, warn the guns' crews to stand by!'

The two men departed on their respective errands.

Travers was on the bridge in less than five seconds, and when the sub had told him what he had seen he went to the engine-room telegraph and increased the revolutions of the engines to fifteen knots.

'I'll shove her on at fifteen,' he remarked. 'Can't go more than that in this sea. By the way, how far off did you say she was?'

'About five miles, sir,' the sub and signalman said together.

'Right,' nodded the skipper. 'In twenty minutes we should be up to her, whoever she is. Sub, have the men warned, and get the guns and torpedo tubes manned. I don't expect for an instant she's anything but an innocent tramp, but we'd better be ready. These Huns are up to all sorts of dodges, foul and otherwise.'

'But what about the gun flashes, sir?' the sub-lieutenant queried.

'M'yes,' said Travers slowly. 'The flashes certainly complicate matters. I don't expect people go blazing off guns in the middle of the night for the good of their health. Someone must be pretty scared, I should think. However, have everything ready.'

'Aye, aye, sir.'

The men, sleeping in their clothes, as was their habit at sea, came tumbling up, but less than thirty seconds later there was another development when the wireless operator clambered on to the bridge.

'I wants th' captain!' he exclaimed, ducking his head as a whiff of spray came rattling against the weather screens like a volley of small shot.

'Here I am,' said Travers. 'What's the matter?'

'About a minute ago, sir, I heard a ship making SOS by wireless! She made it twice, and then suddenly stopped! There's somethin' else makin' signals, too, but I can't make head nor tail o' what she's sayin'! There's somethin' happenin', sir?' He seemed very excited.

'Phew!' whistled the skipper joyfully. 'Don't say we're going to have a run for our money at last! How far off d'you think the signals came from, Sparks?'

'They were comin' in strong, sir. I should say a matter o' ten mile or less.'

'Right. Go down and keep your ears glued to your receivers, and if you hear any more, let me know at once. By George, sub!' he added, rubbing his hands and turning to Munro. There appears to be dirty work going on somewhere, eh?'

'There does, sir,' the sub agreed.

The time seemed to pass very slowly as the *Tavy* forged ahead. Five minutes passed . . . ten minutes . . . a quarter of an hour.

'We ought to be barely a mile off her by now if she's stationary!' murmured Travers disappointedly. 'But I'm blowed if I can see a sign of anything!'

Twenty minutes . . . twenty-five minutes. Still nothing in sight.

The skipper growled something under his breath.

'Where on earth's she got to?' he exclaimed. 'Shove her on at seventeen, sub. I think she'll stand it.' He was getting impatient.

Munro turned the handle of the telegraph until the dial showed the requisite number of revolutions.

The destroyer moved on, making heavier weather of it as she gathered speed, but it was not until thirty-five minutes had elapsed that the lieutenant made a muffled remark, wiped his binoculars carefully, and applied them to his eyes.

'I've spotted her!' he cried. 'She seems to be steering to the south-west'ard, and we're overhauling her pretty fast! Starboard a little, cox'n! Steady so!'

Before very long the dark hull of the stranger was visible with the naked eye. She seemed a fairly large ship, and was apparently about a couple of miles off and steaming twelve knots. The *Tavy* was gaining fast.

'Make a signal telling her to stop!' Travers ordered. 'Then ask her name and where she's bound.'

The signalman pressed the key of his flashing lamp in the longs and shorts of the Morse code. He did it for quite ten minutes without stopping, but no reply was forthcoming. At the end of this time the two ships were barely a mile apart, and unless the steamer, now plainly visible as a craft with one straight funnel and two masts, was keeping an extremely bad lookout, she must have seen the destroyer's signals. But no, nothing happened.

'These chaps deserve to be sunk!' Travers grunted disgustedly. 'I'll put a shot across her bows; that'll wake her up!'

He leant over the bridge rail and gave the necessary orders to the men at the gun below.

As the weapon was discharged there came a brilliant flash and a loud report, and presently the plugged shell pitched into the water several hundred yards ahead of the steamer.

It was a summons she could not afford to neglect, and putting her helm over, she turned round in her tracks and steered straight for the destroyer.

'Tell her to stop!' Travers ordered again, noticing that she was still moving through the water and approaching fast.

Hardly were the words out of his mouth when the fun began.

The steamer sheered abruptly to port, dense clouds of black smoke pouring from her funnel as she increased speed, and then, when she was barely half a mile off, the brilliant red flash of a gun broke out from her side.

Those on board the destroyer heard the report, and a shell screamed through the air like an infuriated demon and raised its spray fountain some distance beyond them. Before it had pitched, other gun flashes were sparkling up and down the stranger's side. She was a merchant ship from her build and appearance, but was evidently powerfully armed. She was firing furiously.

The attack was quite unexpected, but the *Tavy* was not unprepared.

'Open fire on her!' Travers yelled hoarsely, dashing to the telegraphs and jamming them over to 'Full speed'. 'Sub, I'm going to run past her! Nip down on deck and stand by to fire the foremost tube when you sights come on!'

The *Tavy*'s guns roared out in reply, and albeit the violent motion of the ship and the water breaking on board made the shooting rather wild, the shells seemed to be pitching somewhere near the target.

The steamer still fired rapidly, until the air was full of an awful, horrible whining; but at first her shooting was not too good. Perhaps the destoyer offered a very small target, or perhaps the stranger's guns' crews were not very expert; at any rate, most of the projectiles seemed to be falling harmlessly into the sea about two hundred yards beyond and astern of the *Tavy*.

The whole affair was over in less time than it takes to read a description of it. The ships were approaching each other fast on parallel and opposite courses, and would pass at a distance of about eight hundred yards.

The hostile shells began to fall closer. Travers heard a violent explosion from aft, and glancing round, saw the lurid flame of a detonation close by the after funnel. Someone screamed, and then the air seemed full of flying, whistling splinters. The ship had evidently been damaged, for her speed dropped fast. But she still moved through the water.

Another shell, falling in the water about twenty yards short, raised a gigantic spray column which fell on deck and drenched every soul on the bridge and forecastle. It then ricochetted over the bridge, passing so close that the air disturbance whisked the cap off Travers' head and carried it neatly overboard.

But in another instant the sights of the foremost torpedo tube came on, and the sub pulled a lever.

The torpedo leapt out of its tube like a great silver fish and landed in the water with a splash. The stranger evidently saw it fired, for she circled round to avoid it with her guns still firing heavily.

Another hostile shell, bursting in the water, sent a number of fragments whizzing across the destroyer's forecastle. Two men of the foremost gun's crew were hit, and dropped to the deck, but the others, pushing them aside, went on loading and firing, loading and firing, as fast as they could.

The stranger, at very close range, offered an enormous target, and the destroyer's weapons, small though they were, could hardly miss her. Shell after shell drove home, for they could see the brilliant flashes of the explosions as they struck and burst. The *Tavy*'s guns were smaller than those of her opponent, but the latter was enduring terrible punishment, and her fire was weakening rapidly.

Then, quite suddenly, a great column of water mingled with smoke and flame, leapt into the air at the steamer's side. There came the awful, shattering roar of a heavy explosion. The torpedo had gone home.

When the turmoil died away, she had ceased firing. The torpedo must have struck her forward, for her bows were deep in the water and her stern was high in the air, with the propellers still revolving slowly. She seemed to be sinking fast.

Travers was still staring at her speechless, when the sub came on to the bridge chuckling with glee.

'I got her!' he shouted excitedly, pointing at the sinking ship. 'By gum – I got her!'

The skipper said nothing. He had an awful feeling at the back of his mind that perhaps he might have sunk a British ship.

She had fired on him first, it is true, but would that absolve him from sinking her if she did turn out to be British?

The *Tavy* had five men killed outright by the shell explosion aft, and another two wounded at the foremost gun. She was leaking and badly damaged, too, for when the engineer officer came on to the bridge, a little later, he reported that one boiler was hopelessly out of action, that the starboard engine was damaged and could not be used, and that one shell, penetrating the side below the waterline in the stern without bursting, had drilled a hole through which several compartments had been flooded. However, he added cheerfully, the hole had been plugged temporarily, and the ship was in no danger, while she could steam at ten knots with her other engine.

The stranger's bows, meanwhile, were under water, and she was sinking fast by the head. Men aboard her could be seen lowering boats, and circling round, the *Tavy* approached to render what assistance she could.

But before whe reached the spot, the steamer flung her stern high into the air. She hung poised for a few seconds, and then, amidst a cloud of steam and smoke, and with the muffled roar of collapsing bulkheads, slowly disappeared from view as if sucked down by a gigantic magnet.

The destroyer approached the scene and stopped her engines. The sea was covered with wreckage and a film of oil which prevented the waves from breaking, and switching on her searchlight, the *Tavy* swept the water for any signs of survivors. One or two were seen, the whaler was lowered, and after a prolonged search and with no little risk, one officer and twenty men, some of them badly wounded, were rescued. All the remainder had gone to their fate.

Travers waited anxiously. Suppose she were a British ship after all? Suppose he had been responsible for the drowning of some of his own countymen?

But, no! The sub, who had been superintending the embarkation of the survivors, came on to the bridge soon afterwards. He was half beside himself with excitement.

'She was the German auxiliary cruiser *Pelikan*, sir!' he almost shouted.

'The *Pelikan*!' exclaimed Travers, a wave of thankfulness surging through his heart. 'Are you quite certain, man?'

'Absolutely, sir. I got it from one of our — er — prisoners! You remember those flashes we saw?'

'Yes.'

'Well, she was sinking a British steamer!'

'A British steamer!' echoed the skipper. 'Did they pick up any of her men?'

'No, sir,' the sub-lieutenant replied venomously. 'They didn't. They left 'em to sink or swim! Said the weather was too bad to lower boats!'

'Too bad for their boats when we could lower our whaler!' cried Travers, clenching his fists in rage. 'The wretched cowards! I'm glad we had our revenge and sent a few of 'em under! I'd like to shove the survivors overboard after 'em, but suppose I can't, worse luck! Is someone looking after 'em?'

'Yes,' said Munro with a grin. 'At present they're sitting round the galley fire drinking hot Bovril!'

'We're a jolly sight too soft-hearted!' Travers retorted bitterly.

Some fifteen hours later the *Tavy*, minus her after funnel and looking very battered and war-worn, limped into a certain port. The news of her exploit had already been transmitted by wireless, and when she steamed slowly up the harbour on her way to the dockyard, the crews of all the other ships present thronged on deck and cheered themselves hoarse.

The next day a brief announcement from the Admiralty appeared in the morning papers:

On the morning of Thursday last the German armed steamer *Pelikan*, which has lately been responsible for the sinking of several British steamers on the Atlantic trade routes, was encountered in the English Channel by HM destroyer *Tavy* (Lieutenant Robert H. Travers, RN). After a brief but spirited engagement, the enemy was sunk by a torpedo. One officer and twenty men, three of whom have since succumbed to their injuries, were rescued. Our losses were very slight.

Albert Richard Wetjen

DUTY

Perhaps the greatest pleasure in compiling a collection such as this – apart from introducing the reader to some favourite stories – is the opportunity to include the work of a neglected writer. This I shall now do with 'Duty' by Albert Richard Wetjen, whose work has been delighting me for almost half a century. He writes about the sea with the same conviction as Melville, the same authenticity as Conrad and in the same vivid colours as Jack London. Yet how well known is he today in comparison to those three masters of the sea story? Scarcely at all! His books are hard to come by, and I doubt if one of his short stories has been in print for twenty years or more. Yet here is a man who is a supreme master at depicting all the excitement of the high seas.

I first came across Wetjen (1903–66) in the pages of such magazines as Wide World, Collier's *and* Sea Stories, *and then read the six novels he wrote about a tough and resourceful captain named Shark Gotch, published between the two world wars. It was not until some years later, however, that I discovered just what a true son of the sea he was. Born in London of a sea-faring family, he went to sea at fourteen and was shipwrecked twice in the next two years: first due to a fire when in the Bay of Fundy, and second because of fog at Cape Race, which left him stranded on a swamp for five weeks before he was rescued. These experiences prompted him to begin writing when he was eighteen, and further adventures while sailing all over the world as well as serving in the British Merchant Navy during World War I gave him all the raw material he needed. Wetjen (the name is Norwegian in origin) always maintained that he began writing because he disliked hard work, yet as the following story shows, he brought a craftsman's eye to his composition and a born storyteller's instinct to his yarns. I hope that, when the reader has finished 'Duty', he or she will share my opinion that Albert Richard Wetjen deserves to be much better known . . .*

Captain Todd was dying. It was, in fact, little less than a miracle that he had survived so long . . . six blistering days in an open boat since the *Seramis* had caught fire, blown up and gone down. He had been in a bad way when he had first been hauled into the stern sheets from where the explosion had flung him in the water, his left side caved in, his grey moustache singed, his bald head smeared with blood and burns. Yet he had clung to consciousness and command, driven by some inner force, by some hard instinct that had made even the fourteen other survivors regard him with awe, for most of them were hard men, too. Mr Evans, the young third mate, knelt beside the captain in the glow of a tropical dusk and was badly afraid.

'You'd like a drink, sir?'

Captain Todd shook his head and managed a faint smile.

'Water's about done . . . No sense wasting it on me.'

He breathed heavily for a moment and the boat rocked as the men moved aft to watch the end. The bosun stood up, a squat, sturdy figure with a harsh, lined face, towering over the two officers in the stern sheets.

'About gone, ain't he?' he said, wiping his mouth with the back of a hairy hand. The third mate did not answer, but Captain Todd smiled again.

'About gone, bosun,' he admitted. He stared at his third mate. 'You'll be in charge, Mr Evans. The only officer left. Your best chance is to make the coast of Africa. Steer dead east and you can't miss. You've got a chart and sextant and such.'

'I'll manage, sir,' said Mr Evans hoarsely. He was not much

over nineteen, and was not sure of himself. A first command for him. An open boat and thirteen men. He tried to lick his parched lips and shuddered.

'There's a tin box in my pocket,' said the captain wearily. 'And the ship's papers and money. Box holds jewellery consigned to owners. I promised to deliver it to Mr Welsh, the junior partner. It's something special. If . . . if you get through you'll see to it.'

'I'll see to it, sir.'

'That's right.' Captain Todd tried to pat his third mate's shoulder. 'Take over and carry on.'

'I'll carry on, sir.'

The bosun wiped his mouth again and shot a glance at the intent men crowded behind him. He said nothing. Captain Todd gestured for the third mate to empty his pockets and then sighed as if with relief.

'That's all, Evans. Good luck!'

He died soon after dark, coughing once or twice and then growing still. Mr Evans stared down at the black tin box he held in his lap, at the canvas-wrapped bundle of the ship's papers and money, at the heavy revolver that had been the captain's. He was motionless so long, was so quiet that the bosun finally bent and shook him.

'Better get rid of him, eh?' he suggested, jerking a thumb at the stern sheets. The third mate nodded, his face ashen, and horror in his eyes. The bosun stepped by him, bent, gave a little grunt and a heave that was followed by a splash. The third mate shivered and closed his eyes. The bosun noisily brushed his hands and sat down, close to the third mate.

'Let's have a look at the stuff,' he suggested. 'Something to pass the time.'

He took the box from beneath the other's unresisting hands, found a key attached to it by a thin chain and impatiently called to one of the men to light the hurricane lamp.

'I never knew the old man was packing bullion,' he ventured. 'Bring that lamp aft!'

They crowded closer, as many as could before the bosun swore at them and warned them to keep the boat on an even keel. One man held up the lamp and the bosun opened the box. The contents were done up in neat tissue-paper wrapped packages and he unfastened one or two, letting the dim light fall on ropes of pearls, diamond bars, emerald stick pins and such. There was a murmur from the men, and it was that which finally roused the third mate.

He looked up, suddenly aware that they were crowding him, suddenly aware they had the box open and were putting out horny fingers to poke at the contents.

'Here, that's enough of that!' he said shrilly. 'Get 'midships The bosun stared at him curiously, in a manner almost speculative.

'There's a lot of jack here, sir.'

'What's that got to do with you? It's ship's property.'

There was a small silence, and the men's eyes glistened in the lamp-light. The bosun hesitated a moment and then reluctantly replaced the contents of the box, locked it, and handed it back.

'A breaker full of water'd be worth more'n that to us,' he ventured with heavy humour. A man bent and whispered in his ear and he reached up to grip the whisperer's arm, silencing him. 'Not now,' he said out of the corner of his mouth.

'Did you speak, bosun?' inquired Mr Evans, hitching himself into the stern sheets, and shuddering.

'About water, sir,' said the bosun. 'Just said water'd be better than them jewels right now.'

'Yes, we could do with that,' agreed the third mate. He slipped the box into his pocket and took hold of the tiller. 'Better trim that sail, bosun. The night wind's coming up.'

He felt exhausted as well as afraid. His voice was strained, and it sounded unnatural even to himself. The men moved away from him, talking in low tones, but he did not hear what it was they were saying. He had so much to think about. He had to collect his thoughts, strive for calmness. It was a hard time for him. Always before he had had older men over him, to order and advise, to take up the slack if things went wrong. But now he stood alone and he had only been an officer for one short year. Always before he had thought himself a pretty clever sort of fellow, but now he was face to face with a stark reality, and he realized how pitifully inexperienced he was, how uncertain. He was not even full grown to manhood, and he had only tradition to support him.

317

He gripped the tiller with his shaking fingers and headed the boat to the east. It was not likely they would ever reach the coast. A clear four days' run, even if the wind held fair, which in that latitude it almost certainly would not. And to-morrow would see the last of the water. He felt crushed by the sense of responsibility. He had never even remotely realized what it meant, not even when he had taken over his first bridge watch and the captain had left him alone to handle the vessel. He had little petulant twinges of anger when he thought of it. It wasn't fair; wasn't fair of Captain Todd to die; of the mate and the second to perish in the fire. He was the least fitted of them all to be faced with what he was faced with now. And there was no way out. He was the last officer, and in charge. He had taken over. Carry on!

It was a hushed dawn. The eastern sky grew opal white, yawned to the zenith, and then flickers of pink and gold sat along the edge of the world. The sea turned from the gloomy purple of night to the brighter purple of day, and golden lights played in the long hollows of the quiet swells. The horizon blazed abruptly and the rim of the sun showed angry red. The sea was like blood where it ran to meet the sky and the last of the night wind whispered out to nothingness.

The men awoke slowly, yawning, scratching themselves and muttering from dried lips. They began to sit up, look about, at first with eager faces that quickly settled into sullen, bitter lines as the memory of their predicament returned to them. The bosun got up, stretched himself and tried to spit. He stared about, taking in all the horizon.

'Not a damned sail,' he said. 'An' the wind's gone.'

Mr Evans said nothing, but stared at him, wondering at the subtle menace of the other's hoarse voice.

'We ain't got a chance,' someone muttered. The bosun scratched his unshaven chin.

'Not a chance,' he agreed. 'An' I'm choking. Might as well have the last swig now instead of waitin' fer noon.' He heard the men getting up behind him, and his eyes, fastened upon Mr Evans, grew hard. 'Come on, fellers!'

He bent over the water breaker and he had the bung half-out when Mr Evans lurched to his feet. A foot kicked his hand aside, and he looked up with an oath.

'Get out!' the third mate choked. 'Get out, damn you! And leave that alone. I'll tell you when we drink!'

He held Captain Todd's heavy revolver in his hand, and the bosun stared, fascinated, at the big barrel. The other men had grown motionless, watching the scene. Mr Evans's face was drained white and his eyes were burning. There was even a suspicion of trembling in his lips, but he held the gun with a steady hand. The bosun recovered his confidence after a moment and rose, sneering, his thumbs in his belt.

'Gettin' funny, eh? All right, kid. It's a long way to the coast.'

'I'm in command here,' said Mr Evans, tensely. 'We'll keep to the same schedule that Captain Todd laid down.'

The bosun stared at him for a while and then shrugged and rejoined his companions 'midships, talking to them in a low mutter. The third mate relaxed at last and sat down, putting his gun away. He was shaking all over, and deep down he was terribly frightened. Yet he had a little feeling that he had done what was right, had asserted that authority passed on to him. He looked at the thin band of gold that adorned his cuffs and nodded to himself. Just one little band, but it made all the difference.

They drank the last of the water at noon, one man at a time coming aft on the word and receiving his ration from the third mate's hands. There was only a drop or two left for himself, and when he had drunk, he carefully replaced the bung in the empty breaker. The men watched him with burning, savage eyes in which the beginnings of strange deliriums were to be seen. The beat of the hot sun seemed to addle the brain. They were tortured and going mad. Time passed. The wind died, and they sat motionless on an oily sea.

It was just after a red dawn, two terrible days later, when Mr Evans was suddenly jarred to a semblance of consciousness. The tiller was kicking in his hand and a cool wind was fanning at his back. He forced his eyes to open, and, peering round, he saw that the sky was sullen with clouds and there was a little chop on the water, disrupting the smoothness of the sea. The sail filled and water began to ripple along the boat's hull. The men stirred and came to life; then out of the growing wind there swept a series of sharp squalls, black and furious. They were like madmen in the boat as hissing sheets of rain fell to port of them, to starboard, astern of them. It seemed as if the gods were playing, were delighted to watch their sufferings. One man leapt overside with a hoarse cry and started to swim towards a wall of water that churned the sea not a hundred yards away, so close, they could feel the gusts of cold air that emanated from it. He did not swim far. A lean fin slid into view from nowhere and the swimmer disappeared.

And then, as if that had appeased the gods, a squall came right upon the boat, heeling her until her starboard gunnel was all but buried and flooding her with water. The men stood up, staggering, tried to dance, ripped off their clothes to let the cool wetness drench their parched skins. They held their mouths open and up towards the sky. They croaked and laughed, and only the third mate thought to fill the breaker, constructing a crude funnel out of the canvas sea-anchor, and holding the bailing-bucket upright between his feet so that would fill, too.

But nature had not done with fortune, for right upon the heels of the squall, as it whipped away to leeward, the boat abruptly found herself in the very midst of a shoal of fish, like to mullet. The surface of the sea literally boiled with these creatures, and obviously being pursued by some foe, they leaped and floundered in desperate attempts to escape. Dozens flopped over and into the boat itself. The men used their shirts and caps to scoop up others. In less than half an hour, when the shoal had gone in the wake of the squall, the bottom boards were thick with gasping food.

They ate it raw, with the few hard ship's biscuits that yet remained. And then they were sick, and after that they ate again. Later, when the sun came out, they split some of the fish and dried them. They made more or less successful attempts to cook some over the flame of the hurricane lamp. And then they relaxed and slept, the brackish water washing about them as they lay on the bottom boards; the boat heeled steadily now, running before the fair, strong wind that would take them to the African coast. And Mr Evans was filled with relief as he held the kicking tiller and stared at the dancing sea ahead.

'We're all right,' he kept saying to himself. 'Lots of food and water now. A few more days and we'll make it. We're all right.'

He felt strong again. His face was bright, though those two terrible days of calm had left the mark on it. He had been very lucky, he had to admit, to run into a squall and a shoal like that, but that was the way at sea. He steered all through the morning, and presently the men began to awake and stir again, to talk among themselves.

'We're all right now,' called Mr Evans, cheerfully. 'And you might relieve me at the tiller, bosun.'

The faces of the men turned to stare at him as they absorbed his words. The bosun got up and came aft, hitching at his belt, wild-looking and menacing with his heavy growth of whiskers and his burly body.

'Going to make the coast, eh?' he said carefully, looking down at the third mate. Mr Evans nodded, smiling.

'I don't guarantee where, bosun, but according to my reckoning we ought to reach Sierra Leone.'

'Going to head into Freetown, eh?'

'We ought to strike the coast a little north of it, and we can easily run down . . . But why . . .' He was suddenly aware that all the men were regarding him intently, with strange eyes, speculative again. And he stopped.

The bosun turned his head to regard the men and then faced Mr Evans again, grinning a little.

'Coast's pretty wild south of Freetown, ain't it?'

Mr Evans shot him a startled look of surprise.

'I don't know. I've never been there. Why?'

The bosun shrugged.

'Well, I have. And supposin' we miss Freetown and go on south a ways.'

It came to Mr Evans that there was something behind all this. The men were acting now just as they had acted immediately after Captain Todd's death. They had been subdued when thirst and hunger racked them, and now they were fed again . . . what was in their minds?

'Have you gone crazy?' Mr Evans demanded. 'Why shouldn't we put into Freetown? I should think you'd be glad to get ashore.'

One or two of the men laughed.

'Aw, don't act innocent, kid!' someone drawled.

It was not until the third mate saw the bosun's gaze fastened on the black tin box that protruded slightly from his pocket that he really comprehended. And then a dull red flooded his face.

'None of that!' he said sharply. 'We're going to Freetown!'

The bosun shrugged.

'Now what the hell! There's a lot of jack tied up in that box. We can split it and no one'll be any the wiser. Land on the coast and work up to Freetown later. Tell 'em we wrecked the boat an' everything went down with it.'

'You'd better not talk that way, bosun,' said Mr Evans, stiffly.

Some of the men swore.

'Don't waste time arguing with him!' 'Do it up right, bose!' 'You can't talk to a damned kid!'

But the bosun took no notice and continued, half-wheedling, half-explaining.

'Why not? What the hell! We been wrecked, ain't we? Lost all we 'ad! We oughta get something for it . . . And there ain't no one but us knows about the stuff anyway.'

Mr Evans's face was white and tense now, his eyes steady and hard. He had toughened since that night when Captain Todd had died. He had tightened up; he had gathered ballast and a new firmness. He was not afraid now, only a trifle shocked and astonished.

'Forget it!' he snapped. 'You must have gone insane! That jewellery has no value. It's sample stuff!'

The bosun spat deliberately, balancing himself with the boat's lifting across the bright sea, the wind tugging at his shirt and ruffling his tangled hair. He laughed.

'That's why the old man kept it in the safe, hey? Why you're making a fuss about it? Sample stuff me eye! Now listen, kid . . .'

'I'm in charge of this boat, bosun. And don't talk to me like that!'

The other shrugged, placating.

'All right then. Listen, *sir*! . . . Suppose we do go straight to Freetown. We can split the stuff before we gets there, and we can keep our mouths shut afterwards. If there's any inquiries, jest say there wasn't time to get anything off the ship. They ain't going to search distressed seamen. It's a cinch!'

'You'll get your pay,' said Mr Evans firmly. He met the concentrated battery of eyes without a tremor. 'You'll get your pay and a passage home, and I suppose the Line will give you something for new outfits as well as other jobs. As regards ship's property . . . you don't know what you're talking about! Besides, I tell you that jewellery has no value. It's nothing . . .'

'Our pay?' sneered the bosun, shutting him off. He spat aside and laughed. 'Don't be a fool! What's a bit of pay beside what you got there? Your whack'll be the same as ours.' The utter hopelessness of making the man believe him came to Mr Evans, and he grew obstinate and angry.

The bosun hitched at his belt and took another step forward, and Mr Evans put his free hand inside his pocket where rested Captain Todd's gun.

'You stay where you are!' he snapped. 'You stay 'midships. This box and the ship's money goes to Freetown, untouched.'

The bosun hesitated and licked his lips, watching the bulge of the gun.

'Didn't you say you wanted me to relieve you at the tiller?' he said mildly. 'You'll be wantin' to sleep.'

'I've changed my mind,' said Mr Evans. 'You can go 'midships and stay there.'

There was a short silence, and then the bosun shrugged.

'All right, kid,' he said insolently. 'It's your damned funeral!'

He went back to his companions and they held a long conference, the low mutter of their voices drifting ominously aft. Mr Evans tightened his mouth and surreptitiously wiped a trickle of cold sweat from his forehead. He wished for the hundredth time that Captain Todd had not died, or that the mate had lived to take charge. They would know what to do. Should he avoid trouble by letting the men have the box and the ship's money and then report the matter when they had all reached civilization? But no, if he did that they would guess his purpose and would see to it he did not talk. He had an instinctive feeling about that. They would not trust him. He was an officer. He braced himself and forced his attention to the compass beside him, to the coast ahead. There was nothing to do really but carry on. So the day waned and night fell, and Mr Evans had a hard job to keep awake . . .

It was towards dawn when they rushed him, slipping quietly

over the stretchers and almost reaching him before the uneven rocking of the boat jerked him out of a doze. They closed in then, cursing, and Mr Evans stood up, shouting, with sudden hysteria and fright. He shot one man, and with the unshipped tiller he stunned another. He fought like a wildcat, with a desperate sort of madness, shouting all the time. They drew off at last, cursing and sullen. It was hard to get at him, backed against the stern sheets as he was.

'All right,' the bosun said through the darkness. 'All right, kid. You gotta sleep some time.'

Mr Evans never had any clear recollection of the hours that followed. He did remember that he could hardly sit upright, even with the tiller to brace him. He weaved with each motion of the boat, sometimes almost toppling forwards or sideways, as if the muscles of his waist had lost all resiliency. His eyes were like balls of fire, heavy and aching, the lids falling, always falling so that he had to set his teeth to keep them up. His body had become one vast weariness, and his brain seemed on fire, throbbing with the one thought that he must not sleep. He remembered the men watching him; visions of waiting faces, sneering faces, laughing faces swimming before him as in a haze. He was not even aware of the passage of time, not aware that another day had passed and another night had come while the boat slid forward over the sea. He only knew that suddenly there were stars again, and a colder wind, and that the boat was rocking uncertainly as the men came aft again.

'Get out!' he shouted, standing up and waving his gun. The boat slid sideways and wallowed in a trough as he let go the tiller, but none of them cared. Mr Evans was later inclined to think that he was asleep even while he was fighting, for he could remember only the strangest things about the affair. Such as a man's jagged teeth bared at him; such as a fist looming enormously before his eyes; such as one of the men stopping to blow his nose. He was always impelled, however, by the savage thought that he must stay awake and defend that ship's property which Captain Todd had rendered to him; and it made him savage that he could not stay awake. He was even savage in his dreams, for he did dream horribly, and fought and twitched after the men had overcome him and laid him on the bottom boards with much argument and cursing.

He came to, the third mate, to discover himself on his back, the shadow of the sail moving across his face and the clear blue sky edging about the billowed canvas. He stared blankly upwards at first, then grew aware that he was thirsty, and tried to sit upright.

'Woke up, eh?' said the bosun, not in a bad humour. He was steering. 'Might as well as saved us all that trouble, an' then you'd have been more comfortable.'

Mr Evans tried to lick his dry lips.

'How long . . .' he started, and the bosun grinned, almost friendly now.

'You been under more'n a day, what with that crack on yer head and you needin' sleep. Larry there got you with an oar blade.'

One of the men laughed and looked pleased.

'I see,' said Mr Evans hoarsely. He was aware now of a splitting headache and dried blood in his hair and down his face. The bosun leaned forward and, gripping his shoulder, aided him to a sitting position.

'Thirsty, eh?' He filled a pannikin from the breaker and held it out. One of the men, sitting aft of the sail, scowled.

'No sense coddlin' him, bose. Drop 'im overside, says I!'

'You shut your trap!' snarled the bosun, suddenly ugly. 'I'm running this gang now. We ain't aimin' to bump anyone off 'less we has to, an' maybe we c'n bring him round.'

'Can it!' growled another man. 'We need the kid to navigate, don't we?'

'I'll see you damned first!' said Mr Evans, indignantly. 'You're mutineers!'

'Now, kid,' soothed the bosun. 'You be good an' you'll see mama again.' They all laughed, then, and Mr Evans flushed red, bit his lip and subsided. He felt that he had miserably failed in his duty. He could not imagine Captain Todd letting the men take charge like this.

They made him take a sight at noon, which he did more to satisfy his own curiosity as to their position than to please them. The coast was now a low purple line ahead, and he scanned the chart with care, surprised to find he was a great deal farther north than he had suspected. There would be a better chance to make Dakar, French Senegal, than Freetown, Sierra Leone. He said nothing of that, however.

'We're north of Freetown,' he told the bosun, sullenly, when they questioned him. That worthy grunted.

'That's all right. We're going to land and see if we can get something to eat, an' rest up, and then we'll coast down, or maybe figure out something else.'

'What are you going to do with me?' the third mate demanded. The bosun shrugged.

'Ain't much we can do 'less you wants to be sensible and come in with us. We'll give you an equal whack and, I promises, there won't be any double-crossing neither.'

Mr Evans stared at him and stared at the other men. Some of them were hard-bitten, he knew, and would stop at little or nothing. But some were reasonably honest mariners, carried away by the unusual circumstances, by the prospect of sudden wealth, by that madness which comes to the majority when all recognized authority is removed. And Mr Evans hesitated. After all, why should he be concerned? The jewellery wasn't his, nor was the ship's money. He believed the bosun would see him through if he agreed to the man's proposals. And no one would know. He had only to say that everything had gone down with the *Seramis*. He could go home and get another ship and forget the whole incident. There was nothing . . . and his thoughts suddenly checked as he lifted an arm to wipe sweat from his forehead, and the dull glint of the thin gold band on the cuff caught his eye. No, nothing, except that he was the only officer left and Captain Todd had said . . . There was, after all, tradition; the game to be played.

'I'm not a thief!' he said bitterly. 'You can go to hell!'

'You're a damned young fool!' exclaimed the bosun. 'I been stoppin' some of this gang 'ere from bumping you off 'cause I thought you'd come around. What the hell! You've only got a third mate's pay, an' that won't make you rich!'

'It's ship's property you're stealing,' said Mr Evans doggedly. 'And I was left in charge of it. You can't get away with anything like that.'

The blood congested in the bosun's face and his eyes grew ugly.

326

'All right. You leave that to us. The point is you ain't comin' in?'

'No!' muttered Mr Evans. 'I can't! Don't you see, I can't?'

But they could not understand him, and there was a small, tight silence. Then someone said:

'Wasting time, that's all. If you'd listened to me –'

'Shut up!' snarled the bosun, furious. 'We ain't bumping 'im . . . not the way you want it. Give 'im a break. 'E's only a fool kid, and there's no sense us takin' the chance of swinging.'

Mr Evans stared up at him, holding his throbbing head.

'Then what are you going to do with me?'

The bosun spat with deliberation.

'Nothing else for it, kid. We'll leave you ashore.'

The third mate was appalled. Ashore on the African coast, miles from civilization, even from a native village. Without food or weapons. And with no knowledge of the jungle. He did know the coast was sparsely settled; there were savage beasts and more savage men. He set his jaw. His face was ashen.

'That's murder,' he said shakily. 'You might as well kill me now.'

'You got a chance anyway,' the bosun reminded him. 'You can 'ead for Freetown.'

The bosun was inwardly troubled, but he was also obstinate. Now he had actually accomplished what he wished, brought off his coup and obtained the jewels, twinges of fear were his. It had all seemed so simple and obvious out on deep water, with death likely to come any moment; but now, with the coast ahead, with safety not far off, with policemen and gunboats somewhere around, he began to sense complications. Supposing one of the men got drunk in Freetown and talked too much; or flashed some of the loot? It looked as if they'd have to chance that, but he couldn't chance letting the third mate come with them, the way he was feeling. Obstinate young fool! Choked up with a lot of officer ideas! On the other hand, the bosun did not feel able to kill the youngster; at least, not in cold blood. He began to understand the perplexities of leadership, but he also understood his companions well enough not to let them sense this. His outward demeanour was carelessly confident.

'You got a chance that way,' he repeated to Mr Evans. 'If we puts you ashore.' He looked at the other men, all staring at him, some of them uneasy, a few scowling and plainly angry. 'By the time 'e gets through the jungle, we'll be clear,' he explained.

'If 'e *gets* through,' said someone dryly, and someone else laughed, breaking the tension. The matter was tacitly accepted. After a while, when unobserved, the bosun leaned forward and tapped the third mate's shoulder.

'If we don't get clear 'fore you show up, you remember it was me who gave you the chance, eh?' The bosun wanted to keep a sheet-anchor to windward and his eyes were uneasy. 'This ain't all my doin's. That's a tough crowd there, and them jewels —'

Mr Evans stared at him.

'I'll see you to the devil first!' he cried passionately. 'You'll turn them over to me now or take the consequences. Don't be such a fool, man! That jewellery isn't worth —'

'Shut up!' snarled the bosun, hardening. 'You can't kid me! Ashore you'll go. An' I hopes you do croak!'

The afternoon waned, and just before dusk they ran the boat into a convenient little sandy cove, backed by palms and jungle and sheltered by low headlands. They beached the craft after a sharp tussle with the surf and a narrow escape from a half-hidden reef.

The men tumbled ashore, laughing excitedly, running up and down and stumbling on unfamiliar legs. They stretched themselves. They were safe at last after the terrible days on open water. Even the bosun went so far as to run like a boy to the edge of the trees and pluck handfuls of leaves and coarse grass, rubbing them hungrily between his hands. Mr Evans, left to himself, climbed stiffly out of the boat.

It was in his mind to launch it and get away alone, but he knew the effort was far beyond his strength; and even if he did succeed in pushing the boat out of the shallows, he would never be able to get past the reefs and through the surf without aid. Besides, the bosun had the ship's papers and money, and the box of jewellery. Reluctantly, filled with a sullen anger and a mortification that he was beaten, he slowly went up the beach to where the bosun was directing the lighting of a fire.

They cooked the last of the dried fish, cooked some land

crabs they knocked over, and ate them together with a faintly bitter orange fruit they discovered in a small grove fringing the cove. They made clumsy cigarettes of dried leaves and toasted seaweed, the craving for tobacco strong upon them, and they sat around the fire coughing their lungs out in the salty, acrid smoke; but they were moderately content. The night fell like a dark curtain, and a chill came to the wind. The men began to argue.

'We ain't had a look at the stuff yet! Open 'er up, bose!'

'No sense bein' fools about it,' the bosun grumbled. 'We ain't going to split now. If we do you'll start to fight an' gamble, and that'll mess everything proper. We'll wait till we sight Freetown and then divvy it.'

There was some grumbling at this, but, in general, the bosun had the men with him. They demanded, however, that he let them at least see the contents of the black tin box, and count what ship's money had been brought along. The bosun swore, but finally consented, drawing the box and the canvas-wrapped package of papers and money from inside his shirt. There was a general shuffling as the men gathered round.

Mr Evans was entirely forgotten. He sat cross-legged outside the circle, staring nervously around at the dark walls of the jungle from which came the rustlings of the night wind and the faint cries of birds and small rodents. It was terrible, all Africa looming at his back, mysterious and secret. Once a low, ominous drumming reached his ears. Once some larger animal gave a high-pitched scream. Mr Evans shivered and was afraid. He stared at the moving shadows of the men hunched round the fire, and his anger at them abruptly dispersed his fears. He would never live this down. He had been trusted and had failed. If he could not command a small boat, how could he expect, some time, to be given command of a big ship? He got up, shaking, feverish, quite white and very tense. He had to do something!

The bosun was having trouble fitting the key to the box, for it had become bent during the various scuffles it had been through. No one heard Mr Evans come up and stare over the bent shoulders of the small circle. Each man was intent and partially hypnotized by the dancing flames. Then it happened, and why it should have happened, Mr Evans had never any

329

clear idea. He only knew he was suddenly and furiously angry at them all, filled with a petulant, childish rage that they should have so calmly thrust him aside and ignored him, forgotten his rank, laughed at his youth. He made a convulsive jump, scooped the tin box and the canvas bundle right out of the bosun's lap, and then he was gone, running down the beach and into the thick darkness.

There was a period of utter astonishment that held the men still. They hardly realized at first what had happened. Blinded by the fire, they were only aware that something or someone had leaned out of the night and taken their treasure. The bosun was the first to recover, lunging to his feet with a bull-like roar and a furious oath.

'That damned mate!' he choked and lugged Captain Todd's revolver from his pocket. He could see nothing to fire at, and a man near him jostled him roughly.

'That's wot you get bringing him ashore with us,' the man snarled.

The bosun knocked him down, and there was a brief mêlée that lost precious moments before the other men could stop it. They scattered then, each one swearing and raging, to search the beach and the jungle fringe; but once out of range of the firelight they were baffled and impotent. As the first of their rage wore off they grew uneasily aware of the brooding jungle wall, of the mysterious calls and rustlings. And at the last they drifted back to the fire and gathered about the bosun who was uneasily glancing from one to the other.

Mr Evans did not stop until he was entirely out of breath and exhausted, and then he discovered himself to be in the midst of all but impenetrable darkness. He could not even see a star above. It seemed that even the air was thick and heavy. Whichever way he groped he encountered underbrush on the scaly barks of trees. Once, he gulped convulsively as a pair of luminous eyes flashed into his for a moment and then vanished. Some animal raised a hair-lifting snarl on his right that set him running and blundering in a panic again. But at last he dropped, half-unconscious, to earth, holding the tin box and the canvas bundle to him. Then he sank into a coma-like sleep.

He awoke, alert, hours later, when a faint greyness began to penetrate to him and the jungle took on a ghostly visualness. He heard men shouting to one another, and far-off crashing and cracklings as they worked their way towards him. He got up, shaking from weakness and hunger, and, keeping as quiet as he could, he worked forward again. Once, he heard a shot, evidently the bosun firing at some shadow or animal, and after that there was only the noise of the jungle. The sounds of pursuit faded and died. Mr Evans sat down and thought a long time, and then he made a rough but efficient sling of what remained of his jacket, fastening the tin box and the canvas bundle to his shoulders. He could not go back the way he had come, he knew. The bosun and the others might hang around for days looking for him. They would be fearful that he should escape to inform on them; furiously angry at having lost all they had gained, or thought they had gained. Knowing the coast not at all, utterly unfamiliar with wood-lore, the third mate of the *Seramis* squared his shoulders, got a bearing from the sun and, heading first towards the sea, he turned, after sighting it, to walk north along the coast.

The consul at Dakar, French Senegal, had known many strange things to occur along that savage coast, but none stranger than the one but recently brought to his attention. First, had come a French official with word of a mad young man brought into town by some natives who had found him with other natives miles and miles to the south. A mad young man, the consul would agree, to be wandering about without food or weapons, with a black tin box fastened on his back and with a lot of wild talk of mutineers and a sinking ship. At present, the mad young man was in hospital, unable to see anyone; but later on, since his nationality was obvious, no doubt the consul would be interested ... The consul quite understood, sent a few wires and forgot the matter for some three weeks. Then he hastily re-read a brief report the authorities had handed him, and stared perplexed at the gaunt youth his clerk had ushered in.

'So you are the third officer of the *Seramis*, wrecked by fire in mid-Atlantic? Let me have the story, Mr Evans.'

The gaunt young man then sat down, dressed in a rumpled suit of borrowed whites, fumbling awkwardly with a borrowed solar topee he held between his scarred hands. His eyes were sea-blue, the consul noted, very wide eyes and very intent as if they had seen many things. His cheeks were sunken. He possessed countless small scars which the jungle had given him. His hair, cropped short, held a touch of grey at the temples, and about his mouth there were etched fine lines. He made the consul vaguely uneasy, but he sent the masters of three ships away while he listened to the story of the *Seramis*. He heard it through and absently played with a rusty, battered tin box that lay on the desk before him, with a filthy canvas-wrapped bundle, now opened, to one side of it.

'I don't remember much,' said Mr Evans simply when he had done. 'Not after I got away. And then some natives looked after me.' He was extremely vague.

The consul stared at him and brushed a fly impatiently from the back of one hand.

Nineteen. A boy of nineteen! Third officer of a cargo-boat, winning through all that terrible stretch of country. He was appalled.

'I have wired Freetown,' he said slowly. 'If the men reach there they will be held until we investigate further.' He smiled a little and then proceeded to open the battered tin box. 'So you stuck to this all through, eh?'

'Captain Todd told me to see it was delivered, sir. Ship's property.'

The consul nodded.

'I suppose you'd have made the same fuss if it had been a coil of rope . . . or a hurricane-lamp. Ship's property.'

Mr Evans did not quite understand him.

'Captain Todd left me in charge,' he said simply. 'There was nothing else I could do.'

The consul laughed and dipped his fingers into the jewellery in the box, allowing it to drop from his hand to the desk.

'I cabled Sydney about this,' he said slowly, 'as soon as the French handed things over. It isn't worth ten dollars the lot. Your owners were contemplating importing artificial jewellery, and this was a box of samples.'

Mr Evans nodded.

'I knew that, sir,' he said gravely.

'Eh?' said the consul. He grew rigid. Several times he started to say something, but nothing came. Mr Evans frowned.

'I tried to explain to the men once or twice . . . but they wouldn't believe me. It was natural, I suppose . . . for them to think I was lying.'

'I . . . see,' said the consul, slowly. 'But . . . but it was ship's property, so you had to . . .'

'See it through, sir,' Mr Evans agreed.

'You damned young fool!' said the consul, and then, sitting back, he began to laugh with a hysterical note. Mr Evans grew slowly red, his eyes puzzled.

'I don't understand, sir,' he said stiffly. 'I may be a fool . . . Oh, I see. Because it was artificial . . . Well, what else could I do?'

The consul stopped laughing abruptly and stared at him, smiling slightly but with a little pain round his heart. Nineteen years old. Grey at the temples already. Lines in the face before its time. Steady and serious blue eyes. Youth was so in earnest. To suffer and all but die. For some vision and some ideal . . . Lord, what had they to do with life and facts? Mr Evans had compressed his lips.

'I'm sorry if you think me . . .'

The consul made a gesture that silenced him. Wasn't it, after all, the principle that counted? The sense of duty? Where would the world be if there weren't some fools to think of duty? He glanced aside and caught a glimpse of his own reflection in the sheen of a framed photograph, a little tired, a little white, very lined and a little bent. Twenty years on the coast had done that. And then he stared back at Mr Evans, only nineteen and already with the stamp of life upon him. For a box of cheap junk jewellery, a few ship's papers, and a few pounds in gold. Only nineteen could have made that so serious.

And then there came to the consul a foolishly sentimental thing. He could see the figure of that Centurion they had dug up from the ash-covered ruins of Pompeii; that soldier still in his harness, holding his spear, who had obviously remained at his post of guard while the city went under the earth, not stirring because he had had no orders to stir. The discipline of the Legions! Nothing but duty. And the consul laughed.

'Do you know what I think of you?' he said at last. 'Do you know what I really think, Mr Evans? I think that you will make a very fine captain!'

Norman Reilly Raine

THE LAST LAUGH

A Tug-boat Annie Tale

There haven't been many female sea captains, of course, and in maritime fiction only one of real note – but what a remarkable woman Tug-boat Annie Brennan is to be sure! Tough as any man, resourceful and smart, she runs her vessel, the Narcissus, *with a skill many a mere male would admire. And quite a few of them do – especially those who try to outwit her!*

Annie was the creation of Norman Reilly Raine (1898– 1960), a former stoker turned writer, who late in his life became a leading Hollywood screenwriter. A persistent rumour has maintained that Tug-boat Annie was no invention, but a real woman with whom Raine had once worked. Apparently the two had never got on well, and as Raine was never able to outsmart the lady, he vowed revenge by using her in a story. Such was the reception with which the public greeted this tale, however, that Raine found himself softening towards his creation, and instead of trying to make a fool of a woman bold enough to captain her own ship, he turned her into a hero – and so successfully that, in 1933, a film was made about her, with Marie Dressler in the starring role. Although the stories of Tug-boat Annie may not be as widely read today as they once were, her name certainly lives on. Here, then, is a reminder of the good lady at her engaging best . . .

A wild half-gale, aftermath of a week of blizzards, wailed down the strait of Georgia and churned the waters of Puget Sound to a lather of foam and spouting grey seas. The deep-water tug *Narcissus*, her upper works white with snow and frozen brine, plunged wildly through the last little stretch of clamorous water to the shelter of Secoma Harbour.

Tug-boat Annie Brennan, the tug's skipper, and senior master of the Secoma Deep-Sea Towing and Salvage Company, lifted the back of her chilblained hand to rub her eyes, inflamed and rheumy from lack of sleep and the strain of peering ahead through the tumultuous and snow-blanketed sea miles, and looked through the wheel-house window at the welcoming lights shining through the winter evening from Secoma's hilly streets. She patted the tug's wheel and spoke to Peter, the paunchy, slope-shouldered mate, phlegmatically chewing behind her.

'Well, she done it again, the dirty old tramp!'

'There was times I doubted if we'd get through, Annie,' Peter replied. 'It's been a long drag down from the outside of the island, but we didn't lose a log.'

' 'Course not! Don't talk such hodge-podge,' said Annie indignantly. 'The *Narcissus* never fell down on a job yet.'

She put the wheel expertly over and brought the *Narcissus* around the pierhead and into her place beside her wharf. Ahead and astern of her the other tugs of the company fleet — *Asphodel*, *Daisy*, *Pansy* and others — rose and fell on the swell that came in from the turmoil of the outer harbour.

Tug-boat Annie shivered slightly in her old sweater, and blinked the snow from her lashes as she lumbered across the wharf to the company office to report. She climbed the stairs and flung open the office door, letting in a swirl of snow and icy air, then stood grinning in the doorway and rubbing her hands. She boomed:

'Hello, folks! Here I am!'

'Keep quiet, Annie,' the dispatcher told her sharply, 'and shut that door!'

Tug-boat Annie gazed about her in mild surprise. There was tenseness among the office staff; and in the taut silence she could hear the voice of Alec Severn, her employer, telephoning behind the glass partition of his office. She knew immediately, from his tone, that the occasion was unusual.

She closed the door with such care that only the windows rattled, then tiptoed elephantinely to the centre of the main office and presented her generous stern to the comforting rays of the old-fashioned pot-bellied stove.

'Big salvage job, Annie,' the book-keeper told her in a hoarse whisper. 'One of the largest we've had. There's a big steamer run ashore in the thick weather below the Cape. Listen.'

The voice of Alec Severn carried to them:

'The *Narcissus* has just got in . . . Yes, she's big enough for the job, and she's properly equipped . . . Yes, sir!' Tug-boat Annie, her weariness forgotten, stood like a war charger sniffing battle. Her employer's excited voice was heard again:

'Miss Walker!'

'Yes, sir.'

'Telephone Captain Arthur Hofstead to report here at once. He will take the *Narcissus* out. And tell Tug-boat Annie I want to see her. I suppose I'll have a scrap with the stubborn old –'

He stopped suddenly and reddened, for Tug-boat Annie, a mammoth of quivering indignation, loomed in his office doorway.

'Hmm-mph!' said Annie.

'Oh – hello, Annie!' he said with forced heartiness.

'Hello yerself, ye furry-headed sprat! What's this I hear about Art Hofstead takin' my *Narcissus* out?'

'Now, Annie, listen –'

'I'm listenin'!' she said grimly. 'Go on.'

'Well, you've had a hard trip and need a good rest. And this is going to be a tough job. Be reasonable, Annie. You're not as young as you were, and –'

'I'm twice as young as ever I were,' said Annie, breathing hard. 'But we'll let that pass. What ye're gettin' at is, I ain't wanted no more –'

'It isn't that at all, Annie,' protested Severn despairingly. 'It's –'

'Or mebbe,' Annie went on, warming to her subject, 'seein' I've only had forty years in the business, I don't know nothing' about salvage jobs. Prob'ly that's it.'

'Will you shut up!' Severn shouted. 'I never met such a

336

bull-headed old devil. It was only your health I was thinking of –'

Annie's granite features melted in a sudden grin.

'Me health's fine, ye old gafoozler. And I'm sorry fer kickin' up such a frumpus. But ye shouldn't ha' been such a dumbskull, Alec; ye know well enough if anybody but me tried to take my *Narcissus* out she'd spit up her diesels at 'em. Now, what is this job?'

Severn accepted the inevitable and sat back, his red, goodhumoured face intent.

'The steamer *Utgard*, with a large general cargo from the Orient, is piled up on the rocks at La Push, below Cape Flattery. She went ashore in the blizzard this afternoon about two o'clock. And her underwriters have given us the job of getting her off.'

'What's there in it for us?'

'A hundred and ten thousand – if we salvage her.'

Annie nodded.

'And nothing if we don't, o' course. How bad has she struck?'

'Her pumps are taking care of the water that's coming in, so the radio message said; but the great danger is that the weather might get bad again, and she'd break up. So you'll have to hurry, Annie. Take the *Pansy* and the *Buttercup* –'

Annie shook her head.

'No use, Alec. They ain't big enough for a job like this, especially if the sea kicks up.'

'But we have nothing bigger. And the *Narcissus* can't do it alone.'

'Why didn't they call on that big salvage tug, the *Salvage Prince*, at Victoria. She's closer, and –'

'She's laid up in dry dock. What other tug can we get, Annie? I don't want to lose this business.'

Tug-boat Annie's mastiff face went into a furrowed knot as she cogitated; then her red-rimmed eyes took on an angry glitter.

'It certainly boils me up to admit it, Alec – but we'll have to share the job wid that boatload o' colic across the slip!'

'You mean –?'

'Yeah – Bullwinkle! His *Salamander* is the only other tug in

Secoma powerful enough and fast enough to be any use. Guess I'd better see him and talk terms. He's sure to hold me up, too.'

Severn reluctantly agreed.

'Be careful how you handle him, and get the best terms you can. He doesn't like us, remember.'

'I'll be the soul o' tack, Alec.'

She clumped hastily down the stairs, and after pausing at the *Narcissus* to tell her sea-weary crew to stand by, she barged across to the opposite side of the slip to enlist the aid of the *Narcissus*' most bitter business rival, the big and able tug *Salamander*, Horatio Bullwinkle, master.

Mr Bullwinkle was reclining on the settee in his snug cabin, scanning the evening paper, when Tug-boat Annie, after a jocose rat-a-tat, thrust her head in at the door.

'Hello there, Bullwinkle, ye old haddock,' she greeted him, diplomatically jovial. 'What — don't tell me ye know how to read?'

Mr Bullwinkle sat bolt upright, and regarded her with distaste. He said: 'Get yourself outa here, nuisance!'

'Now listen, pal —'

'Before I throw you out!' he supplemented forcibly.

Tug-boat Annie remembered her mission, and forced a merry laugh as she closed the door behind her.

'Ye needn't look so carbolic. I come to do ye a favour.'

'So you're drunk, hey?'

Disregarding this quip, Tug-boat Annie plunged hastily into her proposition.

'So there it is,' she concluded, striving to keep the anxiety out of her voice. 'Well — what do you say?'

'Mr Bullwinkle's little black shoebutton eyes raked her maliciously.

'Ye need me pretty bad, don't ye? Well, in that case, my terms is sixty—forty.'

Tug-boat Annie's heart sank. But she pretended to misunderstand.

'That's real swell of ye, Bullwinkle. I knowed ye couldn't be such a wart as folks say. Sixty—forty, eh? Just the terms I was goin' to —'

'Yeah —' said Mr Bullwinkle calmly. 'Sixty per cent for me. And forty for you.'

Tug-boat Annie's laugh was razor-edged.

'Ye allus was a wag, Bullwinkle. But I want to be fair. Let's say, fifty-five for us and forty-five for you. Huh?'

Mr Bullwinkle resumed his paper.

'Good night,' he said.

Tug-boat Annie heroically restrained her temper.

'O' course, if ye don't want the job,' she said airily, 'we kin easy get the *Salvage Prince* from Victoria —'

'Think I'm a sucker?' Mr Bullwinkle grinned. 'If you could have got her you'd have had her.' He put down his paper. 'I've got you where I want you now, Annie. If Severn don't like my terms he can lump 'em. Of course,' he added magnanimously, 'I don't mind using me own gear.' He spread his paper.

'Ain't you the horse's neck?' returned Annie, desperately genial. 'Listen — let's make it fifty-fifty —'

Mr Bullwinkle looked around his paper.

'Don't slam the door,' he said, 'when you go out.'

Vituperation, pleading and reason all drew a zero. Mr Bullwinkle's obdurate stand wore her down and at length she gave in.

'I want it in writing, mind,' he warned.

'Ain't me word good enough?'

'No,' he told her, 'it ain't. You might get short of breath at the wrong moment.'

Presently he held in his hand her signed agreement, that upon the successful salvage of the steamer *Utgard*, the proceeds were to be divided: forty per cent to the Secoma Deep-Sea Towing and Salvage Company, and to Horatio Bullwinkle sixty per cent. He folded the paper and placed it in his pocket.

'People finds things like you,' Annie commented bitterly, 'when they turns up a wet plank.'

Harsh daybreak in the strait of Juan de Fuca found the *Narcissus* and the *Salamander* battling with a stiff head wind. When they had rounded, with generous clearance, the fog signal of Cape Flattery, Tug-boat Annie awakened from a three-hour snooze. She rubbed the sleep from her eyes, then raised her stiff and aching body from the bunk. While hauling on her sea-boots her eyes rested on the oily smirk of her late departed husband, Captain Terry, in its plush and gold oval frame, and with it she held grumbling colloquy.

'Who are you starin' at, ye grinnin' ape?' she muttered. 'Pretty nice for you, settin' there on the wall, wid nothin' to do! . . . Ho-hum! Me mouth tastes like the inside of a dead pelican . . . wonder how Bullwinkle's comin' along?' Once more her worried eyes encountered the portrait. 'Ye was a awful trial, Terry – but I wish ye was back wid me again – almost. I get kinda tired, sometimes, fightin' alone. Oh, ye needn't laugh! Ye ain't gettin' on me soft side . . . now where the devil'd I put that other boot? . . . Well, darned if I ain't got me hoof in it!'

She waddled to the window, ruminating. 'Hmmm-m . . . snow and fog as thick as yer head. I'd better get on deck and make sure Bullwinkle ain't stole the propeller.'

When she reached the deck the tugs were proceeding cautiously down the coast. Tug-boat Annie took her post in front of the wheel-house, listening intently for the *Utgard*'s answer to the *Narcissus*' hoarse and frequent whistle blasts.

At length, muffled by the fog, she heard an answering '*Whoo-up!*' from the estimated locality of the Indian hamlet of La Push. She signalled Shiftless, the deckhand, who was at the wheel, and he gave several sharp hoots of the whistle, echoed by the *Salamander*, which was buffeting her way, a diluted shadow in the fog, about two hundred yards astern.

Both tugs swung in towards the shore, and soon, through the mist and steadily falling snow, the stranded steamer became visible. And as the *Narcissus* steamed alongside, stokers and seamen with huddled shoulders and beads on their nose-ends, blew on their frozen fingers and gazed woodenly down at her. The two tugs ranged opposite the steamer's waist, and Annie was about to megaphone up, when the captain appeared. He was tall, and thin-faced, and his eyes, dark-rimmed with worry, held the look of a beaten man. He addressed the *Salamander*.

'I am Captain Hall,' he said, in a high almost piping voice. 'Are you the tugs the underwriters sent?'

'Sure we are,' Annie shouted up. 'Looks like ye're in kind of a conundrum, Captain. How bad are ye damaged?'

'You run away back to your galley, cookie,' replied the shipmaster tolerantly, 'and let me talk to your skipper.'

At this, a raucous laugh from the *Salamander* focused attention upon Mr Horatio Bullwinkle, who, with a flaming red tippet around his thick neck, and his strong, bandy legs braced, stood on the forward deck of his tug. 'That's a good one, Annie!' chortled Mr Bullwinkle. 'Haw, haw haw!'

'That's jest a voice from the stockyards — don't pay no attention to him, Captain!' Annie told the startled shipmaster. 'I'm the skipper o' this tug. And that queer-looking contraption over there's the *Salamander*, what I brought along to save her master from starvin' to death. Now what damage have ye got?'

'For God's sake,' piped the outraged shipmaster, 'don't tell me they sent a woman off to do this job?'

'They did!' answered Annie grimly. 'And I'll mebbe do as good a job o' salvage as you done gettin' your vessel safe to port! Come on — let's get goin'!'

'We might have been all right if the weather didn't blow up stronger, but she's hard aground,' returned Captain Hall dubiously. 'The pumps will take care of what water comes in when we are free, and I'll give you what help I can with my engines and anchors and such to drag us off. It shouldn't be hard.'

'Ye're a kind of a optimist, Captain,' Tug-boat Annie told him. 'Anyways, we'll put our hind foot foremost.'

There was further question and answer, in the course of which Captain Hall had occasion to revise his estimate of Annie's fitness for the job; and when the palaver was over the tugs efficiently made their preparations. And with the arrival of high tide the work commenced.

The two powerful tugs, aided by the steamer, toiled heartbreakingly through the day, but without avail. After nightfall the rising sea added to their difficulties. Heavy steel towing wires parted under the terrific strain, and the towboatmen dodged the back-springing coils, cheating death by the blink of an eyelash, then set to work in the darkness and icy spray, with numb and bleeding fingers, only to have them snap again under the tremendous tension of the panting tugs. After the tide had ebbed again the tugs stood by, diving and pitching in

341

the breaking seas that threatened time and again to wash them out.

Tug-boat Annie remained on deck until dawn, her heavy eyelids kept apart only by sheer, indomitable will-power. She was worn out, not alone with physical fatigue, but through the anxiety of realising that if they did not succeed in releasing the steamer by the next flood tide it might be too late. If the wind shifted, their utmost skill would be useless, and she must be pounded to pieces by the white-crested combers.

Slowly, like a damp, white ghost, daylight dissolved the darkness. Through all of the ensuing period of high water she and Bullwinkle, their animosity submerged in the stress of a common task, brought to bear upon their problem all the tricks and ingenious makeshifts by which, through decades of tug-boat and salvage work, Tug-boat Annie had managed to wrest success from disaster. And then, when it seemed that achievement was farthest from their grasp, the *Utgard* shifted slightly, and a tremor ran through her frame. A sea battered the stricken steamer, and the tugs held on; another sea, and the tugs, with the wires humming like dynamos under the appalling strain, made a final gigantic effort; and the *Utgard*, as though suddenly tired of the fight, moved again, forward, scraped her plates over the shelf of rock on which she had rested, slid clear of her bed, and floated serenely free into deep water, and was towed safely off-shore.

The *Narcissus*, plunging triumphantly through the seas, ran alongside the *Utgard*, from which a pilot ladder was lowered, and Tug-boat Annie, standing on her short forward deck, drenched in spray and beating snow, watched her chance. Grasping the ladder at the proper moment she mounted, heavily but with agility extraordinary in one of her bulk, to the steamer's deck.

'You did a good job, missus,' Captain Hall told her, forcing his drawn lips into a smile.

'I know it!' said Annie, with a complacent grin that turned unexpectedly into a yawn. 'Though it was kinda nip and touch, wasn't it? And yon Bullwinkle done his part noble, too — the long-eared baboon! Now what about towin' ye into port? Damaged the way ye are, it might be dangerous under your own steam.'

'N-no –' said Captain Hall, indecisively, 'I think I'll be able to manage all right.'

'It'll be kinda ticklish, gettin' through the strait in this thick weather – and ye said ye ain't familiar with these waters.'

'I'll be able to manage now, all right.' With his vessel once more afloat the shipmaster seemed to have regained something of confidence.

'Okay, then. And I'll thank ye for a receipt for the work we done.'

In his cabin Captain Hall gave her the receipt – a signed acknowledgement that she had performed the salvage and had delivered the *Utgard* to her master, free of the rocks of La Push, and ready to proceed to port. Tug-boat Annie tucked the receipt away, and Captain Hall accompanied her as far as the waist. She halted and looked out into the fog and driving snow; and when she turned back to Captain Hall her face was troubled.

'I ain't tryin' to gouge ye, Captain, but ye really should take a tow in. If them damaged bottom plates begin to go –'

The shipmaster looked dubious.

'Hmm-m. What's your price?'

'The job's worth ten thousand, to take ye clear in; but ye've had bad luck – say, $7,500.'

Captain Hall considered; then he nodded and was about to speak, when there was an interruption, and they turned to behold the snow-patterned pea jacket and impudently grinning features of Horatio Bullwinkle.

'Big-hearted Annie, at it again!' said Mr Bullwinkle hoarsely.

'What do *you* want, tramp?' demanded Annie, instantly on the defensive.

'I just climbed up to see that ye didn't get away with the Captain's gold fillings –'

'They'll be safer widout you here!'

'And I see I got here just in time. Captain, don't you pay her no $7,500 to tow you in. The job's only worth six thousand, and that's what I'll do it for.'

'You keep outa this, monkey-face!' cried Annie hotly.

343

'Wasn't ye satisfied wid chisellin' me for sixty per cent o' the salvage?' She turned to Captain Hall, with an acidly deprecating smile. 'Ye'll have to excuse him, Captain — he's only a fathom o' gas. I'll tow ye in meself for —'

'Fifty-five hundred, did you say —?' Captain Hall asked Mr Bullwinkle shrewdly.

'No, sir — five thousand was my price — *ouch*! Darn you, Annie — stompin' on my toe like that!'

'I wish it was your face!' said Annie bitterly.

'Make up your minds,' said the shipmaster nervously. 'Who gets the job?'

'Well, jest to make sure he don't tow ye ashore again,' Tug-boat Annie began, 'I'll take ye in for —'

'Forty-five hundred would satisfy me, Captain!' put in Mr Bullwinkle hastily.

'And a good hangin' would satisfy me!' stormed Annie, fatigue and exasperation betraying her at last. 'He can have the job. I'm goin' home, and ketch some sleep!'

'Oh — was you up, Annie?' cried Mr Bullwinkle artlessly. 'Well, don't let me keep you up.'

Burning with wrath, Tug-boat Annie returned to the *Narcissus*. And while Captain Hall and Mr Bullwinkle completed their deal in the waist of the *Utgard*, the *Narcissus* sheered away and was lost in the whirling snow. Captain Hall, noting the direction taken by the tug, called Bullwinkle's attention to it with a puzzled frown.

'There's no harbour at La Push for a vessel of her draught, is there?'

'No.'

'Where's she going, then? She's headed right back for the La Push rocks.'

'Search me,' replied Mr Bullwinkle, too elated at having outbid Annie to bother further about her. 'She was born crazy, I guess. Well; Captain — stand by to take our towin' line.'

In the wheel-house of the *Narcissus*, Tug-boat Annie leaned against the wall, her face white and drawn with overpowering exhaustion. Her eyes were dull; devoid of expression; and as she sipped noisily from a thick yellow mug of steaming coffee she vented an occasional ponderous sigh. Peter, who was at the wheel, eyed her in troubled silence.

'I don't understand this foolishness of wantin' to go ashore at La Push, Annie,' he said at length. 'And we'll have the devil's own time gettin' the boat through the surf. Why don't ye turn in and get some rest? I hate to see ye all wore out this way.'

'Keep quiet, Peter,' she said wearily. 'I know what I'm doin'. Here – lemme take the wheel, whiles you and Shif'less get the dinghy ready.'

Slowly and cautiously she avoided the pinnacles of surf-washed rock that showed faintly grey through the mist, and ran in towards the beach south of the village. Then, while the *Narcissus* tossed and rolled without forward way, Peter assisted her into the dinghy, in which Shiftless already was seated at the oars.

'Gosh, Annie, be careful – that surf is dangerous!' Peter warned her.

'Don't worry. Just hang around till you hear me beller. We'll not be gone long. And after that we'll giddap for home.'

It took all of Shiftless's wiry strength and the combined seamanship of both to effect a landing on the beach. Both were drenched, and the boat half full when at length they got the boat drawn up. Annie helped Shiftless to empty it and drag it up on the sand, assisted by two or three mute but curious Indian fishermen who had gathered to watch the landing. Then Annie staggered heavily up the beach, and disappeared in the direction of the village. She was gone for perhaps a half-hour; and as she came up behind the patiently waiting Shiftless, the renewed life and cheer in her voice made him jump.

'Come on, me fine bozo,' she said heartily. 'We're goin' home!'

'What was ye doing ashore, Annie?' Shiftless asked, between grunts, as he forced the dinghy's bows through the rollers towards the waiting *Narcissus*.

'If you must know – and it seems ye must –' she chuckled, 'I was telephonin' the office to preserve me a box at the opery.'

Once more the *Narcissus* struck her old nose into the seas, homeward bound. The wind had slacked off considerably, but the weather was still thick, and the hooting of two fog-enshrouded vessels ahead of her announced that the steamer

Utgard and her escort, the triumphant *Salamander*, were sloshing their way to port.

'Not that I care, ye saucy rogue,' Tug-boat Annie in her cabin muttered, her eyes, with their red and swollen lids, fixed upon the blarneying grin of her late husband. 'I've made a good sum for the company, wid the salvage, even if it is the short end of the horn. And if Bullwinkle wants to cackle over makin' a bit extra on the towin', he can do it and welcome – the scut! Hmmph! I didn't want to do it, anyway.'

Bracing herself against the wide rolling of the tug, she removed her sea-boots and prepared, with a luxurious yawn, to turn in to her bunk.

There was a rap on the door.

'Oh, drat – who is it?'

'It's me, Annie.' Peter inserted his red and dripping face.

'What's the matter – fog gettin' thicker?'

'Can't hardly see the nose on your face.'

'All right. Keep the whistle goin'. I'll be right out.'

Once again drawing on her cold, damp boots and a heavy coat, and jamming her old felt hat over her eyes, she passed with slatting laces to the heaving deck. The balance of the long day, grey and dense and with a rawness that penetrated every corner of the tug, passed slowly into night; and through the long anxious hours, while the *Narcissus* rounded the invisible headland of Flattery and crept cautiously along the strait of Juan de Fuca towards Puget Sound, Tug-boat Annie dozed on a stool in the wheel-house, and went out on deck at intervals to whip her exhausted body into a semblance of life and wakefulness under the wet lash of the night.

At mid-day Shiftless again pleaded with her to rest. Tug-boat Annie shook her head. There was still a spark in her bleary eyes.

'Funny, me gettin' all wore out like this. Mebbe Alec was right, and I'm gettin' old. But once I get the bull between me teeth I don't seem able to let go. Anyways, I'll have a sleep when the fog lifts, mebbe – Hark!' She interrupted herself sharply, and listened. 'There's a vessel ahead of us there, somewheres.'

They stood motionless, straining; no sound but the creaking of the big wheel; then again, muffled by fog, came a series of rapid, nervous toots, like a summons or an alarm. Tug-boat Annie reached for the whistle cord and blew a string of answering blasts, then pulled the engine-room jingle. The *Narcissus* lost way. And again the urgent signal came out of the fog.

'Might be a seiner out o' Port Townsend — we're about abeam o' there,' Annie commented. 'Although, what she'd be doin' out in this muck beats —'

She leaned forward and dropped the window again. And then, from the wet opaqueness ahead came a muffled megaphone shout.

'*Narcissus* — ahoy!'

Annie and Shiftless turned tense, strained faces to each other. Then Annie grasped a megaphone and scuttled on deck.

'Hello!' she bawled. 'Who is it?'

A minute passed; then the dark grey shape of a small motor tug slid out of the fog and ranged abeam.

'Why —' Annie exclaimed, 'it's the *May Dillon*, o' Port Townsend. What —'

'Hey, Annie —' shouted a dim shape on the other vessel's after-deck. 'Stand by a minute, would ye?'

'Sure! Oh — hello, Harvey! What's the trouble?'

'You've got to turn back, Annie. We've been laying out here since five this morning, waiting to try and stop you.'

'What fer?' Annie asked, with sharp trepidation.

'We got a wireless message at Port Townsend from the *Utgard* —'

'I knowed it! That ape, Bullwinkle —'

'To say she was piled up ashore again in the fog. She struck near Clallam Bay.'

'Is she ashore hard?'

'She's prob'ly a total loss.'

For a leaden second Annie's mind shrank from decision. After all, her salvage job was done — she had the master's receipt in her pocket — and she had earned her reward. She needed sleep, and then a hot, unhurried meal, and more sleep. In the pause of indecision the grooves of weariness about her mouth and eyes were etched perceptibly deeper. Then her jaws closed, and her palm came down with a smack on the *Narcissus*' rail.

'Okay – thanks, Harvey!' she called to the master of the *May Dillon*, and vanished from the wheel-house. A quick jingle rang in the *Narcissus*' bowels, the big tug came about in a swirl of foam, her broad stern squatted down to it, and with the water marbling under her counter she spun the broad, white thread of her wake through the strait along the way they had come.

The *Utgard* was piled up with a broken back. Like a huge grey stricken animal she loomed out of the fog, her bow well on the beach, where the receding tide had left her, and her stern sagging down in the deeper water until the letters of her port of registry were submerged. It needed only the brief inspection that Tug-boat Annie gave her as the *Narcissus* swept out of the fog and past her stern, to know that her case was hopeless beyond salvage. But near the pilot ladder, let down from the after-well deck, the *Salamander* floated, unharmed.

'Tug-boat man, huh?' Annie rasped for Mr Bullwinkle's benefit; but her sarcasm was wasted, for that gentleman was on the bridge of the *Utgard*, as she discovered when she had climbed the pilot ladder to the steamer's deck. As she neared the top of the bridge ladder she heard the voices of Captain Hall and Mr Bullwinkle raised in angry recrimination. They were standing outside the chart-room, glaring at each other, their faces blue with cold, and garments mottled by the freshly falling snow, and the appearance of Tug-boat Annie's untidy head and wet, brick-red features, gave fresh impetus to their dispute.

'Here's Annie now!' roared Mr Bullwinkle. 'See what she has to say!'

'I know my rights, mister!' returned the shipmaster miserably, 'and I mean to have 'em.'

'Ain't you satisfied wid pullin' the man's vessel ashore, widout fightin' him over it, ye ungainly swab?' Tug-boat Annie demanded of her rival. 'Ye've sure extinguished yerself this time!'

'Aw, shut your big mouth – it wasn't my fault! I didn't even have a line on board when we struck. He cast it off against my advice when we entered the strait!'

'After you stopped and tried to hold me up for $2,500 more than our agreement!' the shipmaster countered. 'If you're a sample of Puget Sound tug-boat men —'

'He ain't!' Annie snapped. 'He's a sample o' them there gabardine swine what ye hear tell about. What happened then, Captain?'

'I'll tell you what happened!' blustered Mr Bullwinkle. 'He refused the terms I had a right to ask, since the fog was increased risk, and tried to come through the strait himself. He didn't figger on the closeness of the beach and the abnormal set of the tidal current, and it set him ashore. And here he is.'

'That doesn't alter the fact,' said Captain Hall wearily, 'that this stranding and the one at La Push is all one consecutive salvage operation, which would not be complete until you delivered me into port, as agreed. And since the salvage was not successful, you get no salvage pay.'

'You cast my line adrift —'

'And you put another on board me, to try to drag us off here after we struck, thereby resuming your job. It's all one sequence, I tell you.'

'Wait a minute, Captain,' Tug-boat Annie growled. 'It wasn't Bullwinkle here — it was my company — what the underwriters employed to salvage your ship. He made that towin' arrangement on his own hook. But when we dragged your vessel off the La Push rocks that constituted a complete and successful salvage. What's more' — she fumbled in her pocket — 'I got your receipt to prove it!' — and she produced the receipt.

'You see?' shouted Mr Bullwinkle exultantly. 'By golly, Annie, ye ain't so stupid as you look.'

Captain Hall shook his head with the febrile stubbornness of the weak man unjustly assailed.

'That receipt doesn't mean a thing. It hasn't meant a thing since he put a line on board my ship at La Push to tow me in. And I'll prove it with one question.'

'What's the question?' asked Annie uneasily.

'Wasn't this man your assistant — your employee — in the salvage operations?'

Tug-boat Annie recognised the fatal significance of the question; but being by nature truthful, she did not avoid it.

'Yes,' she answered simply.

'There you are, then. As the principal, you are legally responsible for the acts of your employee; and since he continued the salvage after you left, and failed to complete it, your company cannot legally claim the salvage fee.'

'Oh — so that's how it stands, is it?' said Tug-boat Annie quietly.

There was a short silence. Captain Hall's thin face was chalk-white with strain, and worry had painted dark circles around his deep-set eyes; but his rather weak mouth was set in a stubborn line. Bullwinkle, square-set, husky and formidable, his face red with passion, watched him warily.

The silence was broken by Captain Hall. He held out his hand to Tug-boat Annie.

'I'll ask you to give me back that receipt,' he said.

'Don't you give it to him, Annie old pal,' said Mr Bullwinkle quickly.

Tug-boat Annie turned on him savagely.

'You keep out o' this, ye hairy alligator! You've did damage enough!' She turned to the shipmaster, and asked quietly: 'Suppose I don't give it to ye? What's it to you? Your job's gone, anyway.'

Captain Hall's thin shoulders braced, in a vain attempt at jauntiness. But a lump worked visibly in his throat.

'You're right, of course,' he said huskily. 'It is nothing to me personally, for I'll lose my berth, and probably my certificate through this. But — well, it's still my duty to protect the underwriters. The ship's a total loss, now, and they'll have to pay my owners for full value of vessel and cargo, which runs well over a million dollars. So it's hardly fair to expect them to pay your company an additional $110,000 for an unsuccessful salvage, is it?'

It was a brave effort, and Tug-boat Annie admired his stand. She noted the upflung head, and the discouraged eyes that longed to plead, yet would not. Her own eyes misted with quick compassion.

'No,' she said deeply, 'that'd hardly be fair. Mind, I'm not sayin' that if Bullwinkle hadn't acted like a dirty dog, I wouldn't hang on to this receipt. But – well, us Puget Sound tow-boat men don't do business that way. So –'

She proferred the receipt; but before the grateful shipmaster could take it, Mr Bullwinkle forcibly intervened.

'Have you gone crazy, Annie?' he bellowed. 'Throwin' away $110,000 like that? What about my rights?'

'If you had your rights,' she told him, 'ye'd be buryin' beef bones in somebody's back yard!'

'Annie, listen,' he pleaded. 'You keep that receipt, and I'll go fifty–fifty on the salvage with ye, instead of sixty–forty. No,' as he saw her jaw tighten, 'I'll take the forty, and you keep the sixty!'

'Beginning' to crawl now, are ye? Here, Captain –'

'Here, you!' shouted Mr Bullwinkle, 'I'll not let ye give it to him.'

'Well, in that case –' began Annie. She stepped back a pace or two, deliberately tore the paper into tiny flakes, and with an elaborate flip of her hand threw them in the air. The cold and vagrant breeze caught them, and they fluttered away, lost in the whirling snow.

Mr Bullwinkle's subsequent exhibition of temper deserved a larger audience than the handful of pinch-nosed seamen who had gathered on the forward deck to listen, for it was classic. But Tug-boat Annie and Captain Hall ignored him.

'The underwriters won't forget this – you'll get a lot of their business,' Captain Hall said.

'That's what I figger,' said Tug-boat Annie practically.

'It – it was mighty square of you.'

' 'Twas nothin',' said Annie, grinning wanly.

'Nothin' to who?' demanded Mr Bullwinkle fiercely. 'What about me?'

'Well,' demanded Annie, 'what about you?'

'What right had you to tear up that receipt?'

'If you'll muzzle ye ugly bazoo, I'll tell ye –'

'You'll tell me nothing! ye thick-witted clown –'

Annie tried with strange perseverance and stranger patience to impose her voice over his clamorous outbursts. She said:

'Ye'd do yerself a favour by listenin' to what I have to tell ye.'

'I will not listen! Ye throwed away my salvage fee for a stupid that didn't know enough to keep his ship from runnin'' across fields. Big-hearted Annie!' His scorn was epochal. 'Cheats her owners and doublecrosses me, to make a big shot of herself. What a laugh the Secoma waterfront will have over this!'

Annie watched him, a deep, purposeful glint in her eyes, and determination in the grim set of her mastiff face.

'Are ye through bellyachin' fer a minute?' she asked quietly. 'All right, then. Ye talked about the laugh the waterfront'll have. Well, here's a real hee-haw fer 'em. I'm goin' to give you me note for $5,000 for the salvage ye didn't get.'

'Wha-at?' barked Mr Bullwinkle incredulously. 'You'll pay me $5,000 regardless?'

'I will — or at least me company will. Alec Severn will make good on any agreement I sign. You know that.'

Mr Bullwinkle was wary.

'You kidding me?' he grunted suspiciously.

'I ain't kiddin',' she said soberly. 'O' course, if ye don't want it —'

'I'll take it!' he said hastily.

Tug-boat Annie turned to Captain Hall. 'Kin I use some ink and a scrapple o' paper?'

In his cabin Annie seated herself at a table, a pen grasped in her massive fist. Laboriously she wrote, then waved the paper dry and faced Horatio Bullwinkle.

'There ye are, ye bandy-legged shark,' she said. 'Present that to Alec Severn and he'll exchange it for a cheque for five thousand dollars. Wait a minute — I forgot,' she added, as Bullwinkle reached out his hand. 'First, ye can gimme back that salvage agreement what ye screwed out of me the other night.'

Bullwinkle hesitated.

'Okay,' Annie told him indifferently. 'If ye think it's any good to ye, keep it, and I'll keep this five thousand.'

He handed it over without further hesitation, and received in exchange the paper she had written out, binding the Deep-Sea Towing and Salvage Company of Secoma to pay to H. Bullwinkle $5,000 in lieu of salvage for the time and labour he had expended on the SS *Utgard*.

'And now,' said Tug-boat Annie, 'I'll thank ye to take yer ugly physog out o' me sight, for it's makin' me ill.'

'Annie, this is kinda —'

'Get out!' she roared; and he went.

'Now, Captain Hall, can I take you and your crew into Port Townsend? There's nothin' more I can do for ye here.'

The shipmaster shook his head.

'I've had a radio message that the owners are sending a vessel for us from Anacortes.' He hesitated. 'You seem pretty cheerful — you've made me feel better, too; and I'd like to thank you. But you haven't much to smile about over this business.'

'Shucks!' said Annie, with an embarrassed grin. 'I'll always get along. And spilled milk is soonest mended.' She put a clumsy hand on his arm. 'Don't go to frettin' now. I'll be on hand to put in a word for ye when the steamboat inspectors has ye up.'

She descended the ladder to her tug. As her tug left the *Utgard*'s side and set a course for home, the *Salamander* also gathered way and ran parallel, a few yards distant. Mr Bullwinkle thrust his uncouth head out of the pilot-house window.

'Hey — Annie!' he hailed.

Annie opened the door and stepped on deck. 'What — ain't you dead yet?' she began, but Mr Bullwinkle interrupted.

'Annie, you was an awful sap to give me that five thousand.'

'I know it!' said Annie tartly. 'But if ye'd had manners enough to keep yer trap shut a while back, ye'd have got $44,000 instead o' five — less the premium, o' course.'

'What do you mean?' he asked uneasily.

'I tried to tell ye, back on the *Utgard*,' replied Tug-boat Annie complacently, 'but, oh, no! — you wouldn't listen. I was goin' to give ye a full forty per cent share o' the *Utgard*'s salvage fee, but — well, it's too late now.'

'Sa-ay — what are you getting at?' demanded Mr Bullwinkle, now thoroughly alarmed.

'It's so simple that even you might understand it,' said Annie patiently. 'When you went off in charge o' the *Utgard* I rowed ashore at La Push, and telephoned Alec Severn to insure our salvage fee for the full amount. Then, no matter what happened to the *Utgard*, we'd still be sure o' that $110,000. So I could well afford to give you $5,000, instead of the sixty per cent ye'd have got if ye'd hung on to that agreement, or the forty per cent I'd have gave ye if ye'd let me talk to ye. What's that?'

Mr Bullwinkle's reply was interesting but unprintable.

'Oh, my!' Annie cried, covering her ears in pretended horror. 'Ain't ye ashamed to use language the like o' that? By the way, the Secoma waterfront'll still have its laugh — on'y the laugh'll be on the other foot, now!'

She shut the door, and with a tired but happy sigh stretched herself on the wheel-house settee, and looked at Shiftless with one drowsy eye.

' 'Ome, James!' she said.

Nicholas Monsarrat

NIGHT SHOOT

Nicholas Monsarrat's book, The Cruel Sea, *published in* 1951, *is probably the most famous sea novel of recent times, certainly of World War II. Widely praised by the critics as the classic it has since become, it was hugely successful with the public and was also made into a great film. In some people's minds, the achievements of that book have tended to obscure Monsarrat's other superb maritime works such as* HMS Marlborough Will Enter Harbour *(1952),* The Ship that Died of Shame *(1959) and* The Master Mariner, *the first of a proposed trilogy of books that the author hoped would be his greatest triumph, but which death prevented him completing.*

Nicholas Monsarrat (1910–79), who was born in Liverpool, the son of a surgeon and destined to become a solicitor, instead abandoned this career and proved himself one of the greatest novelists of the sea. He did, in fact, serve in the Navy during World War II, eventually commanding three escort vessels, a corvette and two frigates, attaining the rank of lieutenant-commander, and was also mentioned in dispatches for his achievements. A book about some of these experiences, HM Corvette, *published in* 1943, *launched his reputation and was particularly praised by the* New Republic, *which wrote: 'The experience of patrolling, convoying merchantmen and chasing subs has been related many times during the war, but never with the excellence of* HM Corvette.' *Monsarrat demonstrates precisely the same ability to conjure up the drama and tension of the work of a corvette on operations in the following extract from* East Coast Corvette *published in the same year. It, too, is based on personal experience.*

From far ahead of us, the leading destroyer made the signal:

'E-boats now seem to be moving towards the stern of the convoy.'

That was our corner, and about time too. Starting with a dusk torpedo-attack on the leading ships, it had been an eventful night, in which everyone seemed to have been involved but us; and we hadn't suffered the waiting gladly. Guns had flashed, star-shells burst all round the sky, tracer-bullets advertised a crowded meeting; but it had all been outside our range and we had no excuse for interfering, our job that night being to cover the rear of the convoy. Now, with a bright chance of action, the ship woke up and clocked into place as one of the party.

The change from Defence Stations to First-degree Action Stations meant that I had to leave the bridge and go aft, to take over fire-control of the smaller guns. I always find this change-over annoying: up on the bridge they know everything and see it all happening, aft on the quarter-deck news filters through in driblets or not at all, rumours fly around, guesswork reigns. Each time, before leaving the bridge, I ask them to be sure to tell me what's going on: each time they promise that they will: each time the heat of battle puts a Ministry of Information blight on the news. The ship might be ramming the *Tirpitz*, for all one can tell aft: nothing gets through. To-night was no exception, save that we had our own share of action handed to us on a plate, and weren't right out of the fun; and thus some of this account depends on the post-mortem afterwards, when the bridge-personnel, relaxing, found time to fill in some of the blanks and bring my record up to date.

It was a fine night, almost flat calm, with a glowing three-quarter moon making our camouflage nearly perfect and giving us just the visibility we wanted. But while we were waiting, a signal came through: 'Believed to be four or five E-boats operating.' Shortly after this there was some brisk gun-fire to starboard, and then another signal: 'Two E-boats engaged and damaged.' Said the Captain morosely: 'There'll be none of them left by the time they get to us' — a depressing thought which for some reason they took pains to pass aft to me . . . The whole night now seemed to be in suspense: the ship moved forward very slowly, the look-outs stared out over the water, their binoculars moving in careful regulated arcs; up near the head of the convoy another star-shell, behind a cloud, gleamed like the sunset. We could still do nothing but wait for our chance.

Then, when we were beginning to doubt whether our luck was changing after all, we heard some shouting, coming faintly down-wind towards us.

Now this was not unexpected, since a ship had been sunk a little earlier and the picking up of survivors might have been left to us. The only odd thing was the location of the sound – a good way off the track of the convoy, and in the opposite direction from where boats or men swimming would normally have drifted. That needed explaining, and the explanation (or half of it) came up pretty soon: for about a minute after the shooting was heard, an E-boat was sighted crossing the track of the moon about two miles away. And that was where the noise had been coming from.

'That's odd,' said the Captain. 'In fact, more than odd: almost sinister. We'll stalk that monkey and see what he's up to.'

By now the E-boat, having crossed the moon-track, was invisible again, but we had a rough idea of his course and we laid ours so as to converge at an acute angle. Fore and aft, we were ready to blaze away with all we'd got; and presently we saw him again, about a mile away. This time he seemed to be stopped, waiting. We weren't going to disappoint him, either.

We turned towards him, and the distance shortened. But now, as usual, the after-part dropped back into its Cinderella rôle: our alteration of course meant that we could no longer see him from aft, and there ensued a maddening few minutes when we had no idea what was happening and had nothing to look at except a blank sea. Once again, we might have been ramming a pocket-battleship . . . Then the bridge, relenting, came through with the news we wanted:

'First Lieutenant from Captain: He's about half a mile off, dead ahead, and still stopped. In another minute I will turn to starboard so that your guns will bear. Open fire when I do.'

Nothing could be fairer than that. I crossed the quarter-deck and stood close by the gun aft, my hand touching the open-fire and check-fire gongs: at my side the gun's crew, steel-helmeted, were crouching behind their gun-shield, their fingers crooked round the laying- and training-wheels, their eyes peering out on the bearing where we *knew* the E-boat would appear. In the charged silence their breathing sounded forced and unnaturally loud: the moment had a freezing tension about it, and I felt my skin prickling as we waited, within a few seconds of action.

When the ship was about a hundred yards off, the shouting started again, and this time we could distinguish the words quite easily. They were not what we were expecting, and they were not pleasant: hoping for easy meat in the form of a rescue-ship off its guard, that E-boat's crew were calling out: 'Help! Help. We're English!'

By my side, the gun-layer drew in his breath.

'Bastards!' he said softly. 'Sinking one ship, and then using that to trap another . . . We'll give you some help, all right.'

We began our promised turn to starboard — I felt the after-part of the ship tremble as the wheel was put hard over: she heeled slightly, and the stern swung round; and then the E-boat came into view — fifty yards away, its engines stopped, half a dozen figures roughly silhouetted on the upper deck, and someone on board shouting in a cracked voice: 'Rescue! English sailors!'

That last treacherous effort marked zero hour for both sides, and immediately afterwards three things happened very quickly. The gun forrard let fly with a tremendous crack, scoring a hit directly amidships on the water-line: all the guns aft loosed off, pouring stream after stream of tracer bullets right into the target; and a look-out on the blind side suddenly yelled out above the din:

'Another E-boat to starboard!'

I whipped round. A hundred yards away on our beam was a second E-boat, bows on to us, in a perfect position to run a torpedo. For continuing to cover his proper arc instead of being drawn to the excitement of the main action, that look-out deserved a medal.

They must have seen the newcomer from the bridge at the same moment, for immediately the telegraph clanged and the ship seemed to gather herself up and leap forward as we went to Full Ahead. We passed the E-boat we had hit, still motionless and silent: there was no answering fire, no one trying out their English, and she seemed to be settling by the stern. Then a grey-white cloud of artificial smoke, made by the second E-boat, drifted down-wind between us, and she was quickly lost to view.

There ensued a crowded and confused three minutes, of the sort easier to indicate by asterisks than to describe in detail. There were at least two other E-boats in the vicinity, and they began to make high-speed smoke-rings round us, with considerable skill: our guns kept blazing away, the arcs of tracer fanning out at odd glimpses here and there or at the sound of engines: and throughout it all, everyone on board was coughing, spluttering at the effects of the chemical smoke. Then we came under fire ourselves: a spatter of machine-gun bullets hit the upper works, and the repair parties aft ducked for cover as the noise rang out and the chips of metal began to fly. We could see the tracer coming towards us, and we fired back on the same bearing: the targets were hidden in the smoke, but certainly they were there, playing a grown-up brand of tip-and-run, with us as the ball.

It was at this point that a tracer-bullet went between my legs. I saw it coming towards me, getting bigger and bigger: I should like to say that I then turned round and watched it going away again, getting smaller and smaller. But to claim that amount of detachment wouldn't be true: I did not follow its course beyond the point where, with a business-like hum, it disappeared between my knees – a piece of calculated terrorism which discouraged further observation, as far as I was concerned.

Then suddenly we were alone, in the middle of drifting smoke, with no sound anywhere near us: the players had dispersed, without settling the score. We began a circular sweep, looking for the first E-boat, and meantime clearing up ready for the next round, if there should be one. Aft, the guns' crews were bringing up more ammunition and counting empties; and when this had been seen to and we were ready to open up again, I looked round for signs of damage. There was very little, in spite of the noise and the activity of the past quarter of an hour. One of the bullets had gone down a ventilator cowling and (it was said) chased one of the stokers all round the engine-room; but the only actual casualty was a steward who, having no business to be on the upper deck at all, had stuck his head out to see the fun and had been nicked on the forehead just above one eye. He was all right, though indignant in a general way.

We never found that E-boat, nor any trace of it: judging by the way she had been hit, we didn't really expect to. But she was officially credited to us, by a scrupulous Admiralty: which was the next best thing to collecting the bits ourselves. And as you know, the credit was duly endorsed on the after-gun-layer's shield, for all to see and for him to tell the tale about.

We gave a party to celebrate the kill, and at one end of the wardroom we hung a Nazi ensign, borrowed from the Signal Department. By way of adding point to the occasion, we then shot an imperial line to the assembled company, to the effect that the flag had been taken from the E-boat just before it went down.

How exactly did we get it? We passed so close to the sinking E-boat, we said, that a seaman standing in the stern of the ship had been able to reach out and tear it off. But why wasn't the flag itself torn? The halyard must have given way: the seaman was very strong. How did we happen to have a man standing ready? Well (here the Captain, in danger of flagging, nudged me), in our First-degree Action Stations there was always a man told off for this duty. He was armed with a boat-hook and grappling iron. He got three pence a day trophy-money.

And so on: Finally:

'Germany must be getting extremely short of raw materials,' said the most distinguished visitor present, fingering the exhibit. 'This stuff is of very poor quality – it can't compare with our own.'

After that it was too late to tell the truth.

C. S. Forester

DAWN ATTACK

Like Nicholas Monsarrat, C. S. Forester is best known for a single creation – in his case, the redoubtable Hornblower – yet he actually wrote very widely on maritime subjects. To be honest, I was tempted initially to include one of the Hornblower stories here, but as they are so well known to so many readers – and easily available – I decided on something a little less familiar that would also demonstrate Forester's very real skill when writing about modern naval warfare.

Cecil Scott Forester (1899–1966) was actually born in Egypt and travelled a great deal in Europe with his parents before coming to London for his education. Although he studied medicine for a time, he gave this up for writing and also began to follow a wanderlust that never quite left him. In 1926 he bought a fifteen-foot dinghy, the Annie Marble, and, accompanied by his wife Katherine, proceeded to sail through the rivers of France and Germany. Two years later he published an account of this journey and also began to absorb himself in naval history for a series of books he was planning about a man called Captain Hornblower. The first of these books, The Happy Return, appeared in 1937, and was greeted with great enthusiasm by readers and critics alike. 'This work', one of the latter wrote, 'combines the prowess of a Marryat with the psychological complexity of a Conrad sea captain.' A string of Hornblower adventures followed, as well as a stirringly evocative novel, The Good Shepherd (1955), which told the story of forty-eight desperate hours in the life of a North Atlantic convoy during World War II. The story that follows,

'Dawn Attack', is an equally effective and suspenseful yarn about the same period.

Captain George Crowe sat at the head of a crowded table in a cabin which it would be an understatement merely to call crowded. For the first time since his appointment as Captain D. commanding the Twentieth Destroyer Flotilla he had the opportunity of a personal conference with the greater part of his destroyer captains.

Safely back in Alexandria from the fighting round Crete, he could look round at the grouped figures. There were one or two grey heads, of men older than himself, whom he had passed in the race for promotion, but mostly they were young, eager faces.

In Crowe's hands was a chart, and copies of it were being studied by his subordinates – a chart that contained all the details of the harbour defences of the Italian port of Crotona.

There was nothing romantic about the history of that chart; no beautiful woman spy had inveigled it out of the possession of an Italian officer, but it was the produce of some weeks of patient work. Every reconnaisance plane which had flown over Crotona had taken photographs of the place and the approaches to it, and, naturally, in a high proportion of the photographs there had appeared pictures of vessels entering or leaving.

Correlating these pictures, the naval staff had been able to map out the areas in which ships appeared and the areas in which ships never appeared, and thus had been able to make out a pretty clear picture of the extent of the minefields guarding the port; moreover, by joining on the map the successive positions of the ships photographed entering and leaving, the fairway between the minefields could be accurately plotted.

The photographs of the town itself revealed the places of importance sufficient to merit the attention of the Twentieth Flotilla in the operation which Crowe had in mind. The British

Navy was hitting back; the Battle Fleet was going into the bombardment of Genoa while the Twentieth Flotilla was to take advantage of the protection it afforded to raid Crotona and clean up that pestilential nest of shallow-draft raiders.

Nickleby, the flotilla gunnery officer and the model of all staff virtues, was explaining the various targets to the destroyer captains.

'I've marked the positions each ship is to assume,' he said; 'also the various aiming points. The MAS depot is at the base of the white cliff at the east end of the town. *Potawatomi*'ll clean that up. *Shoshone*'ll have the wireless masts in clear view, so she'll be able to deal with those.

'Now, the oil tanks are below a crest — you can see them marked in square G Nine. *Cheyenne* and *Navaho*, in the stations assigned to them, will be able to hit them. Nine degrees to starboard of the line connecting the church steeple and the factory chimney — that's one of their bearings — and range four two double-o will do the business nicely. *Seminole —*'

Nickleby droned on endlessly, outlining the perfect paper scheme in the stuffy heat of the cabin, while Crowe moved restlessly in his chair and studied the earnest, serious faces. He felt suddenly incredibly wise and, by deduction from that, incredibly old. Nickleby seemed to him much like some young man describing to his grandfather the Utopian world that ought to be established. Something ideally enchanting, but which made no allowance for the inconsistencies of human nature or for unexpected contingencies.

Operations of war never did go the way they were planned. Not even at Zeebrugge, one of the best-planned operations in history, had the attack been able to proceed mechanically. When Nickleby brought his beautiful paper scheme to him for his approval, he had permitted himself to smile, and the smile had nettled Nickleby. But he had let him go on with it; it was just as well for his officers to familiarise themselves with the problems and the objectives of this particular operation, and this was as good a way as any other, as long as their minds remained flexible enough to deal with the inevitable emergencies when they arose.

Nickleby had finished his explanations now and everyone was looking to Crowe for further remarks.

He fumbled for his pipe to give himself time to arrange in his mind what he was going to say, and he grinned benevolently at these young men as he filled it and lit it, and he punctuated his opening words with puffs of smoke, paying close attention to pressing down the burning tobacco. It was queer being forty-two; when he was by himself he felt just the same as he did when he was twenty, but put him with all these young people who treated him as if he were sixty and for the life of him he could not prevent himself from acting like it.

'Nothing' – puff – 'is sure' – puff – 'in a sea fight beyond all others, but' – puff – 'if he places his ship alongside that of an enemy' – puff. 'Who wrote that, Rowles?'

'Nelson, sir,' said Rowles promptly, and Crowe found himself feeling like a schoolmaster now, instead of a father.

'It says exactly what I want to say,' said Crowe, 'and better than I can say it for myself. Everyone quite clear on what he has to do? Very good, then, gentlemen, I think that will do.'

There was no need for any claptrap appeal to sentiment, fine phrases or historic utterances. Not with those men.

The summer Mediterranean produced a summer storm that night while the Twentieth Flotilla was making its way towards Crotona, and, as is the way with the summer Mediterranean, it took only a short blow to raise a nasty lumpy sea.

Crowe, eating his dinner with his staff, noticed the increased motion immediately. The fiddles were already on the tables to prevent the crockery from sliding clean off, and the tablecloth had already been damped to provide enough friction to keep the things more or less in their places, but these precautions were already insufficient.

Holby hurriedly excused himself and left the cabin – the poor fellow was always as sick as a dog in any kind of sea. Crowe cocked an inquiring eyebrow at Rowles.

'Glass is dropping fast, sir,' said Rowles; 'this is going to be a lot worse before it gets better.'

'It might have let us finish our dinner in peace,' grumbled Crowe, and regretted the speech a moment later. He realised that there was at least one profound difference between himself at forty-two and himself at twenty; dinner was much more important nowadays, and he had lost the light-hearted acceptance of the picnic meals served perforce in a destroyer in a heavy sea.

An eighteen-hundred-ton destroyer making thirty knots in rough water behaves in a way to be expected of a ship of her design. The higher a gun is mounted above the water's edge, the more efficiently can it be served, so that a destroyer's guns are mounted just as high as is consistent with stability; and on her deck are mounted four ponderous torpedo tubes; and the fire-control system also demands the loftiest position possible. So that a destroyer is liable to roll just as far as is consistent with the limits of safety.

The *Apache* churned her way doggedly through the short steep Mediterranean waves. The seas breaking over the decks made them practically impassable; first she rolled, and then she corkscrewed, and then she pitched, as the wind steadily backed round. The waves hitting her square in the bows sent continual shudders through her, as though some harsh invisible brake had just been applied, liable to tear the unwary from any careless handhold.

The miracle was that the flotilla was able to keep together at all. Crowe blessed the fact that he had learned to sleep in a hammock; he had one slung for him and slept stolidly in it, flung about as madly as though in a swing; lying in a berth under those conditions was as tiring as not going to bed at all.

During the day the wind died down, although the sky still remained a sombre grey, but the storm, in its passage down the Mediterranean ahead of them, still flogged the sea into wicked waves, each one of which sent its corresponding shudder through the frail fabric of the *Apache*.

They did more than that. The modern art of navigation, with its precise instruments and accurate measurements, is still not quite efficient in the face of Nature at its wildest. Subtle calculations could tell Rowles just how far every turn of the screw had thrust the *Apache* through the water, and accurate meters could tell him just how many turns the screws had made. But they could not tell him – nor could any instrument on earth – just how many inches each one of those waves had held her back.

The marvellous gyrocompass could tell Rowles just what course the *Apache* was steering, but it could not tell him how far she was drifting off to leeward with the force of the wind sideways upon her upper works.

Directional wireless could help him to fix his position, but in wartime, with the flotilla maintaining the strictest wireless silence, it was not so easy, especially as the farther the *Apache* proceeded on her course, the more acute became the angle she made with the British stations on land and the greater the possibility of error.

Rowles was a brilliant navigator – in no other way could he have become flotilla navigating officer – but the most brilliant navigator in the world, with a lifetime of experience behind him, could not, in wartime, conduct a flotilla through a prolonged storm and at the end of it be sure within ten miles of where he was. In time of war, with a surprise at dawn in contemplation, ten miles might mean the difference between success and failure and between life and death.

They all knew that, when they clustered on the bridge together an hour before dawn. Holby was still pale with his seasickness, but Rowles was pale with nervous tension.

He was attempting to check back in his mind the elaborate calculations he had employed – a quite impossible feat. Nickleby was nervous, too, thinking of the elaborate allocation of targets which he had made, and wondering if, supposing he found at this moment that he had made some error, there would be a chance of rectifying it.

Crowe looked at their tense faces; it was an object lesson to him in human nature that these gallant young men, about to plunge into an enterprise of the utmost physical danger, were so much worried at the thought of making fools of themselves that the thought of sudden death did not occur to them at all.

It made him smile momentarily, but he checked himself sternly. At too many gloomy wardroom breakfasts could he remember the hostility aroused by the smiling optimist who comes in beaming.

The light was steadily increasing, and the sea had been moderating all through the night. It was no longer necessary to hold on with both hands to preserve one's foothold on the bridge; there was a hand to spare to hold the glasses to one's eyes in a desperate attempt to catch the earliest possible sight of the still invisible land ahead.

Sub-Lieutenant Lord Edward Mortimer, RNR, was nervous as well. He knew this bit of coast intimately, and he was standing by, ready for his local knowledge to be called into service.

He knew it in peacetime; he had anchored his yacht often in Crotona itself, and many had been the brief cruises he had made from there; he had a store of memories of sun-baked beaches and sunburned bodies stretched on golden sands, of beautiful women in lovely clothes, of exquisite ruins on the grey-green hilltops overlooking the blue sea.

'Is that land?' demanded Holby sharply. Perhaps seasickness had, as it often does, sharpened his senses.

They all peered through the greyness; little by little what Holby had first seen took form and solidity.

'That's not Crotona,' said Rowles, and there was heartbreak in his voice.

'Do you recognise it, Mortimer?' demanded Crowe.

'It's not Crotona,' agreed Lord Edward; 'it's —' Lord Edward ranged back through his memories. It was that Viennese girl — he couldn't remember her name now — away back in those impossibly peaceful years. They had gone picnicking with a couple of mules. A cold chicken and a bottle of wine, and some of that sheep's-milk cheese. He could remember the smell of the *macchia* in the sunshine.

'We're seven miles north,' said Lord Edward; 'eight, perhaps.'

It had been pleasant riding back on that shambling old mule over those eight miles.

'You're sure of that?' said Crowe.

'Yes,' said Lord Edward. He was sure, although he could not remember the girl's name.

Crowe's staff looked at one another and at Crowe.

'They'll have sighted us already,' said Holby.

'No chance of surprise,' supplemented Rowles, turning the iron in his own wound.

Crowe said nothing, for his mind was too active for speech.

'We can adopt the other plan,' said Nickleby; 'the one we

first thought of and discarded. Stay outside the minefield and fire across the neck of the peninsula.'

'Probably that's the best thing we can do,' agreed Rowles.

'Mortimer's right,' interrupted Holby; 'there's the Greek amphitheatre on that hillside.'

Lord Edward remembered that amphitheatre; he had last seen it by moonlight, and he had not been alone.

'Signal "follow me"', said Crowe to the chief yeoman of signals, and then to Hammett, 'Four points to port, please.'

The Twentieth Flotilla wheeled southward like a flight of gulls.

'We've still got a chance of doing damage,' said Nickleby; 'we can signal the other captains to lay on the targets already assigned to them from the new positions. They'll have the sense to know what we're after, and firing over the peninsula might be fairly effective.'

The staff was ready to extemporise, and to make the best of a bad job, and not to admit failure.

'If we strike at once we can still take advantage of surprise,' said Holby. Running in his mind was a whole series of quotations from Napoleon's sayings which had been drummed into him when he underwent his staff training: 'Strike hard and strike quickly.' 'The moral is to the physical as three to one.' 'Victory will go to the side which suddenly produces an imposing force of guns.'

'We're going in through the minefield,' said Crowe, like a bolt from the clear sky. 'Take us in, Rowles.'

His staff stared at him. It had not crossed their minds for a moment that, having given the enemy twenty minutes' warning of their approach, Crowe would still continue to act upon the original daring plan. With a tremendous effort Rowles exchanged his astonished expression for one of a proper imperturbability.

'Aye, aye, sir,' he said, and turned to give the orders to the quartermaster.

The flotilla moved down the sleeping shore and wheeled again at the entrance to the channel.

The rhythm of the throbbing engines beneath their feet changed as Rowles rang down for reduced speed to enable the *Apache* to take the tricky turns.

His nerves were steady enough; Crowe was glad to note that, despite the need for haste, Rowles refused to be rattled into a rash handling of the ship. The flotilla followed behind like beads on a string, winding its way along the channel with invisible death on either hand.

'Make the signal for "Commence firing",' said Crowe, and he glanced at Nickleby, who nodded back in return.

Nickleby would give the word for the signal to come down; most of the signals of the British Navy, including this one, become operative at the moment when they are hauled down. Everyone on the bridge stood tense, waiting for the shore to break out into a thunder of gunfire. Still no shot was fired; the town of Crotona grew steadily more and more distinct as they neared it, the individual houses standing out like cubes of sugar scattered over the hillside.

They could see the cathedral now, and the steeple of Saint Eufemia, the wireless masts and the gasworks – all the aiming points which were to direct the flotilla's guns – and still there was no sign of activity on the shore.

Safely through the channel, the second division of the flotilla diverged from the wake of the leading one and deployed for action. The long 4.7s were training round, and as the signal came down they burst into a fury of fire. The nine destroyers carried seventy-two 4.7s, and each one fired a fifty-pound shell every four seconds.

Crowe stood on the bridge with the earsplitting din echoing round him and grimly surveyed the ruin he was causing. He saw first one wireless mast and then the other totter and fall. There was a solid satisfaction in seeing the shells bursting in the clustered mass of MAS – the motor torpedo boats on which the Italians had always prided themselves.

The factory chimney swayed over to one side and disappeared in a solid block, like a felled tree, and then over the ridge came the satisfactory sign of volumes of thick black smoke; the mixture of high explosives and incendiaries which *Cheyenne* and *Navaho* had been firing had done the business.

A naval bombardment was a much more satisfactory affair than anything that could be attempted from the air; planes might drop bigger bombs, but not with one-tenth of the accuracy of a naval gun, and with none of the chance of correcting the aim which a gun permitted.

The *Apache*'s guns ceased fire for a moment and trained round on a fresh target, and then the cargo ships against the quay began to fly into pieces under the tremendous blows dealt them.

But it was in that interval of silence that Crowe heard the rumble of shells passing overhead. The shore batteries had opened fire at last, but they had never been intended for use against ships within the minefield. The startled Italian gunners either could not or would not depress their guns far enough to hit.

'Make the signal for "Second division discontinue the action",' said Crowe. When he heard the harshness of his own voice – the involuntary harshness – he realised the tenseness to which he had been screwed up, and he wondered vaguely for a moment what his blood pressure was.

But this was no time for mental digressions. The second division was heading back through the minefield, and the first division was following them, with the *Apache* covering the rear.

It was more nervous work going out round the turns of the channel even than coming in, for now they were under the fire of the shore batteries. The silence, now that the *Apache*'s guns had ceased firing, was almost oppressive, but Crowe looked with pride round the ship and saw the anti-aircraft guns' crews motionless at their posts, the lookouts sweeping the skies with their glasses, and Rowles' quiet voice giving orders to the quartermaster.

The shells rumbled overhead, and enormous jets of water were springing up from the sea, first on this side of the flotilla and then on that. One shell, as it pitched, called up a tremendous upheaval of water, which rocked the *Apache*, an echoing explosion, and a pillar of black smoke.

'Shell touched off a mine,' said Crowe to Nickleby. 'Interesting, that.'

Extremely interesting, for the mine must have been near the surface for the shell to have exploded it – near enough to the surface to damage a shallow-draft destroyer as well as a deep-draft battleship. Crowe had suspected that possibility.

They were through the labyrinth of mines now and the *Apache*'s pulses were beating quicker as Rowles called for full speed to take them out of danger. The bursting of a shell in their wake close astern told them how the sudden acceleration had saved them once again.

And then it happened, the shell that struck right between the aftermost pair of guns and burst there. The wounded *Apache* reeled at the rending crash of the explosion, so that Crowe retained his footing with difficulty.

He walked to the end of the bridge and looked aft, but the funnels were between him and the point where the shell struck, and there was no obvious damage to be seen; only the first-aid and emergency parties doubling aft, the hoses being unrolled and the trail of heavy black smoke which the *Apache* was now leaving behind her. But the beat of the screws had not changed, so that the ship's motive power was uninjured.

He felt the *Apache* heel as Hammett began zigzagging to throw off the aim of the Italian gun layers. A whole cluster of jets of water sprang up from the point they had just left – some of the spray even splashed round him on the bridge – and the *Apache* heeled again under full helm on a fresh zigzag.

It was nervous work waiting for the next salvo, and the next, and the next, while the reports were coming to the bridge of the damage – the aftermost guns completely out of action, the ammunition hoist wrecked, along with the after fire-control station.

It was the price of victory, and a cheap enough price at that. It was not merely the damage done to the Italians – the blazing oil whose thick smoke was making a wide smudge over the now-distant shore, or the shattered MAS, or the wrecked wireless station. The success of the raid meant that in hundreds of little places up and down their coast the Italians would have to redouble their precautions, mount guns and sow minefields, station troops and maintain a constant guard, everything draining fresh strength from an already exhausted country.

'Thank you, gentlemen,' said Crowe, as his staff turned to him when the last salvo had fallen far astern.

They were a good lot of fellows, who knew their jobs thoroughly well. A little academic, perhaps, but that was a fault on the right side. Perhaps in the end they would master the finer points of their profession and acquire the art of putting themselves in the enemy's position and thinking like him.

At that appalling moment when they had found themselves some ten miles from where they expected to be, they had only thought about the enemy academically.

They had not realised that surprise was likely to last for many minutes after the initial shock; that the lofty shore which they perceived had been something they were expecting, whereas a sleepy Italian lookout on land had no expectation at all, when he rubbed his eyes and peered through the dawn, of seeing a British flotilla on the horizon; nor had his officers put themselves in the position of the astonished Italians watching the flotilla steam through the minefield. His staff had yet to develop a sympathetic outlook.

Crowe's thoughts began to stray. Today it was the turn for a letter to Susan. A dear girl was Susan; it was a pity he would have to confine himself in his letter to inanities and not be able to give the interesting details of to-day's work. Susan was of the type that would have appreciated and understood them.

What Crowe did not realise was that it was the same telepathic sympathy, the same instinctive estimate of the other's feelings, which made him a success with women and a success in war at the same time.

Douglas Reeman

TROUBLE CARGO

Few lovers of sea stories would dispute The Sunday Times' *verdict on Douglas Reeman, that he is 'one of our foremost writers of naval fiction'. His exciting novels of modern sea warfare (published under his own name), and the superb series of historical tales featuring Richard Bolitho, the midshipman-turned-Admiral (which he writes as Alexander Kent), have won him a huge readership and well-deserved critical acclaim. As he has played an important part in the creation of this anthology he also, of course, more than merits a place in it — though it has been no easy task to find one for Douglas has written very few short stories. 'Trouble Cargo' is, in fact, a rare little item which will probably be unknown to most of his fans and has certainly not been reprinted since its original appearance in that much-lamented travel magazine,* Wide World, *back in 1956. It was actually Douglas' second ever attempt at writing and he recalls that it earned him the princely sum of ten guineas! Interestingly, too, it was published in the magazine as being based on fact 'with only the names changed', but the author now admits it was really fiction posing as fact!*

Douglas Edward Reeman (1924–) served as a Lieutenant in the RNVR and brought an experienced seaman's eyes to his novels when in 1958 he began publishing what has since proved a highly successful series with A Prayer for a Ship. *This was followed by* High Water *(1959) and the highly popular* Send a Gun Boat *(1960). The first of the Richard Bolitho stories,* To Glory We Steer, *was written in 1968, and these books have justifiably earned him comparison with C. S.*

Forester's tales of Hornblower. Douglas has close friends in both the Navy and Merchant Navy and receives correspondence from all over the world, providing him with ideas and background material for his meticulously researched books. The intriguing yarn which follows neatly draws my group of stories about World War II to a close, and also provides a prelude to the final story by Alan J. Villiers, a writer and seaman who stands supreme in Douglas' estimation . . .

Gliding steathily through the Adriatic waters at a depth of seventy-five feet, HM Submarine *Tigress* proceeded on a routine patrol in search of her prey.

In the confined space of the control room, everything was exactly as it had been on dozens of similar occasions. The Officer-of-the-Watch leaned against the plotting table, swinging alert glances over the hydroplane operators who sat at their dials, watching the tell-tale depth needles, their faces blank and indifferent, yet noting every change and new display of temperament by the gauges.

Throughout the boat there was an orderly preparation for the new day, and above the throb of the motors and the whirr of the fans could be heard snatches of conversation, as the crew carried out their routine duties.

The course, green curtain across the compartment labelled 'Wardroom' jerked to one side, and the Commanding Officer, followed by the Navigator, entered the control room and strode stiffly to the chart table.

The CO took a glance around to assure himself that all was well; then, turning to the Officer-of-the-Watch, he said with a sigh, 'All right, Number One, stand by to take her up.'

The First Lieutenant pressed the klaxon, which shrilled throughout the boat, bringing the hands hurriedly to their stations. When all had quietened down, he reported, 'Closed up at Diving Stations, sir.'

'Right, take her up.'

The vessel trembled as the air was pumped into the tanks, and the depth gauges crept slowly backwards.

'Up periscope!' snapped the CO. With a hiss, the periscope rose out of the deck, and he stooped to put his eyes to the eyepiece and follow its progress.

He saw the lens brightening from black nothingness to pale green; then blinding sunlight made him wince, and his eyes water, but he kept his head pressed against the rubber shock-pad, and moved quickly round with the periscope.

Suddenly the others in the control room heard him gasp, as he stopped moving and concentrated on one direction. Less than five-hundred yards distant lay a white-painted schooner, rolling in the gentle swell, her becalmed, buff-coloured sails hanging limp and still.

'Down periscope!' he barked, and even before it started to hiss downwards he turned to the others, a grin on his pale, drawn face. 'It's not much, gentlemen, but it's better than nothing. A schooner, about a hundred and twenty feet long, Italian, I imagine; but I can't understand what it is doing here, a hundred miles from home.'

Without waiting to hear their ideas on the subject, he continued, 'Stand by to surface. Number One, this is a gun action; I'm not going to waste a torpedo.'

The Gunnery Officer and his crew waited under the gun hatch, going through their drill almost mechanically.

'Surface!' called the CO, and again the air was forced into the tanks, sending the boat swiftly upwards.

'Ten feet, sir,' said the First Lieutenant, and as the conning tower hatch opened, the CO scrambled up the ladder, into the bright sunlight, and trained his glasses on the little sailing ship even before the *Tigress*'s deck was awash.

With a clang, the forward hatch heaved back, the gun's crew jumped into view, and within ten seconds the gun swung round, seeking the target; the breech-block clicked home and the Gunnery Officer called up to the Captain, 'Ready, sir!'

Without taking his eyes from the other vessel, the Captain eased over to the voice pipes. 'Come up to the bridge, Number One, and bring our new Boarding Officer with you.' To the signalman the Captain ordered 'Run up the ensign.'

Swiftly the white ensign mounted the submarine's stumpy staff, only to hang limp and lifeless in the oppressive heat. The other two officers mounted to the crowded little bridge, automatically training their glasses on the schooner.

'Ah! They are hoisting a white flag,' said the Captain. 'Signalman, tell them to send a boat, we're going to board her.'

As the aldis lamp clicked and stuttered, almost ineffectual against the sun's pitiless glare, the Captain turned to the young Sub-Lieutenant who had joined him on the bridge.

'Look, Melville,' he began, 'this is your first trip as Boarding Officer, so I'd better put you in the picture. I want you to go and have a good look round. Get hold of the ship's papers, and anything else useful. Find out what they're doing out here, and afterwards tell them to abandon ship. Then come back aboard, bringing their captain with you; he may be useful later on. As soon as you get back, I'll sink her.'

Sub-Lieutenant Melville hastened below to muster his boarding party. His head was awhirl with instructions, and his mind alive to his new responsibilities. By the time he had checked his men, two seamen, a stoker mechanic and a leading signalman, and fastened on his pistol the schooner's boat was scraping alongside. With a clap on the back from the First Lieutenant, he leapt down into the sternsheets, followed by his men, and it was only then that he really became aware of the three other men who were manning the little boat.

'So this is the enemy,' he thought; but a more unwarlike trio it would have been hard to imagine. All were old, rather wrinkled little men, burned a deep brown by countless years at sea. 'Rather like the fishermen on the pre-war shipping posters,' he pondered.

However, ancient or not, they pulled steadily for the schooner, not speaking, but watching him with quick, almost frightened glances. In the waist of the boat, the four British sailors sat, reassuring and solid, their Sten guns across their knees.

As they approached the schooner, it seemed to Melville a really beautiful craft, with high graceful masts, raking bowsprit and golden scroll-work around the bow. Many eyes peered down into the boat and loud, excited talk could be heard as Melville swung himself up the rough, rope ladder to the deck.

He gasped at the sight which greeted him. Literally scores of

376

people thronged about him, shouting and apparently trying to make themselves understood. There were women, too, in fact many more women than men.

This was all very confusing, but time was short. 'Leading Hand,' he yelled above the din, 'get this lot herded up forrard, and then get the skipper for me, if he's amongst them.'

At that moment, however, an enormous, bald-headed man, in a greasy white shirt and duck trousers, shouldered his way through the crowd to confront him.

'Sair!' he bellowed, 'I am Captain of this ship. Please to come below to cabin and I will explain what all these people are having here.'

He said it in such a confident, almost commanding manner, that Melville felt obliged to follow him. In the cool barn-like cabin, the giant Italian produced the ship's papers.

'Before you do anything else, I will explain,' he said. 'As you know, your army is on the march up the coast in my country. The Germans –' here he paused to spit accurately into an old tobacco tin apparently kept for that purpose '– ordered me to evacuate a whole town – that is, at least, as many of the old men, women, and children, as I could take on board – so that their army could set up a, how you say, a strongpoint. Also I have the town's bank with me, that is what these policemen are supposed to be guarding, but,' he chuckled, 'I disarmed them when I saw your lovely ship. I do not want any trouble, you understand?'

Seizing his opportunity to say something, Melville said, 'Yes, but what are you doing right out here?'

'It was a storm,' was the reply. 'It came on us suddenly, and we were blown right off our course; our engine broke down, and as the Germans took our engineer, what could we do?'

Melville went on deck, followed by the schooner's captain. He called the signalman, and instructed him to signal the *Tigress*, and inform the CO of all these new developments.

In the submarine, the information was digested thoughtfully, and the Commanding Officer summed up that which was in the minds of his crew. 'I can't let all those women and children take to the boats, and make their own way home; I don't suppose there are enough boats, anyway. And I can't let that gold drop to the bottom of the sea. Yet I can't unload anything here, and I'm certainly not going to let that gold go to the Jerries.

'Instruct Melville to get the schooner's engine repaired; give him his position and the course for Otranto in Southern Italy; that's in our hands. He should make it easily in a couple of days, and the patrols are bound to pick him up. He'll be needing a couple more men to keep that lot in order, too. See that he's got enough fuel for that engine of his.'

The CO grinned. 'Poor old Melville, I'll bet he didn't expect anything like this on his first trip.'

Aboard the *Maddalena*, for that was the schooner's name, the young Sub-Lieutenant was beginning to get matters sorted out. He had locked ten Fascist policemen in one of the cabins, and all the civilians were herded below in the crew and cargo spaces.

It was apparent that the Italian captain was only too willing to help in every way, and he assured Melville that his crew would do what they could to assist him to get the ship away from 'those blinkin' Germans', as he put it.

'All the same,' thought Melville, 'I'll have to keep an eye on him.'

The stoker mechanic reported that he had the ancient diesel in running order again, and as the two extra British seamen had arrived on board, Melville found himself eager to start the voyage.

'Signalman, tell *Tigress* we're getting under way, and that we'll see them again in time for Christmas.' He saw the light winking back from the submarine, and the signalman turned towards him. 'They say "Good luck",' he said.

His thoughts were interrupted by Leading Signalman Robbins asking, 'Shall I tell the stoker to get us under way, sir?'

He jerked back to reality. Once more, even here, service routine took control. 'Very good. Put one AB on the wheel, and one on the main hatch to keep an eye on the passengers. I also want a good look-out kept. When you've posted the men, come back to me.'

As the man hurried away, Melville turned to the Captain who was lurking respectfully in the background. 'Get your cook to prepare food for everybody; he can have a couple of the women to help him. And don't forget to feed those policemen.'

Seven hours later they were well under way on their new course, south-east by south, and Melville felt a little more confident. The *Maddalena* bowled along at a steady six knots; the Italian captain had set two small steadying sails, to help her on her way.

Night fell, like a thick, velvet curtain, and although there was no moon, it was a fine, clear night, the sort that can be found only near the Italian shores.

Having posted the watch for the night, and assured himself that there were no lights showing, Melville decided to take a few hours' rest. He suddenly realized how tired he was and felt as if he could sleep for a week.

How long he slept he could not say, but he suddenly found himself sitting upright, alert and listening. He heard the crack of a pistol, the thud of something striking the deck, and then the sound of running feet, directly overhead.

Seizing his revolver, he dashed up the companion ladder and on to the deck, where he collided with Robbins who had also been sleeping aft. For a moment he could see nothing, and then, as his eyes became accustomed to the gloom, he saw two of his seamen bending over a body by the wheel. Just forward of them, in the break of the poop, were the uniformed figures of the ten policemen, held against the rail at gun-point by the other British seamen.

'What's happened?' he snapped, 'and who's been hurt?'

'It's the old captain, sir,' replied one of the men. 'He's dead.' The seaman continued, 'He went to see if those coppers were all right, and one of them had a knife, and stabbed him; then they let themselves out with his key, and came aft. One of them grabbed Bill here, and while they were struggling, the others smashed the compass and had a go at the engine. I was up forrard when it 'appened, sir, but I came on the double, and fired me gun in the air. That stopped 'em all right.'

Melville's first emotion was one of sorrow for the old captain, and then a wave of blind rage swept over him. He turned to the seamen on deck. 'Put those swine down in the cable tier, and make sure they're well locked in. I'll see they pay for this.'

To the leading signalman he said, 'Get the old fellow sewn up in canvas; we'll bury him here at sea, as soon as possible. I'm going to take a look at the damage they've done.'

The compass definitely was finished, and further inspection proved that the old engine, too, had been put out of action. 'It'd take the 'ole of Pompey Dockyard to put that right,' observed the mechanic gloomily.

Melville felt more angry than dismayed, and all the more determined to get the ship to port. 'We'll just have to sail her,' he thought, 'and hope that the patrols see us. How I wish we had a transmitter aboard.'

The next hours taxed his patience and intelligence to the full. Somehow he managed to make the Italian sailors understand what he wanted, and which sails he required to be set. While they conformed with his orders, the British seamen, with their usual powers of persuasion, managed to pacify the women and children who had come swarming up from below at the sound of the shots.

The little ship heeled to the freshening breeze, and began to forge ahead through the night, apparently overjoyed to be under sail again, even though handled by an amateur. At least, that was how Melville saw it, as he studied first the stars, and then consulted the ship's grubby charts. 'If we hold this course, we ought to make a landfall near Otranto,' he mused, 'or at least within twenty miles or so.'

Dawn came, with a watery, misty grey light; the breeze showed no sign of slackening, and the schooner seemed to be making a fairly good speed, as she dipped and curtsied over the short, white-crested waves.

The womenfolk and their noisy children swarmed over the decks. Food was distributed, and soon they were loudly engaged in eating and talking as hard as they could. Nobody seemed to be mourning the dead captain, whom Melville had dropped over the side, with a brief prayer, just before day-break.

As he watched the scene on deck, the British officer was approached by the hard-worked leading signalman. 'There's enough food for to-day, sir,' he said, 'and only just enough fresh water.'

'That'll have to do,' replied Melville, 'I hope to sight land later to-day, then we'll turn in and make for the nearest port. We can hand this lot over to the Army when we land. I imagine they will think we're pretty short of ships when they see *us* sail in!'

Sure enough, later that afternoon they sighted land, a dark blue hump on the starboard horizon; a fresh course was laid, the sails painstakingly reset, and the ship began scudding for the shore.

The coastline began to take shape; there was a high ridge of hills stretching either way as far as the eye could see, rocks whitened by the surf, then pale yellow beaches, with a friendly background of green trees. Among the trees could be seen tiny, white houses, a village apparently, and then, jutting out from behind a small, rugged headland loomed a long, stone jetty.

'That fishing village will do,' observed Melville. 'I'll not risk going further without a compass along this coast. Night will be on us in a few hours, and what with these awful charts, and all these people on board, it'd be asking for trouble.'

As they drew nearer the shore, he turned the hands to shortening sail; he was not going to risk smashing the ship on the jetty, after getting this far.

'Hoist the white ensign!' he called. 'We'll do it properly, in case the Army are watching!' This brought a laugh from his men, and the usual blank stares from the Italians.

Nearer and nearer came the jetty, and the mooring lines were made ready, but still there was no sign of any reception committee, only a solitary dog that stood on the slimy stone steps, barking furiously at them.

With a gentle bump they came alongside, and the seamen stood by to make fast to the rusty mooring rings, when suddenly one of them shouted, 'Look, sir, tanks, dozens of 'em!'

As Melville stared, he saw first four, then six, eight, eleven large tanks, rumbling out of the village towards the jetty. Behind them came half a dozen lorries filled with troops.

Melville's smile of welcome faded, and icy fingers seemed to grip his heart. 'Gosh,' he choked, 'they're Italian troops; this village is behind the enemy lines!'

The armoured procession thundered across the stonework and drew up with the leading tank opposite the ship.

The steel door in the leading tank opened, and two officers stepped down, followed by a sergeant with a machine carbine. They walked slowly to the gangway, and then up on to the deck where Melville stood, stiff and white-faced, to receive them.

The taller of the two officers, smartly dressed, and much decorated, saluted. In faltering English he said, 'As you know, Captain, my country capitulated to yours this morning, and I would be honoured to surrender my battalion and this village to you . . .'

Alan J. Villiers

THE WINDJAMMER FILM

Of all the maritime writers who deserve a place in a book such as this, few, if any, have a better claim than Alan J. Villiers, of whom the critic Lincoln Colcord observed so concisely, 'No one loves a sailing ship better or writes of her more faithfully.' There is surely not a sailor alive – even an armchair sailor – who has not dreamt at some time of emulating one or other of Alan's great voyages, all of which have been so superbly recounted in his various books. He is truly the seaman's seaman.

Alan John Villiers was born in Melbourne, Australia in 1903 and went to sea at the tender age of fifteen as a cadet in the barque Rothesay Bay. *He sailed for some five years in various square-rigged ships engaged in the Cape Horn trade, and in 1923 went on a whaling expedition in the Ross Sea, off Antarctica. A spell of journalism followed when he began to demonstrate his facility with the pen as well as the spinnaker, but the call of the sea was such that he soon returned and went on a number of voyages in four-masted barques, including the famous ship,* Parma. *His skill as a captain was tested to the full in 1932 when he won the Grain Race for surviving windjammers with a voyage of 103 days from South Australia to the English Channel. The following year, he bettered this time by a massive twenty days! As if this achievement were not enough, in 1934 he sailed the* Joseph Conrad *a distance of 60,000 miles around the world with a crew consisting mainly of cadets!*

Villiers' life has, in fact, been one long round of voyages, charted in books such as Falmouth for Orders *(1929), Last of*

the Windships *(1934)*, Sons of Sinbad *(1940) and* The Set of
Sails *(1949), which has been described as 'a tribute to the sea as
a way of life – free, unregimented, unmerchandised'. During
the last war he won a DSC for his work during the Normandy
landings, and he has also done much valuable work as a trustee
of the National Maritime Museum. As a man who has sailed so
often as a captain, many of his works would be suitable for this
book, but I can't think of a more interesting – or unusual – story
to conclude this book than 'The Windjammer Film'* . . .

Ronald Gregory Walker was a newspaper reporter on the
staff of *The Mercury*, Hobart. As such, part of his duties
consisted in writing up what news there was in the port in a
column called, exactly why is not clear, 'Shipping Intelligence'.
He often used to say that he did not know that shipping had
any intelligence; and in any case no intelligence was necessary
in chronicling whatever news there was about it.

But that is by the way.

Ronald Walker was deeply interested in the ships and in all
concerning them. He loved the newspaper work too, and knew
that city life held no more interesting job. All his young life he
had been strongly interested in the sea. Ships and travel, sea
and aeroplanes, strange lands – these things moved him. He
had a little yacht he called the *Murmur*, and in her many a
happy week-end was spent. He wrote about yachting matters
for his newspaper and pottered about the ships that came to
port, and his days were pleasant.

Hobart, small though it was, had a lovely harbour to which
strange ships sometimes came – great steamers, with
greenheart bows and slipways cut into their sterns, which were
bound upon Antarctic whaling voyages; big steamers in distress from the storms of the roaring 'forties; game little
crayfishing schooners and, now and again, big sailing ships
with timber from the Baltic.

He did not care about the big Orient and P & O steamers,
carrying to England squatters' daughters whose money might

have been better spent in their own Australia. The spectacle of the big cargo steamers he found interesting but not stirring.

But the sight of a great Cape Horn sailing ship deeply moved him. They did not come often to Hobart; when one did, it was with difficulty that he could be prevailed upon to go home. He loved to go across the broad Derwent in his yacht and to lie in the sun on the cliffs at Bellerive, looking at the loveliness of Hobart at the foot of its mountain, and at the shipping round its wharves, and to dream. He had ideas; he thought deeply. He was not content to find his ideas and to shape his actions from what he read in newspapers, heard other people say, or saw upon the screens of motion-picture theatres.

He was very restless. He loved Hobart and was profoundly moved by the grandeur of its surrounding scenery. But he wanted to see the great world outside.

One day he conceived the idea of making a film of the voyage of a Cape Horn sailing ship. He told me about it – for I was a reporter on that newspaper too – and I said it couldn't be done. How could we make a film? I asked. We had no money. We were not camera-men. We knew nothing about the production side of the film industry, and had no chance to learn. I agreed that the subject was a stirring one and that the film should be made, but I did not see how we could do it.

He said we could. He said there was a moving-picture camera on the market that was almost fool-proof. We agreed, then, that we should get one of these and practise with it the following year – which would have been 1930 – shipping together in a Cape Horn sailing ship to make the picture.

Before we had a chance to buy the camera, we read a letter in the London *Daily Mail*, written by a Mr C. J. Greene, imploring somebody to make a real sailing-ship film while the chance remained. The letter was a serious thing to us. It meant, although probably no one would take notice of its sound sense, the idea was broadcast. We thought that we should have to set out immediately if we were not to be forestalled. We decided immediately to go.

There were many difficulties. We had only a few days to get to Wallaroo, in South Australia, to join the Finnish ship *Grace Harwar* there, loading wheat for England.

We were still without cameras, without money, without

385

anyone to back us – we knew it was hopeless to look for any – and without the slightest experience of motion-picture art.

We hurriedly gave notice to our news editor. Walker raised half the money (about fifteen hundred dollars) on an insurance policy, and I sold my home to get the other half. We ordered cameras and film to be sent to us from Sydney and picked them up in Melbourne.

Six days after we had read that letter in the London *Daily Mail*, we shipped as sailors in the *Grace Harwar* at Wallaroo.

We went aboard late at night with our cameras and film in our sea-bags. We said nothing to anybody of our intentions; we signed as sailors, to do the ship's work. We considered then that it was not the ship's business what else we might have done. We knew about sailing-ship masters and feared that if we opened our mouths about this film, other able seamen might be found and we should lose our jobs. There was also the possibility of the captain cabling to his owner and raising the question of film rights and such things. It is the film producers' own fault that there exists a worldwide impression that the outpouring of gold unlimited is a necessity and even a pastime to any one concerned with the making of pictures; but we were not ordinary film producers, and we had no gold.

So we joined the ship and did our work with the others, and said nothing. In the course of time the *Grace Harwar* sailed. She was a lovely full-rigged ship of 1749 tons, and ideal for our purpose. She was Clyde built, over forty years old; she had an open wheel, and none of those labour-saving devices of later days. She was a genuine sister of the Horn of forty years ago – one of the last full-rigged ships, if not the very last, to go round the Horn.

In Wallaroo we discharged the *Grace Harwar*'s ballast that she had brought down from Wilmington, North Carolina, after discharging a cargo of Peruvian guano there towards the end of 1928. The ballast out, we took the wheat in. Half the crew ran away and others were shipped in their place. We took aboard, from the police, a curious Swedish-speaking negro from the West Indies, who had deserted the Erikson bark *Penang* not long before. He was a prohibited immigrant in Australia, being black, and to avoid a five-hundred-dollar fine we had to take him with us out of the country. He had been cook on the *Penang*; we had our cook, so the negro was to be merely a passenger.

The grain loaded, the hatches battened down and break-waters built up on them, the sails bent and the gear all clear, the water-tanks full, and the negro aboard, the food all stored, the lifeboats lashed down, the wheel gear oiled, we dropped our moorings and put out to sea. That was on 17th April 1929. It was not until 3rd September, 138 days later, that we arrived at our destination. In the interval one of us was killed; a second went out of his mind; a third went overboard. We were short of food and the boat leaked. We tried to make Cape Town in distress, but could not. We saw black albatrosses and suffered terribly off the Horn in the dead of winter . . .

We might have known these things would happen. We had thirteen in our crew – thirteen hands before the mast. I don't remember that we noticed it in Wallaroo before we left. We remembered about it well enough after.

We had a Frenchman, a Londoner, four Australians, and the rest were Finns – Swedish-speaking Finns, mostly from the Aland Islands, where the ship belonged. Only two of the crew had been round the Horn before – the Londoner and I. The Londoner and I had been in more ships under the Finn flag than any of the Finns aboard. He had sailed in the *Olivebank*, I in *Lawhill* and *Herzogin Cecilie*. The Finns were all first-voyage boys, some deserters from other ships, two or three members of the original crew who had joined the *Grace Harwar* in Swansea nearly two years before. The average age of our crew was about nineteen. Three had never been to sea before. But they were all fine boys.

They settled down manfully. They were strong and willing, which is a lot; there was an entire absence of that old bickering spirit which was so evident in sail's heyday, when every fo'c'sle had its boss, its bloodshed, and its undercurrent of cliques and jealousies. We had no fight the whole voyage. I have never seen a fight in a Finnish ship.

We began the voyage well. We knew that winter was coming on, so we prayed for a quick return and run round the Horn. The Horn is bad enough in summer, and we did not want to prolong our passage of the west winds getting there. In six days we had passed to the south of Tasmania. That was good. We had a strong west wind the whole time and a big sea. It was piercingly cold and the little *Grace Harwar* was inclined to throw the sea about her decks a lot. We blew out a sail or two. The first night out the mizen t'gall'nt sail blew out of its bolt-ropes, and we set no sail upon that yard thereafter because the ship had none. There were no spare t'gall'nt sails fit to stand down there. The mizen t'gall'nt yard had to go bare until a new sail was cut and sewn. That was some time.

We did not mind the cold. We did not mind the ceaseless wet at the cold wheel, the seas that slopped over us, the teeth-chattering peril of the work aloft. We laughed at the big seas and thought it a joke when a larger one than usual fell aboard with a shock that made the whole ship tremble and threatened to do her serious damage. What did we care while the wind was fair and we came quickly towards the Horn?

From Wallaroo to Cape Horn is, roughly speaking, about six thousand miles. If we ran nine knots before the strong west winds we should make it in thirty days – say thirty-five or thirty-eight, allowing for some spells of lesser winds and maybe some days hove to when there was too much wind to use. We went that way as all sailing ships do, in the hope of getting strong west winds, in order that if we had to suffer acute discomfort, and cold and wet, and ceaseless work, at least it would not last long, and we would be quickly round. The sailing ship does not mind strong wind, as long as it is fair. We had nothing to fear from westerly gales, which would help us on; it was the wind from the east we feared.

The wind came from the east. It hauled round to south-east and hurled itself on us with all the sting of the Antarctic ice in its frigid and unwelcome blast. We could do nothing with the strong east wind. We shortened down and hove to. This was in the southern waters of the Tasman Sea, between Tasmania and New Zealand, across which we had been making to pass to the south of New Zealand on our way to the Horn. The Tasman Sea is storm-lashed and furious in winter-time; we knew that, but we expected at least that we would have west wind.

The wind refused flatly to go back towards any point west. We held on, giving the ship the full mainsail in the hope that it would hold her head up a little, decrease her leeway, and give us some longitude towards Cape Horn. The newcomers to the sea were sick and utterly fed up with it. They wondered why, if once one ship had sailed that road and met with hell, any others were foolhardy enough to try it after.

The sea froze where it touched the steel of the bulwarks; one of our pigs was drowned; the rain and the sleet froze into the serving of the foot-ropes, and aloft was hell. 'It takes guts, this game, my God it does!' wrote Ronald Walker. He had guts, but he was killed afterwards . . .

We tried our best to beat those easterly winds, hoping always that they would stop, believing that the Wind God would take pity on us, and at least let us come to the Horn, no matter what torment he wreaked on the way. But it was not fair to delay us so, with that accursed wind. The east wind continued, with no slightest sign of ever giving up. Gale succeeded gale; constantly the open decks of the old full-rigger were awash; one had to look lively to the lifelines going to the wheel. At night the look-out men could not go to the fo'c'sle head. The seas came over there green, and if they had gone there they would have been drowned. We began to notice how short-handed we were, with six in one watch and seven in the other . . .

In the end Captain Svensson got fed up with the east wind, and put up the helm to run for Cook Straits, which separate the two islands of New Zealand, intending to pass through that way into the South Pacific beyond if the east wind would not allow us to pass south of that Dominion. We reached Cook Straits after three weeks at sea; and then it fell calm and we couldn't get through. Four days we lay there, wallowing, stagnantly, with Mount Egmont on one hand and the rocky northern shores of the south island on the other. We were about to up helm and stand on northwards to pass right round the northern extremity of New Zealand, when a west wind came at last and saw us through.

We saw the lights of Wellington, capital of New Zealand, and reported the ship all well. The west wind kept with us for a day or two, and saw us clear of the Chatham Islands. We began to think it meant to stay, and that we could come to the Horn without further undue misery.

But then the wind faltered, and stopped again. When it returned it was from the east, with fog and rain and gale in miserable succession. Day succeeded day in sodden misery and cold gale. We went out to so many alternate watches on deck, hoping that while we slept the wind had changed, and were disappointed. We gave up hoping any more. We accepted what was in store for us with sullen indifference. Oilskins were long since useless; there was no dry spot on the ship, or dry rag. The fo'c'sle was washed out time and time again by great seas that swept joyously through the inefficient doors. When the doors were shut the atmosphere was stifling. When they were open the sea swept in. We kept them shut, preferring to die of suffocation rather than of exposure. We hardly ever had warm food. The seas put the galley fire out; and, because the water swept so incessantly across the main deck where the fresh-water pump was, we could not work the inefficient pump for fear of mingling salt water with the fresh, and went thirsty. We were cold, wet through, and hungry. There is no heating system on a full-rigged ship; the very cockroaches and bugs in the bunks retired from active service and might have all died for all we saw of them.

I give an extract or two from poor Walker's diary scrupulously kept until the day he died, the better to describe this section of the voyage. He brought new eyes to it, and a new mind. I had been that way before, and described it before, but had not seen it as he had.

May 16, 29 days out [he wrote]. Looking back, those twenty-nine days seem an indeterminable age. Many strange things have happened in them ... Frenchman and I were sent aloft this morning, in a hard squall, which showed every sign of developing into a real Cape Horn snorter. We climbed into the shrouds at 6 a.m. in pitch darkness. It was raining steadily and big seas were coming aboard. The wind had a cold sting which gradually froze us to the marrow in spite of our heavy clothing, oilskins, and sea-boots. We were up there for nearly two hours while a cold and cheerless dawn broke over the wind-torn sea; and we fought with the sodden sails until the work exhausted us and pained. The rain persistently drove at us, soaking our caps and oilskins; the cold water trickled down through crevices which only water could find. Our fingers were stiff and blue with the cold, and red with blood from tears with the jagged wire gear . . .

At first we shivered when an icy finger of water found its way down our backs or up our sleeves, but soon we were so wet and cold that we ceased to care. Get wet and stay wet is the best policy for sailing ships. The greatest agony of mind comes when you change into comparatively dry, only to know with horrible certainty that as soon as you go on deck again everything will be sodden through once more . . .

May 19, 32 days out. You stand a miserable look-out on the fo'c'sle head for hours with plenty of time for thought, but the antidote for depression lies just behind you, towering into the darkness, sweeping on and on along the rolling road, heaving and stumbling as she meets a sea, rushing on again and on; indomitable, insuperable as fate. Great seas come up to meet the ship, thrusting at her, shouldering one another to get at her like footballers in a mad 'scrimmage'. Up and up they heave gathering for the blow. You turn to watch them. The wind howls in your face and the sea spits at you spitefully, driving its spray above and around. A great sea, a liquid mountain of menace, hangs poised above the ship. Up, up it leaps, shouldering its smaller children aside, the splendid crest whitening where it breaks, lending a touch of colour as the plume of a warrior's helmet. Down, down, sinks the ship, shuddering already at the impending blow.

A hundred lesser blows she has already avoided; this mighty one she cannot beat. She writhes like a living thing, in fear and trembling. She heels over heavily. She hovers frighteningly . . . The stars shoot suddenly past the spars — not so bad, with them out! — careering madly across the sky. The ship receives the blow full, staggering at the impact. A tremor runs through the labouring hull . . . But the shattered seacrest has met its match. The warrior's plume has dropped; the ship rises again, tumbling hundreds of tons of roaring, fighting water from her gushing washports. The sea sweeps her furiously end to end, murderously intent upon human prey. Baulked of that, it shifts whatever is movable, and snarls and hisses at the hatch breakwaters maddeningly intent upon breaking them down . . . But the ship wins. Under her load of hundreds of tons of seething water she rolls on, recovering her poise, steadying herself to meet the next onslaught, and the next, and the next after that. For forty years and more now she has been doing that. Beautiful and game old ship!

On the thirty-eighth day Walker was killed at his work in the rigging.

It was very simple. Just one of those ordinary everyday accidents that nine hundred times kill nobody, and on the nine hundred and first wreak vengeance for their previous failings on some innocent.

We were setting the fore upper t'gall'nts'l, which had not been loosened since its getting in described in his diary. The wind, which for so long had been from something east, had at last something of west in it, and we were giving the ship a little more sail to help her on – not that the fore upper t'gall'nts'l would make much difference really, but the psychological effect was not to be scorned.

Walker went up to loose the sail with a small boy named Finila. It was a little after four o'clock in the morning, the worst time of the day. We had so few in a watch that it was bad to send two men into the rigging, but there were reasons for that. We had coffee at half-past five, and the tradition of the sea is that, if there is any work afoot and it is not finished before the coffee bells, then whatever time is taken up with finishing the work is lost. The coffee hour is not extended merely because some of it has been given up to the ship's work. A good mate will see that his watch receive their coffee-time unbroken.

That was why our second mate sent both Walker and young Finila to loose the fore upper t'gall'nt that fateful morning. It was very securely made fast, with many gaskets to stand against the Cape Horn gale; since it had been made fast it had become sodden with rain, and the canvas had swollen. Ice had formed in the gaskets, and any sailor knows that it may take an hour to get a sail loose in those conditions. With the two of them at it they managed in half an hour, and then we on deck – five of us, with the second mate – began the painful process of heaving the yard aloft by the capstan.

When it was half-way up, the second mate saw that a gasket

was foul on the weather clew. The sail would not hoist properly. He yelled aloft to Walker, through the rain, to go out on the lower t'gall'nt yard to clear the gasket. Walker went, and cleared it. He called down to us that everything was clear. We began to heave again; the halliards carried away and the yard came tumbling down.

It fell on Walker beneath it, and killed him there.

We did not know that he was dead when we rushed up the mast and found him unconscious between the yards. We thought that he was merely senseless. There was no sign of wound, save for some blood oozing slowly from his mouth. It never occurred to us that he was dead; we were too much concerned with bringing him to, and getting him to the deck that we might see the extent of his injuries, and what we could do about them. I tried to bring him to with cold water that had been brought up from the deck. I didn't know how hopeless it was; we wanted to restore him to his senses in order that he might help us with the difficult task of getting him, from high on that swinging mast, to the deck. It was not easy to bring a senseless body down that slippery and pitching rigging.

But he did not come to. We rigged a gantline and lowered him down, gently, carefully.

When we got to the bottom Captain Svensson took one look.

'He is dead,' he said.

Dead! The shock was stunning. We did not – could not – believe it. Nowhere is the awfulness of death more painfully apparent than at sea. Ashore there are diversions, one forgets. There are other people to see, other people to talk to, newspapers to read, traffic to dodge. One is not missed so much. But at sea in a full-rigged ship there is only the one little band, and always the wind moans in the rigging and the sea rolls on. When one is gone no one comes to take his place; there are no diversions; nothing happens to deaden sorrow and make up for the loss of the one who is gone . . .

We buried him from the poop next day, with the Finnish ensign at half-mast and the crew white-faced and deeply moved. I do not know anything more moving than sea-burial; not the committal of some poor corpse of a steerage passenger, from high on the steamship's promenade deck in the dead of night, lest the saloon passengers be put off their dancing for a moment, but the last sad rites over a shipmate's bier in a Cape Horn windjammer. We had all known him so well! At sea like that you see the utmost innards of a man, what he is made of. No pretence of city life, no masking of real intents and real character, will pass here – you see all. We knew poor Walker and we liked him well, and this was his end . . .

The captain read some prayers; we sang Swedish and English hymns. There was a short address. The ship was hove to, sadly wallowing, with the moan of the wind in her rigging now quietened by her deadened way, the surly wash of the sea about her decks now softened . . . We carried him to the rail, tilted the hatch; there was a dull plop and it was all over . . .

We put the ship before the wind again and sailed on.

It was the fifty-seventh day before we got to the Horn. It was June then, and the Horn is hell in June, as Masefield says. But for us it was not so bad. We had a gale from the west, and though the sea ran huge and the cold was almost overpowering, the old ship ran on and we were glad.

We wanted to come round the Horn now more quickly than ever, that we might forget something of the tragedy of the other side of it. Death is a worrying thing at sea, especially when its cause is bad gear that might have killed another of us. At the wheel, on the lonely look-out, aloft on the yards, sleeping in the wet, cold fo'c'sle – we remembered the one who had died, turned the details of the tragedy over and over in our minds, until it was not good for us longer to remain in that saddening belt of the wild ocean. A boy screamed in his sleep; he had dreamed he saw Walker's wraith, coming in the fo'c'sle to call us.

The ship began to leak in the height of a gale; the pumps jammed; the water seeped in, and we could do nothing about it. Through a night of storm and snow-squall fury we were huddled on the poop, not certain that the ship would live to see the morning. When the morning came one of the boys was swept overboard by a big sea. What could we do? Many had gone like that, and the wind ships could only run on . . .

But the wind was a little quieter then. We did not run on, though it seemed futile to try to save him. We jammed the wheel hard down and brought her shivering and groaning into the wind. We rove off new ropes into the lifeboat tackle blocks with mad speed; one of us was aloft in the mizen-top, seeing where the floating figure had gone. It was coming on nightfall then, with rain-squalls and gale in the offing. We saw he had grasped a lifebuoy flung to him, and still lived. But for how long?

We got the boat over and six volunteers quickly leaped into it, the mate in charge. Nobody was asked to go, nobody hung back.

We dropped astern and the boat seemed a futile thing, rising and falling in those big seas. It was queer to see the green bottom of the old ship, when we rose on a crest, lifted almost bodily from the swirling water. When we dropped in a trough her royal yard swept wild areas through the grey sky, and we saw little else. Soon we could not see her at all, when the boat sank deep in the valleys between the huge seas. We had no idea where the boy was now. We could not see him. How could we? We could see nothing there, not even the ship. Maybe it was madness to look.

We pulled this way and that hopelessly; yet we could not go back. It began to rain heavily. None of us had oilskins. Frenchman was in his underpants, just as he had come from his bunk. (It was our watch below.) Sjoberg, from Helsingfors, had been laid up with neuralgia. But now he pulled at his oar, coatless, wet through, hungry, and tired, yet not noticing any of these things and intent only on the saving of this second life. We did not want to lose one more. One was enough to give to Cape Horn – more than enough.

The mate, at the steering oar in the stern, swept the sea with his sharp eyes this way and that. There was a chance that we could not find the ship again if the squall came down heavily and shut her out. That had happened with the Swedish bark *Staut*, in much the same circumstances. She put out a boat to save a man fallen from the mainyard, and a squall came down and she lost everybody – man overboard, those who went to rescue him, boat and everything. We remembered that. There was nothing in the boat to sustain life. We had thrown the water-casks and bread-barrel out to make room and to decrease the weight of the boat.

Then in the last moment of light we saw him! It was a

sea-miracle, if ever there was one. He was only three crests away from us! We had been on the point of giving up . . . We lay to heartily and soon had the boy back on board. We pulled him over the stern and went back to the ship, which had been watching us and now ran slowly down-wind towards us. The boy was unconscious and nearly frozen to death, but he lived. He was amongst the lucky ones . . .

A few days afterwards we were round the Horn, and immediately the temperature rose about twenty degrees and our spirits rose with it. In reality we ran into a nasty snow-storm off the Falkland Islands which was every bit as bad as anything the Pacific side of the Horn had given us. But we were in the Atlantic then and did not mind. Blow on, old gale! We did not mind. We knew then that we should quickly come to warmer latitudes, and south-east trades, and so to the north-east trades, the Azores, and then home. . . . But we did not count upon home too much just then . . .

We took advantage of the Cape Horn currents to pass between the Falklands and the mainland of South America, which is an unusual way for sailing ships to take. Once past the Horn we made good progress; it seemed that the Pacific had wreaked the ocean's wrath on us and delivered us to the Atlantic with the gruff greeting: 'Here, these dogs have had enough. Treat them well.'

We were glad, and as the days and the weeks slipped by, came to forget a little what had happened earlier in the voyage. But the sea was not done with us yet.

The second mate went mad with awful suddenness. We had no warning of it. We did not expect anything like that.

We knew that he had worried much over Walker's death, since he was officer of the watch. But it was not his fault. It was not anyone's fault. It was just one of those terrible inexplicable things that are always happening, yet never seem to remove from this earth persons that might well be done without. In the fo'c'sle we worried much, too, but we had each other for company. There is no one more lonely than an officer of a sailing ship. We carried only two, first mate and second. They were rarely company for each other, for when one had the deck the other slept. The captain, as in the sailor's style, kept to himself, and spoke to the sailmaker for company. The mates led lonely lives, finding what companionship they could in their own minds. The result was that when something came to unhinge the mind of our second mate, there was none to see how perilously near he was to breaking down. Nobody noticed until it was too late . . .

We had an awful time with him. About that I would have little to say. It was not his fault, poor devil. We were all very sorry for him. We had to keep constant watch on him for the rest of the voyage, lest he do himself harm. He tried to kill himself three times. It was very worrying. We tried to make for Cape Town to put him aboard some steamer we should see there in the shipping lanes, but the wind changed and we could not make Cape Town. We saw no other ships. We were 104 days at sea before we saw the sign of a steamer, and then it was only a smudge of smoke on the horizon. The sailing ship goes her own way about the world, far from the shipping lanes and away from the busy routes of steamers. She may see other sailing ships, but rarely, until she reaches the shipping lanes of the North Atlantic, anything of steamers.

We found the south-east trades and went up the line. Now the days were pleasant and the sun shone, and flying-fish leapt in fear from the bone of foam under our forefoot. We saw some whales; one of them stayed with us three days. He was not frightened. We had no propeller nor honking engines to frighten him away. He played about us merrily, and when I tried to photograph him, blew spray on the lens.

On the hundredth day we came to the line. Here it fell calm, and we made little progress. We were lucky though; once I spent three weeks in the Atlantic doldrums, in a big four-master bound from Melbourne to St Nazaire. In the *Grace Harwar* we were becalmed only four days, which was nothing. Then the wind came again and we sneaked slowly on.

By then the ship was very foul; her top speed, with a strong wind, was a little more than seven knots, and more in favourable conditions. But she had not been in a dry dock for over two years, and her bottom was very foul. She had lain long months at anchorage on west coast ports, and in Luderitz Bay in south-west Africa. There are no places worse for fouling ships and fouled ships cannot sail.

Another worry now beset us. We were short of food. We had

never had too much. Now as the days passed each took with it the last of some item or other of our small sea-stock – now it was the last rice, the last margarine, the last sugar, the last smoked beef, the last peas. We soon had little but some rather bad potatoes, black sugarless and milkless coffee, and a little bread. There was a small pig which we had been keeping to kill in the last emergency. Here it was. We killed it, only to find that it was diseased and could not be eaten. Maddening discovery! We ate a little, risking it, and soon became violently ill. Still would not throw the bad carcass into the sea. We put it in a cask beneath the fo'c'sle head, fearful to throw it overboard lest we were left with nothing at all.

It was now imperative that we should see a steamer quickly and get some food. We saw no steamers for a week, though we were creeping steadily into the North Atlantic, which was their stronghold. Then we saw a few; a big passenger ship going down to Buenos Aires in the early morning mist. I do not believe a soul on that ship saw us. She was a long way away, and she did not come closer. We saw others later and ran up signal flags asking them to stop. They took no notice. They could not see our signal flags, lying stagnant in the calm. We had no other means of attracting their attention.

It was not until four months had passed from the beginning of our voyage that we received some food. It was on the night of the 123rd day at sea when the Scots steamer *Orange Leaf*, bound to Trinidad, came into sight. We signalled her with a flash-lamp the captain had, and she stopped, telling us to put out a boat and come across. We put out the boat and pulled over about half a mile of greasily heaving sea to where she was hove to.

Being a Scotsman, she gave all she had.

The name of the *Orange Leaf* was indeed blessed amongst us.

She gave us cases of smoked beef, half a cow from her refrigerator, a case of milk, flour, and fresh vegetables, together with a sack of sugar and some other things. She gave us tobacco, but it was real strong sea-stuff – plugs – and our young boys could not smoke it because it was too strong.

A day or so after meeting the *Orange Leaf* we came past the Azores, still with winds that were sometimes good and sometimes baffling. Fifteen days after that meeting we lay at anchor in Queenstown Harbour, Ireland. I was never more pleased to come to a voyage end.

At last I could send a cable to poor Walker's parents and let them know their son was dead. He had been dead three months and more then – a hundred days – and they did not know anything about it. But the newspapers got the story home to Australia quicker than I could, and the first his parents knew of it was a grim paragraph in a paper.

From Queenstown we towed round to Glasgow, and there I left. No one in the ship went back to her. Another crew of young boys came across from Finland, sent by the owner there, and with them a young man as master who had been with me in the *Lawhill* as able seaman eight years before.

The grain was discharged, the ship went down to the Bristol Channel, and loaded coal for La Guaira, in British Guiana. She had reached that port after a wild passage of some forty-five days, intending then to go on through Panama to Peru for guano, or across the South Atlantic and so to Australia for grain. But world freight markets collapsed, and all that she could do was to return again to Mariehamm, Finland, in ballast, there to lie in wait at anchorage, with only a watchman aboard, for the upward trend in Australian grain freights or a good offer from the break-up yards – and the end . . .

The real sea film was made. That part of the adventure was satisfactory. The 6000 feet of negative developed with 98 per cent perfection, which was an act of God in no way due to me, except that my ignorance – not always a bad thing, at least in comparison with a little knowledge – helped me. When Ronald died we had exposed some 6000 feet of film. I was half inclined to throw cameras and film over the side there and then. What did I know about them? How could I carry on? I didn't even know how to load the cameras.

But I went on, not with hope, but because it seemed the only thing to do. There was no sense in giving in without a trial. I taught myself to load the magazines, using for the first few a red light (which would have spoiled panchromatic film) made up from folds of red bunting lashed round a hurricane lamp. I had an idea of the different exposures necessary in the various lights, from watching Walker at work. I could guess what would make a good picture. The ship helped me in that respect; wherever I pointed the camera I could not help but have perfect composition. All her angles were lovely; every scene she showed was beautiful. The sea helped me with the light. It was generally good.

So I went on with the job for a hundred days, not knowing even whether the cameras were working properly, half afraid that they were not, afraid the film wasn't keeping (much of it was panchromatic and not guaranteed), not a laboratory or dark room did we have, no cool film tanks for the tropics.

When at last I reached Glasgow I had half a mind to throw the film off the dock. We went ashore the first night and found that the talkies had come. The days of silent film, which were standard when the *Grace Harwar* sailed, were dead. The negative I had was silent. I didn't know then how much of sound could be faked. I had spent all I had and all that I could borrow; Walker had risked everything and lost his life. I had no idea what the film would be like and had pretty well given it up for a total loss when Walker had died. I had never counted on its being good.

I knew that I had 250 dollars to collect from a publisher in London: this amount would just pay for the development of the negative. But if I had the negative developed I would be broke. I had no job. The film was probably no good. What then? There was nowhere else to get any money.

I risked it. I spent the 250 dollars, and had the negative developed. It would cost, I was told, another 500 dollars for a print. I did not have the 500 dollars and I never saw the print. The negative, however, was good; I set about the forlorn task of trying to interest someone in it, of getting some producing firm to make, from that basis, the final picture – the picture that Ronald Walker and I had set out to make. It was to be a simple real picture of sailing ships and the sea, without story, without sex, without fake; we had always thought the subject lovely and stirring enough without false additions. There are enough pictures faked.

That picture was never made! I hawked the film about in London for months, up and down Wardour Street, in Soho, the heart of London's executive filmland.

There was, I found, no machinery for the marketing of such

a film as I had brought. Film-producing concerns did not want outsiders – and amateurs at that – to bring them in completed negatives, no matter how good they might be. They wanted to make them for themselves, no matter how bad they might be.

I tramped up and down in Wardour Street in dejection. I thought of going to America, but did not have the funds. There was a lot of gush in the British newspapers about the excellence, the world-dominating chance, of British films. I learnt nothing to impress me with the truth of these optimistic statements. I learnt only how the producing companies feared the unusual and what had not been tried before; how deep-rooted was their terror of anything that did not happen to be the fashion of the moment. Crime films? If one company made a crime film that succeeded, then they all rushed to make similar 'masterpieces' that differed so little that the public soon tired of them. Historical plots? Newspaper heroes? We have seen them all . . . I suppose that American producers aren't much better, but, from a showman's point of view, they turn out a better job . . .

My adventures in trying to dispose of the film were more harrowing than those of the *Grace Harwar* in getting it.

I got into the hands of some promoters who talked a lot, said little, had a huge office, and never did anything. They said they were going to exploit the film. They made a print; at last I saw what Walker and I had done. Here was the raw material for a real film! But no one could see it. By the grace of God we had fluked a grand sea picture; by the stupidness of man the public never saw it.

After a while my promoters had a film trade row. They split. My film went with half of them. I lost track of them for a while. It didn't matter much; I was pretty well fed up by then. I had no capital for producing the film by myself, and had no way of getting any. I knew nobody in the film world . . . The film was aground in Wardour Street, and it didn't look as if it would ever be floated again.

But at last a British firm did become interested in it. They liked the negative and appreciated the beauty of the sea part. They acquired it, and set about the discovery of some way of making it into what they considered to be a box-office picture. They brought England's poet laureate, John Masefield, to their studio to see the film, and he was much impressed. It would have fitted splendidly into a film version of his famous 'Dauber'.

After a long time they hit upon a story. They made interior sets of fo'c'sle and cabin in their studios. Here the dialogue sequences were made. They did not do so bad a job. They called the resultant film – one-third real and two-thirds fake – *Windjammer*. The director, who had never heard of the film until it was brought to him, put his name in letters a yard high on a title-sheet to himself; Walker's name, incorrectly initialled, was grouped with mine, in very small letters, together with the men who had done the studio photography, as the 'photographers' on a title-sheet along with all those other persons who, for some mysterious reason, had to be given 'credits'. Well, the director could have his glory . . .

Afterwards the film was sent out to the movie houses, many of whose managers were afraid to book it because it had no theme song, and there was no woman in the story.